Iris Gower was born in Swansea to an Army family. Married early, she was a mother of four and a well-published author by the time she was in her mid-twenties. She still lives in Swansea with her husband in a house on top of a Welsh hill facing the sea she loves. She is the author of the highly successful *Sweyn's Eye*, *Cordwainers* and *Firebird* series of novels.

ARIAN

Iris Gower

CORGI BOOKS

TRANSWORLD PUBLISHERS
61-63 Uxbridge Road, London W5 5SA
A Random House Group Company
www.rbooks.co.uk

ARIAN
A BANTAM BOOK: 9780552140959

First published in Great Britain
in 1994 by Bantam Press
an imprint of Transworld Publishers
Corgi edition published 1995

Addresses for Random House Group Ltd companies outside the UK
can be found at: www.randomhouse.co.uk
The Random House Group Ltd Reg. No. 954009

The Random House Group Limited supports The Forest Stewardship
Council (FSC), the leading international forest certification
organisation. All our titles that are printed on Greenpeace approved
FSC certified paper carry the FSC logo. Our paper procurement
policy can be found at www.rbooks.co.uk/environment

Typeset in 10/11pt Linotype Plantin by Photoprint, Torquay, Devon.
Printed in the UK by CPI Cox & Wyman, Reading, RG1 8EX.

4 6 8 10 9 7 5 3

**To Suzanne and Craig
with love.**

CHAPTER ONE

The farmhouse was dark and filled with menace. The walls were closing in on her. In the pale light from the window the outline of the man was silhouetted, he was drawing nearer to the bed where she lay. His hands were rough upon her, pressing her backwards. She was trying to scream but she had no voice. He was on her, hurting her, taking her in an act of violence that should have been an act of love. She must find her voice and then the pain would stop.

The scream pierced the night air and the silence was shattered. She woke to stare up at the stars through the jagged roof of the shed. They were sharp and clear above her in the soft spring air. Around her was the smell of night, the dampness of the grass outside, the pine scents of the wooden walls of the mean shelter that was her home.

Arian Smale sat up, gasping, trying to shake off the nightmare that still seemed so real. She was shivering and yet perspiration beaded her face like tears. But she was safe. They were gone now, the ghosts of her past, all gone. Even the farmhouse was no more.

Arian pushed aside the rough covering of blankets and edged towards the open door, still kneeling. She poised on the hillside, stared down at the town below her, her home town, Swansea.

To the west, the waters of the bay washed the silver shore, calm and peaceful in the chill of the night. In the folds of the surrounding hills, elegant houses stood bathed clean by moonlight, grand structures where the rich of the town lived.

To the east was the familiar surging power of the copper works sprawled along the banks of the river Tawe. Fierce sparks flew towards the heavens, dousing the moonlight.

The furnaces were being tapped at the White Rock copper works.

She remained on her knees for a long time, thinking about the past, about the sorrow caused by the men who had been, who had passed through her life. A fine collection of specimens they were, between them they had brought her enough grief to turn her against men for ever.

Her father was Robert Smale, owner of a run-down newspaper, a man who had fancied himself as a gentleman farmer. In drink he had been violent, she'd felt the weight of his hand more than once. His only gift to her, her only inheritance was his love of words.

Her uncle Mike had been no better. Known locally as Mike the Spud, he was a coward who had sold her out to Price Davies, the man who was the source of all her nightmares.

But Price Davies was dead now, like the others, all three men gone from her life but leaving it marked like a soiled footstep in crisp clean snow.

She sighed heavily. She needed company. She was becoming maudlin and fanciful. It was the life she led, living rough, roaming the hillside like a dispossessed spirit trying to find rest. And she was hungry, her empty stomach aching for food.

It was almost dawn. A rosiness was creeping over the land, warming the earth to life, and the folk at Honey's Farm would be up and about by now, smoke would be pouring from the chimneys and the everyday sounds of the cattle moaning softly in the byres would be heralding the morning.

Irfonwy O'Conner, the farmer's young wife, would be fresh faced and beautiful in her contentment with her lot, she would welcome Arian, *had* welcomed her when no-one else had wanted to know her. Fon was a true friend, a woman who deserved all the happiness life handed her so generously.

Arian rose and stretched her arms towards the heavens, she flung back her head and her long hair streamed silver gold down to the waist of her thick flannel skirt. Her shawl slipped to the ground, resting there, a splash of colour on the early morning greyness of the landscape. She felt like some pagan goddess, part of the contours of the hills, part of nature. Such fancies for a woman with nothing.

The trees were springing into life now, down there, below in the valley. Soon the blossoms would appear, the spring would come fully into its own and the world would seem a more kindly place.

She began to walk from the land that had been her father's once, before he had thrown it all away, towards where the smoke rose as she had known it would, from the chimneys above the rooftop of Honey's Farm.

The farm door stood open and from inside came the heady smell of bacon. Arian lusted after food. It was a long time since she'd eaten.

Fon O'Conner was plump with approaching mother-hood, her spotless apron emphasizing rather than conceal-ing her condition. She took Arian's arm, concern written all over her honest face. 'Morning, Arian, come in and sit by the fire, have a bit of breakfast with me, I'll be glad of another woman's company, mind.'

Arian moved silently into the welcoming kitchen and watched as Fon deftly lifted bacon from the pan and transferred it to a plate. She looked happy, there were no lines around her young eyes, no bruises on her mind or body. Why should there be? Fon was a happily married woman joyfully awaiting the birth of her second child.

They were about the same age, Arian realized, she and Fon O'Conner, though Arian was so much older in experience. But then Fon had been loved and courted and given a roof over her head by a strong man, she had been cosseted from childhood, she had not experienced the pain of rejection.

'We are so different,' Arian spoke her thoughts out loud, her voice cracking with lack of use. 'You are a good woman and I . . . well I am a whore, I have known men carnally, I am of little worth.'

'Rubbish!' Fon put down the pan and sat at the table, but her hand shook as she poured tea from the brown earthenware pot. 'You have had a difficult time of it, you were . . . were . . .' Her voice trailed away.

Arian shuddered as the nightmare drew nearer again, taking shape and reality. She felt pain and the stirring of anger.

'You couldn't help what that vile man did to you,' Fon said reasonably. 'Price Davies was sick in his mind, you must know that.'

Arian didn't speak and Fon leaned forward and took her hand. 'I owe you a great deal. If it wasn't for your courage . . .' Her words trailed away.

Arian smiled and her face was illuminated, beautiful in it's fine-boned thinness.

'What you have here you've won by your own hard work.'

'Huh!' Fon twisted her lips into a wry smile. 'Hard work is right. I have a stepson eating me out of house and home, a real handful is Patrick, and April, growing up she is, and me not knowing enough to talk to her like a mother should.'

Arian nodded gravely. 'You see, all this is part of your warmth, you take in the children of other women and make them your own.'

Fon didn't reply, she sipped her tea and watched in silence as Arian ate her breakfast, her manners dainty in spite of her hunger.

'Why are you looking at me like that?' Arian asked at last and then, almost immediately she frowned. 'You're not going to tell me to pull myself together, are you?'

'Right then, I won't tell you, but you know what I think. That it's about time you stopped living like a gypsy and found yourself an aim in life.'

'An aim in life?' Arian felt the stirring of anger again deep within her. 'What do you suggest I do?' Her meekness didn't fool Fon for one moment. 'Perhaps I could become a shilling stand-up selling myself in Swansea public bars. That's all I'm good for, isn't it?'

'Don't talk like that!' Fon's voice was sharp. 'Stop feeling sorry for yourself, Arian.' Fon rose to her feet. 'I've offered you work and a home here, more than once, but do you take the chance to make a fresh start?' It was Fon who was angry now.

'Oh, no, you've lost all your courage, you'd rather wallow in self-pity, rather live rough in a run-down hut on the hillside. Forget the past, it's over and done with. Look to the future now while you have your youth and strength and yes, your beauty.'

Arian rose and clutched her hands together. 'It was a mistake to come here.' Her voice shook a little. 'I thought you would understand, just a little.'

Fon was at her side, holding her close in an embrace, rocking Arian gently as though she was a child. 'There, there,' she smoothed back Arian's tangled hair, 'I *do* understand, I understand you've been through so much, you've suffered, no-one is denying that but you can't go on brooding over it for ever.'

Arian extricated herself, she felt uncomfortable being close to any human being, even Fon.

'Thanks for the breakfast.' Arian straightened her shoulders and stood quite still for a moment, not knowing what to do or where she would go next. She was tired of the open countryside, tired of sleeping rough in the shed or beneath hedgerows, but what else was there?

'At least let me give you some fresh clothes, yours are soaked with dew. You'll catch your death if you don't take care.' Fon smiled. 'Go on, you might as well have them, none of my skirts and bodices fit me now.'

'I'm all right as I am,' Arian said, 'you've given me enough. I don't want to live for ever on your charity.'

'Oh, what am I going to do with you?' Fon's voice was filled with exasperation. 'I'm so sad seeing you like this, your spirit gone, your intelligence wasted. Are you going to allow a pig like Price Davies was to ruin your life for ever?'

The very name of the man who had once been her lover had the power to freeze the blood in Arian's veins. She shuddered as though the winter winds were upon her and suddenly she felt unutterably weary. 'Don't worry, I'm a survivor. Hasn't your fine handsome husband told you that more than once?'

'Aye, Jamie has told me that,' Fon agreed, 'but he's a man, a darling man but a man none the less. He doesn't understand, not really.' Fon rubbed at her brow, 'I understand only too well, that it could so easily have been me that man attacked.'

Arian moved to the door. 'I feel better now, a little food and a little indulgence in self-pity has cleared my mind. I'm going, I'll leave you to get on with your chores in peace.'

Arian looked round the warm, welcoming kitchen which reflected Fon's life, where everything was clean and cheerful, and she envied her. But then, not too much. Arian waved her hand to encompass the neat room, the blazing fire, the spotless cloth on the table. 'I can't ever see me conforming to what other women feel is a normal way of life.'

'You will, when the right man comes along.' Fon followed Arian to the door putting her hand on Arian's arm: 'Are you sure you won't stay awhile, help me with the milking and such? I could do with another pair of hands, you know I could.'

Arian shook her head. 'It's not for me. You know I couldn't settle to it, but thanks.'

Arian found herself hurrying away, back up into the hills to where she had found a sort of peace these last months. She walked past the shed as though driven, onwards, upwards towards the farmhouse that once had been her home, the place she had been born and the place where part of her had died. She needed suddenly to face the ghosts of her past and to fix them in the past where they all belonged.

She breasted the hill and saw, with the same old shock of recognition, the burnt-out shell of the farm building. The chimneys pointed heavenward, jagged, blackened like bad teeth. She moved inside the stone walls and looked up at the

12

sky through the skeleton frame of the roof, and suddenly there were tears in her eyes.

Here her father had beaten her in his drunken excesses, here the man she'd thought loved her had held her prisoner, had raped her. The word fell, flint-like into her consciousness. The man who had hurt her was dead but it did not make the pain go away, and if she couldn't begin to face the future with some shred of dignity, she too might as well have died in the fire that had raged through the farmhouse.

She stood there for a long time, recalling the past, examining it, exorcising it, and at last Arian lifted her eyes to the open skies above the burnt-out rooftop and made a pact with herself. She would not remain Price Davies's victim, she would shake off the semi-madness that had gripped her, she would live again, make an effort to force her life into some kind of shape, and sense.

Perhaps if she tidied herself up, took the clothes that Fon had offered, she could go into Swansea, look for a job and then for decent lodgings and then she might just begin to find her self-respect again.

Self-respect, the words seemed nothing more than a distant dream. Could she do it, could she find the courage from somewhere to make a fresh start?

Arian sank down onto a flat stone that now held the warmth of the spring sunshine and tears came to her eyes. She knew them for what they were, tears of self-pity and weakness but she couldn't stem them, not if hell had her.

'Damn the woman.' Calvin Temple stood before the blazing logs that burned brightly in the ornate marble fireplace. 'I'll be thankful when the whole sordid business is over and I'm free of her for ever.'

'Lord Temple, may I speak as a friend as well as your solicitor? Are you sure you wish to go through with this? Divorce is not a pretty thing, even these days. We may be on the threshold of a new century but mud still sticks to

13

both sides and you will come in for some criticism, don't be misled about that.'

'Alun,' Calvin said slowly, 'could you live with a woman who cheated on you, bore a son and then confessed that the boy had been fathered by another man? Could you live with that for the rest of your life? Because I can't. I want to sever all relationships with Eline and her bastard child for ever. Is that so difficult to understand?'

'No, it isn't,' Alun replied, looking away in embarrassment, 'but Lady Temple might accuse you of throwing her out into the street, of bankrupting her, all of which is true.'

'Don't call her that,' Calvin snapped. 'She is Eline Harries, always will be to me.'

'But she has rights,' Alun reminded him gently. 'She is your wife, at least for the time being.'

'I know,' Calvin rubbed at his eyes. Even the mention of her name had the power to hurt him still. 'I know, but she is living with William Davies under my very nose. How else am I to deal with the situation? I am embarrassed and ashamed.'

He paused and rubbed his eyes. Not even to Alun could he confess that he was hurt beyond reason by Eline's betrayal.

'Another thing,' he said, 'I couldn't let my title and my inheritance pass to another man's bastard and that's final.'

Alun conceded the point. 'Of course not, you're right. Forgive my questions, I see they are futile. Divorce, however unpleasant, is the only solution.'

'Will it take long, before I'm free, I mean?' Calvin felt he was supplicating, like a child in difficulties, almost begging to be left some trace of dignity.

'No, it won't take long, not with the obvious evidence of your wife's infidelity,' Alun said softly. He moved to the door, 'I'll be in touch.'

When he was alone, Calvin moved to the window and stared out into the gardens. He saw that the trees in the orchard at the far end of the grounds were beginning to blossom. Spring was touching the earth, the world was warming into life but when would he be able to face life again without feeling as though he was in some way crippled?

Calvin, impatient with his mood, squared his shoulders. He was like a woman with the vapours, he told himself. It was high time he pulled himself together and got on with living instead of merely existing.

Outdoors, it was chillier than he'd thought it would be and yet the bracing air tasted like wine as Calvin set out on foot towards the town. He had little idea where he was going but he needed to shake off the claustrophobic atmosphere that hung over his house. Since he'd been without his wife, Stormhill Manor had not felt the same. It was, now, just another building, it was no longer home.

It was only a short walk into the busy heart of Swansea. The market was thronged with people, and the tang of spring vegetables along with the aroma of freshly baked bread hung enticingly upon the air.

Calvin felt restless. He was a man without direction and he recognized himself as such with a dart of dismay. Money he had aplenty but he needed more than that. He needed an interest in life, a goal, an ambition but one that would not, ever again, involve him falling in love with any woman.

He would eventually need a suitable wife, one who would play the hostess, provide him with heirs and one who would do his bidding without question, but that was something he would think about later on, when his wounds had begun to heal, perhaps.

Calvin suddenly felt the need for a drink of ale. He almost ached for the company of fellow men, and the cheery, smoke-filled bar of the Castle Hotel seemed to beckon him through the portals.

There was a card game taking place in the tap room and now and then a jubilant laugh from one of the players cut through the hubbub of masculine voices.

Calvin sat near the roaring fire and the old chair creaked beneath him. He took off his hat and saw with a sense of satisfaction that the landlord was at his side in an instant, waiting to serve the unusually well-dressed customer whose very appearance shouted wealth and breeding.

'Ale,' Calvin said pleasantly, 'and a toddy on the side will do nicely.'

'I'll send the girl along at once, sir,' the landlord said, his plump face half hidden by a bushy moustache. 'She's new, so if she's a bit slow, like, perhaps you'll make allowances, sir.'

Calvin stretched his feet towards the blaze and meeting the eyes of the man sitting opposite him, nodded in recognition.

'You're looking well, Jamie O'Conner. In town for the day?'

'Sure, that's right.' Jamie was a handsome man with the far-sighted eyes of a farmer. 'Whenever we meet,' he smiled ruefully, 'it's usually in the company of our womenfolk at some fair or other.' He coughed in sudden embarrassment. 'Sorry, I understand you've had some difficulties, you and Eline.'

'That's right,' Calvin said briskly. The clink of glasses made him aware of the girl at his side. He turned. She was thin, wraith-like almost, but there was no mistaking the silver hair, upswept now into a knot but the glow undiminished. He had met Arian Smale some time ago, happy and fresh she'd been then, tagging along with a fine young man, Eddie Carpenter was his name, as Calvin remembered.

He sighed. Things changed. The talk about Arian Smale in recent months had pointed to a very different person to the carefree, confident Arian Smale he had first met.

'Thank you,' Calvin said. 'How is your friend Eddie getting along? Is he a doctor yet?' He looked away quickly. This girl with her haunted eyes and hollow cheeks was yet another reminder of the time when he had been in love with Eline, blindly in love, more fool him. Oh, yes, Eline had taken him places, introduced him to people who, in the normal course of his life, he probably would not have met, worthy people indeed but not his kind, he was better off without them.

'We lost touch. She took a deep breath as though realizing how surly she must seem. 'Grateful enough he was for your help though, sir, I'm sure.'

His help?' Oh yes, he had funded the boy's training. Calvin had forgotten that, the money had been of little enough consequence. The girl placed the mug of foaming ale on the table and Calvin, glancing at her saw that her eyes were lowered, her shoulders bent in an attitude of subservience. Pity, an unwanted emotion, swept over him. The girl was so pale that her skin was almost transparent. She was, it seemed, beaten into submission by the fate life had meted out to her. Well, whatever stories lie behind her demure façade, that was her business and none of his.

As the girl moved away, Calvin turned his attention to Jamie O'Conner. The man was leaning forwards on the wooden settle, his legs stretched out before him, his pipe clenched between his teeth and he was watching the girl with a look of concern. Calvin wondered what he was thinking. At least the man wasn't a gossip, he kept his own counsel.

Perversely, Calvin suddenly wished to draw the man out, make conversation with him.

'Farm thriving?' He asked casually and Jamie took his time in deliberation before answering the question.

'Pretty busy this time of year.' Jamie smiled suddenly and his face was transformed. He was a man that most women would find irresistible and it was clear he was a man at peace with the world and himself. Calvin envied him.

'Early lambing always means work for everyone on the farm but I've got the excuse of coming into town for some seed. Could have sent the labourer sure enough but I felt the urge to bend my arm over a drink as a change from driving a plough.'

Calvin had liked Jamie O'Conner when he'd first met him and now he found himself warming to the man even more.

They were from different worlds and yet Calvin recognized the strength of purpose in him.

'You are a lucky man,' he said almost absently and Jamie nodded.

'Aye, I've got my land, a fine wife, a son and now another babbi on the way. You could surely call me lucky.'

Calvin raised his hand without turning, calling for another drink. His arm met something soft, and there was a sharp intake of breath behind him and the crash of smashing china.

Calvin was on his feet in an instant and turned to meet the apologetic eyes of Arian Smale.

'Sorry, sir,' she said quickly. 'I hope there's no ale on your sleeve.'

The landlord hurried across the sawdust-covered floor and bellowed angrily, his face red.

'For God's sake, was you born awkward?' He raised his hand as if to cuff the girl but Calvin grasped his wrist.

'No harm done,' he said easily. 'In any case it was my fault not hers.'

'She's a trouble-maker, that one,' the landlord said staring down at Arian with baleful eyes. 'Needs teaching a lesson and I'm just the one to do it. Whatever I try to do for her, she treats me like I'm dog shit, pardon my language, sir.'

He turned to Arian, 'Get out into the kitchen, out of my sight,' he said. 'I'll deal with you later.'

Arian was removing the sacking apron from around her waist with an air of resignation. She ignored the customers and faced the landlord.

'I'm not going to let you hit me,' her voice was cold, 'and I'm not coming to your bed, whatever your threats or promises, I'd rather leave here.'

'What and go back to sleeping rough?' The landlord sounded incredulous. 'Nothing but a tinker you are and what I say is—'

The rest of his sentence was cut off as Jamie shouldered him aside and took Arian by the arm. 'You are coming home

18

with me,' he said. 'You know Fon wants you to stay with us, give her a hand, like.' He gestured around the room. 'There's no need for you to work at this sort of job and you know it.'

'Thank you, Jamie,' Arian said quietly, 'but you've got enough mouths to feed without me adding to your burdens. Don't worry, I'll soon find something else.'

'What about working for me?' Calvin was surprised when the words came out of his mouth. He certainly hadn't meant to say them.

'As what?' Arian was looking at him with suspicion in her eyes. Calvin noticed that the lashes sweeping her cheeks when she looked away from him were dark in contrast with the lightness of her hair.

'As a servant, what else?' he said easily. 'I've a housekeeper, new at her job, and a cook who is growing old, and both of them could do with help.' He shrugged, 'It's entirely up to you. I live up at Stormhill Manor if you are interested.'

He picked up his hat and dropped some money on the damp table top. 'Here, landlord,' he said, 'that should compensate you for the loss of your mug of ale.' He smiled, 'As for the loss of your barmaid, I don't think you'll mind that very much, will you?'

Outside, in the clear air, Calvin took a deep breath. What was he about, taking pity on the girl? She probably was trouble as the landlord claimed. Arian Smale had been involved in several scandals already, considering she was just a slip of a girl. He shrugged as he strode away from the hotel. Arian Smale was nothing to do with him, she could go to hell her own way for all he cared.

Arian hurried from the hotel and regardless of the bite of the rough cobbles against the thin soles of her shoes began to run after the retreating figure of Calvin Temple. His offer had been a genuine one and though she didn't relish fetching and carrying for the rich of the town, neither did she relish the thought of sleeping outdoors again, not after having had a bed, however humble, in the upper reaches of the Castle Hotel.

'Sir,' she said breathlessly, 'I'll take the job if it's still on offer.'

'How good of you.' Calvin's shoulder seemed to hunch away from her as though he was embarrassed at her nearness.

'Can I come up to the manor now. Please,' she added as an afterthought.

'That will be all right.' Calvin glanced at her with a complete lack of interest that somehow piqued Arian. She knew she wasn't looking her best, her hair needed washing and her clothes were faded and torn but all the same, she was used to seeing lust in the eyes of any man who took the trouble to really look at her.

She knew about Lord Temple's troubles. Everyone in Swansea had heard that he'd been cuckolded by his wife, that he'd learned that the child she'd borne was not his and had cast her out without a penny to her name, and that he'd even closed down Eline's business enterprises, cleverly depriving her of any profit from them.

Arian had worked for Eline briefly, but that was before Price Davies had started his campaign of hatred against her. Arian shivered, pushing away the painful memories.

'Are you cold?' Calvin Temple looked down at her, his eyebrows raised, a frown creasing his forehead. He was a handsome man but there was an impatience about him, about the way he moved, even about the way he spoke.

'I'm all right,' Arian said with feigned indifference. 'I'm used to being out in the weather.'

The drive leading to Stormhill Manor was tree lined and long and when the impressive structure came into view, Arian took a deep breath wondering how Eline Temple could have brought herself to give up all this for a love match with a cobbler in some poky rented room.

Calvin Temple led the way into the spacious hallway and when a young servant girl bobbed a curtsy to him, he gestured for Arian to be taken to the kitchens.

'Tell Mrs Bob to find her something to eat and to see to it that there's a room ready and some warm, clean clothing, er . . .'

'Bella, sir and if it please your lordship, where can I get clothes from, none of us her size, see?'

Calvin glanced first at the maid's rounded body and then he turned to where Arian stood, slight and delicate.

'I see the problem.' He put his hand in his pocket and took out some money. 'Run out and fetch some clothes then, Bella. You can be trusted to buy skirts and undergarments, can't you?'

Before Arian could protest, he turned away. 'Don't worry,' he said dryly, 'it can come out of your first month's money, you won't owe me a thing.'

He opened the doors to what appeared to be the library, numerous volumes of books ranging the walls, protected by glass doors. A cheerful fire gleamed in the hearth and a leather-topped desk and chair took precedence over any other furniture in the room.

The doors closed and Arian was suddenly shut out. She almost stepped back a pace as though she'd been slapped and then she looked into the curious face of the maid.

For a moment they stared at each other in silence and then Bella sniffed. 'I know who you are, that Arian Smale what killed her own father, that's who you are.'

Arian moved closer. 'Well if I am,' she said with menace, 'don't you think you should be wary of me in case I feel the urge to strike again?'

This was a prospect Bella obviously hadn't considered and she backed away nervously. 'I didn't mean nothing, I 'spects you had your reasons. Look,' she said coaxingly, 'I'll take you to Mrs Bob's kitchen and while you have a nice drink of milk I'll run out to the shops and get you some clothes.'

Arian followed the girl to the regions below the stairs from where the mouthwatering aroma of cooking meat drifted upwards. A woman of uncertain years stood over the huge range, her thick ankles jutting like tree trunks from beneath the hem of her skirt. Her shoes gaped, as though the leather was unable to cope with the spread of her feet.

'Mrs Bob,' Bella said with a deference that wasn't lost on Arian, 'this is a new maid that the master's taken on.'

'Oh, what are your duties, girl?' Mrs Bob lifted the lid of one of the saucepans and sniffed at the contents before adding a little seasoning.

'I don't really know,' Arian said, 'I suppose I can do whatever needs doing.'

'That's what I call talking good horse sense.' Mrs Bob looked at her more closely. 'Don't talk like no maid to me, though, you been edycated I'd say.'

'She's Arian Smale, you know the one that killed her dad,' Bella chimed in and stepped back quickly. 'I'd better go and get them clothes then.' Hastily, she donned her coat and disappeared through the back door.

'Sit down gel, have a cup of my special tea.' Mrs Bob indicated a chair and Arian felt that she was being done a great honour.

'Thank you.' She sat at the table that had been scrubbed to within an inch of its life and gratefully took the hot cup of tea that Mrs Bob poured for her.

'What's all this then, girl?' she asked, 'More to the tale than that silly fool Bella knows, I'll be bound.'

'It's a long story,' Arian said slowly, 'there was a fight, my father had a gun in his hand, he had already put a bullet into the shoulder of another man when I came into the house. I tried to take the gun away from him.' She shrugged, 'It went off, my father was killed.'

'That's that then,' Mrs Bob said, 'you'll hear no more about it, I'll see to that.' She poured some more tea. 'There hasn't been a great deal of luck in your young life by the look of you, *Duw* we'll have to see that changes from now. You'll have a good job by here with us if you work hard and get along easy-like. His lordship don't bother us too much except when things go wrong. Fair, he is, mind and we won't have nothing said about him.'

She rose to her feet. 'Now how about peeling some spuds for his dinner? Thin I want them peeled mind, they cost a pretty penny these days so there's no wasting good food, understand?'

'I understand.' Arian found herself smiling. Mrs Bob might be strict, a martinet even, but she had a good heart. She had taken Arian's word about the killing without question.

Arian shuddered and pushed the thoughts of her father away into the recesses of her mind where all her unhappiness lay. There were enough bad memories hidden there to last her a lifetime.

By the time she went to bed it was past midnight. Arian lay in the unfamiliar room listening to the breathing of Bella in the bed opposite. The maid had forgotten to buy her any nightclothes when she went on her shopping jaunt and so Arian had climbed beneath the blankets in her shift.

'Arian,' Bella whispered and Arian turned over, the springs creaking a protest beneath her.

'What?' she asked quietly.

'Do you mind talking a bit?' Bella asked. 'I can't always get off to sleep straight away-like, a bit afraid of the dark I am, see and Mrs Bob won't allow no candles in bedrooms.'

'Go on then, talk if it helps,' Arian said in resignation. She ached, her eyes were heavy, but Bella's next words brought her awake at once.

'My dad used to hurt me,' she said. 'I don't blame you for killing your dad, not if he was like my dad.'

Arian bit her lip in silence and Bella, encouraged, continued to talk. 'Used to come to me when I was in bed, he did,' Bella said in quiet despair, 'used to lift up the bedclothes and get in with me. Hurt me bad, he did, mind, and me afraid to call out for someone, anyone to come and take him off me. Is that why you killed your dad?'

'No,' Arian said gently. 'My father had a gun, he was drunk, all I did was try to take the gun away from him. It was an accident.' She leaned up on one elbow and looked across at the lump of Bella's body in the other bed.

'I'm sorry about what your father did to you,' she said softly. 'Some men are just evil.'

'Not his lordship though,' Bella's voice was suddenly warm. 'A saint he is, a fine man, he don't do nor say nothing smutty-like, it was awful the way his wife treated him.'

'Aye, well that's none of our business,' Arian said softly, 'now I've had enough of talking, I've just got to get some sleep.' She turned over to face the wall, hugging the rough blankets close to her. She felt warm and protected and for the first time in many a long night, she felt safe even from her nightmares.

CHAPTER TWO

The house in World's End was typical of those surrounding it; tall, and hidden away in a damp, cobbled court. The room at the back of the building was small and cramped, the walls though freshly painted were marked by patches of damp. The curtains on the window hid cracked panes of glass that none the less shone with much polishing. In one corner of the room stood a bed draped with the same cheap, bright material as the windows. It was clear that no effort had been spared to make a home out of one room.

A young woman sat in her chair nursing a small child, an expression of tranquil happiness on her face. On the hob beside her bubbled a pan of *cawl*, the succulent smell of lamb and vegetables drifted to the small, cobbled yard outside.

William Davies lifted his head and sniffed the soup appreciatively, glancing through the open door of the small workshop that in reality was little more than a shed, into the single room where Eline sat holding their son, his face softened; she was beautiful and she was his.

William Davies was a strong, handsome man with just a wing of white streaking his hair. He wore the leather apron of the cobbler and in his hand was a dog, the clamp cobblers used for holding the leather-upper to the sole. He was sitting astride a small bench with an iron last between his strong thighs. Nails jutted from between his teeth and he removed one and deftly hammered it into place in the leather sole of the boot he was mending. He paused as though becoming aware of the silence from within the room.

In a quick movement, he rose and stood in the doorway of his mean workshop. Across the small distance that was the back yard, Eline looked up and met his eyes. She smiled and Will felt his blood flow faster. Would he never cease to want this woman who slept in his bed, who held his son at her breast but who was wife to another man?

He left his work, crossed the cold yard in a few quick strides and moved into the warmth of the room where was all he held dear in the world.

He knelt on the floor and leaned forward, his lips longing to feel her mouth open in passion beneath his. 'Eline,' he murmured, 'I love you.'

He kissed her and his hand brushed her breast, touching lightly the silky head of his son. He wanted to hold them both to him, his woman and his son.

'Come on now, love,' Eline spoke softly, 'stop working, you've done enough for today, see, the light is going.'

'I'll stop working if you come to bed with me,' he teased. 'It's about time I had some cosseting.'

'It's about time you washed the smell of leather from your hands,' Eline said though her voice was gentle. 'About time you took your son off my hands so that I could cut some bread and put out the supper.'

He sighed. 'You are a hard woman Eline, I don't know why I put up with it.' He eased the baby from her arms and Eline fastened her bodice but not before William had glimpsed the sweet fullness of her breast.

He put the baby into the sagging armchair and placed cushions around the child. 'Sleep now, son, I want to make love to your mother.'

'No, Will,' Eline protested but even as she spoke, her eyes were upon him, aware of his arousal. He took her in his arms and drew her against him, his hands slipping from her waist to the firmness of her buttocks. She drew a ragged breath, and with a sense of triumph he knew she wanted him as desperately as he wanted her.

It was a few short steps to the bed and he gently drew her down, stretching himself out beside her. He buried his head against her breasts, and her hands were in his hair, pressing him to her.

He loved her so much that he wanted to possess her every time he looked into her beautiful eyes and saw his desire reflected there.

He took his time, arousing her to the depths of passion he knew she possessed and when he finally joined with her, she gave a shuddering sigh and clung to him as though she was drowning in a beautiful sea of emotion.

Later, Will sat opposite Eline at the small table in the cramped room and watched as she ate delicately, like a dainty bird. She pushed her dish away and then her slim fingers curled in the handle of her cup. Will, looking at the delicate hands now reddened with work, wondered if she missed the skills that she once held so dear.

Eline had been a successful designer, a worker in leather whose talent, genius some might say, had helped her rise to the heights in the shoe-making business. Not only could she fashion the leather but she could draw beautiful designs and create them in masterly style. But now, because of him, she had lost it all.

'Why are you staring at me like that?' she asked, a smile curving her lips.

'Because I can't believe how lucky I am to have you,' he said soberly. 'Eline, the fine house, the luxurious life-style, most of all your work – do you miss it?'

'Wait here, *bachgen*,' she said softly. 'Let me show you what I've been getting up to in between feeding our son and looking after you.'

She went into the tiny scullery and he heard a drawer being opened. Eline returned, her face flushed with excitement and with some sketches held out before her like an offering.

'I haven't entirely given up on my ambitions,' she said. 'Calvin thought he'd left me with nothing, but he couldn't take my love of you and neither could he prevent me wanting to design shoes.'

Will looked in amazement at the fine drawings deftly executed. The footwear seemed to spring alive from the paper, bold riding boots intricately tooled side by side with dainty, feminine slippers. He was silent for a long time and Eline sighed heavily. 'Don't tell me, I've lost it.'

'Lost it?' Will said incredulously. 'My love, you are better than ever. These are fantastic.' His face softened, 'Do you realize that the great Hari Grenfell began her business right here, in World's End?' He took Eline's hand and kissed it. 'I was her apprentice so I know what difficulties she overcame before she was a success and what Hari can do, you can do, my love.'

He smiled as he looked into her eyes, love flowed between them, an almost tangible thing, and Will reached forward, unable to prevent himself from touching Eline's cheek.

'I'll make your designs a reality myself, my lovely, talented lady,' he said softly.

A shadow passed fleetingly across Eline's face. 'I wish you could have said wife.' She forced a smile. 'It *will* come right, won't it, all of it?'

'Once your divorce from Temple is over and done with we'll be married. I can't wait for that day to come.'

Eline hugged him, resting her cheek on the top of his head.

'Are you really going to make shoes from my designs?' Her voice was almost wistful.

'Of course,' Will said at once. 'I'll sell them, too, just see if I don't.'

'How will you do that?'

'Quite easily,' he said, smiling. 'I'll take a few pairs around with me as samples, show them to my customers. I'm sure to get some orders.' He paused.

'I'm glad you haven't given up on your designs, Eline, and don't worry, we'll soon build up a nice little business here, perhaps in a small way at first but it will grow, I'm confident of it. We won't always be poor. One day I'll be able to give you everything you could ever want.'

'I've got that already.' Eline rubbed at her eyes and he saw a tear glint on her lashes. He stood up and put his hands on her waist. 'Now, how about a bit more of that soup before I get ideas into my head again?'

Eline pushed his hands away in mock anger. 'You are insatiable, behave yourself William Davies.' They smiled at each other and Will knew that he would work day and night to make Eline happy.

It was the next morning when Eline woke that her plan of action became clarified in her mind. She would ask her old landlady for help. Mrs Jessop had enjoyed caring for baby William once, she might just be persuaded to look after him again, if just for a short time every day.

Before Will and Eline had set up home together, Eline had been at her wit's end how to cope with her life. Calvin had thrown her out of their home, had left her with no means of support. She could hardly blame him; she'd hurt and betrayed him, made him look foolish in the eyes of his neighbours. She knew the pain she'd caused Calvin was unforgivable. No wonder he was bitter.

Still, he hadn't been blameless; he'd left her destitute, she and her son in fear of starving. It was then that Mrs Jessop's kindness and sound common sense had saved the day.

With the older woman's help, Eline had found herself a job scrubbing floors at the public bar of the inn across the road from Mrs Jessop's boarding house. She'd had a room to call her own and Mrs Jessop had treated her like a daughter. Those were the dark days and she hated to remember them. But now, she had Will, she had their child and with a little bit of effort and planning, she could work again. What more could she want?

Mrs Jessop's pleasure at seeing Eline was gratifying. She held out her arms and welcomed Eline indoors, settling her in the chair in the best parlour, pressing tea and biscuits upon her and all the time with a happy smile on her face.

'Well then, how are you getting on with that fine young man of yours?' She took the baby from Eline's arms and unwrapped him from his shawl, staring down at the small sleeping face with delight.

'I can never thank you enough for bringing Will and me together, Mrs Jessop,' Eline said softly. 'My only regret, if there is one, is that I'm not married to him.'

'Well you can't have everything in life, but then, you've got the most important things so no grumbling, is it?' Mrs Jessop's eyebrows were raised. 'There's this lovely boy for a start.'

'I know,' Eline said, 'and now I think I've found the courage to work at designing again, to try to build up a business so that Will doesn't have to work himself to death.' She smiled coaxingly, 'But I'm going to need your help, Mrs Jessop.'

'Well if you're going to ask me to look after this little angel face then don't give it another thought. I'd take him off your hands any time and pay *you* for the privilege.'

Eline bit her lip. 'There's the problem,' she said, 'I can't pay you anything, at least for a start.'

'Am I asking for anything? You'd be doing a lonely old lady a favour, mind. When do I start, right away?'

Eline laughed. 'Why not?' She flexed her fingers, 'I'm itching to take up a pencil, I can't deny it.'

'Will you go to Mrs Grenfell to sell your shoes?' Mrs Jessop placed the baby over her shoulder and rubbed at his back and Emlyn pulled at her hair, his eyes wide with curiosity.

Eline shook her head. 'I'll be working with Will. Between us we'll make a new start and enjoy ourselves in the process, I shouldn't wonder.'

'Not too much enjoying, mind,' Mrs Jessop laughed. 'You don't need no more babies for a while.' She settled the baby in her lap and gave him a spoon to play with. 'No harm in going to the Grenfells or the Millers, mind,' she said pursuing her train of thought. 'Big business people them and fine folk too, not toffee-nosed like some with money.'

'I know,' Eline said softly, 'but they move in the same circles as Calvin. They meet him socially and might feel they can't openly side with his faithless wife. I wouldn't like to be an embarrassment to anyone.'

'Tush!' Mrs Jessop exploded. 'Where there's business and money there's no thought of embarrassment, you surely realize that?'

'I suppose you're right,' Eline said, 'but no, we'll go it alone, we'll make a success of it, you'll see.'

'Oh, I don't doubt it,' Mrs Jessop said. 'Right, get off with you, talking never did get the work done.'

It was fascinating for Eline to watch the way Will worked at the leather, bringing her visions, sketched on paper, into real solid shapes and designs. The first design he tackled was a pair of heavy riding boots. They were cut to curve around the calf of the leg with support as well as comfort in mind, and the instep was tooled with a fancy design of spurs and stirrups, a motif repeated around the edge of the boot.

She had given him patterns of several pairs of good stout ladies' boots in a variety of sizes; boots were a necessity especially on the cold winter days. Her one frivolity was a pair of evening pumps in kid with a plunging 'V' shape cut over the toes and with beading running from instep to heel. It took Will days of solid working to accomplish the task she had set him and all the time Eline was worryingly aware of the cobbling work he was leaving undone.

'I can't see any working woman wearing those,' Will said, when at last he held up the finished pumps. They sat in the palms of his big hands, small and elegant and quite insubstantial.

'These, I presume, you will offer to the fine ladies of the town. They are lovely but they are an extravagance, Eline.'

'I know,' Eline said ruefully, 'practical shoes are more likely to sell but I couldn't resist just one flight of fancy.'

'I have a good feeling about them,' Will said firmly. 'This pair of pumps is likely to bring you more attention and more custom than any of the other shoes, worthy though they are.'

Eline smiled. 'It's good of you to indulge me, Will, but I think I'll stick to the more practical designs for the time being.'

Will didn't reply but there was an enigmatic smile on his face that Eline did not fail to notice.

'What are you up to Will Davies?' she demanded. He drew her to him and his hand moved to her breast but she pushed him away quickly.

'None of that, not in working hours. Mrs Jessop wouldn't approve.'

'Damn Mrs Jessop,' Will said amiably. 'She's not here, is she?'

He drew her closer again and with a sigh, Eline succumbed, her hands on his face, her eyes shining. 'I love you Will Davies,' she said softly.

William's words proved to be prophetic; the fine pumps sold almost immediately to one of his richer customers. 'I knew it!' Will said in triumph. 'I just knew those pumps would appeal to one of my ladies.'

Eline was sitting at the table, her pencil in her hand, the light from the small window falling on her drawings.

'Oh, so you have "ladies", do you?' Eline said, her hands on her hips, her tone severe. 'I wonder what else you do with them other than mending their shoes?'

'Oh, I have my methods of charming the customers, but only the beautiful ones of course,' Will replied.

He leaned forward and kissed her mouth. 'Now, stop carping and get on with it.'

'With what? ' Eline was genuinely puzzled. Will slipped his arm around her waist, drawing her to her feet.

'Now don't look so appealing or you won't be getting on with anything except looking after your man properly.'

Eline pushed him away, frowning. 'Stop your teasing and tell me what you are talking about: get on with what?'

'Oh, didn't I tell you?' Will said innocently. 'Mrs Walter Rogers wishes for several more pairs of pumps *and* a new pair of riding boots as well.' He winked 'Her lover bought the fancy riding boots and now Mrs Rogers wants a pair just like them. But we mustn't tell her husband.'

'Will!' Eline hugged him. 'Oh, my love, that is the best news I've heard for ages.'

'Aye, well don't forget what I had to do to get you these orders, will you?'

Eline leaned back in his arms. 'What did you have to do?' she asked, her head on one side, an uncertain smile on her lips.

'Well . . .' Will paused tantalizingly, 'I had to be nice, very nice to my lady customers.'

'Oh?' Eline's voice had taken on an edge of anger and Will threw back his head and laughed out loud.

'It's a good thing that all my ladies have very handsome husbands or lovers otherwise I might have been called upon to make even greater sacrifices.'

Eline slapped him playfully. 'You monster, let me go, I've got an idea for a design.'

'So have I,' Will said. 'I don't think my ideas and designs can be put off much longer.'

Eline moved out of his arms quickly. 'Go away, do some more work. We can't live on love alone, mind.'

'We could try,' Will said sighing, 'but I suppose I'd better be a dutiful husband and go out and earn some wages.'

When he had gone, Eline twisted her hands together. 'Husband' – how fine the word sounded when applied to Will. But she had a husband, she was married to Calvin, Lord Temple. She sank down into her chair, her elation vanishing. How she wished he would get the divorce over quickly so that she could be free of him.

She felt a knot of apprehension inside her. She had hurt Calvin badly, he had doted on the son she'd borne within the marriage, the child he thought was his. What if he chose to punish her now by staying married to her, forcing her to live an irregular relationship with Will for ever?

Perhaps she should see him right now while the baby was with Mrs Jessop. It would not be tactful to take her son with her, it wouldn't exactly endear her to Calvin to flaunt her infidelity in his face.

She took up her shawl from the peg on the door, drew it around her shoulders and stood for a moment looking around the room. What a difference to the life-style she'd enjoyed as Calvin's wife.

While at Stormhill she had, apparently, everything she desired. The manor was enormous, with huge rooms hung with fine drapes; meals appeared on the long table in the dining room with apparent lack of effort, sumptuous stews and dishes of meat and fish that would tempt the poorest appetite. And yet there she had not been happy, she had wanted something else from life, had known exactly what it was, and now she had it – the love of William Davies – she regretted nothing.

She smiled as she looked round the cramped room; a cheerful fire burned in the black leaded grate and if a patch of damp appeared from time to time on the back wall, a touch of whitewash soon disguised it.

Outside the air was balmy with the scents of spring, the blossoms festooned the few trees that grew in World's End and the sound of birdsong was pleasing to Eline, smothering for a moment the apprehension that filled her.

How would Calvin receive her, would he have her ordered away from the premises without even talking to her? She wouldn't be at all surprised. And could she blame him? He had been good and kind, a considerate, loving husband and she, well she had been faithless.

It was a long walk through the maze of streets and up the hill towards Stormhill Manor, and every step she took increased her sense of doubt at the wisdom of what she was doing.

At last she arrived at the gates and began the walk along the tree-shaded drive. It was a strange feeling, looking up at the big house, it was as if living there was something she had experienced in a distant dream.

She hesitated at the front door; should she go to the back like one of the servants? But that was absurd. She was still Calvin's wife, she must behave as such or she wouldn't even get past the servant who opened the door.

Eline's surprise as the big door swung open was reflected in the face of the girl who stood before her. She was dressed in a neat black skirt and a white blouse, and an apron was tied around her slender waist. Her hair, silver and gold in

34

the glimmer of sunlight was tied away from her face but there was no mistaking the sheer beauty of it.

'Arian!' Eline said. 'What on earth are you doing here and dressed like that?'

'I'm working here,' Arian stepped back and allowed Eline into the hallway. 'I suppose I'm a servant. I do any and every job that is asked of me.'

'Oh Arian, and you showed such promise when you worked for me,' Eline said. 'Surely you can find something better than this?'

Arian shook her head. 'A lot has happened to me since I was in charge of your workshop, you must know that, Eline. Anyway, Lord Temple was kind enough to take me in when I was desperate. I'm grateful now for a roof over my head and some warm food in my belly.'

Eline sighed. 'You've had a bad time of it, Arian, but I don't suppose you want to be reminded of it. Is Calvin at home? I must see him.' She wondered briefly if Arian was warming Calvin's bed. From what she remembered, Arian had hot blood in her veins; she had fallen under the spell of Price Davies quickly enough. But that thought was uncharitable and, to be fair, Arian had been eager to learn from Price Davies; she had learned as much about the shoe trade as the cobbler was willing to teach her. Of course that was before everything went sour on her, before the strange fire at the farmhouse in the hills, the full story of which even now was shrouded in mystery.

Eline chided herself. Who was she to judge Arian or anyone else, come to that? She was living in sin with Will and with a baby borne to one man while she was married to another. Not exactly a pillar of moral rectitude was she?

'He is in,' Arian's voice broke into Eline's thoughts. 'Shall I tell him you're here?' She looked curiously at Eline. It was clear she knew what had happened between the couple, everyone in Swansea probably knew about the way Calvin had thrown his wife out with little but the clothes she stood up in.

'Where is he?' Eline asked softly. 'I don't want him to have the chance to turn me away without hearing me out.'

'In the library, I think,' Arian said quietly. 'But don't tell him I was the one who let you in.'

Her heart was beating swiftly as Eline made her way across the polished floor of the hall towards the double doors of the library. Her hand, reaching for the door knob, was trembling.

Calvin rose to his feet as she entered the room, the pen still in his hand. 'What are you doing here?' His voice was hostile, his eyes unfathomable.

'I'm sorry,' Eline said, 'I was afraid you wouldn't see me if I was announced.'

'Your fears are well founded. What do you want?'

'To talk about the divorce. You are still going ahead with it aren't you?'

'Why?' Calvin said bitterly. He moved closer to her. 'Not regretting leaving me are you, Eline?'

She looked down at her hands. 'I hurt you, Calvin. You are a fine, decent man. You deserved better.'

He caught her shoulders abruptly and drew her close, his mouth hovering above hers. 'You are tired of your life of poverty, you want to come back to Stormhill Manor, is that it?'

She shook her head. 'No, my home is one room in World's End and that's just where I want to be.'

She saw him flinch. He was frowning as he released her abruptly. 'What then, is it money you want? Your motive in coming here is not one of love and I see no regret in your eyes. Clearly you are happy as you are. Surely you haven't come just to ask futile questions?'

'I don't want your money, Calvin. We don't live well but we manage. I just want to know when the divorce will be over and done with, that's all.'

'So that you can marry your cobbler, is that it?' Calvin said fiercely. 'What if I were to deny you, Eline, keep you tied to me?' He turned and caught her close to him once more.

'You are a fool coming here. I could claim my conjugal rights and not one man in the world would blame me.' His voice was harsh.

Eline looked up at him without fear. 'You won't do that, Calvin, you are far too much of a gentleman to force yourself on any woman, especially me.'

His mouth came down on hers, crushing, bruising, and he held her close to him. There was no tenderness in him and yet Eline felt no fear, simply pain that she had wounded Calvin yet again.

She drew away from him. 'I'm sorry, I was wrong to come,' she said. 'I have no right to ask you anything.'

She walked to the door, her head high and Calvin's voice stopped her.

'Eline, you will have your divorce, I've set the process into motion. It's only a matter of months and then you will be free to marry your cobbler. One thing more, I have disowned your son. If you wanted to fight me in a court of law I dare say you would have grounds, the boy was born in wedlock after all.'

Eline turned and looked at him. 'I think you know that I won't fight it. I accept you have no responsibility for him.' Her voice faded as she saw his pain. 'I've done enough to you. All I hope is that one day you will find someone else to be happy with.'

He gave a harsh laugh. 'I love you, Eline,' he said and there was a note of despair in his voice. 'I've tried to conceal that fact from myself but now that I have seen you again, held you in my arms . . . For Christ's sake why are you torturing me, just get out of my sight.'

She left the house quickly, tears burning her eyes. She had her answer, she would soon be free but at what cost? She hurried down the drive, no longer revelling in the soft sounds and sights of spring. She had ruined Calvin's life by her faithlessness and that was something she would never be able to forget.

That evening, Will sensed something of her mood and took her gently in his arms, pushed back her hair and looked down into her eyes.

'What is it, Eline, why the long face?' He pressed his lips against hers for a brief moment and then held her away from him. 'Tell me, I know something is worrying you.'

'You are not going to like it,' Eline said softly. 'Promise you won't be angry.'

'Come on, stop prevaricating,' Will said, 'spit it out. I'm not going to take up wife-beating just yet.'

'I went to see Calvin today.' Her words seemed to fall into a well of silence and Eline almost felt the tightening of Will's muscles.

Very slowly he released her and moved away, standing at the window although it was far too dark to see anything out in the yard.

'Why?' The word seemed hard, flint-like, and Eline moved to Will and put her arms around his waist, resting her head against his broad back.

'I just wanted to know when I would be free,' she said almost pleadingly. 'The divorce, it should be over within weeks so Calvin said.'

'And what else did Calvin say?' Will's voice held a chill. 'Did he ask you to come back to him? Did he tell you he still wanted you?'

'Please, Will, I meant it for the best but I see now it was a mistake,' Eline said quickly, fear sending wings of pain through her.

Will turned suddenly and pushed her away from him. 'He did, don't deny it, he said he wanted you. Did he hold you in his arms, did he kiss you Eline?'

'No,' she said miserably, aware that she did not want to lie to Will but too afraid to explain what really happened.

'He did, he held you, tried to persuade you to go back to him.' Will's voice was low, 'Don't lie to me, Eline, please. This is too important.'

'Yes, yes!' she said. 'He said he loved me still, he held me and kissed me but I didn't consent to it, I told him it was you

I wanted. Will . . .' She held her arms to him pleadingly, 'Please Will, I'm sorry I went there. It was foolish but I didn't mean anything to happen.'

'You could have rebuffed him,' Will said. 'You could have done many things but you didn't, did you?'

'Will, I felt sorry for him, he *is* still my husband after all.' Immediately the words were spoken Eline knew they should never have been said. Will's face turned white, his jaw tightened and his eyes seemed to penetrate her very soul.

'So, you felt sorry for him, he is still your husband and did he claim his rights over you, did your pity extend to the bedroom, Eline, did it?'

'No!' Her voice was ragged, 'No Will, how could you even suggest it?'

'You let him hold you and kiss you and you felt sorry for him. You've just told me that the man is still your husband so why shouldn't you indulge in a little lovemaking to pass an afternoon? How can I believe anything you say, Eline?'

'I hate you!' Eline said fiercely. 'I hate you Will Davies, seeing how little faith you have in me. I'm sorry I ever came to live with you.'

Will stared at her for a long moment and then, without another word, picked up his hat and coat and left the room. Eline heard his footsteps ringing on the cobbled yard outside, she heard the slam of the gate as if it was a death knell and then there was silence except for the ticking of the clock and the shifting of coals in the grate.

She sank into a chair and put her face in her hands. The tears came hot and bitter and, after a moment, she put her head down on her arms and the sobs racked her body.

Later, she rose and washed her face and patted her hot cheeks with the towel, and misery washed over her afresh. She had made two men unhappy today; the man she was married to and the man she loved, quite a record by anyone's standards.

She pushed the kettle onto the flames and made herself some hot tea, then climbed onto the bed beside the sleeping form of her son.

'Emlyn,' she said softly, 'your mother is a foolish woman. I wish I was wise and sensible but I'm not, I'm nothing at all without your father.'

She looked at the clock, the public bars would be closing and soon now, surely quite soon, Will would be home. To pass the time, she washed and brushed her hair and then pulled on her nightgown. She climbed onto the bed again and stared at the flickering lamp; it was running low on oil, soon it would go out and then, by then, Will would definitely be home.

But the lamp flickered and fizzled and went out and the smell of oil hung in the air. Now there was just the light from the fire and Eline stared at the embers of coal as if they could give her hope.

The sound of singing came from the street and then faded into the distance, the last of the revellers had gone home to their wives and their beds. She had to face it, Will was not coming home, not tonight or any night, he had finished with her, he had believed the worst and had put as much distance between them as possible.

She snuggled down beside the baby and held his warmth against her breast. Tears came afresh and ran salt into her mouth and Eline's sense of despair plumbed new depths. She was no good without Will, she was half a person, she would be unable to function without him.

She turned her face into the pillow to muffle her sobs but crying didn't ease the ache inside her. 'Oh Will,' she whispered, 'please come back, I can't live without you.'

At last, she fell into an exhausted sleep, and when she woke, in the early hours of the morning, the place where Will slept beside her was empty.

CHAPTER THREE

Arian's back ached, the floor under her knees was hard and the water in the bucket at her side was rapidly cooling, making cleaning the slate flags of the huge kitchen doubly difficult. After only a few weeks at Stormhill, she was finding the menial work tiresome.

Lord Temple employed only a skeleton staff; it seemed that on the departure of his wife, he had sacked most of the servants, anyone who could remind him of the happier days of his marriage. Later, he had taken on just those who were essential to the running of the manor, a cook, and a housekeeper. Bella, the maid, was the only one he had retained from the old staff and that, she claimed, was because he felt sorry for her. She was so clumsy that it was doubtful she would find a position elsewhere.

Mrs Richards was a grey figure, her title was of housekeeper but like everyone else in Stormhill Manor, she took on more than one role. Her duties kept her above stairs, she saw that the bedrooms were cleaned and the sheets fresh on the master's bed. She instructed Bella in the correct method of placing coals in the grates to obtain the maximum heat at the minimum of expense, for the accounts too, were her province. Mrs Richards prided herself on saving money even though it was apparent that Lord Temple was very wealthy.

'A penny saved is a penny earned,' she was fond of saying though the rest of the servants were not quite sure what she meant by that. However, Mrs Richards was perceived as being very wise and so her words were listened to with respect.

Mrs Bob was the mainstay of the household, she ruled the kitchen with good humour and as much hard work as her age would allow. She was a fine cook and had learned to make meals that were nourishing and easy to serve, adding the garnishes and sauces that gave the appearance of much time spent over the range but which, in reality took only minutes to prepare. Now, with the coming of Arian, the burden of running a huge manor house was lightened somewhat, though Stormhill Manor warranted a full complement of servants to do it justice.

'Arian, leave that floor for a minute and come by here, will you?' Mrs Bob sounded flustered. She was cooking her favourite dinner of breast of lamb which, with a brisk fire, took only an hour to roast. 'Watch the joint for me while I make some mint sauce. And mind you keep the meat open to the air,' she instructed. 'No popping it into the oven otherwise it will be baked, not roasted.' She paused. 'It might be as well to remember any hints I pass on because one day you might be cook here instead of me.'

She was using the old spit instead of the oven and the fat crackled against the coals sending out a tantalizing aroma of lamb. Arian realized she was hungry. She wiped her hands on her apron, waiting patiently for Mrs Bob to explain what she wanted from her.

'There,' she said at last, her face flushed as she moved from the table where she'd been expertly cutting mint, back to the fire, 'now I need some red wine and some vinegar. Fetch a bottle from the cellar, will you girl?

Arian picked up her bucket and cloth, the floor would have to do for now. In any case, it would be done afresh tomorrow and hopefully then it would be Bella's turn.

She swished the dirty water in the yard and held her hands, one by one under the old, creaking pump, working the handle with difficulty. She looked at her fingers; they were wrinkled like prunes, reddened and rough now, the nails chipped and ragged. She sighed, at least she had a roof over her head, a bed to sleep in and a belly full of good food.

It was cold and dank in the cellar and Arian fetched the wine quickly, hurrying back up the stone steps to the warmth of the kitchen.

Mrs Bob didn't turn from her table where she was clarifying honey for the pudding. 'Mix two glasses of the wine with one glass of vinegar and a few spoonfuls of cullis.'

'Cullis?' Arian asked, 'What's that?'

'*Duw* girl, don't you know anything? Cullis is a bit of old broth, that's all. Adds a tang that the master likes to the sauce. Now get on with it.'

Arian mixed the ingredients into a jug and stood for a moment watching, as Mrs Bob melted the honey and scooped off the scum. She glanced up and saw Arian watching her.

'The secret is to use only the best honey, the poorer quality needs a lot of fussing, you have to add the white of an egg and keep boiling the stuff down, it's not worth the bother but in some homes it has to be done.'

She worked for some moments in silence. 'Right now, add the mint and some cinnamon and boil the lot for quarter of an hour and it's ready. See, it's easy isn't it girl?'

Mrs Richards entered the kitchen, her face unusually flushed. 'Arian, you'll have to serve the dinner,' she said in her peremptory manner. 'Bella's gone and developed a headache.' Her face took on a pinched, disapproving look, 'Comes with her courses every month, convenient if you ask me. Now, change your clothes at once and for heaven's sake do something with that hair.'

Arian looked at Mrs Bob who jerked her head, 'Go on with you, girl, I can manage here.'

Arian mounted the two flights of stairs to the bedroom she shared with Bella. The girl had her face to the wall, she was pale and sweating and obviously unwell.

'Can I get you something?' As Arian talked, she was opening the drawer that had been assigned to her and taking out some fresh clothes.

'No, I'll be all right by tomorrow,' Bella sighed. 'It's always like this, first day on, after that it's not so bad, like.'

'If you're sure then.' It took only moments for Arian to change into a neat clean skirt and crisp apron. She coiled her hair quickly into an untidy bun, cursing at her clumsy fingers, and placed the starched cap on top of her head. 'I'll come up later, see if I can bring you some hot tea.' She spoke to Bella's back, the girl was heavily asleep.

Mrs Bob had the food ready for her to serve; the meal was set out on a tray and covered with a silver lid. 'His lordship don't want no soup tonight so tell him there's extra veg. Mind you give him time to eat his fill before you take him the pudding, he doesn't like to be rushed.'

Arian felt a flutter of nerves that was alien to her. She wasn't used to waiting at table, that was Bella's job. The tray was heavy and Bella, who was a hefty girl, carried it with ease. Arian on the other hand found negotiation of the stairs and the passageway to the dining room quite an ordeal.

It was with difficulty that she knocked on the door, balancing the tray on one hand, her throat dry, fearing the huge silver salver might at any moment crash to the floor.

'Come in.' Calvin Temple's voice was impatient, he wasn't used to being kept waiting. 'About time,' he said as Arian set the tray on the sideboard and lifted the lid. 'What is it?'

'Breast of lamb in wine and mint sauce,' Arian said quickly, her hackles rising at Calvin's tone.

He tasted the sauce and looked up at Arian quickly. 'Who chose the wine?'

'Well, I went to the cellar to get it for Mrs Bob,' Arian said puzzled by his manner. 'Is anything wrong?'

'Very possibly,' Calvin said dryly. 'Please bring me the bottle, would you?'

Arian forgot to bob a curtsy as she hurried from the dining room and quickly negotiated the stairs to where in the kitchen Mrs Bob was sitting down to a cup of tea.

'He wants the bottle of wine,' Arian said quickly, 'Where did I put it?'

She looked among the dishes on the huge table and picked up the wine, staring at the writing on the label without comprehension.

'Oh, my good lord!' Mrs Bob put both hands on her cheeks, 'you've only gone and fetched one of his best bottles

44

of claret and let me use it for the cooking. *Duw*, there's a fool I was, I should have warned you not to take anything from the back of the cellar.'

'Oh, well, it's all wine,' Arian said huffily, 'I can't see that it really matters.'

Mrs Bob stared at her. 'If this wasn't so serious, it would be funny,' she said. 'That claret was laid down by Lord Temple's great-uncle many moons ago. Cost a pretty penny today it would.'

Arian shrugged and returned to the dining room with the bottle. Calvin took it and stared down at the label for a long moment.

'Mrs Bob must be losing her mind,' he said at last. 'This is one of my best wines.'

'It's my fault,' Arian said defensively. 'Mrs Bob has enough to do without running up and down to the cellar. In fact, I might as well tell you now that we are all overworked. There are not enough hours in the day for a small staff to keep a place like this going. I thought a man like you would have the sense to realize that.'

He stared at her for a long time in silence and Arian braced herself; now she would be dismissed, she would be forced to return to living rough on the hillside. Well, she wouldn't wait for his scornful dismissal.

She untied her apron and threw down her cap. 'I was a fool to come here, this work isn't for me.' She pointed to her head. 'I have a brain, I commit the sin of thinking; something not encouraged in the lower orders, is it, Lord Temple?'

'Sit down.' He indicated one of the carved ornate chairs beside him.

'What?' Arian was taken aback by the sudden turn the conversation had taken.

'I said sit down,' Calvin repeated. 'I thought you had a brain and yet you fail to respond to the simplest of instructions.'

Arian sat down. Calvin looked at her for a long moment in silence.

'What would you like to be doing?' he asked. 'What would you use this famous brain for?'

'No need for sarcasm,' Arian said mildly. 'If you must know, I would like to run a business,' she spoke without hesitation.

'I would like to buy and sell leather, I know how to choose the best.' She laughed bitterly, 'I learned from a harsh teacher.'

She thought for a moment of Price Davies, so clever when handling skins, able to discern what texture was needed, the correct amount of resilience, how to cost the leather coming from the tannery to the nearest penny.

'I'm not interested in your past,' Calvin said in a matter-of-fact way that Arian found strangely comforting. 'I'm not really interested in you at all – as a woman – but as a business prospect maybe there's a chance we could work something out.'

'What do you mean,' Arian said, 'work something out?'

'Do you mind if I eat my dinner while we talk?' Calvin said lifting the gleaming cutlery. 'Now that you *have* used my best claret for sauce, I might as well enjoy it.'

Arian waited in a fever of impatience, oblivious of her surroundings; the elegant dining room, the high chandeliers, the sumptuously curtained windows were all part of a backdrop to her. Here was Calvin offering her a way forward for the future but what was the catch?

'Through my somewhat disastrous marriage, I became interested in the footwear business,' Calvin said. 'If I understand correctly, a supplier brings in the leather wholesale to some warehouse or other and the shoe-makers have to buy it in fairly small quantities, is that right?'

Arian nodded, 'French calf has to be imported of course but most skins are easily available in this country, the trick is in choosing the good stuff, you see.'

'What is the competition hereabouts, do you know?' Calvin watched her thoughtfully as he ate his dinner. His manners were impeccable, Arian noted absently.

46

'Well, there's Mr Grenfell of course,' Arian said thoughtfully, 'and Emily and John Miller do a bit of buying but I believe they buy just enough for their own use, they don't have a warehouse as such, not these days.'

'To whom would you sell, then?' Calvin asked and Arian smiled. All these details had been worked out minutely by her during many a long hour when she lay awake in some barn, or cushioned in her broken-down shed.

'There are the small Swansea shoemakers,' she said, 'cobblers who know the best and don't want the bother of going to the tanneries to sort it out. Then there are nearby towns, Morriston, Clydach and Neath and further afield, the whole of the Rhondda valleys, the scope is endless. Eventually even the Grenfells and the Millers would save time and buy from me.'

'You seem pretty sure of yourself,' Calvin remarked, 'but your income from such sources would be small. Surely it should be the bigger towns such as Cardiff and Newport you must aim for?'

'You forget,' Arian said, 'I will be a specialist, anyone who wants the finest kid or pigskin would come to me and pay for the privilege of my expertise.'

Calvin put down his napkin. 'A child and already you are an expert, amazing.'

'Let me see your boots,' Arian said, and Calvin's eyebrows rose a fraction. Good naturedly, he lifted his booted foot and Arian took it on her lap, her fingers tracing the leather as though her finger-tips could see.

'These boots are beginning to crack,' she said. 'The leather wasn't treated properly, see how hard it is where it should be supple.'

'They are almost new,' Calvin protested. 'Where are they cracking?'

'There look, near the instep, where the leather takes the strain of bending. It's not up to the job. It's not seasoned leather but cheap, too quickly cured.'

'You could be right,' Calvin said. 'So you know your leather but can you deal with figures? Can you handle the finance, for if I set you up in business I want nothing to do with it, except to rake in some profits. I don't want you running to me every five minutes with tales of woe.'

'I tell you what,' Arian said firmly. 'Let me do your household accounts for a week or two. I'll prove I can save you money, you'll see.'

'I'll think it over. Leave me now and ask Mrs Richards to come into the drawing room after supper.'

Arian bobbed a curtsy which for some reason caused Calvin to smile and then she was out in the passageway, leading to below stairs.

'*Duw*, you've been long enough,' Mrs Bob grumbled. 'Get the dishes started there's a good girl and I'll take the master his second course. My stomach thinks my throat is cut. I shan't be sorry to sit down to my own supper.'

Arian moved to the huge sink and stared down at the pots and pans. She sighed heavily. Well, if Calvin Temple didn't come up with an offer for her soon, she would leave Stormhill Manor anyway. This was not the life for her. Perhaps she could get a room somewhere, find work on a newspaper; she knew most of what she needed to know about the printing business and what she didn't know, she was confident she could learn.

She had spent much of her time as a child at the offices of the *Cambrian* with her father. She had watched the operators make magic words in the typeface, every letter being cut by hand on a steel punch, every numeral, every punctuation mark taking time and infinite care to produce.

Now there were new machines from America, the Linotype and the Monotype. These machines made the business of printing newspapers so much more swift and effective, but they also made Arian's knowledge little short of obsolete, she realized with a dart of disappointment.

Yet how she would love the challenge of a new career, something to work for, a future with prospects instead of the dead-end job of merely existing in the kitchens of the big house. One thing she was suddenly determined on, even if Calvin did nothing for her, she would make a success of her

48

life. She might never find love, she wanted nothing more to do with men, they only brought hurt and betrayal, but one thing she would have was a career, whatever it cost her.

It was a few days later that Arian learned that there was at least one outcome to her talk with Calvin Temple. Mrs Bob came into the kitchen her face flushed, her eyes shining.

'We're to have more staff at Stormhill Manor,' she said excitedly. 'Lord Temple is taking on a house steward and a footboy as well as an upper housemaid and a maid of all work.'

'I thought that's what I was,' Arian said ruefully, 'Bella too.'

'Well, Bella is going to work as a chambermaid which will be promotion for her, and you, well, girl, I don't know quite what his lordship's got in mind for you.' Mrs Bob sighed. 'It will be wonderful to have some men about the place again, there's nothing gives an establishment a bit of class like some male employees.'

Arian was uneasy. 'I thought a steward's job involved doing the accounts,' she said and her heart sank. If that was the case, Calvin had obviously changed his mind about giving her a chance to go into business.

'Oh, aye and supervising in the dining room, too.' Mrs Bob said. '*Never* serves mind, oh, no, a house steward doesn't demean himself to actually wait at a table, just to watch that others do their duty properly.'

'Seems a pretty pricey idea, to me,' Arian said. So much for her plan of impressing Calvin by saving him money.

'It's only right, though,' Mrs Bob argued. 'I well remember the time when there was not only a house steward in a grand establishment but a butler and under-butler with one or two footmen serving at table and those were the days when there was a tax on male servants.'

Arian was silent and Mrs Bob looked at her sympathetically. 'Don't you fret, girl,' she said kindly, 'there's got to be something good in this for you. His lordship is not the kind to dismiss his servants for no reason.'

Arian didn't reply. Calvin had rid himself of the staff employed to care for Eline and it was quite possible that he'd thought over their little talk and come to the conclusion that she was nothing but a trouble-maker.

It was two agonizingly long days later when he sent for her. He was sitting in his book-lined study, his feet stretched out to a cheerful fire, an open book resting on the table beside him, a picture of how the rich lived – a strange and sharp contrast to the hard work that went on below stairs – and for a moment, Arian resented his position in life, his wealth.

'Arian,' he said, 'I have arranged a room at the back of the house as an office. There you and my new steward will work side by side. It is an unusual arrangement, the books are usually kept by the housekeeper or by the steward alone but in this case, I intend to make exceptions.'

Arian was tongue-tied, she stared at Calvin waiting for him to continue. 'My new steward will begin on Monday. Before then, I would like you to go over the accounts. If there are discrepancies then you must come to me with them, understood?' Arian nodded and Calvin continued to speak.

'The steward, Mr Simples,' he allowed himself a smile, 'don't be misled by his name, will check the books to be sure you have missed nothing. I will give you a three-month trial period and if you prove yourself then we will talk again.'

He waved his hand and Arian bobbed a curtsy and turned towards the door. His voice stopped her.

'One thing more,' she looked back at him. 'I appreciate that the clothes Bella bought for you are not, shall we say, entirely suitable for your new post therefore I would like you to go out and dress yourself properly from top to toe.'

'Thank you, sir.' Arian's tongue felt thick in her mouth and it was all she could do to get the words to pass her stiff lips.

'I know it almost choked you to say it but don't feel in the least bit obligated,' Calvin said. 'You shall receive only your board and lodge for the time being, there will be 'no more wages until you have repaid me.' He turned away and Arian was dismissed.

Downstairs, Arian sat at the table with Mrs Bob and Bella and told them a little of what Calvin had decided.

'So you're to keep accounts, that sort of thing?' Mrs Bob said in disbelief. 'Mrs Richards isn't going to like that at all, not at all.'

'I can't help that,' Arian said, 'In any case, I'll be answerable to Mr Simples, the new steward.'

'Oh, aye, the new steward,' Mrs Bob allowed herself a small smile. 'I think Mrs Richards is having her nose put out of joint in more ways than one.'

The changes that took place at Stormhill Manor caused everyone, with the exception of Calvin Temple himself, tremendous cause for concern. Bella fretted that her rightful place as upgraded chambermaid might be usurped in some way; she was even a little hostile to Arian.

'You're sure you will work in the . . . office?' she asked uncertainly, 'cos we've never had an *office* at Stormhill before.'

'Bella, I'm positive,' Arian said, 'I've got the day off to go out and buy clothes so that I'll look the part. Don't worry so much.'

Mrs Bob was worried about the new maid. She claimed that Bella had taken a long time to train and what if the new maid didn't pull her weight? But it was Mrs Richards who, predictably enough, was the most agitated of all the staff.

'I've never heard such nonsense!' She sat for once at the kitchen table with Mrs Bob and the two younger girls, her pointed nose practically quivering with disapproval. 'A steward to replace *me*, it's an outrage. Is his lordship insinuating that I can't do my job properly?' She looked at Arian.

'And *you*, are to help him, to work alongside this new steward. It isn't quite proper, if you ask me.'

Arian saw no point in replying. In any case, she was too excited about the prospect of going to town to buy her new outfit to worry about the housekeeper's traumas. Mrs

Richards had always been standoffish; she had eaten from a tray in her room, being far too good to break bread with the likes of Arian Smale who had been brought in from the streets, so to speak. And now, in a stroke, Arian had been elevated to a higher position in the household than even the housekeeper, it wasn't proper.

Mrs Richards stared pointedly at Arian, 'Perhaps it's his lordship's bed you are interested in, serving his special needs, so to speak,' she said icily. 'High ambitions you have, my girl, you'd better watch your step. I've heard enough about your background to make a decent woman's hair curl.'

Arian took a deep breath. 'Of course,' she said carefully, 'you'd know all about the needs of men, wouldn't you *Mrs* Richards?'

The woman's colour rose, it was common knowledge that her title was merely a courtesy one, Mrs Richards was a spinster down to the last little fingernail.

'At least I don't throw myself at all and sundry,' she said, her cheeks suddenly pink.

'It wouldn't do any good, if you did,' Arian said coolly. 'I find that men are usually much more discriminating than they are given credit for.'

She rose from the table. 'Well, I'm off out to spend his lordship's money on a new outfit,' she said intending and succeeding in shocking Mrs Richards even more. She leaned forward, speaking to the housekeeper in confidential tones. 'I'd be careful, if I were you. You have already been demoted. If I'm warming his lordship's bed, your next move might well be out the door.'

She left the room then, aware that Bella was suppressing a giggle with her plump fingers while Mrs Bob busied herself pouring more tea. Mrs Richards was as red as if she was suffering a fit.

Serve the spiteful old biddy right, Arian mused. What did she know about Arian's background? How *could* she know what Arian had gone through? The pain and outrage and sheer loss of self-respect were more than anyone could understand, certainly not a dried-up spinster like Mrs Richards. Still, Arian had made an enemy and she was well aware of it.

She strode out from Stormhill at a brisk pace, determined to forget what the woman had said, determined to forget Price Davies and her sordid past. She must live now for the future and the future was looking brighter than it had done for a long time.

Her first stop would be the shoemakers in World's End; Will Davies's shop was becoming known as the place where fine individually designed shoes could be bought at a price a working man could afford.

Eline, it seemed, far from being brought down by her husband's rejection of her, was beginning to flourish as she'd done in the days when Arian had worked for her. She was rebuilding her reputation as a designer, selling her more expensive footwear to the gentry of Swansea.

There might be some element of curiosity in the minds of her customers, the desire to see the woman who had cuckolded Lord Temple and then had the effrontery to set up an illicit relationship with a poor cobbler but her fame as a shoemaker was spreading, of that there was no doubt.

Eline was a talented woman and Arian envied her, she was in love with Will Davies and had found the necessary courage to live with him in spite of the gossips.

Arian's spirits rose, it would be good to smell the leather again, good to talk with people who worked it. Eline always had a fund of ideas and Will – well, Will Davies was a cobbler who had trained with the famous Hari Grenfell.

Arian walked purposefully towards World's End, her footsteps light. Suddenly life was opening up for her, she was filled with hope for the future and if there was an irony in the fact that it was Eline's husband who was the source of that hope then Arian had little choice but to ignore the fact.

Eline heard the sound of the door opening with a dart of delight, her heart began to beat so fast she could almost hear it. She looked up from her drawing and saw Will framed against the pale sunlight. She rose to her feet uncertainly and then he was coming towards her, his arms open, ready to enfold her.

She closed her eyes and felt him draw her close, the scent of him, the familiar touch of him, it was all so dear that tears rose to her eyes.

'I'm sorry,' he said, 'I'm the worst kind of fool to be jealous of you. I just couldn't bear the thought of you being anywhere near Calvin Temple. I'm afraid I'll lose you again, Eline, so afraid.'

'Will, my love, would I be here with you if I wanted Calvin? Sit down, we've got to talk about this, there's air to be cleared and it must be done now.'

She drew Will to the table and sat opposite him, her hands reaching out to hold his. 'I know Calvin turned me away from his door, I didn't have the courage to walk out on him of my own accord, he forced the issue. But did I come to look for you? Think Will, I found a job, I was willing to take care of myself and the baby without anyone's help. It was *you* who came to find *me*.'

Will stared at her. 'That's part of what worries me, you didn't come to me voluntarily, I took you into my home when you were vulnerable.'

'And I came with you because it was what I wanted, I ignored the fact that my good name would be in the dust. Separated from Calvin I would be no more than an object of pity, the cast-off wife and no one would have known any more than that.' She paused and squeezed his hands, 'By living with you openly I've shown the world the reason why Calvin cast me aside, I've become a woman to scorn in the eyes of some people. I think I've proved that I love you, Will.'

'You're right, of course. Forgive me.' He raised her hand and kissed the calloused palm. 'You could have encouraged Calvin, gone back to him, shared the comfort of his mansion but you came home to me. I was a fool to doubt you.'

He knelt at her feet, wrapped his arms around her waist and touched her throat with his lips. 'I love you so much that it's like a pain inside me.'

Eline put her hands on his cheeks and kissed his mouth. 'Prove how much you love me,' she whispered with her lips still against his. He rose at once and swept her up into his arms and gently set her down on the bed.

The shop in World's End, approached from the back, turned out to be little more than a shed, and within was a rough workbench, cluttered with bits of leather, hob nails, a last and other implements of the cobbling trade. Will Davies sat at a bench, hammering a sole into place on a leather boot. He looked up and smiled. He was a handsome devil but no more handsome than Calvin Temple, Arian mused.

'Hello,' she said, 'I'm looking for something special; a nice pair of boots, must be dainty, mind, something preferably designed by Eline herself.'

'You want to speak to Eline?' Will said rising from the bench. 'I'll give her a shout – she's inside the house coping with our son.' The pride in his voice was apparent and Arian could see a little of the charm that had induced Eline to leave her husband.

'Arian Smale!' Eline came forward, her cheeks flushed. She had the look of a happy woman about her. 'There's nice to see you! What are you doing in town, shopping is it?'

'I'm looking for a special pair of boots,' Arian said, smiling, envying Eline's obvious contentment. 'I'm going to work as a book-keeper, at least for the time being and my boss wants me to look the part.' She didn't think it politic to mention that she was still working for Eline's husband.

'A book-keeper is it? Well, I'm glad to see you getting on. I was always pleased with your work, mind, I gave you quite a lot of responsibility and you carried it well, fair play.'

But Price Davies had soon put a stop to that, Arian thought bitterly.

'Well you've come to the right place if you want nice boots.' Will Davies's voice broke into Arian's thoughts.

'Eline has been designing again, she's done so well that we've expanded our premises,' he smiled ruefully. 'Come on in. Right along the passage there you'll find our shop.' He led the way and Eline took Arian's arm, 'It's not much, mind, but to us it's a big step forward.'

William flung open a door and gestured round the large room with the big window facing the front. 'Our landlady has actually let us use this part of the house as a shop instead of us having to sell from the back yard.' He pointed to a row of roughly made shelves.

'Would you like to see some examples of what Eline has done?'

'Will, don't be so pushy. Take no notice of him.' Eline was actually blushing. 'The stuff here is quite ordinary, I'm trying to build up a stock, you see.'

'Well, that's what I'm here for, to see some boots. Come on, Eline, don't be modest. Show me something hard-wearing and smart.'

It was fun to sit on a stool and try on the boots Eline spread out on the floor before her. They were fashioned in leather that was fine even by Arian's high standards and she rubbed her fingertips over a pair of boots in brown, polished leather with kid inserts on the front, admiring them openly.

She eventually found a pair that fitted her perfectly and she didn't hesitate. 'I'll take these.' She paid for them and smiled at Eline's somewhat bemused expression. 'They are worth every penny, don't look so surprised. Where did you buy the leather?'

'I've found a small supplier on the outskirts of Neath,' Will said. 'Why do you want to know? Thinking of going back into the shoemaking business yourself, are you?'

'Maybe,' Arian said, 'the leather fascinates me, I must admit. I know how to spot the difference between good stuff and leather that's lacking in quality.'

'Well, Mr Clifford lives in the Cimla,' Will said. 'He's got a small warehouse there, little more than a shed really but he doesn't mind small customers. I suspect that it's people like me provide him with a living.'

'That's interesting.' Arian made a mental note to go to see this Mr Clifford – he could well prove useful to her. She watched as Will parcelled up the boots, and as she took them she smiled at Eline.

'I wish you luck with your designs and I shouldn't be surprised if our paths cross again sometime.'

Outside in the clear air, she took a deep breath. That could have been a tricky encounter. If Eline and Will had asked if she was still working for Calvin, she would have had to tell them and she was sure they would not have been so helpful. She felt a little ashamed of her duplicity but what good would it have done anyone if she had told Eline who was actually paying for the boots?

She spent most of the day shopping and returned to Stormhill with an armful of parcels feeling she had spent the money Calvin had allocated her as wisely and frugally as possible. She had bought a sensible skirt in dark serge and several crisp white blouses and to top them a coat of warm merino wool – she would need it when winter came.

Mrs Bob greeted her excitedly. 'Arian, the new steward, he's here and he's ever so handsome. *Duw*, if I was twenty years younger I'd set my cap at him, that I would.'

Arian was not interested. She'd had enough of men and she never wanted to be close to one again. She hurried to her room and set down her parcels almost dreamily; there were *some* parts of her chequered past that she enjoyed remembering.

The first to make love to her was Eddie Carpenter. He'd been young, as nervous as she was, but he'd treated her almost with reverence. Their affair had been passionate; he had loved her and wanted to marry her, but even then she knew that he was not the man she wanted to spend her life with.

By now, Eddie might well have qualified as a doctor up in London somewhere. And that turn in Eddie's life, she remembered with warmth, had all been due to Calvin Temple's generosity. Eddie had looked after Eline when she'd been taken sick one day while shopping in Swansea.

His gentle assurance and his knowledge that nothing ailed Eline other than the normal reactions of a woman expecting a child had impressed Calvin to such an extent that he had offered to pay for Eddie's training. Calvin, Arian realized was something of a philanthropist. What's more, he was a very attractive man.

She hastily pushed the thought aside; loving was not for her, she'd had her fill of men, enough to last her a lifetime.

Later, as the staff sat at supper in the huge warmth of the kitchen, Arian had time to study the new steward, the man with whom she would be working. Somehow his appearance gave her a sense of apprehension.

Gerald Simples was certainly handsome; he was swarthy in the way that Romanies were swarthy and his moustache, thick and dark, gave him a predatory appearance that was slightly unnerving.

'You'll be sure to know me next time.' His voice was a surprise – it was cultured and had a slight accent that Arian could not define.

'Sorry, was I staring?' Arian said quickly. 'There's rude of me, it's just that you reminded me of someone, someone I didn't much like.' The last thing she wanted was to encourage the man to think she was interested in him. Indeed, she was almost repelled by the raw edge of masculinity about him.

'That's fine by me,' he said, smiling. 'I'm not here to be liked, I think we shall work very well together, don't you?'

Arian lifted a fork to her lips to save her the necessity of replying. She hardly tasted the food, wishing herself away from the strange presence of the man.

As soon as she could, she returned to her room, a larger one than she had previously occupied with Bella as befitted her new status in the house. As she sank onto the bed, stretching her feet to the fire, she tried to force away the dark thoughts that hovered painfully on the edges of her mind.

But that night, the dream came again. She was being beaten and her body violated, invaded by the man she had come to hate, the man who had died but lived on in her nightmares, and as she came sharply awake, she acknowledged to herself at last the reason for her dislike of Gerald Simples. It was because he bore a startling resemblance to Price Davies.

CHAPTER FOUR

Arian sat in the newly appointed office that looked over the lawns at the back of Stormhill Manor. The smell of freshly sharpened pencils was finer than that of any scent and Arian breathed a sigh of contentment as she turned away from the sight of the large lawns and sturdy trees to study the figures before her.

She had found, in the last few weeks, several discrepancies; small, it was true, but enough to prevent the books from balancing.

Mrs Richards's pique had manifested itself in a deliberate attack on Arian's morals. She had made it her business to learn more of Arian's past and never missed an opportunity to make a sly dig about what she called her unconventional life-style. Her attitude succeeded only in bringing to the fore painful memories that Arian would have preferred to forget, for no-one took the slightest notice of Mrs Richards's spiteful gossip.

With the new steward, though, it was more difficult to be off-hand. He made her feel distinctly uneasy whenever she was alone in the office with him.

And yet, he had a fine mind, there was no questioning that. Columns which it took Arian several minutes to total on paper were done in seconds in Mr Simples's head. To be fair, he was quite ready to teach her a few tricks of the accounting trade but still Arian's instinct was to mistrust him.

'Now let's decipher these accounts of last month,' she said out loud, 'see what a nonsense our good Mrs Richards has made of *them*.'

Arian smiled, amused to realize that she was adopting Mr Simples's speech mannerisms, copying his clearly enunciated words. '*Duw*, I'll be getting above myself if I don't take care.' She gave voice to her thoughts, her tone wry.

'Talking to yourself, Miss Smale?' Gerald Simples had come quietly into the room and stood looking down at her, his dark eyebrows raised. She sat up straighter, brushing back a tendril of hair.

'Just thinking out loud,' she replied. 'I didn't expect you back yet.'

'If you had, you would have reserved your gems of wisdom for me, I suppose?' He peered down at the book. 'There,' he pointed, 'a mistake of two shillings, *that* is an extravagance even for Mrs Richards. I think we'd better go over the books for the last six-month period.'

Arian sighed. There seemed little point in that; the mistakes had been made and however correct the books were, the money would never be recouped.

'Later,' Mr Simples said, 'I want you to go to his lordship and inform him of the money his housekeeper has lost him to date. I make it almost an entire guinea.'

Arian looked up at him. 'Is that really necessary?' she asked. 'It will only get Mrs Richards into trouble.'

'I'm here to do a job, Miss Smale. So are you. We will do it properly or not at all.'

He settled himself at his desk, his back towards her and Arian watched him covertly, trying to decide what it was about him that made her think of Price Davies. It wasn't physical likeness, not exactly, although there *were* similarities in appearance. No, it was some look in the eye, some air of contained power as though Simples could suddenly turn into a dangerous animal.

He glanced back over his shoulder as though aware of her scrutiny. 'Any problems, Miss Smale?' he asked and she shook her head without replying.

It was not often that they were together in the office for any length of time. Mr Simples had other duties that fortunately kept him busy – but when they were, Arian was unable to concentrate on her work, she kept feeling his eyes boring into her although he was in fact acting as though she wasn't there.

She took a deep breath. Her task was to prove that she could handle the household accounts alone, the sooner the better, then she would scarcely ever be alone with the steward.

The work on the books was not difficult; now that she had charge of the outgoings there was an easy method of assessing the month's expenditure. So long as every detail of any purchases was noted in the book, it was normally only a few hours' work to balance the figures at the end of the month. But now that Mr Simples had started delving into the back accounts, goodness knows how long it would take her to sort them out.

She dropped her pencil and became aware that she was being watched.

'Day-dreaming, Miss Smale?' Mr Simples rose and came to stand over her, leaning forward to check the figures on the open page. Arian resisted the urge to move away from him, not wishing to offend. But, as though he sensed her withdrawal, he straightened.

'You don't much like me, do you, Miss Smale?' he said abruptly and she looked up at him in surprise. It was the first time he had said anything remotely personal.

'I've never given it any thought,' she said quickly, and his half smile told her he knew that she lied. 'I certainly respect your acumen,' she said. 'You are sharp with figures and I envy you that.'

'Well thank you, compliments no less, but I still feel that you do not like me. Why?'

Arian shrugged. 'You remind me of someone I'd rather forget.' She looked up at him. 'Unfair of me, I'll agree, but it's something I can't help.'

'Well then, I must prove to you that I am not like that other man. It *has* to be a lover, doesn't it?'

Arian turned away. 'There's no point in talking about

it, Mr Simples. It's my business and anyway, it's all in the past.'

He walked away then, so light on his feet that she scarcely heard him leave the room. She shivered and chewed the end of her pencil. Why did he have the ability to make her feel threatened?

She rose and closed the book with a snap. She had done enough today. She would get out of the room, away from the feeling of being trapped. This was not the way she wanted to live her life – she wanted action, the chance to make a success of a business which would take her away from servitude to any man.

She hurried down the curving staircase and stood for a moment in the hall which was redolent with the smell of beeswax. The door to the library stood open and on an impulse, Arian moved towards the huge bookcase that lined one of the walls.

She looked up at the books and selected one at random. It was difficult to read, the language being involved and ancient.

'A bit ambitious of you.' The leather chair facing the fire swung round and Calvin Temple was observing her, his eyes sharp. 'It's a translation from the French. Are you particularly interested in philosophy, Miss Smale?'

She flushed. 'There is no need to be patronising, sir,' she said quickly. 'My father did edit a newspaper so I'm not without some reading skills, or had you forgotten?'

'Ah yes, Robert Smale, of the *Cambrian*, I *had* forgotten. I apologize.' He rose and took the book from her hands and reaching up, selected another volume.

'I think this will interest you much more,' he said. 'It contains short biographies of the local businessmen. Some of them are leather barons, a subject I know interests you. Perhaps you should seek out one who is eligible for marriage, join him in business, as it were.'

'I don't much like the implication,' Arian said, anger growing inside her. 'I am many things but I am *not* a harlot who sells herself for a price, any price. *I* will make my own way in this life and without marrying a man to do it.'

Calvin's eyebrows were raised. 'How is Eddie Carpenter getting along?' he asked. 'Is he qualified yet? I haven't had a letter from him in some time.'

Arian felt her colour rise 'I *was* Eddie's mistress, if that's what you'd like to call it. That was not for gain and it was my choice. It's no-one's business but my own.'

'The things I have heard about you and the cobbler Price Davies are not true then?' he asked calmly.

'I don't know what you have heard.' Arian felt her face grow hot. She had teased Price Davies with her charms just to learn his skills and in the end she had suffered for it. 'I would prefer it if you did not speak about that part of my life, it is very painful to me.'

'I suppose being betrayed is always painful,' Calvin said and he sounded angry, 'but some of us do not ask for it.'

'I didn't ask for what happened to me,' Arian said, the blood pounding in her ears. 'I was held prisoner and raped by the cobbler you talk about. Does that satisfy your curiosity, sir?'

Calvin seemed taken aback by her outburst. He opened his mouth to say something but Arian went on speaking.

'It was not pretty and I'm not proud of it but it doesn't make me a whore so if you have given me a job with the idea that you can amuse yourself with me between the sheets then you can forget it.'

'I've told you before, I am not interested,' Calvin said his voice suddenly lacking emotion. 'I will not be taken in by a pretty face ever again.'

He moved away from her and the book felt heavy in her hands. Arian felt her anger fade. Calvin had suffered a blow to his pride; he knew what betrayal meant and he was only a man, for all his wealth, a man with feelings which went as deep as her own.

'I don't know what garbled tales you have heard about me,' she said more softly, 'and it would do no good to explain my life to you. I accept that you are not interested so can we just take each other on face value?'

Her voice trembled and Calvin turned to her at once, his hand outstretched. What he might have said faded on his lips as Arian saw his glance move from her to someone in the hallway.

'Yes, Mr Simples,' he said, 'what can I do for you?' He was in charge again, Lord Temple, who owned a fine house and a great fortune and was master of his own fate.

Arian bobbed a curtsy and putting the book on the table left the library, passing Simples in the hallway without looking at him.

'If I may have a word, your lordship,' she heard him saying, and then she was climbing the stairs to her own room, her cheeks still flushed, her hands clasped together to stop them from trembling.

She sat near the warmth of the fire and tried to examine her feelings. For a moment there, she had felt a kindred spirit with Calvin Temple. He had reached out as though in friendship and she would have valued as a friend a man who was not interested in taking anything from her. A man who, like her, had been hurt. But Gerald Simples had ruined the moment. She was right about him, he was an omen for ill in the new life she was seeking to make for herself.

Gerald Simples stood before Lord Temple and marshalled his thoughts. He had heard only part of the conversation between Arian and his lordship but when she had cried rape, it was undoubtedly the truth. He'd heard about Davies's escapades of course, but had chosen to stay right away from any activity involving Price. Now he had met Arian, wanted her for himself, he felt only anger when he imagined them together. But Price was dead, and Gerald was alive and he knew well enough that to be locked in a room alone with Arian was enough to tempt any man to madness. She had an aloofness about her, a touch-me-not attitude that would fool any man into believing her chaste.

Price Davies had been a hothead, and Simples should know. He was his cousin. Recklessness ran in the family; hadn't Simples's own father caused a scandal with a high-society woman? The resulting child, Gerald, was brought up with careless affection by his aunt, Price Davies's mother.

Father had married well, a French woman of high quality. He had found it easy to fool all and sundry with the gift of his silver tongue so that others believed he came of good, monied stock.

Gerald had been brought to France some time later and had found himself reaping the benefits of his stepmother's wealth. He'd had a fine education, and an elegant life-style with no need to lift a finger to work.

When he was sixteen, his stepmother had died and his happy, secure life-style had been snatched away from him. Gerald had disgraced himself by a liaison with some little wench from the lower orders and had been ordered to leave France forthwith.

Gerald, on his return to British shores, had found employment easily enough. Using his stepmother's name, he had worked for a time in a bank in Cardiff. Occasionally, he visited Swansea, gleaning information about the rich of the area.

Lord Temple was helping himself to a drink, obviously not yet ready to talk to his steward and Gerald's mind drifted to the past once more.

He had spent almost a year attending to the business affairs of a rich merchant in London. He had left that position in a hurry but with a pocket full of money. At the age of twenty-five, he changed his name to Simples and returned to Wales and now he was safely ensconced in the home of a lord, no less – not bad going for the son of an adventurer.

When he had returned to Swansea, he had been mildly interested in meeting the woman Price had lost his head over, but he had not reckoned on the strong character of Arian Smale. He had thought to amuse himself with her while he handled the household accounts alone. He imagined he'd earn Temple's trust so that further transactions of a more profitable nature might be made his responsibility.

Still, he thought, he saw what Arian's little scheme was now; it was to get into his lordship's bed and thus get a share of his money. She was, he thought with satisfaction, as devious as he was, they would do well together.

He wasn't fooled for one moment by her claims to honesty and goodness. He had taken the trouble to find out enough of what had gone on up at the farmlands that time when his cousin had died.

A local farmer's wife, a Mrs O'Conner, had been held for ransom, and so was Arian, but that was all just a cover. They, the Smales and his own cousin Price Davies, had all been in the plan together, a plan that had backfired; a fortuitous enough event for Simples, dead men could not talk.

'What was it you wanted, Mr Simples? I'm waiting,' Calvin Temple prompted, bringing Gerald out of his reverie. His lordship sat in his leather chair and smiled with an attitude of tolerance that somehow irritated Gerald.

'I thought Miss Smale would have told your lordship,' he said. 'I have found some discrepancies in the accounts. So far they total to just a guinea but there will be others and I intend to find them, however far I have to search through the books.'

'Don't bother,' Calvin Temple said easily, 'I looked at the books myself prior to engaging Miss Smale or you. The mistakes are honest ones. Don't trouble yourself further about the matter.'

Simples bowed, it seemed that Lord Temple was no man's fool. 'Very well, your lordship,' he said, 'but be sure there will be no mistakes in the future.'

Calvin inclined his head. 'Thank you, Simples.' It was a dismissal. Simples retreated and climbed the stairs towards his quarters, his mind racing – he would have to go easily with this man Temple.

'Oh, Miss Smale. I didn't see you there.' She was standing in the doorway to her room and behind her, he could see the glow of the firelight and the soft drape of a robe hanging over a chair. She was a woman who loved to flaunt her femininity. She thought all men could be bought for the price of her favours.

'Mr Simples,' she replied, 'you found it necessary to talk to his lordship about the accounting errors then?'

'I did,' he said easily, 'I never led you to believe I would do anything else.'

'I hope you didn't make it sound as though the house-keeper was dishonest.'

'That was not my intention. I think you might be a little hysterical; I did rather walk in on – what shall we call it – in *intimate* moment.'

'Intimate, with the door open? Surely not, Mr Simples,' Arian said softly.

'His lordship was just about to respond to your . . .' he looked her up and down, 'not inconsiderable charms. But be not mistaken in me, Miss Smale, I am not a man who is easily fooled by a pretty face.'

He moved on and, entering his room closed the door firmly. Arian Smale might be a fair-looking woman. He would not be above loosening that cloud of hair and burying himself in it, but he was not like his father, a fool to any woman who accommodated him. Oh, no, he had far more self-control and Arian Smale would find that out, to her cost.

Arian looked at the solid wood of the door through which Simples had disappeared and sighed. She closed the door of her own room, returned to the fireside and sank into her chair. So the boundaries were set. She and Mr Simples were declared enemies, he couldn't have made that any clearer. Strange both he and Calvin Temple had used the expression 'pretty face', but while Lord Temple spoke the words with a sense of hurt, Simples's use of the words implied scorn, contempt even. Gerald Simples was a man who would have to be watched, very carefully indeed.

Calvin lit up a cigar and stared around the large room absently. A discreet ball, the card had said, and Calvin, expecting an intimate gathering, had decided to accept the invitation given by a man who was little more than an acquaintance. But simple was hardly the way he would have described the lavish entertainment laid on by Stuart Kingston.

Of the people gathered there, he knew only a handful. The banker, Freddie Elson, was one of them and right now, Calvin realized with a dart of dismay, the plump gentleman was descending upon him, a large glass of port clutched in his hand.

'Calvin, dear chap,' Freddie leaned forward, slightly off balance and it was clear that his glass had been replenished more times than was good for him. 'Calvin, you look at a loss and you can't be alone, not at a party like this. Come along, let me introduce you to a most interesting lady.'

Calvin saw Freddie lift a hand and, as if on cue, a dark, vivacious woman made her way across the room, threading her way through the gathering with complete composure. Her head was high, her soft gown flowing around her perfect figure and Calvin was struck by the way she carried herself like a queen.

'Daphne, my darling, come and cheer up my old friend.' The extravagant gesture of Elson's arm threatened to throw port over everyone near him.

Dark eyes looked into his and Calvin reacted instantly to the sensuousness of the woman. She held out her hand and Calvin took it, touching the softness of her skin with a feeling that he was coming awake after a long sleep.

'Daphne, this dear man is all alone. Calvin, Lord Temple, is very much in need of cheering and you are just the beauty to do it.'

'I'm happy to meet you, Lord Temple. You must forgive Freddie Elson. What he lacks in finesse he makes up for in exuberance.' Daphne's soft voice held such appeal that Freddie, far from being insulted, smiled and kissed her on both cheeks.

'There, I just knew you two would hit it off. I will leave you alone but don't do anything I wouldn't do.'

He weaved his way towards the butler who was carrying a tray of brimming glasses, and Calvin turned his attention to Daphne who was standing so close that he could, by moving his arm, feel the softness of her breast.

He felt aflame with desire. It seemed so long since he'd had a woman, so long since his wife had betrayed him and much too long since he had felt the need to lie with a woman.

'Come, let's sit in the hallway, it's quieter there.' Daphne guided him through the door and then they were sitting close together on the *chaise longue*, her hand resting tantalizingly on his thigh.

'I have been wanting to meet you for some time, Lord Temple,' Daphne said. 'You always seem to me a hugely interesting, if slightly melancholy man. I cannot help but know you've been badly burned and are keeping away from fire in case you are hurt again.'

'You're a perceptive lady,' Calvin said.

Daphne looked away from him suddenly. 'Do you like the poems of Lord Byron?' Her change of mood startled him and it took Calvin a few moments to gather his thoughts.

'He is a cynic,' Daphne said. 'He believes that a woman's vows are as worthless as shifting sand. I think you believe that too, Lord Temple.'

'Calvin, please,' he said quickly, 'I hate being called Lord Temple.'

'Well, Calvin, I understand you have been hurt in love once – would you be willing to try again?'

Calvin leaned forward and touched Daphne's cheek. 'Are you incredibly naïve or are you offering yourself to me?'

Daphne laughed, 'I am *not* naïve so you will have to assume that I am offering myself to you.'

'You know nothing of me,' he said and then longed to bite out his tongue. He wanted this woman. Did her terms matter?

'I know enough. Indeed, I have admired you from afar, as it were, for some time,' Daphne said quietly. 'It was I who inveigled Freddie into getting you here. He persuaded Kingston to invite you to one of his little soirées.'

'You are a scheming woman,' Calvin said, 'and as you know everything about me, you will know I'm not free to take a wife. In any case I don't want one, not precisely at this moment.'

'I know what you want, precisely at this moment.' Daphne looked meaningfully at him and Calvin found himself smiling.

'What are we going to do about it?' Calvin said, his gaze drawn to the soft fullness of her breasts, exposed a little as she leaned towards him.

'Nothing, not right now,' she said. 'Right now we rejoin the other guests, enjoy the party, dance, drink a little wine and we will talk. After that, who knows?'

Calvin felt a sense of disappointment and Daphne smiled knowingly.

'I might not be reticent in saying what I want but neither am I a cherry to be picked at any moment. I choose my time and place – if I continue to be interested.'

Calvin sighed. 'I thought that it would last for aye when lo she changes in a day,' he quoted and Daphne's face lightened.

'You do like the poetry of Lord Byron then? You are not a philistine.'

He rose and held out his hand. 'Come along Daphne, let's enjoy the dance.'

Later, Calvin cornered Freddie and looked down at him thoughtfully. 'Who is Daphne, where does she live, is she married and given to dalliances with other men, is she a whore, what?'

'Oh no, there is nothing whorish about our Daphne.' Freddie protested. 'She is a widow, has been since she was a mere eighteen years.' He paused to sup his drink. 'It's true that she takes a lover from time to time but she is one hell of a woman, a special woman and most of the chaps here would give their right arm to be in your shoes, old man.'

Freddie wagged a fat forefinger, 'But you must treat her right, she takes no nonsense from anyone. One peccadillo

71

with another woman while you are with her and you are out on your arse, old man.'

'She makes great demands for a courtesan,' Calvin said mildly and Freddie looked at him in horror.

'You are honoured by her attentions, man,' he said. 'Don't you know that the Prince of Wales has been chasing her skirts for some months now?'

'What, down here in Swansea?' Calvin asked, eyebrows raised, his cynicism apparent in every line of his taut mouth.

'Daphne has only been back from London for a few weeks,' Freddie said. 'Good God man, what circles have you been moving in?'

'And you mean she has not succumbed to the prince?' Calvin said scathingly.

'No, she has not.' The voice coming from behind him was tinged with ice. 'I choose my lovers, I told you that. It's obvious you don't listen very well. I'm disappointed in you, Lord Temple.'

Daphne turned away. 'Freddie, be a dear and fetch my cloak and call me a cab, will you. I'm going home.'

Calvin watched her leave feeling as if he had been offered a great bargain and had turned it down. On an impulse, he hurried after Daphne and caught her just as she was climbing into her carriage.

'I apologize,' he said, sinking into the seat beside her. 'I am ignorant and I confess it. I've been out of circulation as you well know and I thought that Freddie was being his usual facetious self.'

Daphne looked out of the carriage window and in the darkness Calvin, breathing in the scent of her, felt himself desiring her with an urge that was irresistible.

'I want you, Daphne,' he said. 'I want you so much I can't think straight.'

'Well you must want,' Daphne said at last. 'You must learn that I do not give myself lightly, not to any man. I had a husband once, a husband I did not love, but I respected and honoured him. He died after three short years of marriage. He left me wealthy and independent. I do not need any other man to keep me. I am self-sufficient which enables me to choose my lovers when and as I feel inclined.'

'I understand,' he said, though in truth he was surprised. It had begun to seem to him that most women wanted something from him.

'Since Thomas, there have been only three men whom I have taken seriously. They were fine men and it was I who grew tired of them so don't think you are doing me any favours, Calvin, for it's the other way around.'

He drew her to him and held her close, his mouth against her forehead. 'I wonder,' he said softly, 'might I have the pleasure of your company tomorrow evening?'

She laughed softly. 'I see you are quick to learn. As for your offer, I would be delighted to accept.'

Most of the time Arian, as befitted her position, ate her meals in her room but occasionally, she ventured into the big warm kitchen to eat with the other servants. Because she had begun life at the manor as a maid of all work, she was accepted by Mrs Bob, welcomed even, especially when, as now, there was an item of momentous news to impart.

'Come, sit by here,' Mrs Bob said patting the wooden chair next to her. 'Help yourself to meat and potatoes and while we have our supper, let's get down to brass tacks, is it?'

Bella shifted her chair to allow Arian more room and the new maid stared at her with undisguised curiosity.

'Don't mind Cynthia,' Mrs Bob said. 'She's young but she can keep her trap shut when needs be.'

'Have you heard about the master then?' Mrs Bob asked, her eyes shining like jet beads. 'Can't get over it, me, didn't believe it at first, mind.'

Arian was puzzled, she'd known there was something going on by the strangely knowing smile on Simples's face whenever his lordship was mentioned. It was almost as if he felt he had one up on her by being in possession of information that Arian wasn't privy to.

'No, I don't know anything about what's going on,' Arian said quickly. 'I realize that something *is* going on and it's annoying me to be left out of it.'

Mrs Bob leaned forward on plump elbows. 'He's got a woman,' she said, 'and him still married to that Eline that went off with a cobbler.'

Suddenly Arian felt as though she had swallowed something cold. 'Well, it's only natural that he would want the company of a lady.' Even as she heard herself saying it, Arian felt a sense of displeasure, almost as though she had been betrayed.

'I knows that, but who'd have thought he'd have set up one of them fast and loose ladies? Put her in a lovely house, so I hear, pays her rent and all. A proper beauty she is, too, by all accounts but no better than she should be if you asks me.'

Arian sank back in her chair. She felt as though she'd been slapped. Calvin Temple with a courtesan – it didn't seem possible. And yet why not? Why shouldn't he pay for his pleasures? He could afford it. And wasn't that the way most men took their women?

'There's talk that she's a widow woman,' Bella cut in. 'Knows how to pleasure the gents in the bedroom. I bet she's not a lady in the sheets,' she sniffed. 'I thought better than that of his lordship.'

'Hush now,' Mrs Bob said curtly. 'A man's different to us women, got to have his way, like, when it comes to the ladies, otherwise they fall sick and die.'

God knows where Mrs Bob had heard that one, Arian thought bitterly, but she was not far wrong. A man, it seemed was ruled by his sexual appetites to the point of losing all his senses.

'Come on, girl, you're just picking at your food,' Mrs Bob said. 'Not sickening for something are you?'

'I'm well, thank you,' Arian said. 'I'm just shocked, that's all.'

'I know,' Mrs Bob said confidingly. 'Like me and Bella here, you thought the master was above all that sort of nonsense.' She shrugged. 'But seems he's not and we've just got to accept that it's none of our business.'

Mr Simples entered the kitchen and the silence that descended on the women was almost tangible. Simples smiled.

'I see you have heard the news, Miss Smale,' he said. 'I didn't want to be the one to tell you that your idol had feet of clay, but it's just as well you know the truth.'

'I don't know what you mean.' Arian rose from her chair and moved to the door. She paused, staring at Gerald Simples. 'I have no illusions at all about men – those were taken away from me long ago.'

'I understand,' Simples said smiling. 'I suppose you can even sympathize with this . . . this lady, the one his lordship has taken up with. After all, you both are what I would call experienced in the ways of the world and of men.' He paused as Arian gritted her teeth. 'The only difference between you and this courtesan, as I see it, is that she has the wit to make a good living from her way of life while you. . .' He left the sentence unfinished and Arian, losing control, hit out at him blindly.

He caught her wrist easily and held it so tightly that his nails dug into her flesh.

'Now, now, Miss Smale, your conduct is unbecoming to your position. You are acting more like a fishwife than a respectable woman. But then,' he paused, 'as they say, breeding, or the lack of it, will out.'

Arian wrenched her hand away from his grip and hurried up the stairs, her heart thumping. She was angry with Simples. The more she saw of him the more she disliked him. His resemblance to Price Davies had increased; some mannerisms, and sometimes the twist of his head would send her spirits plunging into the depths of despairing memories. But even Price, animal though he was, had not had the power to fire barbs of speech that would find their mark with such cruel precision.

At the entrance to the hallway, she collided with a tall masculine figure and was held for a moment in sheltering arms.

'Arian, what on earth is it?' Calvin Temple stood looking down at her white face and wide eyes and it was clear that he felt genuine concern.

Arian forced herself to breath evenly. 'It's nothing,' she said, 'nothing I can't handle myself.'

'I saw Simples going below stairs,' Calvin persisted. 'Has the man done something to offend you?'

'No, it's nothing,' Arian protested. 'I'm all right, really. It's nothing for you to concern yourself with.'

Calvin's arms dropped away from her as if he had suddenly become conscious that he was holding her. 'If there is anything, *anything* at all troubling you, please feel free to come to me,' he said.

Arian looked at him, seeing him as though for the first time. Calvin was a fine upstanding man, tall and handsome with a charm about him that most women would find irresistible. Most women, including herself.

'Excuse me.' She moved away and stood for a moment staring at him.

'Yes?' he asked and Arian shook her head.

'It's nothing.' Lifting her skirts she hurried up the two flights of stairs to her room.

She sat on the bed for a long time, facing something that she had concealed from herself for weeks now. She was in love with Calvin Temple. *She* might not have known it, but Simples had realized it at once. And if he could, he would use the knowledge to his advantage, there was no doubt about that.

Arian wished that she could cry, but she was past crying. She had cried away all her tears a long time ago. In dry-eyed misery she stared into the flames of the dying fire until the clock in the hall chimed out the midnight hour.

CHAPTER FIVE

Arian pushed the books aside with an impatient movement and rose to her feet, this was getting her nowhere. However much she studied the figures, she could make the result no different – there was a discrepancy of almost five guineas.

Simples entered the office and stood in the middle of the room, his hands thrust into his pockets. He was almost good looking, Arian thought, except that there was a slyness at the back of his eyes.

'You wanted to see me, Miss Smale?' His tone indicated that he hoped she wasn't wasting his valuable time.

'Yes, I'm afraid I did,' she replied. 'I would like you to go over the figures for last month.'

'Last month? But that's all been taken care of by Mrs Richards. I thought we had decided to allow her to resume responsibility for the books. Your job, as I see it, was to supervise the allocation of money for various services to do with the household, the servants' wages, the buying of new bedding, and so on.'

'We did,' Arian agreed, 'but I thought it appropriate that I still check the books.'

'And?' he asked impatiently.

'And I found a discrepancy, quite a big one. There is a loss of five guineas and I can't understand what's happening here.' She paced about the room. 'Normally, as you know, an error is easy to spot but in this case, there's been an attempt to cover up the loss. It's a deliberate attempt to defraud, I'm afraid.'

'And you think Mrs Richards is sharp enough to arrange a blatant fraud? Because that's what you are implying.'

Arian shrugged. 'I just don't know what to think. Please look at the books yourself. It would help.'

Simples picked up the book and tucked it under his arm. 'I will deal with it later, when I have time. After all, it isn't a major problem is it?'

Arian was surprised by his attitude, she had summed him up as a stickler for detail. 'Well, if you're sure.' She spoke uncertainly and Simples gave her an oblique look.

'You do trust me with the books don't you, Miss Smale?' his voice was edged with sarcasm.

Arian bit her lip. She knew Calvin was trusting Simples with the handling of his huge estate. Simples was dealing with the running of the parklands and there was talk among the servants that he might even be advising Lord Temple regarding his business investments, so it was scarcely likely that he would be very much concerned with a mere household discrepancy.

'Please, don't give it another thought.' She held out her hand for the book. 'I realize now that you are far too busy to concern yourself with such small details. I shouldn't have troubled you.'

'Well that's as may be, but now that you have,' he spoke acidly, 'it's my duty to look into the matter.'

Arian bit her lip. She felt foolish for having involved him in what was, after all, her responsibility. But it was too late to change her mind, he was walking away from her, the book snugly under his arm and she had no choice but to watch him go.

She sank down at the desk and rubbed at her eyes. She had probably overlooked something quite minor and obvious, some expenditure that was wrongly documented perhaps, a figure put in the wrong column, an addition where there should have been a subtraction. She wished now that she had given herself longer to study the books. She should never have called Simples in; it gave him the ideal opportunity to infer she was not up to the job.

Arian imagined his scorn when he spotted the error, for error it undoubtedly was. As he had said, Mrs Richards would hardly be experienced enough or clever enough to handle a deliberate fraud.

Today was her day off. She intended to compile some notes on the leather trade, send out some letters – in short, begin to put some irons in the fire. She still harboured the hope that she might be able to set up in business on her own before very long. In the meantime, she might just as well enjoy her day off from Calvin's business.

She shook the ink from her pen before setting it down and tidied the scatter of papers on her desk. She stretched her arms above her head and wondered if she should spend her leisure time in the fresh air.

She was fortunate, she mused, that she had so much time off. In that Calvin was generous. Arian was given one free day a week instead of once a month as were most servants. But then she was not, strictly speaking, a servant. What was she? A charity case, a girl Calvin had taken in out of pity?

Oh, damnation to Calvin Temple and to Gerald Simples and to the cash books; all this was not really her problem. She would go out to town, visit the boot and shoe emporiums of the Grenfells and the Millers, see if she could find out who were the suppliers of leather to the big businesses.

It was high time she was making some sort of move. She was becoming too comfortable at Stormhill, too complacent. She had her ambitions and if she did not nurture them, they would wither and die before she had the chance to see if she could make them work.

In her room she dressed in her new coat and placed the velvet hat upon her silver-gold hair with a grimace of displeasure. She looked so ordinary, almost respectable. The word made her smile with wry humour. Arian Smale, respectable – that was a new twist to her life.

She left the house by the back door. These days it was never quite clear to her what was her station in life. Once she had been the daughter of a landowner, a man who had also owned the *Cambrian* newspaper. Robert Smale, though dissolute, had once been considered a cut above the lower orders. She squared her shoulders. One day, Arian Smale would be a person in her own right. Then she would use no-one's back door.

It was to Arian's surprise and gratification that she found in Craig Grenfell an enthusiastic listener. She had entered purposely though the large entrance to the Grenfell emporium and had found him supervising the delivery of a new batch of leather. The skins were being stored in the cellars below the building and there, Arian learned, the whole floor had been converted into a gigantic store and workshop.

'You are a friend of Hari's aren't you?' Craig asked. Arian didn't hear him, she was fingering a piece of leather with such concentration that he had to repeat the question.

'I can't claim to be a friend,' she replied seriously. 'I have met Hari of course, and I know of her reputation. Who in the shoe business doesn't? I admire her tremendously and only wish I had a quarter of her gifts.'

Craig thrust his hands into his pockets. 'And are you in the leather business?' He smiled down at her and Arian warmed to him. He was a gentleman, a wealthy man and yet he was prepared to give her some of his time.

'I know a little about good leather,' Arian said, 'and while much of this stock is fine enough, a few shoddy skins have been put in with the good to make up the load. You are being short-changed and I'd suggest you take the matter up with the supplier. Mrs Grenfell has a wonderful reputation but some bad leather would soon damage that.'

'I see,' Craig said slowly. 'And you could pick out these skins for me, could you?'

'Well, it would take some time to go through the load,' Arian said doubtfully, 'but it could be done, certainly.'

'And you could do it?' Craig persisted.

Arian lifted her head and looked at him. He was a fine man, broad of shoulder and clear of eye. Hari was a fortunate woman in more ways than one.

'Yes,' she smiled. 'I would be delighted. I can begin on it today, if you like.'

'That won't be necessary,' he eyed her good clothes. 'You are hardly dressed for it.' He put his head on one side thoughtfully. 'How would you like to work for me on a regular basis?' he said. 'My buyer is talking about retiring soon, perhaps his eye-sight isn't as good as it used to be or his sense of touch. I shall need someone to take over from him.'

'You know nothing about me,' Arian said quietly. 'Why should you give me a job?'

'I do know a little about you, I read the papers *and* I hear gossip – it's inevitable in a town like Swansea.'

'And you are not put off by what you've heard?' Arian asked, the colour rising to her cheeks.

'I take a person on trust until they prove otherwise,' Craig said evenly.

Arian was silent for a while. She smelled the leather, heard from the large workshop next door the clatter of machines and knew that this was where she belonged.

'I'll have to speak to Lord Temple,' she said at last. 'I'll ask him to release me from my position in his household. I'm sure he'll agree.'

Of course he would, Arian mused. He would probably be happy to be free of the responsibility of her. He had taken her in out of pity and she was grateful for that but now she had become a useless part of his household. There was no real position there for her and they both knew it.

Craig smiled and his eyes creased at the corners, he really was a most attractive man. And he was happily married, a state she envied. He was a man she could like if never love.

Though he was far above her socially she was charmed by him. He didn't act as though he was superior, but then, to a man like Craig Grenfell, social standing was not a matter of great importance. Hadn't he married Hari who was from the lower orders?

When she left the cellar, her thoughts were in chaos. She knew it was time she branched out, took charge of her own destiny and yet the thought of leaving Calvin's house depressed her. Then she would never see him, never be close to him. Perhaps that was just as well – he did have a mistress now, she reminded herself.

Arian wandered round the emporium and once caught sight of Hari Grenfell as she swept through the first floor, her glossy hair framing her face, her eyes bright and interested in everything she saw. Arian found herself envying Hari in a way she hadn't believed possible. She had found her way in life with unwavering persistence. She had a fine business, a great talent and the most handsome wonderful husband. Did any woman deserve such fortune?

Arian returned to Stormhill at last, just as the sunlight was dying behind the trees. Even as she entered the back door, she sensed an atmosphere that was far from peaceful. Something had happened while she'd been out and Arian couldn't help but feel a sharp drop in her spirits. She knew instinctively that whatever had occurred, it somehow involved her.

In the kitchen, Mrs Bob was sitting at the big table pouring tea. At her side Mrs Richards was sobbing into a handkerchief, her eyes red, her whole frame shaking.

'What is it?' Arian asked. 'What's happened?' She saw the two women look up startled and then Mrs Bob was gesturing for her to sit down.

'There's been that much rowing going on by here,' she said. 'His lordship asking questions about the accounts and upsetting poor Mrs Richards and that horrible Simples blaming everyone but himself.'

Arian felt her heart sink. It was about the missing money, the error she had found had obviously been reported to Calvin Temple.

'What did his lordship say?' Arian sank down into the wooden chair and rested her arms on the table. 'Did he blame anyone, me perhaps?'

'No, bless you.' Mrs Bob shook her head and a tendril of greying hair fell over her forehead. 'No, he says it must be a mistake, he don't think none of us could be dishonest.'

'*You* are not under suspicion,' Mrs Richards said to the cook. 'It's me and Arian here who will be held responsible. It'll be too awful if we can't prove a mistake has been made.

No good house will ever take us if we're dismissed under a cloud.'

'I'll speak to his lordship,' Arian rose to her feet. 'I'll convince him that it's not anyone's fault, it's just an error in the figuring.'

'That man Simples says it's no mistake,' Mrs Bob said. 'It's a clever way of pinching the money from his lordship, that's what he says.'

Arian felt suddenly cold. In that case, the blame could only fall on herself. Calvin would know, just as Simples did, that Mrs Richards was not capable of such a blatant fraud. As it was Simples who had reported the matter, he could hardly be a suspect. No, it was she who would be accountable.

Calvin Temple, as it turned out, had company and Simples barred Arian's way when she would have knocked on the drawing room door.

'I must see his lordship,' Arian insisted quietly. 'I must try to clear up some of the misapprehensions you've put into his mind.'

'I did my duty, nothing more, nothing less,' Simples said smoothly. 'It was *you* who brought the matter into the open. What did you expect me to do, keep quiet about it?'

'No, of course not,' Arian protested. 'It's just that you gave me the impression the matter wasn't pressing. As it is, you've put me in a bad light.'

'And how do you come to that conclusion?' Simples asked. 'Three of us handle the books; Mrs Richards, you and my good self. On reflection, the matter needed to be investigated and the sooner the better, don't you think so?'

'I suppose so,' Arian said doubtfully. Gerald Simples's words were so reasonable, she felt more than a little foolish in questioning his behaviour. 'Still,' she persisted, 'by reporting the error yourself, it looks as though *you* were the one to find it. That seems to me underhand to say the least.'

Simples shrugged. 'We can do without histrionics, Miss Smale. I did the correct thing by my own standards. If that upsets you then there is nothing I can do about it.'

The door of the drawing room swung open and Calvin Temple stood framed in the soft light from the gas mantles on the walls. He was looking down at Arian, his expression stern. 'Your voices are raised,' he said evenly, 'I can't allow my guests to be disturbed in this way.'

'I must speak to you, sir,' Arian said quickly, and Calvin lifted his hand to silence her.

'In the morning, Miss Smale, I will be in my study waiting at nine o'clock. In the meantime, I would appreciate a little order in my house.'

He turned away and then paused, 'Simples, I need another bottle of port, if you please.' Then the door was closed firmly and Arian sighed in exasperation.

As she turned to go, her head high, Simples followed her into the passageway and caught her arm. 'You are a proud little madam, aren't you?' he said. 'You need a good husband to tame your temper, young lady.'

Arian's eyebrows lifted in astonishment. 'And you are offering yourself for the position, is that it?'

'You could do a great deal worse,' Simples still held her arm, 'and if we were betrothed, I'm sure I could sort out the small matter of the missing five guineas.'

Arian was speechless for a long moment – a sign, Simples seemed to think, of encouragement. He put his arm around her waist and drew her close to him.

'I could make you a fine husband. I could give you respectability, something you have lacked these last few years. It's an offer not to be tossed away lightly.'

'You must be insane, ' Arian gasped, pushing at his chest, aghast at his assumption that his attentions would be welcome.

'I wouldn't marry you if you offered me the world on a silver platter.'

He released her abruptly and Arian hurried upstairs to her room, breathing heavily in distress, anger and fear beating at her with dark wings.

For a moment there, in the darkness of the passageway, she had been a captive again, at the mercy of a man who had no conscience, a man who was unhinged. She had felt the pain of his violence, felt the horror crawl within her at the thought of him possessing her against her will. Somehow, in her mind, Simples had become synonymous with all the bad memories that haunted her past, and in that moment she hated him.

To Arian's chagrin, the meeting with Calvin Temple had to be postponed because he was suddenly called away on family business. Arian fretted about the delay but there was nothing she could do but get on with her plans for taking up the position with Craig Grenfell. Now more than ever, she wanted to get away from Stormhill. True, she would be distancing herself from Calvin but he, like all men, never looked below the surface but took events at their face value.

She would have to look for lodgings, that would be the first move in her bid to make a new career for herself in the leather business. To do that, she needed money. She must see Calvin, have him pay the wages he owed her. She knew that he would be generous and would doubtless let her go without too much trouble. Perhaps he would be relieved to have her off his hands.

She smiled wryly to herself. Fortunately she had worked for him long enough to repay the outlay on her clothing. And the wages she would receive as a buyer would far supersede those she had earned as a dogsbody.

But that was unfair of her. Calvin had never treated her as anything but a lady; she had been very fortunate that he had taken her in to his home, helped her find some measure of self-respect. Suddenly, her throat was constricted, 'Calvin, Calvin, my love, if only things were different.'

It was later that night when she heard strange sounds coming from the bedroom below. There was the crash of china and the noise of a masculine voice cursing.

Arian opened her door, the landing was quiet. She had the bedroom nearest the stairway. It seemed no-one else had heard the commotion. The other servants, with the exception of Simples, slept in the attic rooms, and of Simples there was no sign.

She made her way down the stairs and along the corridor towards Calvin's room. She heard him blundering about and then a thud as though he had fallen.

She opened his door cautiously. The lamp was lit and Calvin was sitting on the floor, a heap of bedclothes around him. He was holding his hand and Arian gasped as she saw the trail of blood running down his arm.

'You're hurt, what's happened?' She hurried towards him regardless of the fact that she was wearing only a nightgown. It became instantly clear that Calvin had supped too freely of wine – his hair was tangled and his shirt was open to the waist.

'More money,' he slurred the words. 'Another old uncle has passed away, God rest his soul.' He looked up at Arian, 'What do I want with more money, tell me? Money I've got plenty of but what about love, tell me that?'

Arian knelt beside him and moved the pieces of broken wash-basin out of harm's way.

'Let me have a look at that cut,' she said softly. 'Here, let me see.' She took his hand, conscious of its warmth as his fingers curled around hers. 'It's not so bad, is it? I'll get a clean handkerchief from your drawer.'

She bound up the cut and helped Calvin untangle himself from the bedclothes. 'Come on, let's get you to bed. Sleep is what you need now.' She put her arm around him and half dragged him to his feet.

'Lie down, I'll go and get Simples. He can help you undress.'

Arian hurried along the corridor and up the stairs. She knocked lightly on Simples's door and after a moment, opened it. The room was empty. Shrugging, Arian returned to Calvin's room.

'Let's get your boots off, Calvin,' Arian urged, using his name without thinking. 'You'll feel better in the morning, I promise you.'

She drew off his boots, struggling breathlessly, knowing he was in no fit state to help her. Panting, she pushed him over on his side and tried to pull the bedclothes over him.

His arm flew out and caught her, she staggered and fell down beside him. She laughed, leaning on one elbow to look down at his face. He was breathing easily now, his eyes closed, his lashes incredibly long, sweeping his face.

Arian had a sudden impulse to kiss him. She bent down and touched her lips to his. He stirred slightly and she raised her head, and it was then she became aware that she was being watched.

Simples was standing in the doorway, a strange look on his face. His eyes met Arian's briefly then he was gone. Arian scrambled from the bed, realizing she was wearing only her nightgown. She looked around her, the broken china on the floor, the bedclothes in a heap and she knew how the situation must have appeared to Simples. He doubtless thought that she had been involved in a drunken orgy with her boss.

She considered rushing after him and trying to explain, but then she shrugged. Why should she bother about him? She'd been doing nothing wrong.

She glanced back at Calvin. He was sleeping soundly and as she watched him, Arian was unaware of the soft contours of her face and the smile that curved her lips.

It was the next day when Simples asked her to come to his room to talk.

'Is that wise?' Arian asked. 'Won't the servants gossip if we are alone in your room?'

'They might gossip a great deal more if they get to hear about you and his lordship.' Simples's words were loaded with meaning and Arian felt a tingling along her spine. She raised her head and looked Simples in the eye.

'Are you thinking of blackmailing me into coming to your bed?' she asked. He flinched almost visibly.

'Nothing so crude, Miss Smale but I do suggest we discuss this privately. Shall we say after we've had supper this evening?'

'Very well.' Arian was tight-lipped. She didn't trust Simples but at least he couldn't get up to much with a household full of servants, not to mention Calvin who was remaining at home for dinner.

She swallowed hard. She would have to speak to him soon, talk to Calvin about the error in the books, convince him that no-one –at least not she – was trying to cheat him. Her heart sank. She must also tell him that she wanted to be free to work for Craig Grenfell.

She drew a ragged breath. Since the night before when she'd pressed her mouth to his, she'd been strangely shy in his presence.

Her opportunity came suddenly. Calvin was crossing the hall just as she was making her way upstairs. He paused and smiled down at her.

'I believe I have to thank you,' he said, his eyes full of laughter. 'I have a vague recollection of you playing the ministering angel, binding up my wounds and putting me to bed. It was very kind, thank you.'

'There's nothing to thank me for, sir,' she said quickly, aware of the colour in her cheeks. 'It was nothing.'

'Well, I'm very grateful,' he said, 'though I must admit that when I woke, the bedclothes were in rather a heap around me.'

Arian laughed suddenly at the recollection of Calvin sitting on the floor in a tangle of bedclothes, his hair tousled, his shirt open.

At that moment Bella walked past, her apron crackling stiffly. She bobbed a curtsy and looked curiously at Arian – she obviously couldn't understand the lack of deference Arian showed their boss.

Calvin stood for a moment as though uncertain what he should say and Arian knew that if she didn't speak up now, she never would.

'I've been offered another job,' she said in a rush. 'It's working for the Grenfells in the leather business. It's what I have always wanted to do.'

Calvin gave the impression that he might take a step backwards though he didn't actually move. 'I see,' he said slowly. 'Well, in that case, you must feel free to do what you wish.' His voice was formal, there was no sign of laughter now. 'I take it you will work till the end of the month?'

'Oh, yes, of course.' She was going to speak about the missing money but the words stuck in her throat.

'Very well. I'll have Simples make your wages up to the end of the month, then.'

'Thank you, sir.' Arian felt strangely as if she'd been given a reprieve. She was not leaving yet, not until the end of the month.

In the silence, Calvin stared at her, his eyes unreadable and then, abruptly, he nodded and turned away.

Arian moved upstairs. She might as well get the meeting with Simples out of the way. In any case, once she left Stormhill, he would be no more trouble to her. And yet even that knowledge somehow failed to raise her suddenly flagging spirits; the end of the month wasn't that far away.

'Come in and close the door, Miss Smale,' Simples said when a few minutes later she stood on the landing outside his room. When she hesitated, he took her arm and drew her inside.

'What is it?' Arian stood against the closed door as though ready to flee and Simples smiled thinly.

'It's all right, Miss Smale, I'm not going to attack you,' he said. 'I am far too subtle a man for that sort of approach.'

'What do you want?' Arian repeated her question and Simples sank into a chair.

'I'll come straight to the point, Miss Smale,' he said, placing his fingertips together and looking at her intently. 'I have come to a decision. I intend for us to be married.'

Arian stared at him as though he had taken leave of his senses. 'You must be out of your mind.' She bit her lip. She had blurted out her thoughts, put them into speech and she saw Gerald Simples's face darken with anger.

'Not out of my mind, Miss Smale,' he said with a dangerous quietness, 'I simply mean every word I say. I will marry you. Make up your mind to it. You and I are meant for each other. In time you will come to appreciate the truth of my words.'

'I'm leaving here,' she said desperately, 'taking up another position. I'll be far away from you, out of your reach. Just forget all your ideas about me. I'm not going to marry anyone, ever.'

He smiled thinly. 'Oh, yes, I think you will, Miss Smale.' He stepped a little closer and she flinched. He rested his hand on her cheek so briefly that she wondered if she'd imagined his touch.

'I will know your charms, believe me, I will possess your sweetness.' He touched a curl of her hair. 'I will tangle my fingers in your glorious locks and will taste my fill of your lips.'

He looked, she thought, like a predatory animal, his eyes were alight, his mouth close to hers and in that moment, she feared that somehow he could make his desires come true.

'Then you will have to take me by force,' she said harshly. 'I'll never come to you willingly, you can count on it.'

'Don't *you* count on it, Miss Smale,' his voice was soft, menacing. 'You will come to me when and as I want. You will give yourself to me – I do not rape and plunder, I wait and get what I want in my own way.'

His mouth was inches from hers. She thought of screaming but somehow knew she would be made to look foolish. 'Keep away from me, Gerald Simples,' she warned, 'just keep away.'

He moved at once and stood looking down into her face. 'My silly, pretty child,' he said, 'don't try to fight me, for I'll have you, you'll see.'

She opened the door and left the room hurriedly, her breathing harsh, her hands trembling. In her own room, she sank onto the bed, her hands over her face. She must run, now while she had the chance, for Gerald Simples's words suddenly seemed prophetic.

CHAPTER SIX

Eline looked around the small room with a feeling of regret. Now that she was leaving the old house, it suddenly felt safe and sheltering. Small and inconvenient though it was, it had been her first home with Will and here they had been happy.

'Come on, Eline,' Will said softly, his arms creeping round her waist from behind. 'You're going to love our new place.'

She leaned back against him. 'I know, it's beautiful – a big kitchen, a workshop and a separate bedroom for the baby when he's older, it's just what we want. Still . . .' her voice trailed away wistfully.

'Still, nothing,' Will said firmly. 'We're moving on to better things. Thanks to your talent.' He turned her round to face him and kissed the tip of her nose.

'Don't look so worried. Soon you'll be free and then we'll be married. You'll be Mrs William Davies, how does that sound?'

'Wonderful,' Eline sighed softly, 'like a dream come true, but you know how people will react when the divorce is made public. I'll be the centre of attention again, tongues will wag and people will point a finger and stare at me, the scarlet woman.' She bit her lip. 'Life is not fair at all. Calvin is seeing another woman, it might well be that he wants to marry again.' She spoke softly. 'It seems he's been to the Assembly Rooms and the theatre with her, so the gossips in the grocers were saying, but no-one condemns him for it.'

Will rested his hand on her shoulder. 'Does it matter what people say? Forget Calvin Temple, put him right out of your thoughts. It's you and I and our child. We are important now, not the past.'

'I know I behaved much worse than Calvin,' Eline said, 'but *he* is forgiven for taking a woman, no, not forgiven, he's *expected* to have a lover just because he's a man and very rich, while I . . .' She paused and took a deep breath. 'Yesterday, a woman in the street actually moved her skirts aside when she was passing me. You'd think I was a paid harlot the way she looked at me. It seems there's one law for Calvin and another one for me.'

'That's just ignorance for you,' Will said and there was an edge of impatience in his voice. 'As for Temple, I'm glad he's resigned to the fact that he's lost you for ever.' His tone softened, 'Look, love, folks will soon forget the matter and find something else to talk about.'

'Will they?' Eline said doubtfully. 'We are shunned by some people as it is. There are those who wouldn't come to us if you were the only cobbler in Swansea.'

'We can do without them then.' Will kissed her lips lightly. 'There are many potential customers outside Swansea's boundaries – we'll go further afield if need be but we *will* make a success of our business.' He led her to the door. 'Already, your shoes are beginning to sell to the rich customers who expect only the best. They want to know that they are wearing something exclusive, that they won't see the same shoes on anyone else. Be happy with the way our future seems to be working out, Eline. Please don't keep worrying about things that are not important.'

Eline squared her shoulders as Will picked up their son and walked out into the street. She paused, unable to resist one last glance back into the small room. She saw the fireplace, dead and black now without flames or coal to warm it. She saw the thin curtains and the worn mats on the floor. It was a bare room, almost an ugly room, but she had made it home. Here she had come to live with the two people she loved most in all the world – William and their son. Tears misted her eyes as she saw even the damp stains on the walls with a feeling of loss.

'Goodbye,' she whispered, and then she left the safety of the small room with the feeling that she was embarking on uncharted, dangerous seas.

Simples cornered Arian on the landing outside her bedroom. She had been avoiding him ever since his fatuous declaration that he was going to marry her. She looked up at him in the soft glow from the lamp and he smiled down at her with a smugness that at once set her hackles rising.

'We must talk, Arian,' he said softly. 'If you value Lord Temple's good name, you'll come to my room after supper this evening.'

'And what if I don't?' Arian responded. 'There's every chance I might go to Calvin Temple and tell him all about your demands and threats.'

Simples shrugged. 'Well then I would likely be dismissed. If that were to happen it would make my story all the more credible. I would be a martyr to the altar of his lordship's shameful dalliance with you. Such gossip about the rich is meat and drink to the lower orders.'

He leaned closer to her and there was the scent about him of power, as though he had her just where he wanted her. His next words sent a chill down her spine.

'I would be free to blacken both your names as much as I wished.'

'I'm sure a man like Calvin Temple would be more than capable of refuting your accusations,' Arian said hotly. 'He has the courage to defy any blackmail attempt and take the matter to law.' Arian lifted her chin defiantly.

'In any case, what could you say except that you saw me helping him into bed?'

'I saw you in your nightwear lying *with* him on the bed, the sheets tossed aside, his arm around you, you were kissing him.' He paused as if to calm himself. 'It was the dead of night. Who would believe it was an innocent meeting if I were to repeat what after all is the bald truth?'

Simples paused for his words to sink in, and then continued. 'Remember, his lordship is a man about to sue

93

his wife for divorce on the grounds of her immorality. It wouldn't look good if he was found to be bedding one of his servants, would it?'

Arian was silent. What could she say? Of course it would be assumed that she and Calvin were lovers. No-one hearing Simples's accusations could believe anything else.

'And then there's his lady friend,' Simples persisted. 'His relationship with her could be construed as intimate. He might be forgiven for taking one lady to his bed but his servant as well? That's too much for even the most tolerant person to excuse. Public opinion is a dangerous weapon; questions would be asked about his wife. Did she deserve to be dismissed from the marital home or was some fault in Lord Temple the cause of the trouble?'

Arian felt that all this was unreal. She couldn't be standing here listening to Simples's blackmailing threats. But what could she do? He was right. Gossip such as he was suggesting wouldn't do Calvin any good at all.

'I'll think about what you've said,' she spoke in a low voice, anger thudding through her brain. 'That's all I'm going to promise, that I'll think about it.'

'Think hard, I'll be expecting you in my room later.' Simples moved away, descending each stair with a precision of movement that jarred on Arian. He did everything precisely, with deliberation, as if nothing was on impulse but every move a calculated decision.

Arian ate very little supper, her mind was in chaos. Should she go to Calvin? Tell him what Simples was about, have the man discredited? It was one way out of her predicament. But on the other hand, to tell the truth openly would be to hand Simples the excuse to declare war on Calvin's reputation. People in Swansea, like everywhere else, loved a good scandal.

Arian shuddered. She didn't want to go to Simples's room. She didn't even wish to be near him. Why did he want to see her in private anyway? He'd told her he was not a man to force himself on a woman, so what was he planning?

She was still debating with herself when, after supper, she climbed the stairs and paused on the landing. What if she decided not to see Simples? Would he carry out his threats to spread gossip about Calvin? She suddenly doubted it. Simples stood to lose a great deal – a good job and a secure future. He would be a fool to make an enemy of Calvin.

She hesitated and then biting her lip, moved on towards her own room. She wanted nothing to do with him. His threats were idle. She would defy Simples, let him do his damnedest.

She sat in her room trying to evaluate the situation. What did Simples have on her anyway, was it just the matter of the discrepancy in the books? Would that be enough to turn Calvin against her? She doubted it. He was far too sensible for that. She washed and undressed, her mind still racing. Doubt crept over her. Could Simples really blacken her name? Did he have something up his sleeve, a card he'd yet to reveal?

Lying in bed, she stared up at the ceiling through the flickering candlelight. The cracks appeared to spread outwards in the shape of a map. There was Wales and England, there just near the window Scotland and a little way over, towards the door, was etched a shape that roughly resembled Ireland.

How foolish she was. That was her last thought as she fell asleep and then she was plagued by dreams, dreams of herself locked in an embrace with Gerald Simples, an embrace from which it was impossible to free herself.

She woke in the morning heavy eyed, the remnants of her nightmares still with her. And yet she felt triumphant – she'd defied Gerald Simples, called his bluff.

When she was dressed, she hesitated a little before opening the door of her room, taking a deep breath, willing herself to be calm. What could he do to her? Here in the home of Calvin Temple she was safe, even from a man as ruthless as Simples.

He saw her later in the back hallway, his face hardened as he stared down at her.

'So you defied me,' he said in a low voice. 'This is not the end of the matter, Miss Smale.' The words came out coldly, like stones falling into the silence. 'I mean to have you for my wife, and I *will* have you, I promise you that.'

She felt panic sweep over her. 'I didn't come to your room because I saw no point in it. You must realize it wouldn't be any good, I could never love you,' Arian paused to wonder why she was even trying to explain things to him, he just wasn't hearing her, 'so what is the use of you wanting me?' she finished lamely.

'I don't care if you don't love me now. Love can grow and if it doesn't,' he shrugged, 'I can live with that, so long as I have you in my bed.'

Arian shivered and squared her shoulders. 'There's no chance of that, believe me.' He took a step towards her and she held up her hand.

'Stay away from me, Mr Simples, just stay away from me.'

He smiled then, slowly, unpleasantly. 'I've told you once before, Miss Smale, I will never force you, not physically. You will come to me of your own free will. My plans are made and I will make it happen.'

Arian hurried away, what if he could somehow make his words come true? Nothing could be worse than being tied to a man like that. He wasn't quite sane, she was convinced of it.

She told herself to be calm and moving towards the chair near the fire, she sank into it, clenching her hands together to stop them from trembling. She was being silly, melodramatic. Of course Simples couldn't force her into anything, certainly not into coming to his bed of her own free will. It was nonsense, the dreaming of an unbalanced mind. Or was it?

Calvin put his hands behind his head, his knuckles sinking into the softness of the pillows. He smiled as he watched Daphne at her ablutions. She was the epitome of charm and grace, she was the mistress of seduction and yet she had a sweet air of innocence about her as she stood naked before him.

Daphne lacked the usual reticence of her own kind; women very rarely revealed their nakedness even to their husbands. He thought, with a sharp pain, about his wife. Eline had been modest in the extreme, always keeping her beautiful body covered. He had only known it by touch but God, he had loved her.

He stared at Daphne's long slender legs. She was elegant and tall and could have been angular had it not been for the fullness of her breasts. Her legs were astride as she washed delicately, the darkness of her hair a contrast to the alabaster skin. He desired her, oh yes, he desired her with every fibre of his being but then desire was easy, love was not.

'Like what you see?' Daphne said smiling archly at him, her soft mouth curved upwardly, invitingly. Calvin returned her smile. He took one arm lazily from behind his head and beckoned to her.

'I like what I see very much,' he said. 'Come here and find out for yourself.'

'But Calvin, darling, I have to go,' Daphne said, 'I've an At Home to attend with one of my best friends.'

'An old flame perhaps?' Calvin felt amused more than jealous as she nodded.

'Well, to be precise, the old flame's wife.' Her cheeks dimpled. 'It *could* all be rather embarrassing darling if I didn't keep my head.'

'Come here,' Calvin said with mock sternness. 'How can I look at you and not be stirred to passion?'

Daphne looked down at him, a glow coming into her eyes. She moved languorously towards the bed, her pupils dilated with anticipated lust, her lips moist.

'I can see how stirred you are, my dear,' she said and gently lowered herself down beside him.

It was dusk when Calvin ushered Daphne outside to her waiting carriage. He stood there until the even clip clop of the horses' hooves had died away and then he closed the door.

Turning, he saw Arian standing in the shadows. She had a stillness about her as though she had been watching him. 'Did you want anything?' he asked, and an expression fleeted across her face that he wasn't able to read.

'Have I shocked you by entertaining my ladyfriend in my room?' he asked moving closer, aware of how small she was, how fine boned. Perhaps it was just the contrast between her and Daphne that made Arian appear almost fey and somehow mystical.

Calvin realized with a dart of interest that he knew very little of the girl's inner thoughts – Arian was an enigma while Daphne was an open book anyone could read.

'Come into the drawing room,' he said, leading the way, 'I think we should have a little talk.'

She stood near the doorway, her eyes not quite meeting his.

'Why haven't you been happy here?' he asked wishing to draw her out of her shell. He realized, in that moment, how reluctant he was to let her go.

'I've enjoyed working for you well enough, sir, but to be honest with you, I think it *is* time I moved on.'

'Move on, to what, though?' he asked briskly. 'To work for someone else? Is that what you wanted? I had the impression you wished to be your own boss.'

Arian straightened her shoulders as though to do battle. She spoke in a rush. 'Working for Mr Grenfell would give me an independence I don't have here.' She was breathless and Calvin knew she was nervous. 'I would be selecting the best skins and doing the actual buying.'

'I thought you wanted your own business?' Calvin insisted. 'That's surely what real independence is all about?'

'Aye, I know,' Arian said, 'but . . .' her voice trailed away and Calvin felt himself relax.

'But you thought I'd forgotten all about it?' he supplied, feeling more in command of the situation now.

She nodded, almost miserably. He looked down at her, saw shadows in her eyes. She felt he had failed her.

'Well, in truth, it had gone out of my mind just lately,' he said, 'but what I have done is looked at suitable premises for you.' A glimmer of a smile appeared on his face. 'I hadn't forgotten you entirely, you see. Arian, I would like you to realize your ambitions, I want to help.'

'Thank you, sir.' Her tone was stilted and Calvin felt there was more to her urge to get away from the manor than met the eye.

'Is this sudden urgency anything to do with the missing money, by any chance?' he asked quietly. 'If so, please don't give the matter another thought. I haven't.'

'No, it's not that. It's nothing, just that I don't want to work here for evermore. I want to get out there, make my own mark on the world.' She grimaced. 'Perhaps you'll think all that presumptuous on the part of a servant.'

'Not at all.' His tone became businesslike. There was no fathoming women, he decided, it was useless to try. 'There's a warehouse to let down at the docks, needs a bit of work but the construction is sound.'

It seemed that Arian would turn his suggestion down, and suddenly Calvin knew he didn't want to lose sight of her – she interested him.

'It's the chance you always wanted,' he said smiling. 'Have your ambitions changed or is it that you are afraid of the challenge?'

He saw the rich colour suffuse her cheeks, her chin lifted and her eyes seemed to glow angrily.

'There's a silly thing to say.' He heard the Welshness of her voice with amusement – the lilting sound was a contrast to her usual even tones. 'It's just that I feel obligated to Mr Grenfell, that's all.'

'Don't worry about Craig,' Calvin said. 'I'll square things with him, he's an understanding sort of a chap.'

Arian seemed undecided, she looked at him doubtfully and small white teeth chewed at her lip. She was little more than a girl, Calvin thought, and yet by all accounts she had lived the life of an experienced woman.

'Is there something else bothering you?' Calvin sensed an uneasiness in her that was so strong it almost reached out and touched him. She shook her head abruptly and a stray curl of silver-gold hair fell over her forehead.

'No, nothing's bothering me, but there *are* a few things I must think about, sir. Could I talk to you later about the warehouse and all that?'

'Of course,' Calvin said quickly, 'no-one is going to force you into doing what you don't want to.'

Was he mistaken or did a strange expression fleet across her face? He turned away abruptly. He was being far too concerned with this girl – she was none of his business. He had enough on his plate already, with his divorce imminent and Daphne growing more and more tiresome every day.

And yet when he had left her and was seated in the comfortable leather chair in his study, he could not help seeing her face, soft, petal-like and the bright tendril of hair falling childlike over her brow, and he was strangely affected by the image.

There was something about Arian, he realized, that brought out his protective instincts. 'Rubbish!' he said the word out loud. All that he wanted was to bed the girl – why didn't he face the truth? As for emotional entanglements, he could well do without that sort of complication in his life. He rose abruptly and moving to the sideboard, poured himself a stiff drink of porter.

Arian sat in her room and stretched her bare feet out towards the fire. She was lost in thought, her brow furrowed, her hands twisting nervously at the folds of her nightgown. It had become clear to her, as she'd brooded in the semi-darkness, that she must get out of Stormhill, find rooms of her own, be independent. Calvin could scarcely be accused then of having a relationship with his servant.

The gentle knock on her door startled her. She glanced up at the clock and sighed. It was bed time and no doubt Bella had arrived with her milk drink, the last of the evening.

'Come in,' she sat up straighter in her chair and turned with a welcoming smile that quickly faded.

'Mr Simples,' she said icily, 'I wasn't expecting you and as you can see, I'm not dressed for visitors.'

He closed the door and came further into the room, his eyes drinking in every detail of her appearance. Arian felt almost naked under his scrutiny.

'So your ideas of running a business are coming to fruition, then?' he said slowly. Arian was suddenly angry.

'I'll not only have my own business but my own home,' her voice low, 'then you won't be able to spread any lies about me and his lordship.'

'You haven't thought all this out, my dear Miss Smale,' Simples said with maddening reasonableness. 'If you were to leave, it would appear that his lordship had grown tired of you, cast you aside as he did his wife. This would not recommend you to a future employer, now would it?

'Then there's the discrepancy in the books. Didn't you wonder why Lord Temple has never brought it up again?' He went on without waiting for a reply. 'I think I rather gave him the impression that it was your . . . er . . . little blunder. I excused you of course, said I knew what it was like to be short of money, told him it wouldn't happen again and that I would be personally responsible for you in future. Lord Temple was very understanding but how would any future employer react to that little story, which his lordship would be honour-bound to confirm, should it get out.'

Arian felt anger run through her veins like hot wine. She wanted to strike out at Simples, to tear at his smug face with her nails. She took a deep breath and forced herself to be calm.

'How dare you do such a thing?' her voice was low. 'You know I didn't make any error or take any money.' She gave a short laugh 'And you say you care for me. You must be mad.'

His face darkened. 'Be careful, Miss Smale, that you do not go too far.' His eyes were suddenly like ice and Arian heard warning bells in her head.

'Of course,' she said more evenly, 'you would make it a point of making known my so-called dishonesty to anyone you considered a threat to your plans?' Arian's spirits sank. She saw clearly just how far Simples would go in order to get his own way.

He began to talk more quietly, even menacingly. 'I'm not willing to let you out of my sight. I need you to be close to me so that I can keep an eye on you.'

Arian felt her face grow hot with anger. 'I don't want you keeping an eye on me,' she said fiercely.

He took her arm. His grip was light but she felt almost mesmerized by the way his face was close to hers, his eyes, those strange eyes, were staring into hers.

'I know too much about you, Miss Smale. There have been other, later . . . errors shall we call them? in the accounts. In any case, I will not let you go. I will do anything – and I mean anything – to anyone who tries to take you away from me.' He paused for his words to sink in.

'So you see,' Simples continued, 'you'd better accept his lordship's offer. I intend to have you close to me here at Stormhill.' He paused, looking at her as though he would like to press his mouth to hers.

'Look on the bright side; there would be the prestige of running your own business, you would be free, independent, up to a point.'

Arian looked at him sceptically. 'But would I be free?'

Simples smiled. 'As free as you can be, Miss Smale but then none of us is entirely without obligations.'

'Please leave,' Arian said in a low voice. 'I'm very tired and I think I'd better get some sleep. There's a lot of work ahead if I'm to run my own company.'

'Indeed.' Gerald Simples moved towards her and Arian fought the desire to turn away from him. She stared levelly into his face, her expression forbidding any familiarity and after a moment, he silently let himself out of her room.

Arian sank back in her chair, her thoughts in chaos, but one thing was clear; Simples was dangerous and would stop at nothing to get what he wanted. She was inclined to believe that it was he who had tampered with the accounts, he who had misappropriated the funds, all so that he would have more of a hold over her.

Somehow, she must manage to keep him at arm's length at least until the divorce was over and done with. Once Calvin was a free man, she could tell Gerald Simples to go to hell his own way.

Events moved swiftly, for it seemed that once Calvin made up his mind to something, he acted on it at once. The premises on the docks were eminently suitable and Calvin saw to it that a room was furnished as an office.

'A substantial amount of money is lodged in your name in the bank,' he said as he handed her down from the carriage and led her along the edge of the water towards the office. Gerald Simples was a few steps behind them, with a pile of books under his arm.

'Yours is the easy part,' Calvin said. 'You only have to get the business under way – a simple job for someone as talented as you.'

She knew he was teasing. She knew, too that now she had to really start making her contacts. She needed to find suppliers who would sell her the leather, and customers who would pay her well for the expertise she would offer.

She bit her lip nervously. 'I'm sure it's going to go well,' she said shakily and Calvin laughed as he pushed open the door of her office.

'I feel I should carry you over the threshold or something,' he said softly, bending towards her. She looked up into his face and saw that his mouth was very close to hers.

She never knew if it was on an impulse or if he'd calculated his next move but then Calvin's mouth was on hers. The kiss was light enough, it probably meant nothing to him, but Arian was aware of a feeling of pain deep inside her. She realized that she'd wanted him to kiss her and now that he had drawn away, she felt a sensation of loss.

She took a deep breath, becoming aware that they were not alone. Simples was standing behind them, his face averted but the line of his shoulders showed his tension. A few yards away a group of men in good suits were glancing at them in amusement and Arian moved inside the office, her face aflame with colour.

'Gerald here is going to help you set up your accounts,' Calvin said. 'He really is a first-class man.'

'I don't need any help.' Arian concealed her dismay by bending her head to straighten a blotting pad on the new desk.

'It's just for a few weeks,' Calvin said, 'until you have chosen your own staff.' He smiled. 'I wouldn't like to leave such an attractive young lady alone on the docklands, it wouldn't be proper.'

Arian realized he was half teasing her but he was right all the same; she had no option but to accept the presence of Gerald Simples, at least for the time being.

'It's very kind of you,' she said to Calvin and then forcing herself to smile, she included Simples in her glance.

'And kind of you to spare me the time, Mr Simples,' she said not meeting his gaze.

'I must be going,' Calvin said, 'but I have taken the liberty of lending you the services of our own Bella for the time being, so that everything is seen to be above board. Can't have you and Simples being talked about, can we?'

When Calvin had gone, Arian sank down into her chair. The first thing she must do, she decided was to send a letter to Craig Grenfell. When she'd informed him of her change of plans he'd been very generous, requesting her services as a consultant if she was still interested.

Her spirits lifted. This was really too good an opportunity to miss. If Mr Grenfell wanted her help, it would be the first step to supplying his stocks of leather herself.

She drew a sheet of paper across the desk towards her and saw with surprise that it was headed with her name and the address of the business.

'That was my idea,' Simples said quietly. 'I hope you can see how useful I can be to you.'

'It was a very good idea,' Arian said quietly. 'At least my correspondence will look businesslike. Thank you Mr Simples.'

Bella entered the room with a tray, her face beaming. 'You didn't know I was in by there, did you?' She said. 'Got you a little kitchen an' all, his lordship has.' She looked at Arian with a little sideways glance. 'Very fond of you, he is, mark my words.'

Briefly, Arian's eyes met those of Gerald Simples and she saw a gleam of triumph before she looked away again.

'Don't be silly, Bella,' she said quickly. 'His lordship has an eye for a good business venture, that's all.'

Bella's grunt revealed quite plainly what nonsense she thought that was. She placed the tray on the table and stepped back a pace. 'I got to do some shopping now,' she said, 'but I won't be long and I'll be back to make you some luncheon.'

When Bella had gone, there was silence in the room. Arian looked down at the headed notepaper. The empty sheet seemed to mock her and a sudden sense of panic filled her.

'One step at a time, Miss Smale,' Simples said calmly. 'Just take one step at a time.'

She drew the sheet of paper closer and dipping the pen in the ink, she began to write.

CHAPTER SEVEN

'Dirty whore!' The words hit hard like stones, and as Eline looked into the face of the woman who had spoken them she saw there such venom that a chill ran down her spine. 'Whore,' the woman repeated, 'living tally by here among us respectable women, aught to be burned for a witch you did.'

Taylor's grocery shop was full of customers and Eline felt the colour run into her cheeks, emphasizing her embarrassment. She drew herself up and looked her accuser in the eye.

'There's nothing dirty about me . . . Mrs Willett . . . isn't it?' Eline's voice was surprisingly calm. 'Unlike some people I could mention, I take a pride in my appearance.' She looked pointedly at the woman's skirt bedecked on the hem with mud from the roadway. Slowly, her eyes rose to the torn bodice and the worn shawl. 'I may be many things but not dirty.'

'Oh clever clogs is it?' The woman said pushing up her sleeves. 'Calling me dirty, eh? That's fighting talk that is mind, don't take that from no-one, I don't.'

'Really, Mrs Willet,' Eline said coolly. 'I have no intention of brawling with you like a fishwife. You called me names and that sort of abuse could land you in trouble with the constables.'

The woman paled at the mention of the law. She tugged the grubby shawl closer and quickly retreated towards the door. 'Well I'll not shop in by here while the likes of you are being served,' she said, her jaw thrust forward aggressively. 'Cast out by your husband you were for having a bastard child and now you are living in sin amongst us respectable folk.' She appealed to the other women who stood around in ragged groups uncertain how to respond.

'Divorced!' she said the word on a gasp of horror. 'This woman is going to be *divorced*. Are we going to put up with having someone like her mixing with us?'

The proprietor came forward shaking his head apologetically. 'Please, both of you, just go,' he said, his plump chins quivering, revealing his distress. 'I'm sorry, missis,' he said to Eline, 'but just keep away from my shop, I beg of you, I don't want any trouble in here.'

Eline gave him a long cool look and he rubbed the sweat from his brow. 'I got to make a living like everyone else,' he was apologetic but determined. 'Please, just go.'

She left the shop with as much dignity as she could muster but Eline was trembling as she walked back along the street towards home.

'What's wrong?' Will was on his feet the instant she entered the shop, putting his arms around her, hugging her close. 'What's happened, Eline, tell me?'

She sighed heavily, 'There was a scene in Taylor's shop. One of the women called me a dirty whore. We were left alone in World's End among the outcasts of society. That's where we belong and we should have stayed there, not moved to this more *respectable* district.'

He tipped her face up so that he could look into her eyes. 'You are no whore,' he said softly. 'You are a woman in love. We are a couple, we will face this together as we've faced everything else.'

Eline knew he was right – they had sacrificed everything to be together. She wasn't going to allow a sharp-tongued harridan to upset her. And yet she was upset.

'It will get worse,' she said quietly. 'Once the divorce is over and the proceedings are splashed all over the newspaper, it will be the talk of Swansea. Can our business survive the scandal, Will?'

'Look, it's the rich who are buying your shoes,' he said. 'They have enough scandals to last a lifetime so they are not going to bother about you being divorced are they?'

'I don't know.' Eline sank down on one of the stools in the workshop and toyed with a piece of leather. 'The rich might be up to all sorts of things in private but they take care not to be found out.'

Will took her hands in his and knelt before her. 'Look, Eline, if things get too bad we can move away from Swansea. We'll get married quietly and live where no-one knows us.'

'I won't be chased out of my home town,' Eline said firmly. 'I was born and raised on the outskirts of Swansea and I'm not going to give in to the gossips.'

'That's my girl,' Will hugged her. 'I hoped you'd say that. Now, go and see to our son - he's been sleeping for the past hour – and me, well I've got plenty of work to do,' he smiled a little ruefully, 'because my prices are cheaper than those of any other cobbler, apparently. You see, the poor are not above giving me their business in spite of me living in sin with a scarlet woman!'

Eline forced a smile but as she walked through the workshop towards the kitchen, she felt somehow as though she had been besmirched. The words of the woman in the shop still rang in her ears; 'dirty whore', that's the reputation she would have to live with, her son would have to grow up with, and Eline didn't know if she could bear it.

Craig Grenfell smiled down at the young lady who was sorting through the heaps of skins in his warehouse, watching with amusement as she indicated those which were inferior. She was wearing a plain brown skirt and loose brown jacket. Her hair, a splash of brightness against the drabness of her clothes, hung in a plait down her back. She really was a lovely girl, clever too.

'These must be sent back to the suppliers,' she said glancing almost absent-mindedly over her shoulder. 'I don't think for one moment you will be reimbursed for the poor goods but at least you will have proved that you can recognize rubbish when you see it.'

'Well Miss Smale,' he said, thrusting his hands into his pockets, 'I think from now on, I'd be better off giving my custom to you.' He took out a folded sheet and handed it to her. 'My first order is for French calf. I'll trust you to see that it's the best quality.'

She looked up at him, her eyebrows raised. 'But you know the French suppliers,' she said. 'What's to prevent you doing the ordering of the goods yourself as you used to?'

'I'm getting lazy,' Craig said. 'As you said, I've accepted rubbish in this batch of leather. The truth is I wish to spend more time with my family.' He shrugged, 'I don't need to work too hard these days and in any case, I think an enterprising young lady like you deserves help on the climb up the ladder.'

And he did. In some ways Arian reminded him of his wife. Hari had gone into business with nothing but her knowledge and skill at shoemaking – the trade taught her by her father – and now she had become a household name and he was achingly proud of her achievements.

He smiled to himself, and, he was not above being influenced by a pretty young face either. Arian Smale was a lovely girl with soft silver-gold hair, a fine-boned face and a *very* nice body. Craig sighed, if only he was the sort to take infidelity lightly he might well be tempted to lure Arian into his bed. But then, Hari would have him hung, drawn and quartered, at least.

He became aware that Arian was smiling at him, almost as though she could read his thoughts. 'You'd better be going,' he said softly and her eyes glinted with amusement.

'Yes, I think I better had.'

Craig returned to his office and shut the books with a snap of finality. He might as well finish work for today, go home and make love to his wife. Hari was a beautiful woman, like fine wine she had matured well and what's more, he loved her dearly. But he could still enjoy the thrill of looking at a young, lovely woman couldn't he?

Arian sat in her office and stared out through the window. Her first move had been made now; courtesy of Craig

Grenfell, her business venture was under way. Excitement filled her. She had passed her first test, for here in her hands was confirmation of her very first order. She had written to the suppliers of French calf and had received their reply.

She sighed. There was one hitch – because she was a new name to them, the suppliers wanted the money put into their own bank before delivery was undertaken. This she had reluctantly discussed with Simples, but he had assured her that this was the usual practice and so she had taken the appropriate steps to have the money transferred from the account Calvin had set up for her.

The huge bill for the calf had frightened her at first but she reasoned that it would be cheaper to order in bulk and keep some of the stock for herself.

'You are looking very pleased with yourself, Miss Smale.' Simples appeared in the doorway. 'I hope you have had a good result from the suppliers you contacted?'

'Yes, thank you Mr Simples,' Arian said. 'I am grateful to you for giving me their address. Where did you get it from, by the way?'

'It was passed on to me by a very reputable businessman,' Simples said softly, 'a Mr Miller, Emily Miller's husband. He is a very trustworthy person, I assure you.'

'Of course he is.' Arian looked at Simples, wondering why he felt obliged to help her succeed in business when it would make his foolish idea of marriage even more remote. Perhaps he hoped to ingratiate himself with her – hadn't he said he wanted her to come to him willingly?

Whatever his reasons, at this moment she was grateful for his help. She would never find him attractive, never want anything, not even his friendship, and yet his co-operation was necessary to her at this juncture and so she forced herself to be polite. 'I'm grateful, Mr Simples,' she said and somehow, his smile made her more than a little uneasy.

When Arian returned to Stormhill that evening, it was to find Mrs Bob in a state near hysteria. 'That parsimonious, mealy-mouthed woman! I'll swing for her so I will.' She hammered the table top with her fist as though taking her anger out on the scrubbed boards.

'What woman? What's wrong?' Arian sat down and Bella handed her a plate of meat and potato pie, her face full of avid enjoyment.

'Glad I came back early from your place,' she whispered, 'I'd have missed all the fun otherwise.'

'Hush Bella,' Mrs Bob said irritably, 'I'm telling this tale so just keep your lip buttoned.' She sank down into her chair and faced Arian.

'Left us, gone to another situation, she has, and her spreading gossip about the folk within this household right, left and centre.' She paused briefly for breath. 'Do you know what the butcher-boy told me, do you?'

Arian shook her head and waited for the flood of Mrs Bob's angry words to continue.

'Mrs Richards has been spreading the story that you are warming his lordship's bed, the evil, old horse-face has the gall to talk about his lordship and you and that Daphne woman all being involved in immoral doings. Making his lordship out to be a right womanizing, boozing no-good, she is.'

Arian glanced at Simples. He saw the look and she knew he recognized it for what it was – Arian's way of telling him that he could no longer threaten to blacken Calvin's name, it had been done more than adequately by the housekeeper.

'Jealous she is, of course. That's what's at the bottom of it all,' Mrs Bob continued. 'Just because his lordship took on Simples here, and then to go and put you in charge of the books, well that really got up her nose.'

Arian sighed. 'Don't worry on my account,' she said quietly. 'I lost my good name a long time ago and I don't give a damn what people say about me now. I am sorry though for his lordship. He doesn't deserve to be accused of things he hasn't done.' She looked directly at Simples and he had the grace to turn away.

'I wonder if all this gossip will affect his lordship's chances of getting rid of that wife of his,' Mrs Bob said uneasily. 'I know she's living openly with that cobbler Will Davies and has a son by him. It's a disgrace. His lordship deserves better than that but still, people might draw their own conclusions about why she got involved with another man in the first place.'

'No doubt there was fault on both sides but I know his lordship loved Eline very much,' Arian said quietly. 'I know her quite well. She's had a tough time of it and she's certainly not the loose woman some people try to make her out.'

'Well, I dunno about that,' Mrs Bob said doubtfully. 'Been married before she has, mind, then had his lordship for a husband and now got a lover. Not doing too bad, is she?' There was a glint of humour in Mrs Bob's eyes and Arian responded with a smile.

'Don't let's argue about it,' she said, 'but remember, things are not always what they seem to be.'

If there was a double meaning in Arian's words, both Mr Simples and the cook chose to ignore it. Arian finished her supper in silence and then rose and stretched her arms above her head. Suddenly conscious of Simples's eyes upon her, she dropped her arms to her side quickly, afraid he might take her action as one of provocation.

'Thank you for a lovely meal,' she spoke to Mrs Bob. 'Now I'm tired I think I'll go to my room and read for a while before I go to sleep.'

'Oh, I nearly forgot to tell you,' Mrs Bob covered her mouth with a work-roughened hand in a gesture of dismay.

'Tell me what?' Arian asked. 'Another bit of gossip is it?'

'No, more important than that,' Mrs Bob said with an irritating desire to delay saying what was on her mind. 'His lordship wanted to see you, said you was to go to the drawing room when you had eaten.'

Arian nodded and left the room, climbing the stone steps up from the kitchen with a feeling of exhilaration. Calvin wanted to see her and somehow the thought made her very happy.

'Come.' His voice sounded mellow as it reached her through the closed double doors of the drawing room.

Arian obeyed him and bobbed a curtsy as she stood on the threshold of the large room with the heavy drapes closed over the long windows.

'Why is it I feel you're mocking me whenever you do that?' Calvin said easily.

'I don't know, sir.' She didn't pretend to misunderstand him – he was an intelligent man and sometimes she felt he could see right through her.

'You were not born to be subservient,' Calvin continued, 'and I believe the events in your life have only reinforced the stubborn streak in you.'

'If you mean I'm the independent sort, sir,' Arian said quickly, 'then you're right.'

'Sit down, Arian,' Calvin said easily. 'We are alone, there's no need to be formal.'

She sat on the edge of one of the finely worked chairs. The old wood gleamed and the satin upholstery had grown mellow with age.

'You have spent quite a lot of your money,' Calvin said, resting back in his chair, apparently at ease, though his eyes were clear and direct as they looked at her.

'Yes, I have,' she said, wondering if he was going to put a curb on her outgoings. After all, it was *his* money, not hers. She felt a tremble of annoyance – he was supposed to be trusting her with the business.

'Have I done anything wrong in your opinion?' she asked and was irritated by his quick smile.

'Don't be so prickly, Arian,' he said. 'I am not criticizing. There's plenty more money where that came from, it's not that.'

'What then?' Arian asked more cautiously. 'Have you any reservations about my judgement?'

'It's this company you are buying from,' Calvin said. 'I know nothing of them. They are French I believe?'

'Indeed,' Arian replied rather haughtily, 'you buy French calf from the French. Their representative was very trustworthy, he spent a great deal of time with me. I decided then to buy in bulk so I'll have a fair stock of my own leather.'

'I see.' Calvin looked thoughtful and Arian had the feeling he was not reassured.

'Some of the stock has already been sold to Craig Grenfell,' she spoke quickly, feeling that somehow it was important to convince him that she knew what she was doing, 'so I've already recouped most of my outlay. With the rest of the calf, I hope to make my profit.'

'Then you are happy with the goods that this French company have supplied?'

'I saw some excellent samples of leather. I had to decide to buy at once or miss a bargain. The ship sails from France next week.'

Calvin was silent for a moment then he sat forward in his chair. 'Arian, would you like me to make enquiries about the French company, to assure us both that they are reliable?'

'That's really not necessary. The representative named some eminent people who are buying from his firm.' She wished Calvin to keep out of her business. 'I would like you to leave me to sort it out,' she said. 'Try to trust me to run things my own way.'

'Very well,' he said and she felt she was being dismissed.

'Are you sorry then?' She couldn't leave the matter alone. 'Sorry that you put me in charge of so much money, I mean?'

He came towards her and smiled down at her easily. 'I will have to bide my time before I answer that question,' he said. 'I'm sure of one thing – that you are entirely trustworthy whatever the evidence to the contrary.'

She coloured, knowing he was referring to the lost five guineas. At least he didn't believe she'd taken the money and she was inordinately pleased at the revelation.

'As for me, I have made a few mistakes recently and seem to be losing my grip on business matters. I have made losses but fortunately nothing irretrievable.'

'I won't lose your money,' Arian said and even to her own ears, her voice sounded a little desperate. She knew that Simples had been handling Calvin's interests and a shiver of apprehension gripped her. If mistakes had been made, they were Simples's mistakes, so what if he was wrong about this French company?

'Don't look so worried.' Calvin's voice was gentle. 'I am not in the workhouse yet.'

He was very close to her and Arian felt the magnetism of him strongly. She knew that she found him attractive, she had done from the night she had helped him into bed and she had pressed her mouth to his. If she was to be honest, perhaps even long before that. But now she felt more . . . she had an overwhelming desire to protect him, to hold him safe in her arms, to . . . God! She was all sorts of a fool.

His hand was on her shoulder and his fingers seemed to burn into her skin. 'Arian . . .' he said, 'sweet, serious child.'

She wanted him to kiss her, to hold her close, to touch her breasts, to make love to her. He moved away.

'Go along then, I won't trouble you again. You are quite right. You must run your business as you see fit and I have no right to interfere.'

Disappointment swamped her. She felt as though a door had been slammed in her face. 'Thank you, sir,' she said and moved woodenly across the room. What made her think for one moment that he would want her? She was shop-soiled goods and, what's more, not of his class. He had the beautiful Daphne to take to his bed; what need did he have for a girl from the farmlands, a girl who had known other men?

In her room, she sank trembling onto the bed and stared down at her hands. They were bare of rings – she belonged nowhere and to no-one. Perhaps, she thought ruefully, she should take up Simples's offer of marriage after all. He was a man and he wanted to make her respectable.

'Fool!' she said and the word fell softly into the silence. Arian kicked off her shoes and then knelt and put a few more coals on the dying fire.

She felt alone and empty. She might as well face it, she was in love with Calvin Temple, which was absurd; all he felt for her was a vague sort of pity, a wish to help her make something of her life. And why should he feel anything more?

He knew something of her past, he certainly knew about Eddie who had been her lover. He had helped Eddie get on in life and, in the same way, he was attempting to help her. That was all.

She undressed, washed and drew on her cotton nightgown and all the time she was fighting the tears. It seemed there was a heavy weight of grief within her for the innocence she had lost. She wanted to be clean, to be whole again, to be worthy of the love of a man like Calvin Temple.

Suddenly she flung herself face down on the bed. She wanted to be loved by him. He fascinated her, he was a tall handsome man, but it was more than that, he had a mind that seemed to be in tune with hers so that he almost knew what she was thinking before she did.

She felt the tears constrict her throat and told herself she was crying for something she could never have. She pressed her mouth into the pillow not to cry out loud. She felt old pain and fear rise up within her, old nightmares that had ceased to trouble her seemed to come alive again.

She didn't hear the door open, or hear the light footsteps approaching across the carpet. But she did feel hands on her shoulders – kind masculine hands.

Eagerly she turned, thinking Calvin had come to her but the breath left her body as she saw that it was Simples bending over her, his face full of concern.

'What's wrong, Miss Smale?' he asked. 'Has anyone hurt you?' He leaned closer to her and she resisted the urge to pull away from him. He was only trying to be kind she told herself sharply.

She shook her head. 'No, it's just that I suddenly felt so alone.' She hated herself as soon as the words were out of her mouth. Why was she giving Simples any excuse to get close to her?

'You are not alone, Miss Smale.' He spoke softly and in the glow from the fire he appeared simply handsome without the air of menace that usually surrounded him. Arian felt herself relax a little. Simples had said that he would never force her and in that, at least, she believed him.

He knelt beside her on the bed and with a crisp clean handkerchief he dried the tears from her eyes. 'Never think you are alone,' he repeated. 'I am always going to be here to take care of you. You must know that, I've told you plainly enough.'

She felt she should make him go away and yet his concern was strangely comforting. 'I'm all right, now, thank you,' she said quietly.

She felt suddenly vulnerable in her cotton nightgown and she was aware that the buttons were open and the softness of her breasts was clearly visible. It was to Simples's credit that he didn't try to take advantage of the situation as some men might have done.

He touched her cheek lightly. 'I know what you are thinking, Miss Smale,' he said, 'and don't think I'm not moved by your . . . your state of undress but I am not the sort of man to force any woman, let alone the woman I am in love with.'

'No,' Arian protested, 'you don't love me, Mr Simples. You don't know me.'

'Very well, we won't argue about it.' Simples moved away from her and Arian took a deep breath, savouring the relief she felt at his willingness to accept defeat so easily.

He seemed to lift his head, as though listening and then he looked at Arian. 'Come to the door with me, Miss Smale. Make sure it is closed securely and try to get a good night's sleep, that's the best thing for you just now.'

She obeyed him and meekly crossed the room behind him. In the doorway, he held onto the handle and turned to her. 'Remember, get a good night's sleep now. You need it.'

Arian saw a shadow over Simples's shoulder and across the landing. She was aware of Calvin standing looking at her. She realized how the situation must appear; she in her nightgown with her hair dishevelled and Simples bidding her have a good night's sleep.

She lifted her chin. Well, she had no reputation to lose so why should she worry what he thought? She closed the door and retreated towards the bed and now her eyes were heavy and dry, there were no more tears. Tears were futile, they solved nothing.

The next day in the office, Simples acted as though nothing untoward had taken place the night before. Observing him, Arian wondered at his steadfast belief that some day she would marry him. She shivered. Now in the cold light of day, she knew that she could never even like him, let alone accept him as a husband, not if she was left alone for the rest of her days.

And yet he was quite a good-looking man, although his mouth was perhaps a little narrow, and his eyes held a remote expression, as though his thoughts were guarded. Yet last night his expression had been far from cold when he had looked down at her in compassion.

What was it about him that repelled her then? Was it only his passing resemblance to Price Davies, the man she hated still even though he was dead?

With the thoughts of the past came a reminder of the feeling of affinity she felt for Fon O'Conner. Fon had been a good friend to her in the bad days, had shared with her some of the ordeal of being imprisoned and in danger. Fon, however, had escaped unscathed. She was happy now, her bad memories erased by her husband's love. Fon was the lucky one.

Arian felt she would never know what it was like to love and be loved in return. She had never been part of a normal family, even during her childhood. She had been afraid of her father, afraid of his anger and his violence after his drinking bouts.

She smiled wryly. Perhaps she should settle for being a courtesan to a rich man. To Calvin Temple, a voice said inside her head and a feeling of warmth filled her at the very thought of belonging to him even in some small measure.

Well Calvin did not want her, not in that way, not in any way. She heard Simples talking quietly to Bella in the small kitchen and she forced herself to concentrate on the work in hand.

'Mr Simples?' she raised her voice so that he would hear her above the sound of the kettle singing on the stove. 'Could you come in a moment please?'

He came at once, his crisp collar making his skin seem darker. His moustache was trimmed and elegant, and his suit was immaculate. Why couldn't she like him just a little? It would make life so much easier.

'The ship should be in dock now, shouldn't it?' she asked. 'The one with the calf, I mean. Wasn't the *Marie Clare* due in today?'

'I believe so Miss Smale. Shall I walk along to the shipping office and enquire?'

'That would be very kind,' Arian said, forcing down the feeling of unease that had suddenly gripped her. If anything was to go wrong with this, her first order, she would have failed before she'd begun.

She went to the window and watched as Simples stopped to talk to a group of sailors. Impatiently she urged him, in her mind, to get on with his job. She was anxious now, worried that the ship had been delayed or worse. What if it had gone down with all her stock of precious calf?

She was being foolish and she knew it – she was over-reacting to her own sense of fear. She turned as Bella came into the office with a tray of tea, giggling and blushing, and Arian looked at her curiously.

'It's them sailors, Arian,' Bella said, 'talking to me by the back door they was, telling me that two beautiful women like us shouldn't be here alone, might get eaten up by big bad sailor boys. Aren't they awful?'

'Don't encourage that sort of talk, Bella.' Arian's voice was sharper than she'd intended and Bella looked at her askance.

119

'They was only joking, mind,' she said. 'Good boys they are, known some of them for years. It's only the foreigners you have to watch.'

'I'm sorry, Bella.' Arian sank into her chair and accepted a cup of tea. 'I'm a bit on edge this morning.'

'Aye, I can see that.' Bella looked at her from under her eyelashes. 'Don't know what to make of you working by here mind,' she ventured. 'Not a job for a girl, is it? You could have his lordship like a shot, be his . . . what do you say, mistress?' She sat in the chair opposite Arian – familiarity that would never have arisen had Arian not once been a servant just like Bella herself.

'He got an itch for you, mind,' Bella continued. 'Anyone can see that. Take you to bed like a shot he would and be good to you, mind.'

Arian drank her tea without replying. How wrong could Bella be? Calvin was not interested in Arian as a woman; he had told her that once in plain English. He wanted to help her, that was all.

'Then there's Mr Simples,' Bella went on remorselessly. 'He's daft on you. He would like to put a ring on your finger, make you his wife. What more could any girl ask than the love of a fine upright man like him?'

Arian sighed. 'Bella, you make a lovely cup of tea but I can do without the advice, thank you.'

'Oh, right, be like that then,' Bella said, 'but there's tears when a woman takes on a man's job, you mark my words. No good will come of all this business stuff.'

It seemed that Bella's words were to be prophetic. Gerald Simples returned to the office with a frown creasing his forehead and Arian stared up from her empty order book with fear breathing a cold breath over her.

'What's wrong?' she asked. 'Hasn't the *Marie Clare* docked yet?'

Gerald Simples closed the door and approached the desk. 'Oh, yes,' he said, 'it's docked all right.'

'Well then?' Arian urged, her eyes wide as she tried to read something from Simples' expression. He shrugged.

'It's just that the load of calf is not aboard,' he said bleakly. 'Something has gone very wrong.'

Arian sank back in her chair and a sense of despair swept through her. She put her hands over her face and tried to hold back the fear that beat with dark wings against her temples.

'Don't worry, Miss Smale,' Simples's voice reached her as though from a long way off. 'I'll sort it all out, don't you worry now. Just you leave everything to me.'

She looked up at him with fresh hope. 'Do you mean it? Do you think you can find out what's happened?'

'I would do anything for you, Miss Smale,' Gerald Simples looked at her gravely, 'anything.'

Why was it then, that when he left the room Arian was not reassured? Why did the fear still lie like a heavy burden inside her? She rose from her desk and stared through the window, seeing the sailors strolling along the pier or the cold pewter waters of the docks. All she could see was Calvin's face in her mind's eye and hear his voice as he told her that he had lost his touch as a businessman. Perhaps he was right and she was just another one of his mistakes. Perhaps she should get out now before she lost him any more money. But no, she would wait for Simples to return. He would do his best for her, she felt that in her bones, and for the first time, she knew the faint stirrings of gratitude to the man.

She returned to her desk. All her resolve and sense of purpose seemed to have vanished. Hope had been short-lived. Her optimism had withered on the vine. She was defeated by the first hurdle. Where was her spirit, her sense of adventure, her longing for achievement? It had all gone, lost somewhere in a sea of uncertainty and Arian Smale no longer knew which direction she must take.

CHAPTER EIGHT

Fon O'Conner contemplated the sky above Honey's Farm with the attitude of a woman seeing the clouds for the last time. She trembled with fear as she stared through the window and bit her lip to keep from crying out in panic.

'Can I fetch you something, Fon?' April Jones's voice was tremulous. She chewed her nails and regarded Fon with fearful eyes. Fon made an effort to control herself.

'It's all right, April. Jamie's gone for the doctor. I'm going to be just fine, I'm only having another baby so don't you worry.'

'You're not going to die like my mammy, are you?' April asked biting her lip, her eyes large and luminous, her little-girl figure blossoming into an early womanhood. The child was far too old for her years in many ways, Fon thought distractedly. How on earth was she going to cope with April's growing up, when she didn't feel in the least equipped for it?

'No I am not going to die!' Fon said firmly. 'I'm a young healthy woman and giving birth to a child is the most natural thing in the world.' She wished she believed it but she had once had an inbuilt fear of childbirth that she believed she'd overcome. At the side of the bed, in the roughly made wooden cot, slept Catherine, her daughter, not yet a year old. It was too soon for another baby, much too soon, she thought in panic.

Catherine's birth had not been easy. Fon had been tense, her body struggling against what was an act of nature but to Fon it had all been just as bad as she had feared. The tearing, burning pain seemed to go on and on and when at last her child had come into the world, Fon had been so exhausted that she scarcely felt anything for the red-faced scrap that was her daughter.

Patrick came into the room and plumped himself on the bed, his face grave. 'Are you sick, Fon?' he asked in a sombre voice. Fon's face softened.

Her stepson was grave with concern, like an old man, and yet his face still held the rounded contours of childhood. 'No, of course I'm not sick. I don't know what all the fuss is about,' she said in as easy a tone as she could manage. 'I'm going to have a baby, that's all Patrick. A little brother or sister for you.'

'I don't want a brother and I've got a sister,' Patrick said firmly. 'And I've got April, haven't I?'

'Aye, you got me, Pat,' April said rubbing his hair across his eyes playfully, 'but I'm not your real sister, mind. Cathie here is your real sister.'

'Well you live with us,' Patrick said with implacable reason. 'You're *like* a sister and Cathie's too little to play with me.'

Fon bit her lip as a pain spread insidiously around her stomach, like iron fingers gripping her body, squeezing painfully and centring in her back. She sucked in her breath, feeling as though her bones were being pulled apart. She turned her face to the pillow so that the children would not see her distressed. Why didn't Jamie come back? Why didn't he *hurry*?

'Take Patrick and the baby downstairs, April,' Fon said when the pain had subsided. 'I feel like a little bit of a rest.'

'All right then,' April said eagerly. She took Cathie carefully out of the cot and held her gently. 'I don't mind having this one, she's good as gold, but you, Patrick, I bet you'll plague me to make you a bit of toast or some bread and jam.'

'Butty and jam.' Patrick, taking the bait, leapt off the bed, his eyes alight. 'I'm starving.'

'You look starved,' April said with heavy irony. 'Come on, brat, I suppose I'd better make some tea while I'm at it.'

When Fon was alone, she stared up at the sky outside and watched the clouds loiter along above the hills like sheep.

There was a hint of rain in the air and at any moment, the clouds threatened to turn into heavy mist and drown the fields of Honey's Farm.

Another pain wound cords of tautness about Fon's body. She gasped and clung to the sheet, biting her lip to prevent herself from crying out. Soon now, the doctor would come and give her something to ease the pain. For God's sake, she needed it. Why was she so prolific, she who didn't want to bring children into the world? It really was ironic.

She could hear the children arguing downstairs; April, who would soon enter her teenage years, was feeling her superiority over the much younger Patrick and was obviously insisting on the boy doing something that he was not too happy about. Fon grimaced, guessing it was something simple like washing his hands before he came to the table. To her relief, the door downstairs opened and she heard Jamie's voice.

'Be quiet!' he commanded and immediately there was silence. Fon heard footsteps on the stairs with a mingled sense of relief and apprehension. She knew that she would be acutely embarrassed to have the doctor examine her which was foolishness – he was probably so used to watching mothers give birth that it meant nothing to him.

The door opened and Jamie immediately seemed to fill the room. He was a big handsome man, rugged and with the look of the open air about him. His very presence gave Fon confidence and she managed a smile.

'How are you doing then, Mrs O'Conner?' The doctor appeared from behind her husband's shoulder. He was dwarfed by the larger man. 'Nice to see you again. I hope you recognize me, I'm doctor Eddie Carpenter and I'm here to see that this baby is safely delivered.'

'Eddie!' Fon's surprise was quickly followed by a feeling of relief. Eddie, she had faith in, she'd seen him at work on the farm before he'd even qualified as a doctor.

'Eddie,' she took his hand, 'you've grown a beard, *duw* you're looking so well, so smart.'

He was gently feeling her stomach, his hands gentle yet searching. 'You seem to be doing all this very well, Fon. You'll be just fine, nothing to worry about.'

His words brought Fon a warm glow of reassurance. She felt herself relax as he smiled down at her.

'You've done this before, Fon and the second time is always easier, I promise you.'

As he talked, his hands were busy beneath the sheets. He grunted and nodded and Fon, watching him, felt at once that he was pleased with her progress.

'Ah, yes, the head is nicely in place. He feels a big lad and you are a small mother but I know you'll do very well.'

Fon glanced at Jamie. His eyes were anxious and she smiled at him in reassurance. 'Don't worry, love,' she said softly, 'you just go about your business and leave me to mine.'

'That's the way,' Eddie said winking. 'Right then, bring some hot water, Jamie and let the midwife up the minute she comes.' He patted Fon's arm. 'She'd better hurry, mind, or we'll be doing this one all by ourselves.'

His words proved to be prophetic. Fon's labour moved from stage to stage with very little trouble, perhaps because Eddie was there, talking, soothing, being Eddie, her old friend.

Then the pains changed, she was bearing down, grunting in her throat with the effort of pushing her child into the world.

'Good girl,' Eddie said. 'That's fine, you're almost there, Fon, easy now, not too hard. Now bear down!'

The effort took all her strength. She closed her eyes tightly, feeling the sweat beading her brow. Almost with a sense of detachment she pushed as hard as she could, knowing Eddie was helping her.

There was a sudden sense of release, the burning sensation in her body miraculously was gone and into the silence came the sharp cry of a new-born child.

The midwife entered the room, her face red from hurrying, her eyes apologetic as they looked down at Fon.

'*Duw*, there's sorry I am,' she said, gasping a little. 'I've missed the show then, have I? I'm just in time to sweep the stage, so to speak.'

'Aye, we've managed nicely,' Eddie said pleasantly. 'We have a good mother here, nurse. The way she's going she'll soon have a brood of fine sons just like this one. Yes, Fon, you've got a son.'

He put the baby into Fon's arms and the midwife clucked in exasperation, 'Just like a man, no blanket for the babbi. Here, let me wrap him up.'

Fon looked down at her son with a sense of amazement – the screwed-up face and the bush of red-gold hair appeared so beautiful to her. The baby began to cry again and Fon felt herself melt with tenderness.

'It's all right, my darling,' she said, 'it's all right, mammy is here.'

Jamie was at her side then, staring down at her with pride. 'You've given me a boy this time, Fon, my colleen,' he said, his voice hoarse. 'A fine brother for Patrick and Cathie, sure enough.' His arms, open to receive their son, and his eyes meeting Fon's, were filled with warmth.

'He's a fine, handsome boy,' Eddie said triumphantly, as if he alone was responsible for the child. 'Good lungs, fine, sturdy limbs. You'll have a good farmer there, Jamie.'

'Right, you lot,' the nurse said firmly, 'out of here while I see to the mother and baby. A nice cup of tea wouldn't go amiss, mind.'

Jamie returned the baby to Fon's waiting arms. 'Well done, colleen,' he said softly, 'well done.'

Fon's eyes filled with tears. She had done it, she had safely come through her labour. Her sense of achievement was exhilarating. She had matched Jamie's first wife – she had produced a fine son. She sighed. She must be the happiest woman in all of Swansea.

Sarah Frogmore was restless. She was a married woman with a fine child, she had a wonderful home and an apparently devoted husband – everything a woman could want, so it would seem to the outside world.

She leaned back in her chair, her needle falling idle. She had come a long way from being the daughter of a cobbler, a woman with a not too innocent past, to this, the lap of luxury. Now she was Mrs Geoffrey Frogmore, respected in a society that once would have shunned her.

She smiled ruefully. Her father too, had done well. John Miller had married Emily Grenfell, a woman from the upper classes, a woman who had made a great deal of money. It was Dad's good luck that Emily had fallen in love with him and had become his wife, thus raising his standard of living to heights beyond his imaginings. Not that John Miller was an adventurer. He loved Emily as much as she loved him; they made a fine pair and it was clear to everyone that they had a good marriage. Sarah envied them.

She looked up from her needlework lying idle in her lap and watched her son pore over one of his books. Jack was advanced for his years – he was not yet four and could read very well. That skill was due to Geoffrey's intense interest in his son and his urge to educate the boy.

A shadow fell over her face. Geoffrey was out yet again with his friend Chas. He had stayed out all last night, no doubt sleeping at the apartment he rented so that Chas and he could be together as often as possible.

He did make a show of being a happy family-man when his father was around. Old Mr Frogmore had a touching faith in his son's ability to be a good husband and it was in Geoffrey's interest to foster this belief. Geoffrey, if he was to benefit from the inheritance willed to him by his father was obliged to convince the old man that he was a lusty, loving husband.

Sarah sighed, if only it was true. She failed to understand why Geoffrey preferred Chas's bed to hers. She could not fathom the reason for one man loving another but she had come to accept it – there was nothing else for her to do. And yet she was hungry, hungry for love and affection, hungry for a man's arms around her.

Her sewing fell unnoticed to the floor as she thought over her past life and loves. There had been a few men in her life including William Davies. She smiled wryly. Last she'd heard he was living with Eline Temple in some mean house in World's End. What sort of life was that? She thanked her lucky stars she'd not married him. And yet his love for her had once been real enough.

As youngsters, they had explored each other with eagerness, had made love under the hot sun, had tasted together the joys of the flesh. She sighed. What she would give now for one night of passion with him.

The maid entered the room bobbing a curtsy. 'If it please you, Mrs Frogmore, Mrs Miller is here to see you.'

'Wait just a minute or two and then show her in,' Sarah said inclining her head, barely able to conceal a self-satisfied smile. Emily, the once proud and haughty Emily Grenfell, had to wait on her pleasure.

Emily came into the room a few minutes later and if her smile was a little forced, she made an effort not to let it show. Sarah was not slow to notice that Pammy wasn't with her.

Sarah didn't mind that Emily was alone, as she didn't particularly want to see Pammy. She had never regretted that Emily had adopted the girl, for Pammy was the fruit of an illicit match between Sarah and Sam Payton – a black sheep if ever there was one – and it was an episode in Sarah's life that she'd rather forget. There had never been any love for the child in her heart; Sarah knew that she should be ashamed to admit such a thing but it was the truth. Now that she had her son, she felt even more distant from her daughter. Her love for Jack was overwhelming. In any case, Pammy was part of her past that was best kept well hidden.

'Emily, how nice to see you. How's my father? Keeping well, I hope?'

'John is fine,' Emily said. 'He sends his love.' She sat down and plucked off her gloves. 'The best thing I ever did was marry your father,' she said softly.

'The second best was adopting my daughter,' Sarah said, unable to resist rubbing in the fact that Emily had no child of her own.

'I have never ceased to be grateful for that,' Emily said gravely. Sarah, waited, wondering to what she owed the honour of the visit – it was rare that Emily made a social call.

As though reading her thoughts, Emily spoke. 'I just felt it was time I called on you. I wanted to be sure that everything was all right.' Her eyes went to the small boy who was looking over his book curiously. 'Jack is a fine son. You are so very lucky, Sarah. I do hope you realize it.'

Jack smiled and spoke with a charming lisp, 'Where is my grandpapa?'

'He'll be around to see you later, I expect,' Emily said. 'Come here, I've got some sweeties for you.'

Sarah suppressed a smile. They all fell in love with Jack. He was a handsome, intelligent boy and as she watched him, love for him filled her so that tears came into her eyes. If only, she thought ruefully, she and Geoffrey had a vigorous relationship in the bedroom, she would be completely happy.

'I know how lucky I am,' she said softly, 'but then luck comes in different guises.' She saw Emily look at her in surprise 'Oh, I have some finer feelings, whatever you think of me,' she said bluntly. 'I envy the relationship you have with my father. I can see that there's real love between you and that's something very rare.'

Emily smiled and her face was transformed. 'You're right,' she said, 'John and I are as much in love now as when we first met. I have a thrill of pride and pleasure whenever I see him entering a room.' She paused. 'I take it that nothing has changed between you and Geoffrey then? Love hasn't grown?'

Sarah bit her lip. 'Emily, my husband is not a man who loves women, not passionately anyway. Oh, yes, he loves me after a fashion, and he loves Jack to distraction but you must understand he is different.'

129

'Different? How?' Emily was uncomprehending and Sarah wondered at her naïvety. Emily was older than she, had been brought up to riches and luxury, but for all that she was quite unsophisticated in some ways. Sarah decided to shock her.

'My husband is in love, physical love with another man,' she said flatly, and she saw, with a certain sense of satisfaction, the colour drain from Emily's face.

'You must have heard about such things,' Sarah said impatiently. 'It is nothing new.'

Emily seemed to recover her composure. 'Of course it's not new,' she said. 'It's as old as time just as prostitution is, but no-one expects it to affect them personally.'

Sarah saw Emily's glance rest on Jack who was once more absorbed in his books.

'Geoffrey was capable of doing it with me,' – she knew Emily would be embarrassed by her crudeness but some devil within her drove her to hurt her stepmother whenever she had the opportunity – 'just enough times for me to conceive his child, and even then it was with his eyes tightly closed and him thinking of his lover.'

Emily looked away and stared through the window. When she spoke, her voice was low. 'How can you bear it?' she asked. 'For a husband to be unfaithful with another woman is bad enough but how can you fight another man?'

'I can't,' Sarah said quietly. 'I've tried, God knows I've tried but Chas comes before everything.' She paused. 'Everything except our Jack and, of course, the inheritance.'

'Sarah, it's no wonder you are sometimes bitter,' Emily said and her sympathy was evident. 'To live with a man knowing that he is . . . different must be very difficult.'

'He is kind,' Sarah said. 'He is more considerate than most husbands in many ways. Perhaps that's how he can live with the guilt of his secret passion.'

'And Jack . . . ' Emily's voice trailed away. Her eyes were sad as they rested on the small boy.

'Jack will never know the truth about his father,' Sarah spoke emphatically. 'He will grow up believing that we are a normal healthy family with no skeletons in the cupboard.'

Sarah could see by Emily's face that she doubted such a thing could be possible.

'But brothers and sisters,' Emily said. 'Will Jack not miss having a family?'

Sarah, who had thought along these lines herself more than once, felt her resolution harden. 'He will have a brother or sister,' she said firmly. 'What Geoffrey has done once, he can do again.'

It was only when Emily had left that Sarah's thoughts crystallized into action. Speaking of her wish for another child out loud, discussing it with Emily had suddenly made it seem a reality. She felt a fresh determination fill her. She would prepare her strategy very carefully, coax her husband into her bed with reasons rather than feminine wiles, reasons why it was desirable to have another child.

She would play on Geoffrey's one weakness – his love for his son. She would tell him that Jack needed a family, someone to whom he could turn when his parents could no longer be around.

She found herself looking forward to Geoffrey's homecoming as though waiting for a lover. He would be late, he usually ate dinner with Chas, but just for this once that suited her purpose.

She bathed and perfumed her body and when that was done, she dressed carefully in a satin nightgown and then brushed her hair out until it gleamed. She hesitated on the landing and then went into Geoffrey's room and climbed beneath the sheets.

He was later than usual and Sarah was almost asleep when she heard his door open. She tensed, her heart was beating swiftly as she waited for him to approach the bed.

'Sarah,' his voice was muffled, 'what do you think you are doing?'

She sat up and looked at him as he stood beside her, his face almost comical in its dismay.

'I want us to have another child, Geoffrey,' she said

without preamble. 'Jack needs a brother or a sister. It's not right that he should be an only child. He'll be lonely, you must see that.'

'Sarah,' Geoffrey turned away from her, 'I can't, I just can't, you know how I feel.' He sank down beside her. 'I love Chas. He's everything to me. It would be a betrayal.'

'You are *my* husband,' Sarah's voice trembled. 'I'm not asking for your love, Geoffrey, only your child.' She held out her hand imploringly, 'You gave me Jack, can't you give me another baby, Geoffrey, please?' She heard the note of desperation in her voice and knew that she wanted more than another child. She wanted, needed to be held in a man's arms, to be made to feel alive again. She was young, too young, to live the life of a nun.

'I'm sorry,' Geoffrey's voice was flat, 'the answer is no. I can't, Sarah. You knew what I was from the beginning. You settled for the money and for our son.'

Sarah climbed out of the bed and wound her arms around Geoffrey's thin shoulders. 'I'm not so bad, am I?' she whispered, her mouth against his neck. 'I'm attractive still, aren't I?'

Gently, he pushed her away. 'Of course you are attractive.' He sounded desperate. 'You are a beautiful woman but I just can't pretend to be what I'm not.'

Sarah began to cry then, tears rained down her cheeks, hot, angry, bitter tears that racked her small frame. After a moment, Geoffrey took her in his arms.

'Look, Sarah, I love you, in a way, but not in the way I love Chas. Try to understand me, won't you?' He paused but Sarah was too hurt to speak.

'I respect you as my wife. You are a wonderful mother to Jack – I couldn't ask for better but . . .'

He rose and moved away from her. 'Don't cry like that, Sarah. I can't stand it.'

She couldn't stop. Now that she'd started, all the pain and frustration of her life of celibacy came pouring out of her.

'I've tried, God knows I've tried to be content,' she said, 'but I have needs Geoffrey, just as you have needs.

I am a woman, my blood is hot. I want loving, Geoffrey and if you don't give it to me I must find a lover or go mad.'

'No!' Geoffrey's voice was suddenly harsh. 'You must not take a lover. What would my father think? What about our son if he found out that his mother was a whore?'

'I *am* a whore,' Sarah was suddenly angry. 'You knew *that* when *you* married *me*. Oh yes, we knew all about each other's little ways, didn't we Geoffrey? Except that I didn't know until I was tied to you by law. You cheated me Geoffrey, you cheated me.'

He was white with anger but he was calm. 'Very well, if it means that much to you then I will give you another child,' he said. 'Fetch me the brandy. Perhaps if I am drunk enough I will be able to betray my true instincts.'

Sarah's surge of hope faded as quickly as it had come. She knew she didn't want Geoffrey that way. If he couldn't bear to make love to her unless he had drink inside him then she didn't want him.

'What then, Geoffrey, when you are drunk? Will you put out the light so that you can pretend I am Chas, your precious man-friend?'

'Sarah,' Geoffrey's voice was low, 'do you have to make it all sound so cheap and sordid?'

'What you do with Chas *is* cheap and sordid.' Sarah moved away from the bed, her humiliation and pain were almost insupportable. 'I will never come to your bed again, Geoffrey. I will never again beg you to love me.'

'Sarah,' he lifted his hand in supplication, 'I'm sorry. I can't help the way I am.'

'Go to hell,' Sarah said flatly and left his room.

It took Sarah only two weeks to find the man who she deemed suitable to father her child, two weeks of sifting the evidence of all the available men in her circle. She was not looking for love, nor even for a long-term affair. She wanted only to assuage the hurt and pain that Geoffrey's attitude had built up within her. She needed to banish the look of revulsion on his face, to see again desire and need in the eyes of a virile man. And like a raging thirst, she wanted a child so that she could prove to Geoffrey that even if he didn't want her, there were those who did.

She smiled to herself as she leaned back in her chair and thought of the man she would soon take to her bed. 'Look out, Calvin Temple,' she whispered, 'you are in for the treat of a lifetime.'

CHAPTER NINE

Arian stood just within the closed doors of Calvin's library and saw with a heartmelting feeling of concern that he appeared tired and dispirited. He had sent for her, an unusual enough occurrence these days, though the way Bella had framed it, the request for her presence in the library had been more in the way of command.

'The shipload of calf has not arrived then?' he asked, not looking at her but playing with a pen, rolling it between his fingers, unaware of the droplets of ink staining his hands.

'Not yet.' She paused uncertainly. 'There's every like-lihood that the company have just made an error, perhaps the calf was delayed at the French docks.' Arian felt an overwhelming urge to reassure him. 'Simples is trying his best to sort things out.'

'Ah, Simples,' Calvin glanced at her briefly. 'You trust him, then? I imagined you were not too fond of Mr Simples.'

'It could be that I have misjudged him,' Arian said carefully. 'He certainly seems to be doing his best for me just now.'

'First impressions can usually be relied upon,' Calvin's words were enigmatic and Arian waited for him to continue. 'On the other hand, it's only fair to give everyone a chance to prove themselves, one way or the other.'

Arian was a little puzzled by Calvin's attitude. What was he trying to say? She would have spoken, asked him what he meant but a knock on the door silenced her.

'Yes, Bella, what is it?' Calvin spoke impatiently, dropping the pen onto the desk as the maid bobbed a hasty curtsy.

'It's a young lady to see you, sir,' she said breathlessly. 'Mrs Frogmore, she says her name is but she was Sarah Miller before marriage and a right little minx she was too if . . .' Bella's words died away as Calvin held up his hand.

'Show her in, Bella,' he said abruptly. 'I presume she's not applying for a position in the household so a character reference is hardly necessary.'

Arian moved towards the door. It seemed her meeting with Calvin was at an end and she had the unsatisfactory feeling that there were things they should have spoken about but had failed to do so.

She glanced with some curiosity at Sarah Frogmore. Arian, too, had heard some of the scandal about the girl's past but then who was she to judge? She'd been the subject of enough scandal herself and not all of it justified.

She forced herself to smile when she noticed that Sarah's gown was daringly cut to emphasise her rather splendid figure, and an absurd dart of jealousy pierced her. What did it matter who visited Calvin's house? It was nothing to do with her and she would be making a fool of herself to think otherwise. Calvin was not bound to her in any way. He was simply her employer, he liked her and trusted her, but nothing more.

Sarah nodded to Arian and paused for a brief moment before sweeping into the library. The door closed and Arian stared at the polished wood panels as if trying to see through them, wondering what was being said within the room. She could think of no reason why Sarah would want to see Calvin; so far as she knew, they had no business contact, no other sort of contact either.

After a moment, she sighed. It was nothing to her, what Sarah Frogmore did or what she wanted with Calvin. In any case, she was probably here on some quite humdrum matter.

Arian smiled softly. Calvin was a law unto himself – he did just what he wished, came and went as he pleased, he had no keeper, needed none, asked no-one's permission, certainly not that of Arian Smale.

She moved away slowly, almost reluctantly. She had work to do, problems of her own to think about and nothing would be cured by standing in the hallway feeling jealous because another woman was shut in a room alone with Calvin Temple. It was about time Arian was honest with herself; she meant nothing to Calvin, her head knew it, she just had trouble convincing her emotions that it was true. She shrugged and mentally shook herself and yet the strange feeling that somehow Calvin was being taken away from her persisted.

When Arian had gone, Sarah faced Calvin and her courage almost failed. 'May I sit down?' she asked, glancing up at him standing tall and so very masculine at her side.

'Please, forgive my rudeness. I was taken by surprise by your beauty.' He smiled and she was aware that his words were meaningless, spoken lightly in order to put her at her ease, to charm, and charm her they did.

He indicated that she take a seat and she smiled up at him warmly. Honesty, she decided, was going to be the best policy. Calvin Temple was no man's fool and would not be taken in by feminine wiles.

'In return for that pretty compliment, may I say that you are more handsome than I'd realized but then we have only met over dinner in other people's houses.' She moved restlessly, unwilling to blurt out the reason for her visit. 'I'm very happy I came to see you.' She knew she was prevaricating and she saw by his curious glance that he knew it too.

'And why have you come to see me?' His question was blunt but his smile still warm and interested. He moved to the table and held up a dazzling cut-glass decanter. 'May I offer you some claret?'

'That would be lovely.' Sarah knew quite well that Calvin had expected her to decline, to ask instead for some tea but she felt she needed a drink to give her courage – her mission now seemed bizarre, almost ridiculous.

When she took the drink from him, she looked up into his face. 'I have come to ask you a very great favour,' she said simply. 'I want a child and I feel it would be a privilege if you would agree to be the father.'

He stared down at her in silence, his eyebrows raised and nervously she rushed on, 'I can't have my husband's baby. I would rather not go into the reasons for that but I assure you it's the truth. I desperately long for another child and I have been very careful and deliberate in choosing you to be the father.'

'I'm flattered,' Calvin's tone held a touch of derision, 'but my dear lady, it's out of the question. We scarcely know each other.'

'Does that matter?' Sarah looked up at him beseechingly. 'I'm not asking you to love me or even to have an affair with me, just lie with me, give me a child. Would that be so difficult a task for you?' She faced him squarely. 'Don't you find me desirable?'

She saw Calvin frown. 'I'm a red-blooded man. Of course I find you attractive, even beautiful, but to lie with you just to give you a child is out of the question. Don't you realize what complications that might cause?'

'There would be no complications,' Sarah urged. 'A son or daughter born to me and Geoffrey in wedlock would be seen to be *his* child. There would be no repercussions for you.'

Calvin shook his head. 'You must be out of your mind, madam. I'm sorry, it's impossible, it really is.'

Sarah put down her glass and rose to her feet. 'Please, don't give me a flat refusal now, just think it over. Given time, it might not seem such a strange request.' She went to him and touched his hand, looking up into his face imploringly. 'I am an experienced woman, I admit I have had more than one lover, and as for you,' she shrugged, 'you are estranged from your wife. She is living with another man. We could have a good time together. What would you have to lose?'

She put her finger over his lips as he would have spoken. 'Don't say anything now but please, please think about it. You could be the means of bringing me so much happiness.'

She turned away from him before he could protest once more that what she asked was impossible. Awkwardly, she let herself out of the room, aware then that he was striding after her, opening the large front door, smiling down at her, drinking in her appearance. She felt a dart of triumph – there was interest in his eyes. He was susceptible then, after all.

When she was once again outside in the freshness of the day, Sarah fanned her hot cheeks with her hand and a small smile played on her lips. She would best Geoffrey yet. She would have a baby and have the attentions of a fine man into the bargain.

Now that she had spoken with him, been close to him, she was more than ever convinced that Calvin Temple, Lord Temple would be a fine father and a fine lover too. In spite of her high-minded protestations about longing for a baby, Sarah knew that she would be thrilled to be in the arms of a man like Calvin. There was strength of character in every noble line of his face.

She would have her way with Calvin, she felt it in her bones, by hook or by crook she would have him in her bed and then Geoffrey would learn that if he didn't give her what she wanted then she would take it from someone else.

'We must go to France.' Simples was standing looking down at her and Arian felt herself grow tense. 'There is no other way to secure the load of calf. We must confront the directors of this company, make them honour their obligations. You might have been hasty paying in full.'

'I know and something has to be done,' she said. But to go to France with Simples – she couldn't think of anything worse. She moved to the window of the office and stared out at the waters of the dockside without seeing them.

'His lordship is in deep trouble as it is, he mustn't lose any more money. It could prove disastrous.'

Arian doubted the truth of Simples's words. Calvin had certainly not given her any such impression. And yet his tense look, his open statement that he had made mistakes, perhaps he was in trouble. Either way, she knew that she had no choice in the matter.

'All right,' she said, 'you make all the necessary arrangements Mr Simples and I'll pack some clothes. We'd better sail as soon as possible.'

Simples left the office quietly and Arian sank down into her chair. The books before her were a mockery, the orders she'd so diligently sought were unfulfilled. Her customers were still waiting for the delivery of leather she had promised so confidently.

She hid her face in her hands and the tears, so hot and angry, burned her lids. She would not cry, she told herself fiercely. Crying was for weaklings not for the likes of Arian Smale. She sat up straight in her chair and squared her shoulders. Crying did no good at all, she'd found that out a long time ago. But then it was easy to be hard when there was no-one on earth she cared for. Now she cared about Calvin she couldn't hurt him.

Later, she stood in her room in Stormhill and looked around at the familiar drapes, the ornate black fireplace, the pretty flowered tiles that surrounded the grate, and sighed. She felt she was leaving a safe haven and going out into the world where all was uncertain.

She placed the letter of explanation she had written Calvin on the mantelpiece and, after a moment's hesitation took up her bag and left her room, closing the door carefully behind her.

She had not faced Calvin with her plans for the trip to France for obvious reasons; he would ask questions and not only would he disapprove of her travelling with Simples but she would have to confess that she knew of Calvin's financial problems.

Calvin would be generous, he would urge her to forget the calf, he would doubtless insist that he could bear the loss without too much trouble but she would not allow that – she had made the blunder, she would put it right.

Simples was waiting for her at the back door. He too, had a bag in his hand and he was smartly dressed in a dark suit and a high-collared shirt. His eyes were approving as they rested on her neat black skirt and coat and the hat pulled down over her brow.

'The *Marie Clare* sails at midnight,' Simples said, 'an unearthly hour I know but the captain has to obey the tide tables.' He smiled, 'Not even the redoubtable master of the *Marie Clare* can alter the rhythms of the sea.'

Arian was in no mood for humour so she led the way out of the house and began to walk briskly down the drive. Simples went quickly back into the house, then caught her up and walked beside her. She knew it must appear most odd to the servants. The idea of a young lady going off alone with a man on a journey to foreign lands was so outlandish to a girl like Bella that she just wouldn't understand the motives behind such a venture. Mrs Bob, with her common-sense attitude would probably tell Arian she was being all sorts of a fool, warn that she would be the subject of a great deal of gossip in the servants' quarters.

Arian shrugged. It would not be the first time or the last that tongues had wagged behind her back.

'Come along, Miss Smale. We can get on board and make ourselves comfortable, at least.'

She walked with Gerald Simples towards the docklands in silence, very conscious of the man at her side. She felt her instinctive distrust of him rise up within her and she wondered at her madness in accompanying him to a foreign country.

She was tempted, for a moment, to turn back to Stormhill before it was too late but the thought of Calvin's worried expression prevented her and doggedly, she went onward towards the waiting ship.

The *Marie Clare* was set to ride on the rising tide, an old creaking vessel, three masts pointing skyward, beautified by the moonlight that streaked across the bay from Mumbles Head to the jutting arm of the Swansea pier. Arian felt a catch in her breath – she hadn't realized how much she loved her homeland until she was about to leave its shores.

'Take my hand, Miss Smale,' Simples said as he mounted the gangway leading up to the side of the barquentine, and as it seemed churlish to refuse, Arian allowed him to help her upwards above the dark waters of the dock and onto the lilting deck of the ship.

'I hope you won't feel sea-sick,' Simples said, releasing her hand, 'but in any case, the coast of France is not very far away.'

No-one seemed around to greet them and Arian followed as Simples led her across the gently moving deck towards the upper deck.

'You wait here,' he said as he made his way across the sloping boards, 'I'll find the master.'

She watched him for a moment and then glanced back at the shore almost with a sense of unreality. What was she doing here in the darkness on a strange ship, trusting herself with a man like Simples, crossing the sea to a foreign country? She shivered, and yet some stirring of excitement began to filter into her mind. This was an adventure, she told herself. A visit to a foreign land was something that most people never experienced in a lifetime. Arian knew she would have enjoyed it had it been someone, anyone, by her side other than Simples.

He reappeared after a few moments and gestured for her to follow him. Simples led the way below, negotiating the steps easily and waited for her to join him. She felt embarrassed, her skirts rising so that her legs were revealed but Gerald Simples didn't appear to notice. He opened a door and gestured towards a small cabin.

'You can wait in here out of the weather,' he said. 'The master thinks there's going to be a bit of a squall but nothing to worry about.'

Arian didn't like the way Simples was taking charge and yet what could she say? He was clearly trying to be as helpful as possible and his attitude was one of remote deference. It was almost as though they were strangers.

She looked around and saw by the charts spread out on the table that this was the captain's own cabin. She sank into a chair and put her face in her hands. She wished she was back at Stormhill with Calvin Temple sleeping in the room near by, within easy reach should she need him.

But she had to prove to him that she knew what she was doing. She couldn't allow him to think she'd failed at the first obstacle fate put in her way. Calvin had trusted her with his money, that was something it would pay her to remember. She straightened her shoulders and lifted her chin. She would do her level best to sort out the matter of the missing supply of calf, and would either fetch the load home with her or somehow recoup the money she had spent. She was determined on it.

The ship seemed to heave into motion, and there was, quite suddenly, a feeling of activity. The sounds came from the deck above of sailors calling to each other, the creaking of the timbers increased alarmingly and the ship plunged like a live creature as the sails cracked in the wind. They were on their way to France, and there was no turning back now. She was in the hands of Gerald Simples and she had no alternative but to trust him.

CHAPTER TEN

'I don't know where they've gone, sir, but both of them have just vanished. Spirited away, they've been.'

Calvin looked at Bella with a sense of irritation, knowing that the maid was revelling in this latest piece of gossip.

'Was there no message for me?' He tried to keep his voice even but within him there was a turmoil of feelings he could not explain. There was anger, yes but there was also a sense of outrage that Arian Smale would go away without a word and with a man she professed to dislike.

'No message, sir.' Bella remembered with a dart of unease, seeing Simples in Arian's room, tearing a piece of paper to shreds but it couldn't have been of any importance, could it?

'Very well, Bella, you may go,' Calvin said, turning away from the avid interest in the girl's eyes. He heard the door close and leaned back in his chair trying to reason with the chaotic thoughts that filled his mind. Why should he worry what Arian Smale did? And yet, he felt betrayed.

Was it possible she joined Simples in embezzling funds from him? Calvin clenched his teeth together. He had put considerable resources at Arian's disposal. So far there had been no sign of any return for the money, even the supply of calf had failed to materialize.

His instincts told him that Arian was no crook, nor that she cared for Simples enough to do a deal with him and then abscond with the proceeds. There must be some simple explanation for the disappearance of both Arian and his steward, it was just that at this moment he couldn't think of anything plausible.

He'd had his doubts about Simples for some time. There was no denying that the man's advice so far on money matters had been anything but sound. Calvin could stand the losses – the bulk of his fortune was secure and the amount of money he had invested in Simples's schemes had been small – nevertheless, there was something underhand going on and he intended to find out what it was. The losses couldn't all be put down to the fluctuations of the market.

He rose to his feet, feeling suddenly restless. He wondered if he should go to see Daphne, spend a few hours in her warm arms and forget Arian Smale. He hesitated. Daphne was an exciting woman but she was very demanding, almost overbearing; sometimes she could be almost tiresome. Lately he felt she was beginning to get bored of his company – she sometimes turned from his arms with impatience. That was not the relationship he wanted with his paramour. Indeed, did he want a paramour at all? Wouldn't he much prefer the arms of the fragile, independent Arian Smale?

He laughed without humour. He was like a love-sick juvenile, not knowing quite what it was he wanted but with an itch that needed to be scratched. He somehow felt jaundiced with the whole of womankind; they used a man and then, when the whim took them, betrayed him as thoughtlessly as they would cast aside a used garment.

He returned to his desk and with an act of deliberation drew his unopened mail towards him. He should occupy his mind with other things. Women; how they could hurt and anger if they so chose.

One envelope revealed a scented piece of note paper containing a brief message from Daphne. It seemed she would be unable to see him for a little while, 'other matters' needed her attention. Another lover no doubt.

The final letter held news of his divorce. Soon, he would be a free man. Free – that was ironic. He moved to the sideboard and poured a large measure of brandy.

Sarah walked into the hallway of Stormhill not seeing the elegant staircase nor the haughty-faced young maid who had admitted her. Her heart was beating swiftly and a pulse in her throat seemed to throb with a life of its own. She could hardly believe her own temerity. She had been turned away from Calvin's home once, would he reject her again? Well whatever the outcome, she had to make one last-ditch attempt to get her own way.

He was seated on a large *chaise longue* and Sarah had forgotten how handsome he was, how lean of hip and broad of shoulder, and Sarah caught herself looking him over as though he was a prize stallion. The irony of her thoughts was not lost on her.

She paused, savouring the moment, thinking how wonderful it would be to lie with a real man again, to be desired, caressed, brought to fulfilment.

'Come in, dear lady, come in. Very good timing on your part, I'd say.' He sounded a little drunk, and suddenly she felt triumph build within her.

Within the drawing room the drapes were discreetly drawn against the afternoon sunlight. On the table stood a half-empty bottle of fine brandy.

'Make yourself at home,' Calvin said making a grandiose gesture of his arm, 'while I pour us a drink.' He filled two glasses and handed one to her and then smiled for the first time.

'How nice to see you,' he said with more than a touch of irony in his voice. She felt he was laughing at her but she didn't care. Her senses were alert to him, she wanted him and by God she was going to have him.

He didn't wait for her to speak, but replenished her glass which she realized with a sense of surprise she had emptied in one gulp.

She sat beside him and stared at him, mesmerized as she lifted the glass to her lips. The drink seemed to give her back some of her confidence and with an easy movement, she removed her coat. She knew she was looking her best, the bodice of her gown was cut low to reveal the swell of her breasts and she saw Calvin's involuntary glance pause at her neckline.

'Very charming,' he said softly and then, deliberately, he put down his glass and leaned towards her.

Sarah took a deep breath as he took the glass from her hand and bent over her, his mouth warm against the cleavage between her breasts. Her breathing became ragged as desire filled her. She needed a virile man, she knew that, she had always known it and subjugating her natural instincts had not come easy to her.

She put her arm around him and pressed him to her, her hand sliding down between his thighs. She sighed with satisfaction, knowing that he was roused.

Sarah wanted to tear off her clothes, to feel him penetrate her willing flesh. She wanted to moan with ecstasy beneath him, to make up for all the long months of her celibacy. And yet she was wary of this man, he was an unknown quantity to her. Calvin Temple was not a man to be manipulated as all the rest of her lovers had been – he was in control, he would call the tune and she would obey him.

He emptied his glass and she watched him impatiently. His eyes mocked her – he knew she wanted him and he was making her wait, almost as though he was taking some sort of revenge.

She saw his hand open the buttons of his shirt and she licked her dry lips. She felt she would die if he didn't take her quickly.

He stood before her quite naked, magnificent in his manhood then he came to her and began to undress her with almost casual haste. For a moment she felt like a whore.

She closed her eyes as he pressed her back against the cushions. She felt his hands begin to thrill and tease her. Her bodice tore as he caressed her breasts, then he roughly pushed at her skirts and she gasped with shock and pleasure. She arched her back, silently begging him to come to her, to possess her.

When he joined with her, she cried out and sliding her hands over his strong buttocks, pressed him closer. She moaned as he moved slowly at first, teasing, bewitching. Then she was lost in the thrill of the moment, her senses reeling, her nerves tingling as his movements increased in urgency.

The magic seemed to go on and on, the delight that he was giving her she would have killed for. She flung back her head and heard her voice, unrecognizable, crying out in joy. She clung to his broadness now, crying tears of happiness, her body floating on a tide of released tension. She was fulfilled.

She stayed with him in his room all night, not even giving a thought to her son. Geoffrey was nothing if not a good father – he might be worried about her but his child would come first.

She roused herself from a languor of happy exhaustion to see Calvin standing with his back to her, already dressed. Hearing her movements he turned to look at her as though he'd never seen her before.

'There will be a carriage outside waiting to take you there. Good-bye, Sarah.'

When he left the room, she stared at the door in disbelief. He couldn't have just walked out on her, he couldn't. She needed him, for God's sake.

She rose and dressed with trembling hands, and pausing, she looked at herself in the mirror. For all that he had gone, left her as a man leaves a whore, she had only gratitude in her heart for Calvin Temple. He had made her feel like a woman again, a whole, red-blooded woman.

She sighed heavily. Perhaps it was her lot in life never to find the love of a fine man like Calvin. She had Geoffrey's regard and loyalty up to a point – she had his ring on her finger – but there was such a lot she had given up for that privilege.

It was only when the carriage which Calvin had ordered for her jerked to a halt outside her own home did doubts and worries assail her. What would Geoffrey say about her long absence? She drew a deep breath as she alighted in her own driveway. What could he say? He had his own peccadilloes and he could hardly begrudge her one small fling.

He was not at home when she entered the house and

Sarah questioned the maid with a thoroughness which nevertheless left her with very little information. Geoffrey, it seemed, had gone out early taking their son with him and had not said when he would be back.

Sarah bathed at her leisure, luxuriating in the hot scented water, thinking of the past hours spent with Calvin. How she had enjoyed their love-making. She began to make plans. Even if she were to have caught for a baby, why reveal that to Calvin? She could ask him to spend more time with her, just to make certain that she had achieved her goal.

She smiled to herself. In spite of his abrupt departure, she was sure that Calvin Temple had enjoyed their encounter as much as she had. Otherwise why stay with her for such a long time?

It was only later as she dined alone at the long candle-lit table, that Sarah began to really worry about Geoffrey and more so about Jack. It was late for the little boy to be out. He was normally in bed long before this.

She ignored the curious looks of the servants as they brought her food. She had very little time for the people Geoffrey had hired. They were his responsibility, he saw to their wages and ensured that they performed their duties. Sarah, for her part took it all for granted. She was meant to be waited on, meant to be pampered. Had she not given her husband the son he wanted so badly?

Night came and there was still no sign of Geoffrey or their child. Sarah called the housekeeper and spent an entire hour with her but the woman could add nothing more to what the maid had said earlier.

She spent a restless night wondering where Geoffrey could be. Had he taken their son to visit his grandfather, old Mr Frogmore, who doted on Jack? But no, Geoffrey would have had to explain the absence of his wife and he would never show the old man that there might be any sort of rift between them.

Anger poured through her like wine. Geoffrey must have taken Jack to the flat he provided for his paramour. The thought of Jack in the same room as Chas set her teeth on edge, and jealousy flared through her, an unreasoning jealousy of the man her husband loved. What if her husband had gone for good?

She punched the pillows wishing she had Geoffrey here so that she could rant and rave at him, call him all the foul names under the sun, threaten to expose him to his father. She fell back in the bed, relief flowing over her. Of course, Geoffrey would have to come home – he needed his father's approbation and would do nothing to anger the old man, not while he held the purse strings.

In the morning, Geoffrey called early and Sarah was subjected to the indignity of being summoned to his presence in her dressing robe.

He looked at her coldly. 'I take it you have found yourself a lover,' he said and it was not a question. 'I have expected this for some time and have made provision for it.'

'What do you mean?' Sarah asked, lifting her head high, feeling that perhaps she had been too sure of her power over him.

'I have taken my son to live with me,' he said. 'You may keep this establishment. I will make you an allowance but I will not live with you any longer.'

'You can't take Jack to live with Chas,' Sarah said angrily. 'I will not allow it and neither would your father approve of such an arrangement.'

'I have found a house for Jack and me, and most of the staff will be moved to my new home,' he said. 'Chas will have his own apartment in town. He will act as tutor to our son, visiting every day but don't worry, Sarah, he's not an evil man and he's very fond of Jack. He would do him no harm, I do assure you. Chas loves *me*. Hard as you may find it to accept that possibility, it's the truth.'

'And what is your father going to say about it all when I tell him about you and your precious Chas?' Sarah said challengingly. 'Answer me that, Geoffrey Frogmore.'

'My father will never know, not if you're to keep this house and the generous allowance I intend to make you.

In any case, you might consider what even a hint of such a thing would do. It would kill him.'

'Well you are not going to take my child from me,' Sarah said uncertainly. 'Jack belongs with his mother. You can't be so inhuman as to keep us apart.'

'You didn't think of that when you stayed out all night,' Geoffrey said calmly. 'Just as well I was at home with him or he'd have been in the hands of the servants. It's not good enough, Sarah and I'm not having it.' He paused and stroked his beard. 'I will allow him to visit but he'll no longer be subject to your whims.'

'You would rather him be influenced by your behaviour, would you?' Sarah said angrily. 'You and that man lying together, it's disgusting.'

Geoffrey shook his head. 'You'll never understand, will you? Chas and I are loyal to each other. You, on the other hand don't know the meaning of the word. You were born a strumpet and a strumpet you will remain until the day you die. Do you think I want Jack growing up knowing what a whore his mother is?'

She opened her mouth to protest but Geoffrey lifted his hand. 'I've nothing more to say to you, Sarah, you may go.'

'You won't get away with this,' Sarah said wildly. 'I'll blacken your name all over Swansea. I'll make everyone realize what a misfit you are.'

Geoffrey shook his head. 'No you won't do that, Sarah. You are motivated by greed. You couldn't exist without my money, that's why you married me. In any case, not even you would want to destroy our son. What of his future with a father in prison?'

Sarah put her hand to her mouth to stop the flow of angry words. She knew, with a sinking of her spirits that Geoffrey had beaten her. She moved to the door and stood for a moment looking back at him.

'Very well then, go. Get out of my sight. But I'll never give my son up, believe me, I'll win him back even if it takes me years to do it. Wait until he's grown. What will he think of his father then?'

She flounced out of the room and hurried up the stairs, tears of rage and frustration pouring down her cheeks. How dare Geoffrey take her son away with no thought for how she would feel? She clenched her hands into fists. She hated him. She wanted to slap Geoffrey's sad little face – she could never forgive him for what he had done to her, never.

Arian jerked awake. She was cramped and stiff from sitting in the chair in the small cabin of the *Marie Clare*. The boards groaned beneath her feet as the ship dipped gently from side to side. She rose to her feet and rubbed at her neck. How long had she been asleep? She peered through the porthole and saw that the ship had docked; she was in France. The dawn was beginning to streak the sky, and there were a few sailors strolling about the docklands.

She opened the door of the cabin and went onto the deck. The cold salt breeze stung her face and she was aware that she was suddenly very hungry.

There was no sign of Simples. Arian moved about the deck looking for someone to search for him. She saw one of the sailors glance at her curiously and she lifted her head and moved towards him.

'Have you seen Mr Simples?' she asked but the man shook his head uncomprehendingly. She bit her lip. It seemed that most of the crew of the *Marie Clare* were French and it was possible that the sailor had no idea what she was talking about.

'Your Captain,' she said slowly, 'where is he?'

'Captain Marchant, he leave the ship.' The man pointed to the gangplank leading onto the quayside. Arian approached it and looked into the dark waters but the sailor was shaking his head as though to deter her from attempting to go ashore alone.

She fumed impatiently. Where on earth could Simples be? Would he have gone to the calf company without her?

The man brought her a cup of thick black coffee and she nodded her thanks. It was hot and sweet and brought some of the feeling back into her cramped limbs.

It was beginning to get light when Arian decided she could wait no longer. She fetched her bag and took out the address of the calf company. She would go ashore and find out if anyone knew where she could find the offices. It seemed they were here on the dockside somewhere, so it shouldn't be too difficult to locate them. In any case, she had a suspicion she would find Simples there before her.

Arian edged her way along the gangplank and with a sigh of relief stepped onto the firm ground of the dockside. She looked around, wondering which direction to take and then moved forward impatiently – she had to do something, she couldn't stand here all day hesitating.

She made her way towards a huddle of warehouses and turning a corner hesitated as she saw a group of sailors laughing together, one of them holding a bottle of wine aloft. He turned as though sensing her presence and smiled down at her, speaking rapidly in French, and reaching out he gestured for her to come forward.

She held out the piece of paper with the address of the company she was seeking but the man scarcely looked at it. Instead, he rested his hand on her shoulder, speaking to her softly, in a suggestive manner that chilled her.

She made to shake him off but he dipped his hand into his pocket and brought out a handful of money making a gesture towards her that was quite graphic in its meaning. Arian stepped back in horror. It was clear he thought she was a cheap stand-up touting for trade. The docklands of France, as those of Swansea, were a place of rich pickings for any woman of the streets.

She shook her head and the man took out more money laughing down at her, and it was apparent from his attitude that he and his friends were the worse for drink.

She strode away and turned to see the man staring after her. He spoke violently in rapid French and Arian looked round to find she was surrounded by jeering sailors.

The men fell back suddenly and Arian was relieved to see Simples come forward. He spoke rapidly to the sailors in French, she heard and recognized the word 'Gendarmes' and the men seemed to melt away into the shadows.

Simples turned to her. 'Arian, things haven't turned out the way I expected, I'm sorry . . .' His words trailed away. Arian didn't see the police come up behind her. She felt her arms being jerked behind her back. They were one each side of her, two burly gendarmes propelling her forward, uncaring that she was stumbling over the rough stones.

She couldn't believe it. She was being taken away by the police with little ceremony. Why, what did they think she had done wrong?

'Mr Simples, what's happening?' she called but there was no reply. She was thrust into a creaking carriage and the nightmare journey through the unfamiliar streets began. She was uncomfortable, unable to sit back because of the way her arms were tied and every jerk of the carriage threatened to throw her to the floor.

The journey seemed to last for hours but at last the carriage came to a halt and she was thrust into the roadway. She fell to her knees but was hauled upright by rough hands and pushed forward into the entrance of what appeared to be a police station. Perhaps now, she thought, everything would be sorted out and she would be released.

An official-looking man sat upright behind a desk. His face was impassive as he talked to her in rapid French.

She shook her head. 'I'm sorry, I don't understand,' she broke into the tirade, 'I'm a stranger here.'

The man shook his head and muttered something to one of the gendarmes and then she was being dragged away. Unceremoniously, she was pushed into a cell and the door was slammed behind her with a ring of finality.

She fell against the rough wall and for a moment, lay there dazed. She shook her head to clear it. This could not be happening to her, it must be a bad dream, a nightmare. She'd had so many nightmares in her life this was surely just one more.

As her eyes became accustomed to the gloom, she saw that she was not alone. About twenty other women were crammed into the cell, most of them asleep or unconscious.

A young girl near to her spoke softly in French and Arian shook her head. 'I don't understand.' She heard the desperation in her voice and knew she was near to hysteria.

'You English?' the girl said and Arian turned to her eagerly.

'Thank God,' she said thankfully. 'You speak English.'

The girl nodded. 'A leetle, only.'

'How long are they going to keep us here? What will happen?'

'More slow, you must speak,' the girl urged. 'I not know much words.'

'What is going to happen to us?' Arian said trying to calm herself and speak more distinctly.

The girl shrugged 'They keep us weeks, two or three, they turn us out then, back to the streets.'

Arian put her hand over her mouth. She couldn't stay here for a day let alone a few weeks. She forced her trembling limbs to support her and then she called out loudly through the bars of the cell door.

'Please come and help me! Help!' she shouted.

The young girl tugged at her arm, shaking her head urgently but Arian was too overwrought to heed her.

'I must get out of here!' she called. A man appeared and snarled some words in her direction, and once more the girl at her side tugged her arm.

'Just let me talk to someone,' Arian pleaded and her heart lifted in hope as he began to unlock the door. The girl cowered back against the wall, and too late Arian realized the man was not going to help her but punish her.

He stepped inside the cell and, looking with disdain at her, spat on the ground. Without warning he slapped her full across the face and she fell, her head spinning with pain, unable to see for the lights that danced before her eyes.

The next blow caught her kidneys. She was unable to protect herself, as her hands were still tied. She gasped, drawing up her knees to protect her stomach. He rained blows upon her back and her head until Arian felt he would kill her.

She heard the young girl say something and she heard a harsh slap of the flat of the man's hand on the young face. But he went away, slamming the door behind him, the key grating in the lock.

'You be good and quiet.' The girl lifted Arian's head onto her lap. 'It will be worse if you make 'im much anger.'

Arian felt one of her eyes begin to close. She drifted off into semi-consciousness, thinking disjointedly that she was a girl again with her father coming home drunk from the public and venting his rage on her.

The darkness that was creeping up on her was welcome and she allowed herself to sink into it with a sense of relief.

It was morning when she woke and for a moment, Arian felt a sense of total confusion. She didn't know where she was except that the place was damp and the smell around her was nauseating. Then she remembered that she was in a French prison and she sat up abruptly, groaning as she felt the bruises on her face and body.

Most of the women around her were still asleep but one young girl was attempting to wash at the mean bowl of water that apparently had been pushed through the bars of the cell. Arian recognized her as the girl who had befriended her the previous night. The girl turned and smiled and indicated the bowl.

Arian crawled forward, her legs trembling, and as a wave of faintness washed over her, she realized it was many hours since she'd eaten a meal.

'Have water now,' the girl whispered, 'before everyone else uses it.'

The water felt good on her face though Arian flinched as she inadvertently brushed her bruises. She dried her skin on the hem of her skirt and then sank down in her corner, thinking ruefully that even in this hell-hole there was a sense of guarding one's own territory.

Some hours later, she was alerted by the sound of the cell door being opened. She felt rough hands drag her to her feet and then she was being propelled into the corridor.

She tried to struggle and was immediately struck across the face so that she fell heavily against the rough stone wall. Hauled upright, half unconscious, she was half pushed, half dragged up a flight of stairs and led along another corridor. Then she was in a bare room with Simples standing looking at her in concern.

He spoke rapidly in French to the gendarme who seemed anything but discomfited by the tirade. He shrugged and replied laconically.

Simples untied the ropes that bound her and then held her in his arms. Arian was too exhausted, and too grateful for his presence, to protest.

'Thank God, I managed to talk some sense into these foreigners,' he whispered. 'They intended holding you on charges of fraud, something to do with the calf company.'

Arian clung to him, still not fully conscious, her head aching, her body sore and bruised. She heard Simples continue speaking without fully understanding what he was saying.

'I've had to tell them that you are my responsibility, that I will take charge of you, otherwise they are not willing to release you.'

He put his finger over her lips as she would have spoken. 'Be careful, I'm not sure even now they believe me that you are innocent or that you know nothing about this company. All you did was to give them an order for calf.'

Arian leaned against him wearily, resigned to allowing him to sort everything out for her. It should have surprised her that Simples spoke very good French but somehow it didn't. Nothing about him surprised her any more.

A man in plain clothes entered the room and spoke to Gerald in French. Gerald nodded, obviously agreeing to something the man was saying and quite suddenly, the gendarme standing to attention became almost festive in his attitude. He smiled at Arian and shortly a woman came in carrying the bag Arian had brought ashore.

She was led to a washroom, given a clean towel and some of her own clean clothes. She washed and changed with little enthusiasm. A quick look in the cracked and damp-speckled mirror was enough to show her that her eye was swollen and black and she was looking far from her best. But at least they were releasing her, doubtless the authorities had seen the error of their ways and were trying to make amends.

She was taken back to the bare room and saw that a priest had joined the company. He scarcely looked at her bruised face and seemed engrossed in the papers the gendarme was holding before him.

'What is it?' Arian whispered, as Simples came to her side and shook his head. 'Just say what I tell you to and then we will be out of here,' he whispered urgently.

The priest stood before them and spoke some words. Arian listened in bewilderment. Was she being asked to swear that she was not guilty of fraud? She didn't care – so long as she was let out of the prison she would say anything they wanted her to.

She clumsily repeated the words Simples spoke. Her tongue felt thick, she felt faint and ill, her head ached intolerably and all she wanted to do was to lie down somewhere where it was quiet and dark and comfortable.

It was only when her lifeless hand was lifted and a ring slipped onto her finger that she realized what had happened; she had married Gerald Simples.

She would have pulled away but he held her fast. 'Hush, it's the only way out of here,' he warned. 'If I'd refused to marry you we might both have been kept in prison.'

He held her close to him and spoke in her ear. 'Remember, we are in a foreign country, their ways are not ours.'

Arian's feelings were in turmoil as she allowed him to lead her out into the street where she breathed in the fresh air with gratitude. She saw the gutters were being hosed down with water and the shops were slowly opening their doors. Everything seemed strangely unreal, like a bad dream.

Simples helped her into a carriage and then they were heading away from the police building and towards the outskirts of the town. The sun was lightening the sky, it promised to be a beautiful day. Arian suddenly began to cry. Here she was sitting beside a man she disliked with his ring on her finger.

She looked up at him, challengingly. 'You always wanted this, didn't you?' she said. 'It's all your fault. I hate you. I'll never forgive you for this.'

'Don't be absurd,' he said sharply. 'Did I ask you to go ashore alone? You were safe while you stayed aboard ship. I would have sorted everything out for you if you'd only given me time.'

He was right and she knew it. 'Well there's no chance of me coming into your bed,' she said in a low voice. 'You might have married me but you can't make me do anything against my will.'

'Do you think I wanted to marry you like this? I have some pride, though you don't seem to realize it,' Simples said coldly. 'You must come to my bed of your own free will or not at all.'

'Well you can guarantee it will be not at all,' Arian said drawing as far away from him as she could.

When the coach stopped outside a small squat building near the docks, Simples helped her down. 'Behave as naturally as you can,' he said. 'We have to stay in the country until matters are cleared up and if you venture out alone again I won't be responsible for you. Do you understand?'

Arian nodded and allowed him to help her from the coach. 'I will mention that you had a nasty fall,' he said calmly. 'That will explain your bruises.'

'How long do we have to stay here, then?' Arian asked apprehensively and Simples looked at her with raised eyebrows. 'Until we have sorted out the stock of missing calf and found out just who is guilty of fraud.'

The motherly woman who opened the door to them clucked in sympathy as Simples made an excuse about Arian's injuries. She spoke in rapid French and Gerald took Arian's arm. 'Come along, Mrs Simples,' he said evenly, 'let us find our room.' He led the way up a creaking staircase to a sun-filled bedroom.

Arian looked in dismay at the big bed and tried to quell the rising tide of fear that threatened to overwhelm her. She was trapped here in France, married to Gerald Simples and tonight they would spend the night together in this room. Would he be true to his word and leave her alone or would he turn in the night and force himself upon her?

She sank onto the multi-coloured quilt and stared down at the floorboards. It was as if her strength had deserted her. She seemed no longer in charge of her life and somehow it didn't seem to matter what happened to her now; she felt tired and ill, she had been imprisoned and beaten and all she wanted to do was sleep. She curled up on the bed and closed her eyes. Her body ached, her head felt on fire. If only she could sleep then everything would be all right, the nightmare would go away.

She was aware of a hand on her brow and opened her eyes with difficulty.

'You are going to be all right,' Gerald was leaning over her. 'I'm your husband and I'm going to take care of you. There is nothing for you to worry about.'

Arian turned her face into the pillow and wished she could die.

CHAPTER ELEVEN

Eline stared through the window at the women who'd gathered outside the shop. They were pointing and gesticulating, their faces accusing, angry. Eline unconsciously squared her shoulders; it was clear that news of Calvin's divorce proceedings against her was now common knowledge.

Quite how such information spread so quickly among the poorer quarters of the town she didn't know but then bad news had a way of travelling swiftly. She and Will would have to prepare themselves to face the barrage of antagonism and abuse usually heaped on those unfortunate enough to have their mistakes aired in public.

Calvin would come out of it all mainly unscathed. He was now a free man, there would be not a spot on his reputation. He was aggrieved, the injured party, betrayed by the wife who had cuckolded him. Eline could see the headlines in the *Cambrian* as though they were there before her, already in print: 'Shameless woman bears a child by her lover and flaunts her faithlessness in her husband's face.'

No doubt the townspeople would say she deserved to be cast from polite society, and scorned by her neighbours, never mind that since their parting Calvin had done his own share of flaunting of women. He'd been frequently seen with his paramour in public but then there was one law for men and another for women. Calvin had not feared to take that awful Daphne woman anywhere he chose, yet he was seen as the wronged one and Eline as a woman who deserved to be ostracized.

She felt Will come up behind her and slip his arms around her waist. 'Don't worry. In a little while we'll be able to get married,' he said softly. 'The gossips will forget, they always do. There will be something else to occupy them soon, you'll see.'

She turned in his arms and buried her face in his shoulder, her heart was thumping in fear. 'Perhaps they won't ever forget, perhaps they will never buy shoes from us again.'

'Don't worry so much,' Will urged. 'The gossip will pass, you'll see. Remember, my darling, we are together, free. That's all that matters.'

A few days passed before Eline found the courage to venture outdoors. She needed to do some shopping at the market in Oxford Street to replenish the larder, she was low on flour and potatoes, as well as meat.

She knew she would have to face her hostile neighbours sometime. She expected comments, pointing fingers, and she would just have to put up with it all until the scandal was forgotten.

She was at the vegetable stall in the market when she was confronted by a woman she'd never seen before. The vitriolic tone of the stranger's voice startled Eline as she was putting away her change into her purse.

'You are a scourge on us all.' The words fell harshly into the sudden silence. The chattering around Eline had ceased as though on a hidden signal, and women were watching from a distance wondering how Eline would react.

She stared challengingly at the woman who was neatly dressed, her collar white and carefully ironed, her hat firmly in place on her greying hair.

'You are an abomination in the eyes of respectable womanhood. We can do without your sort shopping by here in Swansea market alongside us God-fearing folk.'

'Excuse me,' Eline said, forcing down the rising tide of anger and panic that filled her. 'What business is it of yours what I do? You don't know me or anything about me. What right have you to accost me like this?'

'I have every right as a church-going woman to point out how disgraceful your behaviour is.' The woman raised herself to her full height. 'I have the right of any virtuous woman to accuse and deride a harlot who walks in my path. I

162

speak as a God-fearing widow-woman and I speak for many when I say you should be driven out of our town.'

'Look,' Eline said quietly, 'I have no quarrel with you. I am going about my own business, so just let me pass in peace. There's nothing more to be said.'

By now the group of watching women had drawn closer, staring at Eline in self-righteous piety, pleased, it seemed, to have someone to accuse of immorality.

'Mrs Coppleworth is right,' one woman called. 'It's your sort that leads our men astray. I know what you are, Eline Temple, an alley-cat who will lie with any man who offers you his services.'

'Don't be absurd,' Eline said loudly. 'I have not taken anyone's husband and I refuse to justify myself to rabble the like of you.'

A clod of earth struck Eline's face and she lifted her head defiantly. The flat of a stone caught her cheek and as Eline stepped back a pace, Mrs Coppleworth's voice boomed out, loud, almost hysterical in tone.

'This woman is the lowest of the low,' she called. 'People of our sort do not get divorced, it is a shame and a sin.' She turned, aware that she had a rapt audience. 'She,' the woman was fairly quivering with righteous indignation, 'she would go to the bed of another man while tied in the holy bonds of matrimony. This . . . this whore is a scar on the fair name of womanhood.'

Eline saw with horror that the women were arming themselves with stones. This could not be happening, not here and now in the familiar streets of Swansea.

A figure stepped in front of her, as a stone was hurled past her face.

'Stop this at once!' The woman was puffed up with anger. She stood arms akimbo, hands on generous hips, protecting Eline from the crowd of incensed women.

'So it's you, Nina Parks, the strumpet from the Mumbles,' Mrs Coppleworth shouted. 'Go back where you belong. You're no better than you ought to be either. You and Eline Temple are cut from the same cloth, whores both of you. Shared a husband once, we've not forgotten that, mind.'

'Shut up!' Nina Parks almost spat the words at Mrs Coppleworth who stepped back a pace. 'Shut your mouth. I'm going to deal with you in a minute. In the meantime take you, Maisie Scott,' Nina pointed a finger. 'I know you take Tom the Milk to your bed most Sundays when your man is out fishing, so what right have you to judge any woman?'

She paused, savouring the sudden silence, her eyes flickering over the now cowed group of women. 'And you, Delyth Jones, your husband has an eye for the young girls and you look the other way 'cause you can't bear him in your own bed.' She turned to survey the crowd. 'All of us here know that's the truth so I challenge anyone to call me a liar.'

Predictably none of the women wanted to draw attention to themselves, not when Nina Parks was in full flood. She turned triumphantly.

'And as for you Moriah Coppleworth, you drove your Billy to drink with your cant and your Bible thumping, drove him into an early grave, you did, mind. What age was he? Twenty-six, twenty-seven? Glad to be out of it, he was.'

No-one spoke, even Moriah Coppleworth was abashed, her head hanging low.

'Now get back home, all of you. Read the Good Book. See what it says there about casting stones and then look at yourselves in the mirror if you can bear to.'

The women dispersed slowly, muttering low, afraid that Nina Parks would launch another attack on them. It was Mrs Coppleworth who paused and stared belligerently at Eline.

'You won't always have *her* to speak up for you,' her voice was harsh. 'You will have your come-uppance, you'll see. God does not sleep, mind.'

'Oh clear off,' Nina said impatiently. 'Go and make someone else's life miserable. That's all your sort are good for.'

Eline let out a heavy sigh of relief as the woman turned away. Nina looked at her with a wry smile.

'God preserve me from a good woman, I always say.' She put a hand on Eline's arm. 'You haven't carved out a very easy path for yourself, have you, love?' she said softly. 'You never did, not even when you was married to Joe but you was very young then, mind.'

Nina's voice shook a little. 'I suppose I loved Joe more than you ever did, bore him children, gave him myself. You and him were never meant. God help you, you have the knack of marrying men you don't love.' Her voice was without censure. 'Go on, do your shopping and don't let them wicked, gossiping women stop you.'

'Thank you, Nina,' Eline said quietly. 'I dread to think what might have happened if you hadn't come along.'

'That's as may be. In future you must attack first, Eline. Don't let them women get the upper hand over you; none of them is without sin and you remind them of that.'

She stood for a moment, looking at Eline and there were memories in her eyes. She swallowed hard. '*Hwyl*, Eline, bye. Take care of yourself now.'

Eline stood alone in the middle of the busy market. She was trembling but she knew if she gave in to her fear she would never feel safe on the streets again. Determinedly she set out towards the butcher's stall, her throat a hard lump of unshed tears.

It was strange how Nina had come from the past like a ghost bringing thoughts and images Eline would rather forget. The days Eline had spent in Oystermouth as Joe's bride had been unhappy ones; she'd not been accepted then, either. Perhaps she was destined to be a misfit, never to find a place in any society. But all that she would forgo. Respectability was only an empty word; her true happiness lay with William and with their son. Lifting her head high Eline moved onwards through the crowds that thronged Swansea market. An outcast she might be, but she was loved and that was all she desired.

★ ★ ★

Night was falling. Arian sat on the bed and watched as Gerald Simples lit the candles in the small bedroom. The light sprung around the room, warming the patchwork quilt on the bed into colour, softening the contours of the old heavy furniture, throwing shadows that danced mystically on the cracked whitewashed walls.

With his back to her, Simples began to undress and Arian bit her lip, knowing that she was in an impossible position. 'Come along, Mrs Simples,' he said, 'you might as well try to make yourself comfortable. You can't sit there on the edge of the bed all night.'

'Don't call me that!' Arian said irritably and she flinched as he stood naked before her, his broad shoulders blotting out the glow from the candle so that it made an aureola of light around his dark hair.

'Why not?' he said easily. 'It's your name.' He climbed into bed, turned his back to her and pulled the bedclothes up around his shoulders. Arian shivered. It was cold in the room, there was no fire and her body ached for sleep.

After a time she undressed and, in her petticoats, climbed beneath the blankets, feeling the warmth with a sense of relief. She moved right to the edge of the bed, keeping as much distance between herself and Gerald Simples as she could.

Slowly tiredness overcame her. She desperately needed sleep, her head ached and her body was sore and exhausted. She felt languor, sweet and soft, steal over her and then she gave herself up to the weariness that slowly overtook her and she slept.

She woke suddenly. It was dark. She felt a body against hers, strong and masculine and with a sense of horror and embarrassment she realized that in the night she must have turned towards the warmth of another human being – she was in Gerald Simples's arms.

She tried to see him in the dark. He was breathing evenly, clearly asleep. She tried to edge away from him but he grunted and wound his arms around her waist. She knew that he was unaware of his actions, as she had been

166

of hers. She was still so weary, so in need of rest that she relaxed. What did it matter if in the throes of sleep they held onto each other? In the morning she would make her position more than plain; she wanted none of him and, once they were home in Swansea she would seek advice on how to escape from the awful situation she had found herself in.

Her last thoughts before sleep once again claimed her were of the ceremony in the jail. It could not be legal; everything would be sorted out and it would be all right in the end but for now she simply must sleep.

In the morning she opened her eyes to find Gerald Simples looking into her face. He was only inches away from her and she had one arm flung around his broad back. For a moment she didn't know where she was. He was smiling, his teeth white, his hair tousled across his forehead. She sometimes forgot in her dislike of him what a handsome man Simples was.

She moved sharply away from him and he smiled. 'Good morning, Mrs Simples.'

She rolled away from him and climbed out the other side of the bed without replying. Anger poured through her, anger at herself for allowing him to get close to her.

'Don't make any mistake,' she said firmly, 'once we are home again, this sham of a marriage will prove worthless.'

'Really?' he said rising from the bed and standing near the windows stretching his arms. 'What makes you think so?'

'It was under duress,' she said, 'and a pretence just to get us out of the jail.'

'Not at all,' Gerald Simples said evenly. 'It was a perfectly legal ceremony performed by a Father Alain, a properly ordained priest. Face it, Mrs Simples, you are my wife whether or not you like to think so.'

'We'll see about that,' Arian said hotly. 'Now get out of here while I wash and dress.'

Ignoring her, Simples drew on his trousers and moved to the wash-stand. 'I intend to use this water and if you choose to wash, you can fetch your own water from the pump outside.'

He calmly poured the water from the jug into the basin. Arian turned away in futile anger. She listened to the sounds of his ablutions, the scrape of razor on his chin, with a sense of unreality. These were things you shared with your nearest and dearest, with your husband. But then Gerald Simples was her husband. With a sense of despair, she knew that she believed him when he said the marriage ceremony was legal.

'You might have made me your wife in name,' she said hot with anger, 'but in name is all it will be! Remember that.'

He didn't reply but continued to shave and Arian sat amongst the bedclothes staring at his broad back, hate and anger pouring through her like wine.

Later Gerald left the boarding house without a word and Arian had no means of knowing where he had gone or when he would return. He had not confided his intentions and she was quietly seething at the way he had left her alone, knowing she would be afraid to venture outside after what had happened.

She ate, with little appetite, the breakfast an aged lady dressed in black set before her. 'Good morning,' she ventured. 'Did Mr Simples leave any message?'

The old lady shrugged and spoke in a torrent of French. Arian sank back in her chair, knowing it was useless – she would just have to contain herself in patience as best she could until Gerald chose to return.

The day passed slowly with Arian feeling uncomfortably in the way. What she imagined was a boarding house was little more than a cottage with a spare bedroom apparently let on occasions to passing travellers.

When she attempted to spend some time alone in her room, the old lady entered, gesticulating wildly, her eyes bright, her grey hair in wisps around her thin face. The young girl at her side was carrying a broom and a handful of old rags. The old lady spoke quickly nodding towards the bed and Arian gathered that she was in the way; the bed was to be made up and the room tidied, presumably to receive other visitors.

Arian was at a loss to understand the old lady's questions, accompanied by excited waving of her bony hands, until the young girl intervened.

'Are you to stay here more nights?' she asked haltingly. 'Madam wishes to know this.'

Arian shook her head. 'I don't know how long we will stay but for tonight, yes, I think so.' The day was passing and Arian had no way of knowing the tide times. All she did know was that if Gerald Simples didn't return soon there would be no alternative other than to stay until morning.

It was all his fault. If he didn't think of telling her his plans, then even if they were sailing on a late tide, he would just have to pay madam for another night's lodgings.

Supper was a simple meal of paté, crisp fresh bread and a glass of wine. Arian fumed with impatience. Gerald had been out of the house for hours now. What was he doing? If he was visiting the offices of the calf suppliers then she should have been with him. What did he think he was doing, behaving in such a high-handed manner?

In the cool of the evening she ventured outside into the cobbled courtyard, overcome with the need to leave the confining walls of the small cottage. Her mind was in a turmoil as she asked herself how she'd allowed such an absurd situation to develop. She had come to France with the best of intentions and she'd been thrown in prison, ill-treated and beaten like a common thief.

She looked down at the thick band of gold on her finger. She had allowed herself to be tricked into marriage. No, not tricked, not really, she admitted to herself – in her desperation she'd have done anything to be out of that terrible jail. Still, there had been some solitary hope in her mind that the marriage would not be legal, that somehow, once she was safely home, it could be dissolved. And yet Gerald seemed so sure they were tied together for good. She sighed in despair. This was surely some nightmare from which she'd wake.

She sat in the slant of dying sunlight and stared out across the street towards where the masts of ships rose above the rooftops. She thought longingly of home, of Stormhill, of Calvin Temple whose lips she had kissed so sweetly. She placed her hands on her hot cheeks. She was in love with Calvin Temple, an impossible dream which might just have come true but now there was an impenetrable barrier between them – her marriage to Gerald Simples.

When he returned home at last, Arian could not wait to talk to Gerald. 'Well?' she challenged when they were together in the small bedroom. 'What's been happening today while I've been kept prisoner here?'

He ignored her outburst and sat on the bed easing off his boots. Finally, he spoke. 'I've been to see the people at the French calf company.' He gestured impatiently. 'Sit down and listen to me. I've been doing my best for both of us and I don't need any histrionics from you.'

'Why didn't you take me with you then? I had as much right to speak to the suppliers as you. No, I had *more* right – the business transaction was mine.'

'I thought after the events of the last few days, you were better kept off the streets,' Gerald said smoothly. 'In any case, these people feel more comfortable dealing with a man. Can't you understand that?'

Arian subsided onto the bed. There was a lot of sense in what he said and yet anger still burned within her. 'Go on, tell me what's happened.' She spoke as quietly as she could.

He sighed heavily. 'Several firms have been bankrupted by this farce; it seems that the calf business was nothing more than a front for a shady, not to say fraudulent, deal.'

'You mean Calvin's money is lost? I've been a gullible fool, grasping at what I thought was a wonderful bargain. What an idiot!'

'There's worse to come,' Gerald spoke dryly. 'Lord Temple might well be investigated for his involvement in all this and if that's the case he can kiss goodbye to his good name and possibly his fortune.' Simples failed to meet her eye.

'How can this be? Calvin had never heard of this company before. I can speak up for him.'

'Don't be so naïve,' Simples lied effortlessly. 'I'm telling you I've handled money in Lord Temple's name for some time. It was the only source from which he gained any profit. He will be implicated up to his neck – he's not the paragon of virtue you believe him to be. Lord Temple might even go to prison, unless . . .'

'Unless what?' Arian was suddenly fearful, her mouth dry as she stared into Simples' face.

'Unless I take the blame.' The words fell into a silence and Arian tried to comprehend what that would mean.

'But then *you* would go to prison,' she said. 'How could you bear it after seeing me in that awful place? In any case, what would you gain from it?'

'I would be set up for life by the gratitude and money Lord Temple would shower upon me.' He stared at her levelly. 'And I'd probably be let off lightly as a mere pawn in the game. I'd certainly be willing to take the chance if . . .' his words trailed away and Arian swallowed hard. She knew what he was going to say but she had to ask anyway.

'If what?' She felt her legs tremble and she bit her lip waiting for his answer.

'If you will come to my bed.' He watched her reactions carefully, and when she didn't answer he spoke again.

'I know you don't love me but love can grow, given a chance,' he said persuasively. 'I would be good to you, I would treat you with respect always, you know that.'

'But why should I give up my freedom for Calvin Temple?' Arian asked but her voice lacked conviction.

'I think we both know the answer to that, Mrs Simples,' he said. 'You fancy yourself in love with him. You wish to protect him but you and he are worlds apart. It could never be but at least you can preserve his good name.'

'I don't know,' Arian said. 'How can I be sure you are telling me the truth?'

'I'll be taking you to see the authorities involved, people who are already conducting an investigation. Then I will ask the police to talk to you. Perhaps then you'll be convinced I'm telling you the truth.'

Arian closed her eyes. She was so confused. Could she allow Simples to take the blame for what must have been nothing but carelessness on Calvin's part? She couldn't believe him guilty of anything underhand whatever Simples said. But what if he was? Could she bear to be Simples's wife just to save Calvin from disgrace and possibly imprisonment? She tried to imagine Calvin in the dank smelly hole of a cell where she'd been put, imagined him enduring the indignities that she'd endured and she shuddered.

'All right.' She straightened her shoulders. 'We'll go to see these people and when I know you are speaking the truth, I will make my decision.'

They again spent the night in the same bed, back to back, with Arian scarcely sleeping at all. Her mind raced around like a rat in a trap. She didn't want to be Simples's wife, she didn't even like him. And yet what was the giving of her body? What did it really matter? She had not ever seen virtue as something to be prized.

When she was a young girl she had given herself freely to Eddie, her first lover, and had enjoyed him shamelessly. She had even survived the attentions of Price Davies, so would giving in to Gerald Simples be so bad? At least he said he loved her and would respect her.

She knew, in her heart, there was no question to be answered. She would do anything if it meant saving Calvin from imprisonment. She didn't for one moment believe him guilty of anything underhand. If he was in trouble over the leather company then it was all a mistake on his part – he was nothing if not honest. She curled up in the bed, her knees drawn to her chin. This could be her last night of being her own woman. Tomorrow she might have to agree to receiving Gerald Simples as a husband. She wanted to cry but tears would not come. In any case, hadn't she learned a long time ago that tears solved nothing?

In the morning she was heavy eyed and headachy and she dressed without caring that Gerald Simples was in the room with her. What use was modesty now? She was his wife, would be his wife in fact as well as in name once their inquiries were completed, for she knew instinctively that he would prove to her all that he'd said was true.

He took her into the nearby town with a name she could not pronounce and led her to the same police building where she had been imprisoned. She shuddered as she entered the doorway and saw again the uniforms of the French police.

Gerald led her along a corridor and then they were entering an office occupied by four men. One of them looked up from behind his desk and nodded in recognition.

'Mr Clerice, would you explain the situation regarding the French calf company to Mrs Simples?' Gerald spoke quietly in English when they were both seated opposite the Frenchman. He inclined his head.

'The people behind this company are in deep trouble, madame,' the man said in a heavy accented voice. 'They have broken many people, robbed them of their money. Some victims were so desperate they have taken their own lives. It is a dreadful business.'

'Lord Temple, he is implicated?' Arian asked, her mouth dry. The man toyed with the bowl of his pipe, and his eyes met hers with a gleam of something she could not quite understand.

'It would seem that way, madame, unless there is someone else to blame for the problems.'

'Like who?' Arian asked, her heart pounding in her breast. The man raised his eyebrows.

'Like whom? Well, that it is my job to learn.' He shrugged. 'It is early days yet. You will appreciate there is a lot of investigating still to do before final conclusions are made.' He rose and looked down at her. 'It might even be you are the cause of the trouble, madame. I keep an open mind until there is proof but in the meantime, do not leave France.' His tone was sinister and Arian shivered.

Gerald rose and took her arm, drawing Arian to her feet. He opened the door and she moved into the passageway before him, panic beating at her like dark wings.

Once outside the station, she looked up at Gerald fearfully. 'Can we be arrested for this?'

Gerald shook his head. 'No, there's not enough evidence against us, not unless I confess, but we *can* be kept here indefinitely. Do you really wish to go to the offices of the calf company now?' he said. 'I warn you that there we will find confusion, books being taken away, offices emptied – it's a sorry sight, believe me.'

'I must find out all I can.' Arian didn't want to believe any of this. She could not understand how Calvin had become mixed up in anything so shady. And yet he'd said he was making mistakes in business, perhaps this was one of them.

The cab ride across town was an uncomfortable one with Simples sitting thigh to thigh with her on the creaking seat, his shoulder against hers, his hand resting lightly on her knee in what she could only describe as a proprietary gesture.

When they reached the mean offices in a narrow street, she saw the name above the door in small, insignificant letters and sighed. The whole place smacked of an illicit business.

Inside, it was as Gerald had described; the rooms were a hive of activity with people scurrying to and fro like ants, carrying books and equipment out of the office and loading furniture into vans.

Simples spoke to one young man in French and the man stopped in his tracks. 'It is bad,' he said in English. 'The company has ruined, it has all gone wrong. People feel, what you say? Cheated, by what has happened.'

'What has happened?' Arian asked and the young man looked puzzled.

'She do not know?' He appealed to Gerald who spoke to him in French.

The young man held out a sheaf of papers and Calvin's signature sprang out at Arian. 'There is been bad dealings, wrong doing by some people and now we innocent ones have lost our jobs.'

174

Gerald looked at her closely as they moved away from the building. 'Do you believe what I've been trying to tell you?'

'I believe you,' Arian said softly. 'But I can't believe Calvin would knowingly cheat anyone. Why should he?' She turned on Simples. 'And why on earth should you take the blame for Calvin or any other person's mistakes?'

'You know why. For the same reason you'll come to my bed as a proper wife.'

'If you are saying that you love me then I don't believe that either.' Her voice was flat. 'You just want to best me, to make me do what you want, to get me into your bed.'

'Come,' Gerald said and she realized he was in the habit of ignoring anything he didn't wish to answer, 'we'll return to the boarding house. I've got a feeling we are being watched.'

The night was drawing in by the time they returned to the little cottage near the docklands. Arian ate little of the supper madame had prepared. Her thoughts were a tangled confusion of impressions and questions, the only thought that was clear in her mind was that tonight she would do what she had sworn never to – she would go to Gerald's bed if not willingly then at least without being physically forced.

'Your dilemma is simply solved.' Gerald leaned towards her across the table and it was as though he could read her thoughts. 'Tonight you become my wife and tomorrow I will give myself up to the police, tell them I was responsible for what I shall describe as a "mistake".' There was irony in his voice. 'You can return home and I will remain here and try to sort all this out.'

He paused and watched as she inclined her head in mute agreement. 'It must be understood that when I eventually return home it will be to a proper marriage. Is it agreed?'

Arian nodded, watching dry mouthed as Simples rose and bowed to the old lady. 'Good night, madame,' he said politely and then he left the room.

Madame looked questioningly at Arian. It seemed strange to her that Mrs Simples's husband should retire to the bedchamber without her.

Arian sat for as long as she could, watching as madame lit the lamps and drew the curtains over the darkened windows and then, at last, knowing she could prevaricate no longer, she rose to her feet.

'Good night,' she said and the old lady inclined her head. Arian mounted the stairs slowly, every one creaking beneath her feet, warning Gerald Simples of her approach. Arian knew that her mind was made up. She would do what Gerald wished and then, tomorrow, she could go home to Stormhill, leaving Gerald behind, and try to set herself free from this ridiculous situation.

She paused outside the bedroom door. Tonight she would have to grit her teeth and allow Gerald Simples to make her his wife. Well, he might possess her body but he would never have her love.

And yet, even though she hated him for forcing her to do his will, she knew that she should be grateful to him for the sacrifice he would have to make. He could spend a long time in prison and she couldn't deny that she admired his bravery. Perhaps he was telling the truth when he claimed to love her. The thought brought her a certain comfort.

She took a deep breath, opened the door and went into the bedroom. Gerald had arranged several candles around the room. The diffused light softened the contours of the huge bed and there he was waiting for her, his eyes grave as they regarded her.

'Well, Mrs Simples, you have come to me at last.'

Instead of answering, she began to undress, facing him, allowing him to see her nakedness. He watched her all the while but waited patiently until she came to him and climbed beneath the sheets. He drew her to him almost as though he was testing her and then he kissed her eyelids, her throat and, when she didn't protest, his mouth moved to her breasts. She lay still as his hands slid over her body, exploring her, taking his time. After a moment, he leaned on one elbow, looking down at her. 'You do not feel anything?' His dark eyes seemed to shine and she stared up at him almost wistfully.

'Last time I had a man it was violent and awful. Can you blame me for being afraid?' She closed her eyes, wishing he would get on with it, get it all over so that she could turn away from him and drown herself in misery but he was determined to try to please her.

'Look at me,' he said, and her eyes flew open. 'I don't want a rag doll, I want a live, red-blooded woman. Give me a chance to prove myself. Don't shut me out like this.'

Obediently, she put her arms around him and then he was above her, poised, waiting for her to accommodate him. He would spare her nothing, that was clear. She must act like a wife, he was determined on it.

She guided him to her, practised in the ways of pleasing a man, knowing that if she was to get the experience over quickly, she must accommodate him. He joined with her smoothly and, with surprise she realized that her body was receptive to him. He did not have to force or hurt her; her body was betraying her.

She sighed as he cupped her breasts gently and when she closed her eyes, it was not in despair but in acceptance. Simples might be all she hated in a man but he was vigorous and his body was smooth and hard beneath her hands. He might be using her but that was all right, she would use him too. Their marriage was a pact, not a love match. She breathed heavily as his passion increased. Tonight, she decided, was not going to be the ordeal she'd expected it to be.

CHAPTER TWELVE

Arian woke to find Simples leaning on one elbow, staring down at her with a strange expression on his face. She stirred uneasily and turned her head away from him but he cupped her chin with his hand and made her look at him.

'It wasn't so bad, was it, Mrs Simples?' he asked quietly. 'I think you might even enjoy being my wife.'

She edged away from him. In the cold light of morning, the whole thing seemed impossible – her marriage to Gerald Simples, a man she did not even like. She felt the colour rise to her face. She had given herself to him, just as he said she would.

'I don't love you,' she said flatly. 'I'll never love you. Is that what you want, a loveless marriage?'

'I had what I wanted last night when I possessed you,' he said. 'To me it was the most perfect night of my life.' His hand slipped down over her throat, lingered there and then moved to her naked breast and his breathing quickened. 'I'll never be tired of proving that you are mine.'

His other arm encircled her waist, drawing her close to him. 'Come, Mrs Simples,' he spoke in her ear, 'it is time to show me what an accommodating wife you are just once again before I give myself up to the police.'

She turned her face away from him, not wanting him, wishing she was anywhere but here, in a strange country in bed with a man whose very scent was unfamiliar to her.

'You liked it well enough last night didn't you?' he asked, his hands caressing her. 'You were ready to welcome me, I could tell that much. Your lips might say no but your body told me differently.' Even as he spoke, he was drawing her beneath him. 'I want to make sure you are really mine before we are separated. Surely you can understand that?'

She yielded to him, it seemed easier than arguing, and let him have his way. She would simply close her eyes and endure his attentions until he was tired of trying to please her.

He was vigorous, he was determined and yet Arian felt unmoved now by his obvious passion. Daylight pouring through the window made a reality of their union and highlighted the absurdity of the way she was allowing him to blackmail her into submission.

She grew tense as his vigour increased, but he was aware of it and kissed her mouth, his tongue probing. She lay unresponsive, which only served to excite him. It seemed he wanted to subjugate her, to force her to do his bidding, whatever she felt. He put his hands beneath her, holding her close to him while he poured his passion into her and then, at last, he released her and fell from her, smiling in his fulfilment.

He lay still beside her in the bed for a long time and then his hand touched her hair briefly. 'I am in love with you, you know that don't you? You will love me, too, given time.'

She didn't answer but tears trembled on her lashes. It was so awful to lie with one man when her whole being cried out for another.

He sighed heavily. 'You will be all right, now. I've made arrangements with Paul Marchant for your passage home on the *Marie Clare*.' He turned and kissed her neck. 'You'll sail with the afternoon tide and tomorrow you will be back at Stormhill. You must tell Calvin Temple nothing about what has happened, otherwise he might feel obliged to come out here and give himself up to the authorities.' He smiled ruefully. 'That would make your little sacrifice all for nothing, wouldn't it?'

His hand touched her face, his finger tracing the line of her mouth. 'What you must tell him is that you are now my wife. Truly my wife.'

If he had forced her, she would have fought him, hated him but he used guile and persuasion and though Arian knew she would never like him, let alone love him, Simples had the ability to make her feel obligated to him. She sighed as he drew her close once again. Gerald Simples, as she was learning, was a demanding husband.

Later she stood in the window of the cottage bedroom and watched as Simples strode along the roadway on his way to give himself up to face the possibility of imprisonment in a foreign country. She felt somehow released – she was going home. She knew she should feel guilty about leaving Simples behind and yet she could only be glad that she was free of him, if only for the moment.

It was with a sense of relief that Arian picked up her bag and descended the creaking stairs. Soon she would lie in her own bed, sleep alone beneath the sheets, with the huge chimneys of Stormhill rising high above her. And in a room not too far away from her, Calvin Temple too would be asleep, the man she loved, the man for whom she would give anything to save from shame and disgrace. She sighed as she paused in the small narrow passageway. It had been worth it, this marriage, her yielding to Gerald Simples. It had all been worth it, hadn't it?

Calvin Temple stared down at the books on the desk before him and frowned.

'So, Brighton, these books have been doctored, is that what you are saying?'

The old man standing behind his shoulder pulled at his grey moustache nervously. 'I would say more, Lord Temple. I would say that you have been embezzled out of a great deal of money.'

'I see.' Calvin pushed back his chair and rose to his feet. 'The investments Simples made in this French calf company in my name are worthless then?' He thrust his hands into his pockets.

'Absolutely.' Brighton removed his glasses and polished them with his spotless handkerchief. 'This company, if it exists at all, must be on the point of collapse. It's all very doubtful. You would be well to keep right out of it all. I am rather surprised that you invested in something that was

180

not entirely reliable in the first place, sir, if you'll pardon me saying so.'

'I was told a check on the company was not necessary,' Calvin said. 'My fault entirely for not keeping a closer eye on Simples. Will I face legal problems?'

The old man shook his head. 'No, I think not. You personally have not received any moneys from this company, it has been all outgoings and no income. You, as well as many other investors, I fear, have been duped.'

'Well someone must have benefited from all this,' Calvin said, 'and I've got a good idea who that someone is.'

Brighton replaced his glasses. 'Well cut your losses, your Lordship,' he said. 'Fortunately you can afford one or two mistakes without too much of a problem but I should fire whoever was advising you; he doesn't know what he's talking about.'

'Oh, I think he does,' Calvin said softly. 'Thank you, Brighton, you have cleared up a number of puzzles for me. I'm grateful for your time.' He held out his hand. 'Perhaps we can do business together again, I could do with a sound adviser, it seems.'

When he was alone, Calvin sat at his desk and stared down at the books. His thoughts were in chaos. He could understand Simples taking him for a ride, but Arian? She seemed so straight in her dealings, so patently honest. He pushed the books away. Well, he would reserve his judgement until he had spoken to her.

As for that charlatan Simples, he should be handed over to the proper authorities as soon as he returned from France. The man had feathered his own nest very nicely during the time he had been working at Stormhill. Had he corrupted Arian too? Was it possible?

There was a knock on the door and the maid bobbed a curtsy. 'A lady to see you, sir,' she said, 'a Mrs Frogmore. She says it's urgent.'

'All right, show her in.' Calvin leaned back in his chair, his anger mounting. Women were all liars and cheats, hadn't he learned that yet? They always wanted something from a man – if it wasn't money it was something else.

Sarah was flushed and her eyes were shining as she looked at him. 'There's glad I am you let me in,' she said and in her excitement her Welsh accent was marked.

'What did you want to see me about?' he said flatly. 'Did you want me to play the stud again? If so, forget it. I'm not in the mood for granting favours.'

Sarah shook her head. 'I'm going to have a baby,' she said softly. 'Your baby, and I'm so happy.'

'Well at least someone is.' Calvin felt slightly uneasy. His instinct to hurt vanished in the face of Sarah's joy and he couldn't help but feel a pang of conscience that he had made the girl with child, knowing that he would not have the responsibilities of fatherhood.

'Sit down,' he said. 'Tell me, what does your husband say about all this?'

'He's left me,' she said simply. 'Geoffrey doesn't care for women, you see.'

Calvin digested her remarks in silence. He felt as if a noose was tightening round him. 'I'm not sure I understand,' he said. 'You already have a child by your husband don't you?'

Sarah smiled. 'He took me as he would take a dose of medicine, an heir was necessary to him, you see.' She came towards where Calvin was seated and rested her hand on his shoulder. 'Lord Temple, Calvin, *Duw*, I think I have fallen in love with you.'

Calvin rose to his feet and stared down at her, knowing he had been foolish in having anything to do with her. 'That's just too bad, Sarah,' he said. 'I am not in love with you. There was never any question of love between us. In any case, you're a married woman and you have obligations to your husband, whatever you might think about him. And then there's your son.'

'And what about our child?' Sarah rested her hand on her stomach. 'He will be a fine boy, I just know he will. Don't you want a son?'

Oh, he wanted a son, all right. A son with silver-gold hair, a son with the fine characteristics of Arian Smale. He wanted a *legitimate* son. What he did not want was to be tied, however tenuously, to a woman like Sarah Frogmore.

'Be discreet,' he said quietly. 'I have just divorced my wife for doing what you have done. I'm not proud of my behaviour but it's done now and it seems you've got what you want. But remember you would have a great deal to lose if Geoffrey Frogmore were to disown you publicly. As it is, the child will be presumed to be his, you yourself said just that. You do understand the position, don't you?'

'There's a question! Of course I understand, I'm not dull,' Sarah said and Calvin could see that she was stung by his attitude. 'I came here to tell you about the baby. I don't mean to talk all over Swansea about it.' There was the hint of tears in her voice and Calvin softened.

'I'm sorry,' he said. 'I really do apologize, I'm a lout. Come along, sit down. We shall have some tea.'

Sarah began to cry quite suddenly and Calvin stared at her in confusion. For a moment he stood there feeling helpless and then, awkwardly he put his arm around her. She looked up at him hopefully. 'Say you'll see me, just sometimes, just as a friend?'

'Yes, of course I will.' He patted her shoulder, knowing that he had let himself in for more than he had bargained for when he had taken Sarah Frogmore to his bed. He turned away from her, closing his eyes and all he could see, behind his closed lids, was the delicate face of Arian Smale.

It was early the next morning when Arian returned to Stormhill and Calvin, seeing her standing in the hallway, her bag at her feet, felt warmth and love well up within him. She appeared tired, her face was pale, her eyes shadowed. She couldn't be involved with this man Simples. She was ignorant of what he had been doing, she must be.

'We must talk,' he said. 'You must tell me where Simples is, there's a matter I must have out with him.' He was leading the way towards the study but Arian stood still in the hallway, her shoulders slumped.

183

'Please, I must get some sleep,' her voice was cracking with fatigue. 'The journey from France, it was so tiring.'

'Of course,' he said contritely, going to her, putting his hand on her shoulder, looking down into her glorious eyes. 'You sleep, Arian. Sleep all you like and then we must spend some time together, we have a great deal to discuss.' He watched as she slowly climbed the stairs. Love overwhelmed him. Why had he not spoken of it before? There was so much time missed. He wanted Arian Smale and her absence had made him realize just how much.

Well he was a free man now and could do what he liked, marry whom he wished and with all his heart, he wished to have Arian as his wife.

Impatiently he watched the clock. It was growing dark and still there was no sign of Arian reappearing from her room. At last he could bear it no longer. He took a lamp and mounted the stairs. He quietly opened the door to her bedroom and saw that she had fallen into bed in her shift, her bare arm hugged the pillow as if for comfort. She was so beautiful, so heart-rendingly beautiful that he longed to sweep her into his arms.

She opened her eyes as though aware of his regard and, for a moment he thought he saw his love reflected in her eyes. Then she looked away.

'Arian,' he said softly, 'Arian, I've missed you so much.' She was silent for a long moment. Then she sat up and the sight of the soft swell of her breasts made him catch his breath.

'I've got something to tell you,' she said desperately. 'Gerald Simples and I, well, we were married in France.'

Calvin felt as though someone had slapped him across the face. 'I don't believe it,' he said. 'You don't even like the man. He must have forced you.'

'Stop,' Arian held up her hand. 'Calvin, such a lot of things have happened since I left here. I've learned things, things perhaps better left unsaid.'

'He's blackmailed you, that's it, isn't it?' He had taken her shoulders and was shaking her and her silver hair tumbled across her pale face. 'What has that bastard got over you? You would never marry him of your own free will.'

Arian sighed heavily. 'Please don't ask me any more questions. I'm his wife, I'm married to Gerald Simples, that's all that matters.'

'You've slept with him?' Calvin could not believe it, she and Simples lying together. The thought made him sick with anger and jealousy.

'Yes,' her voice was low. 'I've been to his bed.' She looked away from him but he could not let it rest.

'He forced himself on you, that's it isn't it?' he asked almost desperately. Arian shook her head.

'No, I went to him willingly,' she said staring at him challengingly.

Calvin rose to his feet. 'But he made you, somehow he made you. You didn't enjoy his attentions did you?'

'Yes, of course I did,' Arian said fiercely. 'Why else would I have consented to be his wife?'

'The man is a charlatan,' Calvin ground out the words. 'He's a crook. I'll expose him to the world for what he is.'

'Don't bother,' Arian said. 'He is probably in a French jail at this very moment serving time for something he didn't do, not intentionally anyway.'

'What do you mean?' Calvin asked flatly. He was puzzled. 'Why should he be in a *French* jail . . .?' He broke off. It was pointless to voice any accusations at this moment, in any event, it seemed that justice was being done; Simples was paying for his crime of embezzlement. 'They suspect him then, the French authorities?'

'He's facing prison whatever.' Arian turned her face away from him. 'Please, go away, leave me alone. I'm tired of men and problems. I just want to be left by myself.'

Calvin moved to the door. 'I don't understand any of this.' His tone was bitter. 'Why you should side with Simples is just beyond me, but then women always have a way of letting me down. I suppose I'm a fool to trust any one of them, even you.' He couldn't keep the edge of sarcasm from his voice.

'Perhaps when you are less tired we can talk about my accounts and you can tell me just what Simples has been up to.'

He left the room, his throat thick with what he could only describe as anger. Never would he admit that the moisture glazing his eyes was tears.

Gerald Simples sat in the small café on the Rue du Bois with his friend Mr Bertrand seated opposite him. 'Well, Gerald, so your wife has gone home before you?'

Gerald smiled. 'I shall soon join her and will be all the richer for our little venture.'

'Ah, you've come out of it well, a small fortune and a beautiful wife – what more could any man ask?'

'You've had your fair share,' Gerald said evenly. He sipped the strong black coffee and leaned back in his chair, stretching his legs before him. 'Soon I'll go home, though I doubt I'll work for Calvin Temple again.'

'You mean he may have found out about your leetle, shall we call it, an enterprise?' Bertrand's thick eyebrows were raised. 'It's possible, the man is no fool so I've heard.'

'He has so much money I doubt he'll miss a little slice of it,' Gerald said, 'and if my little scheme has been discovered, I've my insurance, haven't I?'

'Ah, your little Arian, your lovely wife. You think his lordship is in love with her?'

'I'm sure of it,' Gerald said easily. 'He wouldn't prosecute me, not once he knows I'm married to his little love.'

'But she is beautiful. It must be good to have such a beauty warming your bed. Is she eager, this Arian?'

'Not eager,' Gerald smiled, 'but willing enough, I've made sure of that.'

'How so?' Bertrand's large hand encompassed his coffee cup and he swallowed the bitter drink in one gulp.

'Oh, I have my methods.' Gerald said, wondering at the pinch of disquiet the thought of Arian's obvious love for Calvin Temple gave him.

'You are not falling in love with your wife are you?' Bertrand sounded knowing. 'It is no surprise, my friend. I would fall in love too if I had such luck.'

Gerald had no place for love in his life. Arian was an obsession that would pass and he needed her as his insurance against Calvin's wrath when, and if, his scheme was discovered.

He couldn't fall in love with her; Arian had known other men, indeed, his own cousin Price had possessed her. Gerald had married her with his eyes wide open, she was no shrinking virgin and yet his being stirred when he thought of her so soft beneath him. It excited him to know he could possess her body whenever he chose – she had made a bargain and she would stick to it – and yet it irked to know he would never possess the inner core of her.

'You have gone all, what you say? broody, Gerald. Missing your little wife, you see. Hadn't you better go home to her before she gets into mischief with some other man? Ah, but you cannot, she thinks you are in jail. Right now, she will be feeling sad for you, no? It will do her good. Absence has a way of warming a woman's heart.'

Gerald doubted it, she was probably relieved to be away from him, to be back beneath the roof of the man she really loved. The thought, surprisingly, had the power to give him pain.

'Aye, she thinks I am in jail,' Gerald said. 'She will wait for me to come back to her, she's a woman of her word. She might want another man but she won't take one, not now. By the time I get home, she will be filled with remorse, thinking I've languished in prison.' He paused. 'You know, Bertrand, we will have to think up a good reason for my release.'

Bertrand laughed, throwing back his head. 'Poor petite, she does not know that there is no charge against you, not here in France, at least. Now back in England, that is a different matter. It is there that you have been so clever, diverting funds from his lordship's coffers into our pockets.' He rose to his feet. 'As for an excuse, I should just say there was too leetle evidence against you. That, my dear fellow sounds plausible enough. Come, Gerald, it is time we had a little fun, no good sitting around feeling the need for a woman. I know a nice little house where the girls are all young and willing to please.'

Gerald put some coins on the damp table top and followed Bertrand reluctantly. He somehow didn't feel the need for a woman, not for anyone other than Arian.

But that was foolish of him. He should not allow himself to be dependent on any woman; they only hurt you in the end, abandoned you as his mother had done. No, Arian was nothing to him, just a tool in his little plans, for he would make more money from Lord Calvin Temple, he was determined on it.

The House of Ladies was in one of the back streets of the town. There the lamps filtered a soft light over the large room where men sat drinking freely of the wine that was poured by a young servant girl.

Bertrand spoke to the madam in French and he and Gerald were led straight away up the carpeted stairs towards the bedrooms. 'I want Collete,' Bertrand's tone was firm, 'you, my friend, can have whoever you want. I will see you sometime, I do not promise when.' He added with a grin '*Bon voyage*, my friend.'

Gerald stood alone in the small bedroom and stared around at the silk drapes and the soft lights, feeling as though he was in some sort of unpleasant dream. A young girl entered quietly, her breasts revealed by the thin robe she wore. Her face was rouged and her eyes lit up when she saw that her customer was a personable young man.

She came close to him. Her perfume was cloying, her hands were busy at his belt. Suddenly Gerald knew that he didn't want this, not any of it, not the soft lights nor the attentions of the young whore. He held her away from him, handed her some money and then, deliberately, he left the room.

'Now that you are rested, perhaps you'll be good enough to explain exactly what has been going on.' His voice was cold, distant, and Arian looked up at Calvin Temple as he stood over her, an accuser rather than the man she loved.

'I don't know what you mean,' she said evasively, wondering how much he knew about the swindle and how much, if anything, he had gained from it. 'What do you think has been going on?'

'Don't play games, Arian.' Calvin thrust his hands into his pockets, 'What I *know* is that I've been swindled out of rather a lot of money.'

'*You've* been swindled!' Arian repeated his words in bewilderment. 'But you were the only one who gained anything from the whole sorry business.'

'Gained? What are you talking about? I have lost close on two thousand sovereigns, that is an awful lot of money by anyone's book.'

Arian looked at him searchingly. Could he be speaking the truth? If so, what were the implications for Gerald Simples?

'But the policeman in France said you were involved. I saw your signature on the documents.'

'Huh!' Calvin was angry. 'No you didn't. And if I have made a loss, others might have come out of this with pockets well lined. But not me.'

Arian had married Gerald Simples to save Calvin's good name and now it seemed that her sacrifice was for nothing.

'But Gerald has gone to prison. He's taking the responsibility instead of you.' Her confusion was mounting.

'I doubt that!' Calvin said. 'He might have told you he would be imprisoned but he'll be back any day, just mark my words. He will suddenly have been miraculously released.'

'I don't believe it,' Arian said. 'It can't be true. Gerald wouldn't go to such lengths just to make me his wife.'

189

'He might, if it involved making himself a small fortune into the bargain,' Calvin said raggedly.

Arian put her hands to her hot cheeks. 'But I believed him,' she said. 'I've been so foolish . . .' Her voice trailed away. 'You are telling me everything, aren't you?'

Calvin stared at her with hard eyes and she flinched. 'Are *you* telling *me* everything, Arian? That's more to the point.'

Arian sighed softly. 'I thought you'd go to prison, I thought the French police had a case against you. You're sure you couldn't be blamed in any way?'

She bit her lip, staring up doubtfully at Calvin. If Gerald had been lying, he'd backed up the lies with convincing proof. Could it be he had friends among the French police?

'Arian.' Calvin took her hands in his and she closed her eyes, resisting the longing to cling to him. 'Arian, I think we've both been taken in but somehow we'll make this all right. I'll see that your marriage is annulled, if that's what you want.'

He bent towards her, his lips close to hers and Arian leaned against him, wanting him to make things right for her. 'God, I can't even think straight.' Her voice was low, despairing.

She wanted to tell Calvin that she loved him, that she wanted only him, that it pained her to give herself to another man but that she'd done it for him.

There was a loud knocking on the door. Arian saw Calvin shake his head impatiently. Reluctantly he released her hands.

Arian moved quickly towards the window. She didn't want Bella or any of the other servants to see how distressed she was. Half hidden by the curtains, she saw the door burst open and Sarah Frogmore push her way, past the startled servant, into the room.

'Oh, Calvin,' Sarah's voice was shaking, 'I had to come. Please comfort me. I've been so ill. I've lost the baby, our baby and I can never have another one, not ever. Oh,

Calvin, I feel so distraught, so alone. I didn't know who else I could turn to.'

Sarah pressed herself against him, her face against his shoulder and awkwardly he put his arms around her. 'I'm so unhappy,' Sarah said in a muffled voice. 'I wanted this baby, your baby, so very much.'

Shock waves washed over Arian – she couldn't believe what she was hearing. She saw Calvin give her an agonized look before she slipped from the room. Men, they were all cheats and liars; hadn't she learned that about them yet? How many lessons did she need before she stopped being fooled?

She hurried up to her room and picked up her bag. She would get right away from here, leave all the lies and deceit behind her. She never wanted to see Calvin Temple again. And as for Gerald Simples, when he did come back with some made-up story of how he had been released, it would be to the realization that he had no wife, except in name, for she would never lie in his bed again.

CHAPTER THIRTEEN

The main road wound through the small village of Clydach
along the same line as the turgid waters of the canal. There
were few houses in the village, some of them meandering
up the slope of the wooded hillside like white mushrooms
grown at random. A sprinkling of public houses had been
strategically built along the main thoroughfare for the
convenience of the local colliers and, towards the perimeter
of the village where the road led to Pontardawe stood the
beginnings of what was to be a new nickel works, the dream
of Ludwig Mond and Carl Langer.

Near the centre of the village was a small shop, the
windows and entrance hung with boots and shoes. The sign
above the door, newly painted, read: Davies and Son, boot
and shoe repairers and manufacturers.

Eline Temple was seated at a desk at the corner of a
workroom. She had a pencil in her hand and there was an
unfinished drawing on the sheet of paper before her. She
looked up suddenly and smiled.

'Good girl, Arian. You've finished those boots for Jono
the Mond, I see.' She leaned on her elbows and chewed the
end of her pencil.

At the long workbench sat Arian Smale, her small mouth
sprouting the nails she'd been using on the heavy sole of the
boot on her last. She took the nails carefully from between
her lips.

'Aye, I've finished them, finally, but I hope Will doesn't
get me too many customers like that one. Gone through to
the uppers, Jono had, and him with feet like a cart horse.'

Eline's eyes were suddenly dreamy. 'It's good to have
work though, isn't it? We seem to be doing all right, up
here in Clydach, touch wood.' She smiled wryly. 'With us

all pulling together, we're bound to make a success of the business, if you can grace our little enterprise with such an elevated name.'

Silence followed her words and Eline, watching Arian shrewdly, saw the frown between her fair eyebrows and guessed something of what she was feeling. If the enterprise they were engaged in was small, then Arian's part in it was infinitesimal. It must be hard for Arian to be a cog in the wheel when she'd harboured fond hopes of going it alone. Arian was probably feeling at this moment that she'd failed dismally.

'Your newspaper pieces are bringing in a bit of extra money.' Eline felt the need to encourage Arian. 'Very clever you are with words. It all helps, mind.'

Arian didn't reply and Eline rose to her feet and moved towards her, resting her hand on the girl's shoulder. She was far too thin. Eline felt a dart of concern.

'Perhaps you should ease up on the heavy work around here, do more writing – you've obviously got a talent for it and we've certainly gained some publicity from it.'

Arian met her eyes. 'Well, at least I'm good at something then, better at writing than at selling leather or making shoes.' Her tone was dry. 'Still, you're right. We're not doing too badly, when it comes down to it.' She hesitated as though she were about to confide in Eline and then the moment passed. 'We needed to get away from Swansea,' she said briskly, 'and if I've never mentioned it before, I'm grateful to you for giving me a job.'

Eline watched Arian place the carefully polished boots on the workbench and rub at her eyes with slender fingers. There was a deep sadness there, hidden away behind the girl's tough exterior, and it was not difficult to recognize the reason why. Clearly her marriage to Gerald Simples had not been a success, it had lasted for such a short time. Things must have gone badly wrong. Arian refused to use her married name even when she wrote her pieces for the local press. She was, it seemed, hiding behind a pen-name. It was almost as though she feared her husband might come after her. Well, if Arian wanted to confide her feelings then she would, in her own time.

'I'm glad you came to ask me for work,' Eline said. 'Quite frankly we couldn't have managed without your help. You were a godsend, believe me.'

'I don't know about that. You could have employed a much more experienced cobbler than me, somebody with strong hands and plenty of practice.'

'Ah, yes, but none of them would have worked for just bed and board. In any case, most of the cobblers have families. We couldn't uproot them and bring them here, could we? You, Arian were an answer to our prayers.'

'The arrangement suited us both, then.' Arian picked up a cloth and absent-mindedly polished the leather uppers of the boots she'd just repaired, her long hair swinging over her shoulders in a shimmering curtain.

She really was a beautiful girl, such delicate skin, such fine features. Eline smiled to herself. Good thing Will only had eyes for her, if he had been a womanizer he might well have had his head turned by Arian's delicate looks.

Eline's heart melted at the thought of him. Will had been so angry at the way Eline had been treated by the people of World's End, he'd have gone out and fought the whole of the town if it would have spared Eline pain. Instead, he had accepted her suggestion that they make a fresh start somewhere outside the boundaries of Swansea.

How strange fate was, Eline mused. Arian wanted to be free of her marriage vows and Eline couldn't wait to tie herself to Will in holy matrimony. Soon now, she told herself, very soon, they would be married. Then they could both begin to put the past behind them.

Eline bit her lip. She would try to forget her unhappy marriage to Calvin Temple and all the pain and misery of the divorce. What was past was dead and gone and she must try to look to the future.

Will would be her third husband; she had made two wrong marriages but she knew that this one would bring her lasting happiness.

'*Duw*,' Arian's voice broke into her thoughts, 'you look so happy sitting there. I envy you, Eline, you know that?'

Eline was startled out of her reverie. 'I suppose I'm very lucky but things haven't always gone easy for me, as you well know. I was just thinking about Calvin, how foolish I was to think we could be happy together. I've made an awful lot of mistakes in my life but that must have been the worst.'

She looked at Arian who had suddenly bent her head, her cheeks flushed. 'I know what you mean,' Arian's voice was low. 'I've made my own share of mistakes, too, but you are so happy now, you shine with it.'

'What are you looking for in life, Arian?'

'Something I can't have.' Arian looked directly at Eline. 'I'd give anything to be with one of your "mistakes". I'm in love with Calvin Temple. That's a big laugh, isn't it?'

Eline felt shock waves run through her. Arian and Calvin? She couldn't picture them together somehow and yet why should she be surprised? Arian had worked in Stormhill for some time, had been close to Calvin. Even Eline had to admit that he was a handsome man, a good man. He wasn't to blame for any of the unhappiness in their marriage – she was.

'Perhaps I shouldn't have mentioned it,' Arian said. 'He was your husband and I realize there was bad feeling between you. I love him and there's no point in denying it.'

'Why in heaven's name did you marry Gerald Simples, then?'

'It's a long story.' There was an edge of bitterness in Arian's voice and Eline felt she had probed enough.

'Well, here in this lovely little village, we can make a fresh start,' Eline said cheerfully. 'No-one knows us, or anything about us, except that we make and mend the best shoes the villagers will ever see.'

She sighed. 'I can't pretend I don't miss Swansea – the sea, the rolling sands, the beautiful parklands.'

Arian gave a short laugh. 'Not forgetting the stink from the copper works and the smoke that forever hangs over Kilvey Hill!'

'Well, there is that,' Eline conceded, 'but I suppose I was always lucky. The places where I lived were away from the worst of the dust and smoke.' She lifted her head, listening. 'My son is awake,' she said, smiling. 'I thought the peace was lasting rather a long time. I'll leave you to carry on here and I'll make us all a bit of dinner. I'm starving.'

She took off her leather apron and hung it up on the hook. 'Not that I've been much practical help to you anyway, too busy at my drawings for that.' Eline frowned. It had been one disadvantage of moving to Clydach that she'd had to conceal her reputation as a well-known shoemaker – it appeared to the villagers that she was just a cobbler – but the sacrifice was a small one. Soon she would build up a name for herself again. This was a fresh start, for Arian as well as for Eline.

She moved along the shadowed passageway. The old walls, she noticed, needed a coat of whitewash and there was a damp patch near the ceiling. It was not her property, none of her business if it deteriorated, and yet the thought saddened her.

Eline made her way towards the kitchen, her thoughts busy. There was a lot of headway to make in the business – there was little money coming in and her family still needed to be fed. She sighed. The bit of meat left over from Sunday would have to do; sliced with hot vegetables, it would make a passable enough dinner.

Eline felt her spirits lighten. Soon now, Will would finish making his deliveries. He would come home, take her in his arms and kiss her, and then everything, the hardships, the poverty, all would seem worthwhile.

Arian hoisted the basket of boots higher on her arm. Her load was lighter now that she had made most of her deliveries. She had collected quite a lot of money for the repairs and by God they needed to make some profit somewhere. The last few days business had been slow, to say the least. She glanced up at the evening sky. It was still pale with late sunshine but the clouds were beginning to gather, threatening rain.

The smell of fresh bread drifted towards her from the bakehouse and Arian realized quite suddenly that she was hungry. Eline did her best, cooking nourishing meals with very little means at her disposal but Arian was beginning to feel she was a burden, straining the small resources of the family to the limit.

Fish was cheap, coming up from Swansea Docks but there were only so many ways of making fish appetizing and today, Arian had declined to eat with Eline and Will. Now she was sorry.

Still, she had no cause to complain. At least she had a roof over her head and a job to do and, more to the point, she was well away from the sight of Gerald Simples.

She had, at the first opportunity, taken the wedding ring from her finger and thrown it into the sea, as if by that act she could break the ties that bound her to him. When she had come to Clydach she had reverted to her maiden name, unwilling to be called Mrs Simples a moment longer.

Arian still burned with anger when she thought of how Simples had coerced her into marrying him and, worse, had tricked her into going into his bed. She shuddered as she recalled his embraces and her cheeks flamed as she remembered doing his bidding, helping him to take his pleasure of her. Well one day he would pay dearly for what he had done.

She stopped at the cottage on the edge of the hillside and knocked at the door which was standing slightly ajar.

'*Bore da*, Miss Smale.' Jono Morgan was smiling down at her; a big, beefy man who had worked on the planning of the new nickel works that were coming to Clydach. Already he was an admirer.

'Good morning, to you too, Jono,' she replied. 'I've brought your boots back. Worked hard on them, I did, mind.' It was with amusement she realized she was falling into the Welsh pattern of speech, influenced no doubt by the people in the village.

'Come in, *merchi*. Have a sit down by here in the kitchen. Look fagged out, you do.'

Arian followed him into the warm kitchen that smelled of meat freshly roasted and she swallowed hard as she set down her basket.

'*Duw*, there's pale you are,' Jono said gently. 'I'll make us a nice cup of tea, shall I?'

'Please. Something smells nice.' Arian glanced towards the oven beside which a bright fire burned. 'Just about to have your supper, were you?'

'Aye, I was that. Like to take food with me, Miss Smale? Honoured I'd be, mind.'

Arian hesitated and Jono, seeing her hesitation, spoke quickly. 'It's settled. You'll stay. Miserable, it is, breaking bread alone.'

Arian felt soothed and rested as she sat in the cosy room watching Jono deftly cut the roast meat into slices. Beside the meat, he spooned a mound of vegetables and Arian smiled.

'I'm a woman, not a horse,' she said in amusement. 'I'll never eat all that.'

'Well do your best, *merchi*, and what you don't want you leave, right?'

It was strange and rather nice being called a girl by this big Welshman. Jono was not handsome. His face was rugged, pitted with blue scars that betrayed his past. Sometime, Jono must have worked the mines, his cuts and grazes becoming impregnated with coal dust but now he was to be something high up in the works.

'Know me next time, will you?' Jono was smiling and Arian became aware that she was staring at him. She returned his smile.

'Aye, I'll know you, Jono the Mond. How could I forget such an ugly face then?'

'Oh, a pretty compliment, I must say!' Jono pretended indignation. 'And I thought I was winning you over with my charm.'

'Winning me over with your cooking, more like,' Arian said. 'This meat is done to a turn. You'll make someone a fine wife one day.'

'I can cook when I have to but I'd rather have a pretty young girl in my house, serving my food.' Jono had stopped smiling and Arian realized she'd led him into what was becoming a far too personal line of conversation.

'I'm sure you've had more than your fair share of those,' she said briskly. They ate in companionable silence and then Arian sat back in her chair with a sigh of gratification. 'That was lovely. Now then, about your boots.' She pushed away her empty plate. 'I think you'll find them satisfactory, though try not to wear them down quite so much next time. You'd gone through to the uppers.'

Her attempt to change the subject fell on deaf ears. Jono leaned across the table and imprisoned her hand in his. 'I've had my fair share of young ladies, yes, more than my fair share if the truth be told, but never a girl I wanted to spend the rest of my life with.'

Arian sighed. 'I'm sorry, Jono.' She knew she would have to be honest with him. 'I'm not a single girl, I'm married.'

He jerked back from her, his eyebrows raised. 'Married? Well where's your husband, then? What's he thinking about, letting you run about the countryside alone?'

'It was a mistake,' Arian said. 'The marriage, I mean. I didn't love him and when I found he'd cheated on me, I left him.'

'Duw,' Jono said, 'that took a bit of guts.' He stopped in confusion. 'I don't suppose I should be so familiar seeing as you are a married lady, but I can't think of you as anything but a pretty little girl.'

Arian was flattered. Jono was an honest man and she felt able to trust him with the truth. 'He'll be back from France some day, I suppose, and I don't want him to find me, so please, Jono, don't talk about this to anyone.'

'A man who cheats on you with another woman must be a real waster,' Jono said misinterpreting what Arian had told him. 'Deserves a good hiding, does a rat like that.'

Arian decided to let him believe what he wished, it was far too complicated to explain matters to him. She rose to her feet.

'Well, thank you for a lovely supper.' She looked longingly at the big piece of beef standing on the table. How Eline and Will would love to get their teeth into that.

'Why don't you take this with you?' Jono said, quickly wrapping the meat in a muslin cloth. 'I don't want any more of it and I can't be bothered storing the stuff.'

Arian bit her lip. Jono's kindness touched her deeply. She rested a hand on his arm.

'I wish I could have fallen in love with a man like you, Jono,' she said softly. 'I know you would have cherished me and cared for me . . .' she smiled to relieve the intensity of the moment, 'and kept me well fed into the bargain.'

'Well if ever you need me, I will be here. That is a promise,' Jono said softly.

Arian was aware of him watching as she moved away up the valley road. At least, she thought warmly, because of Jono she was able to take a fine supper home to Eline and Will.

She sighed heavily. This period of hardship was only temporary, she felt it in her bones. There must be better than this in her future. She hoisted the heavy basket higher and taking a deep breath, walked forward with her head high.

Gerald Simples stepped down from the gang plank, glad to leave the unsteady deck of the *Marie Clare* behind him. The master was beginning to get on his nerves. Paul Marchant asked too many questions.

He stared around him, drinking in the familiar scents of Swansea Docks. The salt air and the smell of tar mingled with the acrid stench of fish being unloaded from one of the ships. He thrust his hand into his pocket, staring around him uncertainly. He wondered if he should go to Arian's office on the quayside or take the road straight to Stormhill.

He was slightly uneasy about his reception. It was more than probable that Calvin Temple would still be in ignorance about the way his funds had been diverted but there was always that unlucky chance that, over the past weeks, the books might have been properly scrutinized.

He smiled to himself. He was worrying about nothing. It was unlikely that there would be any hitches in his plans. In all probability, he would continue quite happily investing Temple's money. From now on, he would be careful to take only the occasional 'commission' from the funds. It didn't do to become greedy.

The French end of things he'd managed quite well – a few pockets lined, a bribe here and there, and his connection with the fraudulent company was hushed up. Money usually did the trick, he found, whatever country he was in. The fact that he spoke fluent French also helped oil the wheels on this occasion.

He sighed. It would be good to see his wife again. Arian had submitted most sweetly to his desires and if she wasn't entirely enthusiastic about the marriage, he could put up with that. How many wives were eager in the bedchamber? Not many, if bar-room gossip was anything to go by.

He decided to go by the office first and set out briskly along the quayside. Soon, he thought warmly, he would hold Arian in his arms, take possession of her lithe young body. And if he could never own her soul, so be it.

The office was closed and, peering into the windows, Gerald saw that the desk was covered in dust. It was quite obvious that no-one had occupied the place for some time.

His uneasiness growing, he made his way out of the docks and along the huddle of crowded streets that flanked the harbour, wondering if anything could have happened to Arian. He could only hope that she'd remained in ignorance of what he'd done. If she ever found him out, he could kiss goodbye to her co-operation. She would have nothing more to do with him.

On the hillside, the air was cooler and fresher, the breeze coming in from the sweep of Swansea Bay sweet and clean. It was here on the grassy slopes of Mount Pleasant and the Uplands that the rich of the town had their big houses, fine houses built for style and elegance, built to withstand the ravages of time.

Stormhill stood out from the other buildings, the sheer size and elegance of it dwarfing the surrounding houses so that they shrank into insignificance beneath the crenellated towers and sprouting chimneys of the manor house.

Gerald walked around the back of the building and entered through the kitchen door, breathing in the familiar smells with a sudden, unexpected sense of home-coming. Gerald had never had a real home – he had been little more than a tolerated guest wherever he'd lived.

Mrs Bob was working as usual, rolling pastry, sleeves pushed up above plump elbows. Gerald nodded to her, aware of the curiosity in her glance but, without pausing, he climbed the stairs to the back hallways. The sooner he saw Temple the better.

'Bella!' Gerald called to the young maid, and after a moment she appeared from one of the large rooms, her eyes wide.

'Bella, is his lordship at home?' he asked, his eyes shrewd as he saw the flustered look on the girl's face. Something had happened in his absence, but what?

'He's in the study. Shall I tell him you're here, Mr Simples?' Bella sounded breathless.

'Wait a moment,' Gerald said. 'Where is Arian? Is she at home?'

'Oh, she's gone away, Mr Simples.' Bella clasped her hands together in an agony of embarrassment. 'Went off sudden-like, she did. Don't know where, mind.'

Gerald felt cold. It was clear that his plans had gone awry but how much did his lordship know?

'Go and announce me then, what are you waiting for?' he said abruptly.

Lord Temple was seated at his desk, a pen in his hand, some open books on the table before him. Gerald knew then that the worst had happened – the fraud had been discovered. He mentally shook himself, nothing could be proven. So he had made a mistake, it happened.

Temple was silent, waiting for Gerald to speak. He cleared his throat. 'Is anything wrong, Lord Temple?' he asked solicitously.

'I should have thought you would know better than to ask that, Simples.' Temple sounded as though he was making an effort to contain his temper.

'I'm sorry, sir,' Gerald's composure held. 'I realize that the entire operation has failed. The French calf company was not the sound investment I thought it was. I can only apologize and try to make it up to you.'

'It seems *any* investment you made on my behalf was doomed to failure. It's clear you've embezzled large amounts of money.'

'Not embezzlement, surely, sir,' Gerald said calmly. 'I, and Arian too, made those payments and investments in good faith. It was never possible to know that this company was shaky.'

Calvin Temple rose to his feet then, his face red. 'I could forget the matter of the money,' he said icily, 'it might indeed have been an ill-advised move on your part.' He paused as if to gain control. 'What I can't forgive is that you coerced Arian into marriage, a marriage she didn't want. You used her regard for me to blackmail her into your bed.'

Gerald feigned astonishment. 'Is that what she told you?' he asked.

'Are you denying it?' Temple moved a pace forward as though to attack him but Gerald stood his ground.

'I did Arian a favour,' he said calmly. 'I married her to save her from a French jail. At first the authorities were holding *her* responsible for the whole débâcle. Then, sir, they turned their attention to your part in all this.' He shrugged in what he hoped was a self-deprecating manner.

'I had to work damn hard to get the charges against us dropped, believe me.'

'Arian said nothing about any charges.' Temple sounded uncertain now and Gerald felt a moment of triumph.

'Where is she?' he asked. 'I shall ask her to tell you the truth, all of it.'

'How can I believe you?' Temple rubbed at his hair. 'How can I believe either of you?'

Gerald sighed. 'Go to France yourself, sir. Look at the police records, if you wish. Arian was held in custody until I took responsibility for her. It was only because I took the step of marrying her that she was set free. The police practically stood over us until the ceremony was performed. It was what she wanted, what we both wanted.'

'Get out of my sight.' Temple turned away. 'You deserve each other. I don't think either of you would know the truth if it bit you. Go, leave my house and be thankful you are not facing charges here in Swansea.'

Gerald left the room. This was not the outcome he had hoped for but at least he was walking away a free man. He packed his few possessions and left Stormhill, if with some regrets then with a sigh of relief too. All in all, things had not worked out too badly.

He retraced his footsteps down the hillside. He would find good clean lodgings, make himself comfortable. It would need to be somewhere modest, at least for now – wouldn't do to be seen splashing money about.

Money he had, quite a lot of it; all he wanted now was to find his wife and bring her home. In this, the law of the land was with him, he had the right to bring her to his home whatever her protests. Arian might not come willingly to his bed now, as she'd done in France but she was his wife and as such, she would have to learn obedience. He smiled in anticipation, he would very much enjoy teaching her.

CHAPTER FOURTEEN

Sarah looked around her at the elegant drawing room, the luxurious carpets, the matching drapes, with wry amusement. She had everything a woman could desire, a lovely house, a generous allowance, and yet she had nothing.

She hadn't realized how much she would miss Geoffrey. His presence had been a constant source of reassurance, allowing her a rightful place in society. More, he had given her the feeling of being needed, loved almost. Except in the bedchamber, he had been an exemplary husband. And now he had left her.

Her son, of course, she yearned for. She longed for the touch of his soft cheek against hers, the feel of his silky hair beneath her hands and yet, strangely, she missed Geoffrey's gentle presence almost as much.

She couldn't blame him for walking out on her, not now that she'd had time to reflect on her actions. She had shamed him, taken away his dignity by going to the bed of another man and it had all been in vain, there was to be no child.

Sarah had been devastated when she had miscarried Calvin Temple's baby. She had remained in her bed for days, tended by a hired nurse, a stranger who naturally assumed the child was the product of a happy marriage. But since the nurse had departed, there had been nothing but the loneliness of empty days and even emptier nights. The staff she'd grown used to were gone to Geoffrey's new house and just a few new servants employed to replace them. Hardest of all to bear was the almost certain knowledge that after her ordeal, there would be no more pregnancies.

She rose to her feet. She must see Geoffrey, must speak with him, beg his forgiveness. Perhaps he would come back to her. It was a faint hope and she knew it but at least she must try.

She walked into town, bemoaning the fact that Geoffrey had left her no transport of her own. He had taken the elegant carriage the groom kept polished to perfection and even the stable of fine horses was gone. The big house had become like a deserted ship, she thought in sorrow.

Once in town, she was able to take a cab to Geoffrey's new home on the outskirts of Swansea. She sat in the worn leather seat, hearing the turning of the wheels and the sound of horses' hooves with a sense of isolation. No-one cared if she lived or died, she might as well resign herself to that fact, she told herself gloomily.

Geoffrey's new home was modest, settled in the folds of the hillside overlooking Mumbles Bay. The wash of the sea soothed Sarah and as she climbed down from the carriage a slant of sunlight warmed her. She moved towards the door feeling a little more optimistic.

'Want me to wait?' the driver called after her. 'It will cost a bit more, mind, but it might be worth it, you won't find another cab out by here in a hurry.'

Sarah scarcely looked at him. 'My husband will take me back into town,' she said and then added, 'Thank you,' in a voice that was anything but gracious.

The driver flicked the reigns and the horse jerked the carriage into movement, and Sarah watched for a moment before squaring her shoulders and turning once more towards the house.

'Sunrise' was a two-storeyed building with a flat frontage made of mellow stone. The windows were small. The place was little more than a glorified cottage, no place to bring up her son, she thought indignantly.

She was about to ring the bell hanging outside the porch when she heard the sound of laughter from the garden at the rear of the building. She warmed as she heard Jack's voice and quickly she skirted the bright garden and made her way around the perimeter of the house.

She caught her breath as she saw Jack, his head thrown back, childish giggles shaking his frame. Geoffrey was holding a ball above Jack's head and as Sarah watched, he threw it to the other man who pretended to drop it. Jack immediately snatched it up.

'You're piggy-in-the-middle, Chas!' he said excitedly.

It was then that Geoffrey caught sight of her. He immediately stiffened, a guarded look coming over his face, the laughter vanishing. Sarah felt unaccountably saddened and a little jealous – she had never made Geoffrey look so happy.

'Mammy!' Jack's delight at seeing her was a balm. She caught him as he flung himself at her and held him close, revelling in the warmth of his small body and the feel of his arms around her neck.

She kissed his face all over and hugged him as though she would never let him go. After a time, Geoffrey moved slowly towards her.

'Come inside, Sarah,' he said. 'We can't talk out here.' He gave Chas a look full of apology and unmistakable love, and Sarah, for the first time, understood a little about how her husband felt about his lover.

'I haven't come to cause any trouble,' she said quickly. 'I was lonely. I wanted to see Jack . . . and you, Geoffrey.'

She felt, rather than heard, the sigh that came from Chas. She glanced at him and he appeared fearful and uncertain. She felt sorry for him.

'It's all right,' she said, 'I'm not going to be difficult, I promise.'

She could see at once that she had made the right move. Geoffrey's tone was warmer when he spoke.

'We shall have some tea together. Would you like your mother to stay for tea, Jack? Chas can stay too,' he added defensively.

Jack's smile was radiant. 'Mammy, have you come home to stay?' he asked and Sarah forced herself to swallow the lump in her throat.

'We'll see, my lovely,' she said, her voice thick with emotion and Geoffrey looked at her sharply.

'Sarah . . .' he began, 'I'm sorry but—'

'Don't say anything, not now, Geoffrey,' she said quickly. 'Just let me enjoy my time with you both.'

Inside the house, Sarah saw that it really was quite spacious. The building extended back a long way and though it was not to be compared with the house Geoffrey had given her, it was quite charming in its own way.

They ate a tea of crusty bread and jam and sweet small cakes in the brightly painted, sunlit nursery suite. Chas had tactfully left them. At least, Sarah thought, her husband wasn't so besotted as to live openly with the man.

Jack chatted to Sarah constantly and his conversation centred around his father and Chas whom Jack seemed to hold in great affection. Sarah suppressed the pang of jealousy at the thought that Chas seemed to be supplanting her in her child's life.

Later Geoffrey sent Jack to play outside. 'Find your nurse, there's a good boy. Tell her you need a wash. I shan't be long.'

When the door closed behind her son, Sarah looked at Geoffrey and suddenly she was tongue-tied. How could she ask him to come back to his old life when he was so patently happy in his new one?

'I'm glad I came,' she said at last, 'if only because now I understand a little of what your . . . your friendship with Chas means to you.' She sighed. 'And Jack, he's obviously settled down and is very happy.' Her voice broke. 'I wanted you to come home, Geoffrey, for everything to be as it was before.' She drew a ragged breath. 'Now I can see that a reconciliation is out of the question.'

'I couldn't go back to living a lie, Sarah, but please don't feel too badly about things.' He glanced at her quickly. 'You'll soon make a new life for yourself but I don't think it wise for you to bear a child to another man, do you understand me?'

'There will be no child, not now, not ever,' Sarah said and Geoffrey took both her hands in his.

'I'm sorry, Sarah, sorry for your unhappiness but there isn't much I can do to help you. One point I would reassure you on; divorce between us is not an option I would ever consider, you'll always be cared for financially.'

'I never wanted a divorce anyway,' Sarah said emphatically. She thought of it, the shame of being an outcast as Eline Temple was, the sniggering and sneering, the outright hostility that had driven Eline away from Swansea. She shuddered. 'No, divorce is not for me, Geoffrey.'

'I'm glad to hear it.' He leaned forward. 'Be discreet in whatever you do,' he said. 'That is only fair to me and to our son.' He pressed her hand lightly.

'I know you miss Jack now but, if I'm honest, I feel that you are not cut out for motherhood, you care too much about . . . well, about other things. Believe me, you're better off as you are.'

Sarah felt defeated, too defeated to argue with him. 'Perhaps you're right, Geoffrey, but if you will just allow me to see more of Jack I promise I won't try to influence him against Chas in any way.'

Geoffrey looked at her levelly and released her hand. 'I believe you, Sarah. We'll have to see how everything works out. Remember this though, in many ways you are a fortunate woman. You have money, respectability and your freedom.'

'Yes, I suppose so.' Sarah rose to her feet and looked at Geoffrey regretfully. 'If anything should happen to change things, if you and Chas should fall out, please come back to me Geoffrey. I would be a good wife to you. I mean that.'

'I know.' He looked away from her to the garden where the sun was now slanting long shadows over the lawn. He was a man she no longer knew. In truth, Geoffrey never had been hers, his heart had always been with Chas and now she'd lost even the little of him she'd had. He turned and caught her glance and his eyes were those of a stranger.

'Can your groom take me home?' she asked almost humbly and Geoffrey smiled at her in obvious relief.

'Of course. Goodbye Sarah, take care of yourself.'

She turned once to look back from the carriage window and saw that Jack had rejoined his father and was laughing happily, hugging Geoffrey's legs. Sarah knew, in that instant, that she was leaving one part of her life behind her for ever.

Arian was tired. She had worked hard all day in the workshop and once dusk fell and the light was too bad to see properly, she'd set about delivering the boots and shoes that had been standing stiffly on the shelves as though in an unspoken rebuke because they were lying idle instead of protecting the feet of their owners.

At last the deliveries were done, her basket was light on her arm and she was on her way home.

Home, it had a hollow ring. The one room where she slept and spent the little free time she had, seemed almost like a prison. She was weary of staring at the same four peeling walls and the one old picture of a woman at a well gazing up at a handsome youth, wearier still of witnessing the happiness that was an almost tangible thing between Eline and Will Davies.

Arian was lonely, she felt unloved and unwanted, an onlooker into the lives of others. She tried to tell herself she was a valuable asset to the small business, she could pick out good leather at a glance and she was getting better at the day-to-day tasks of tapping the boots and shoes. She worked hard and earned the small wages that Will was now able to pay her and yet she was unfulfilled, itching to find something else, something that just escaped her grasp. Perhaps that something was happiness.

As she entered the premises of Will and Eline's small shop, she breathed in the scent of *cawl*, the nourishing, economical soup Eline was fond of making and although she was hungry, the thought of making a third at the scrubbed table was enough to take her appetite away.

'Home then?' Eline was setting the table in the warm kitchen, her face shiny from the heat and Arian knew that this life couldn't be easy for the woman who had once enjoyed marriage to Lord Calvin Temple and all the luxuries that state brought.

And yet there was a sheen of happiness about Eline, a glow that pronounced her contentment for all the world to see and that was the sort of feeling that money couldn't buy.

'I've got news for you,' Eline said, leaning on the table, her hands red and work-worn. 'Will and I are going to be married on the weekend.'

'Married?' Arian said in surprise. 'But where? Who is going to marry you?'

It was difficult enough being a divorced woman but to be remarried in any of the local churches was little short of impossible.

'There's a vicar up in the valleys, near the mountains of Brecon, he's willing to marry us.' Eline was jubilant. 'It was Will who found him. A strange man, is Vicar Marriot, a foreigner by all accounts but very liberal in his views. He says that so long as the marriage is registered properly there will be no problem.'

'I'm glad for you, Eline,' Arian said quickly, feeling she'd been tactless, bungling even, in her tiredness. 'I really am happy for you.' And yet there was a sinking feeling within Arian that she couldn't quite identify.

She supposed that being in the house she had served some sort of purpose, she had been a buffer; just in case anyone in the village had found out that Eline and Will weren't already married, her presence would have gone some way to regularizing the position. Now with Eline and Will about to be wed, she was going to be an unnecessary burden, Arian thought dismally.

She ate her meal in silence, listening to the excited chatter pouring from Eline's lips. 'I'll wear my new daffodil-yellow frock and I might as well throw caution to the winds and get a matching hat.'

'You should look very nice,' Arian said forcing enthusiasm into her voice. 'What about shoes? You'll need new ones.'

'Wait here,' Eline rose and moved into the back room, returning after a few minutes with a box that rustled mysteriously.

'I've been working on these in secret, anticipating my wedding day.' With a flourish, Eline brought a pair of pigskin boots out of the wrappings and held them aloft.

'Oh, Eline, they're beautiful!' Arian didn't need to pretend enthusiasm now, the boots were in various colours, the calf dyed and stitched together by Eline's expert hand. The predominant colour was soft gold, giving the boots a richness and a distinctiveness that shouted good taste.

'That's not all.' Eline shook out the folds of paper and produced a cape worked in the same patchwork design and colour as the shoes. 'This is mainly for decoration,' Eline said, 'but a cape will be useful if it's cold up in the mountains.'

'You're brilliant,' Arian said warmly, 'and Eline, you should patent the idea. The capes and matching boots would sell like hot cakes, I'm sure of it. Will you let me contact the papers, put an advertisement in? It could change our fortunes. You must realize how good these things are.' She handled the cape almost reverently.

'It's not new,' Eline said. 'It's the same idea I've used before for the Eline Cape Boot. Perhaps you don't remember that.'

'And if I don't remember, there will also be others who will find your ideas fresh and new,' Arian spoke persuasively. 'These things are multi-coloured. The idea is different enough to capture the imagination, believe me.'

'I don't suppose there's any harm in trying to rouse a bit of interest. Go ahead, Arian. Do what you think best.' Eline returned the cape and boots to the box as she heard a sound at the front door.

'That'll be Will, he took the baby out for a bit of fresh air. He's so good with Emlyn, I am lucky.' Eline stood

212

for a moment looking at Arian as though she would say something else and then, turning, she moved to the stove and began to ladle soup into a bowl.

When Arian had finished her meal she rose to her feet. 'I'll just get on up to my room,' she said. 'I've got to get the wording on the advert just right.'

'You needn't rush away just to be tactful,' Eline said quickly. 'This is your home as well as ours and you spend far too much time alone.'

'No, really, it's what I want.' Arian hurried up the stairs and, once inside her room, stood with her back to the door, her eyes closed. Soon she would have to move on, she knew she couldn't stand the enclosed atmosphere of Eline's house much longer. The happiness in it was suffocating her.

She kicked off her slippers, climbed onto the bed and began to compose an advertisement for the cape and boots. The words flowed easily and Arian grimaced ruefully, she wasn't the daughter of a newspaper man for nothing. Robert Smale hadn't given her much but at least he'd given her his flair for stringing sentences together.

It was a fine day with the sunshine high over the mountains when Eline and Will were married. Arian, holding Emlyn in her arms, felt tears come to her eyes as the beautiful words of the simple service rang out in the empty church.

She remembered with bitterness her own marriage, hastily performed and in a language she didn't understand, tying her to a man she despised. That all seemed so long ago now, as if it had happened in another lifetime. The months had passed slowly since Arian had run away from Swansea, from the unhappy memories and from Calvin, the man she loved.

Will was putting a ring on Eline's finger, Eline was smiling up at him, her face radiant with happiness. Arian sighed. She couldn't imagine a time when she would experience the same sort of happiness herself. Her happiness, if it ever came, would not be in some man's arms but in fulfilment of her ambition to be a successful business woman.

She tried to assess her potential advantages. She had a

213

head for words and figures, unusual enough in itself. She also was able to choose good leather almost by instinct. On the debit side, she had no money, no resources of her own, and she was stuck in a small room in someone else's house from where she would never get on, not unless it was on the coat tails of Eline's success.

No, the answer was to move away. Perhaps to Cardiff, set herself up as a widow and then take out a loan of some kind to begin her own business. Could she get away with it? It was doubtful. She shifted Emlyn to a more comfortable position in her arms, her thoughts still racing. Hari Grenfell had made a name for herself and she'd had nothing but her ingenuity and her courage, and look what she'd achieved. Of course, Hari Grenfell had an enormous talent.

The bridal couple began to walk down the aisle to the strains of the lovely music from the old organ and Arian moved forward and kissed Eline's cheek in an uncharacteristic gesture of warmth.

'I know you'll be happy,' she said, her voice thick. 'This is what you've always wanted, isn't it?'

A man crossed the bare courtyard of the churchyard, a pad and pencil in his hand. He spoke a few quick words to Will and then turned away.

Arian handed the baby to Eline and frowned anxiously. 'It's a reporter, I can spot them a mile off. Don't say a word or your business will be spread all over the country.'

She saw the man approach her and turned away. He was persistent. 'I'm working for the *Brecon and Radnor Express*. Can you spare me a few minutes?'

Arian ignored him, pretending not to hear, then watched uneasily as the reporter shrugged his shoulders and made his way towards one of the deacons of the church.

Gerald Simples sat in the public bar of the Castle Arms and looked idly at the newspaper before him on the table. He was feeling more than a little disgruntled with life; money he had, but he was not able to splash it around and that irritated him. What's more, he knew that he had made a powerful enemy in Calvin Temple and, for some time to come, he would have to watch his step where business was concerned.

And then there was the matter of his wife. None of his enquiries had uncovered any sign of where she had gone and he wanted her, God he wanted her.

He leaned back, the newspaper forgotten as he dreamed of having Arian in his bed once more. She was like a drug. The woman he had married had somehow got beneath his skin and now his body ached to hold her. Arian with her silver hair and lithe young body had become like a thirst he could not quench. True she had never been passionate, whenever she gave of herself it was as the result of a bargain, but he could accept that, just so long as she didn't fight him beneath the sheets.

Sighing, he returned to the newspaper. He turned a page and a large headline caught his eye. THE MARRIAGE OF DIVORCEE it read and the article beneath the headline went on to reveal that a Mr William Davies, cobbler, had married Eline Temple, a divorced woman.

Excitement filled Gerald. That was it. That's where Arian would be, with Eline and Will. Why hadn't he thought of that possibility before?

He read the entire article twice, ignoring the parts about the fashionable leather-wear that the Davies's were designing, and concentrating on the piece concerning a young lady who appeared to be nanny to the couple's child.

The attraction of the writer to the young lady in question was obvious as was his flowery description of her silver-gold hair and her fragile beauty. It was Arian, there was no doubt about it.

Gerald rose to his feet, the address of the newspaper was clear enough. He thrust his hand into his pocket, drew out some coins and laid them next to his empty glass. Then he left the public bar and went outside into the pale sunshine.

'Right, Arian, my love,' he said softly. 'Your days of freedom are numbered. Your husband is coming to claim you.'

* * *

Arian sighed wearily and rested her basket on a wall. It was full of working boots, heavy leather boots with thick soles, and it was all she could do to carry the load around the streets of Clydach. There was no doubt that the business had picked up of late with people coming to the shop from miles around, some of them out of curiosity to see the woman who had been in the papers, the one who had been divorced, but many of them turning out to be genuine customers.

Arian looked up the winding roadway and the thought of climbing the hill was daunting. She was growing tired of tramping around Clydach delivering repairs, sometimes having to call two or three times to the same house before finding anyone at home.

Her back ached and her feet were sore. Not even the soft comfort of the boots Eline had made for her could ease the blisters that chafed her heels.

As she did her rounds she knew, had known for some weeks, that she'd had enough of this life; even being with Simples had been better than the unremitting grind of working for Eline and Will.

Arian thought of returning home to wash at the pump in the yard and then to sit in her room alone, staring out of the window. She was sick and tired of the same view of the backyard and the single oak tree that shadowed her room preventing the sun from ever venturing inside.

She picked up her basket and hoisted it on to her arm; the work wouldn't get done by standing here feeling sorry for herself. It was with a sigh of relief, some hours later, that Arian finished her round and turned to descend the hilly track back into the village.

She would tell Eline tomorrow morning that she was moving on. Quite what she would do, she had no idea but she couldn't stand the rigid boring routine any longer. There was no challenge, no surge of excitement, nothing but the same dullness to be faced day after day.

Dusk was falling and with it the chill of the autumn air. Soon winter would come and walking the hillsides would be even more arduous. Arian sighed, longing for her comfortable life at Stormhill, her warm room, her easy task of keeping the books, the excitement of being near Calvin Temple. She'd been secure there, happy. Why hadn't she settled for all that instead of trying to become a leather lord? The idea now seemed preposterous, bizarre even. What gave her the arrogance to think she could be a success at something as ambitious as that?

Suddenly, before she had time to call out, her arms were grasped from behind, she dropped the empty basket and tried to struggle, a sense of panic beating at her temples. A scarf was tied around her mouth and eyes, and she felt the cruel bite of cord around her wrists.

She wanted to protest that she had nothing worth stealing, but only guttural sounds came from between her covered lips. She tasted the scarf and the smell of it seemed somehow familiar. She kicked out with her booted feet but unable to see, her aim connected only with the air.

The breath was knocked out of her as she was hoisted onto a strong shoulder. The blood seemed to rush to her head, fear was a bitter taste in her mouth. She hung like a sack, unable to move, only able to listen to the heavy breathing of the man carrying her and feel with dread his feet slithering over the uneven land.

She'd heard of robbers waiting in the high reaches of the hills and there were pick-pockets in every large town but here, in the sleepy village of Clydach, such things were unheard of.

The walk seemed to go on endlessly. Her stomach hurt and her head began to ache. She felt she couldn't breathe properly and she longed for the relief of being set down on firm ground.

She began to listen to the sounds around her. She became aware of a horse near by and the creaking of carriage wheels. Hope flared within her, perhaps she was nearing the busy streets and someone would see her plight and rescue her.

She was dumped unceremoniously onto a cold leather seat. She realized she was inside a coach. She felt someone sit beside her, the leather creaking beneath his weight.

The coach jerked into motion and Arian felt herself begin to slip from the seat. Hands lifted her upright, set her back more securely against the upholstery. She was acutely uncomfortable, the cord biting into her wrists. Hands fumbled at her throat and Arian shrank back as far as she could, shivering as fingers touched her bare skin. She could see nothing but she could hear someone breathing beside her.

What did anyone want with her? She had no money, no possessions, nothing. The coach moved forward at a brisker pace, taking her away from the life she had begun to despise but which now, she longed for. The hand began caressing her skin, her throat, moving round to the nape of her neck. She simply sat still, praying that she would not be harmed.

The scarf was removed from her mouth and a finger traced the outline of her lips. She shuddered, dreadful memories were rising to the surface of her mind, memories of Price Davies, of the way he'd violated her. It couldn't be happening again, could it?

'Who are you?' her voice trembled. 'What do you want? I've got nothing, no money, nothing.'

There was no reply and Arian, straining to hear the sounds around her, could detect only the soft breathing of the man at her side. At last, the coach jerked to a halt. She felt the rush of air against her skin as the door was opened, heard the chink of money changing hands. She was lifted in strong arms. She wondered if she should call out but, as though suspecting her intent, a hand was placed across her mouth.

She was inside a building then. She could smell the clean scent of beeswax. She heard the slam of a door shutting and then she was being carried upstairs.

She fell backwards and cried out in fear but the softness of a bed cushioned her. She felt herself being rolled on her side and her cords were being undone.

Crazy images of the past flashed before her eyes – a farmhouse, a fire, death and destruction.

Her hands free, she tore the scarf from her eyes and blinked at the square-shouldered figure turned away from her, lighting the lamp.

He came to her then, looming up out of the darkness. 'Welcome home, Arian,' he said. With a shock of mixed emotions, she realized she was looking into the face of her husband Gerald Simples.

CHAPTER FIFTEEN

'I'm worried, Will,' Eline sat in the small living room, the late sun was on her shoulders and she would have felt good except for the nagging feeling that something was wrong. She pushed aside the patterns that fanned out before her. 'Arian should have been back by now.'

'Perhaps she's been invited for a meal with one of the customers,' Will said easily. 'Jono obviously has more than a passing interest in her.' He paused thoughtfully and then, his face lighting up as he looked at Eline, he smiled. 'It must be very boring for her being shut in with an old married couple like us.'

Eline returned his smile. 'Aye, I suppose you're right.' She looked down happily at the wedding-band gleaming on her finger.

'It's so good, Will,' she said softly, 'so good to be Mrs Davies. I've waited so long for it to happen.'

She looked up as Will came towards her and took her in his arms. 'Come on, Mrs Davies,' he said, 'let's have an early night, shall we?'

'But what about Arian?' Eline said softly, winding her arms around Will's broad shoulders. 'It's past eight o'clock. I *am* worried in spite of your reassurances, it's a feeling that's all. Do you think you should go out and look for her?'

'I do not,' Will said emphatically. 'She's more than capable of looking after herself. Arian's a sensible girl and must be allowed to live her own life. Anyway, where would I look? Clydach's a small place, so she couldn't have gone far. She *must* be with Jono.'

'I suppose you're right.' Eline looked round wistfully. The baby was asleep on the sofa. She could come down and take him to bed later. There was no pressing work to be done and she and Will rarely had time to themselves.

'Come on then, Will Davies, let's go to bed.'

He took her in his arms and swept her off her feet, carrying her like a bride upstairs and into their room. 'You're a temptress, Eline,' he said in a whisper. 'I love you so much it almost hurts, have I ever told you that?'

'William,' she touched his cheeks, drawing his mouth down to hers, 'there are times when it's right to talk . . . but now is not one of them.'

She woke suddenly and sat up in bed. Moonlight stretched fingers of light through the curtains. Eline thought she'd heard a noise downstairs and she looked around anxiously. Will was beside her and the baby was asleep in the small cot. He stretched and turned over and Eline relaxed against the pillows, everything was all right and if she had heard anything it would be Arian coming home. She smiled. It seemed her friend was beginning to put the past behind her and make a new life for herself up here in Clydach. Good luck to her too, it was about time she stretched her wings.

Sleep crept over her and before she finally succumbed, Eline put her arm across Will's bare chest and sighed with happiness. They were together, her family, and all was right with her world.

Arian stared into Gerald's face and anger flowed, heady like a draught of wine, through her body. 'What do you think you are doing?' she demanded, her voice hoarse. 'How dare you drag me away from Clydach? What gives you the right to behave like this?'

'I'm your husband,' Gerald Simples said evenly. 'I have every right to bring you back to my home.'

Arian looked around her. She had no idea where she was – she'd been able to see nothing on the journey from Clydach which had been the whole idea of the blindfold, she realized now.

'And where exactly is home?' Arian spoke more calmly now. There was far more to be gained by reasoning with this man who was her husband than by showing her hostility.

'It's not too far from Swansea,' Gerald said, sitting on the edge of the bed, 'and I think you will find it quite comfortable once you get used to it.'

'I have no intention of getting used to it.' Arian's resolve to be reasonable was short-lived. 'I'm getting out of here first thing in the morning.'

'I don't think so, Mrs Simples.' Gerald put his hand on her bodice and began to open the buttons. She pushed him away but he persisted.

'Are you going to force yourself on me then?' she said challengingly. 'After all you said?' He shook his head.

'You should know me better than that,' he said, 'but I do want to take away your clothes. They are not what I'd call suitable for the wife of a well-to-do gentleman.'

'Gentleman!' Arian sneered. 'You flatter yourself.' She felt him tug at her bodice and the worn material tore beneath his hands. He pushed her back and undid the buttons at the side of her skirt.

'Look at this,' he indicated the hem. 'It's filthy.' He took off her skirt and threw it on the floor. 'Burning is all that these rags are good for.'

His expression of disgust stung. 'I've been tramping the streets, I can't help it if I have to walk up muddy lanes to deliver my repairs, can I? I have to make a living you know.'

Without answering, Gerald unlaced her boots and eased them from her feet. He touched her blistered heels.

'You call this living?' He pulled back bedclothes and indicated that she get into the warmth of the blankets. 'I call it slavery, myself. You'd be better off living with me, at least you'd have clean clothes, a good home and a bit of money in your pocket. And perhaps you'd have the opportunity to begin a new future.'

'I wanted a future as a business woman,' she said, 'and you took that away from me. It's over and done with.'

'Not necessarily,' he said. 'I might yet be able to arrange something for you.'

'And in exchange?' Arian asked, knowing the answer already.

He leaned over her, his face close to hers, and he was smiling.

'In exchange you act as a wife should, that's all I want, Mrs Simples.'

'Stop calling me that!' Arian said. 'My name is Arian. Why can't you use it?'

'Because I don't wish to,' Gerald said formally. 'To me you are Mrs Simples, my wife. That's all.'

'Your plaything in bed, you mean.' Arian spoke bitterly. 'That's all you want, isn't it? My body?'

'I'd prefer to have your devotion, of course,' Gerald said, 'but if that's out of the question I'll settle for what I need most which is, as you so crudely put it, your body.'

'Why me?' Arian asked desperately. 'Why can't you find someone else willing to enjoy your embraces?'

He picked up her torn skirt and bodice and moved to the door without answering her question. 'In the morning, you will find fresh clothes laid out in my room for you. If you choose to wear them, I'll know that you have agreed to my terms.'

'In other words, you'll keep me prisoner here until I do what you wish?' she said fiercely. 'All right then, here, take me.' She held out her arms. 'Come on, what are you waiting for?' Her anger was mounting. 'It's what you want and I'm offering it to you.'

She didn't understand the look on his face as he turned away from her, but her heart sank as the door closed behind him and she heard the sound of a key turning in the lock.

Arian put her hands over her eyes. Her thoughts were in chaos. She'd been snatched from the life she'd come to hate, was that so bad? A new future, Gerald had said. Was it possible?

Her feeling of hope was short-lived. What new future? Her credibility as a buyer had gone, vanished with the fiasco over the French calf. What could Simples possibly offer her?

She curled up in the bed, glad of the warmth of the clothes wrapped around her. Could she have gone on with her old life, she wondered, enduring the harsh winter weather, carrying her heavy basket around with her, tramping all over the hillside delivering repaired boots and shoes, returning to the house that she shared with Eline and Will, continually feeling like an outsider. Was that what she wanted from life?

She closed her eyes wearily. Perhaps Simples presented a way out, perhaps he could find her some work that she would enjoy, then at least she could feel fulfilled as a businesswoman if not as a wife.

It was a long time before she slept and then she dreamed that she had her own leather business, that she was successful and respected in the town of Swansea. In her dream, Calvin Temple featured large; adoring, wooing her with wine and flowers. Nowhere, not even as a shadow, did Gerald Simples appear to mar her dreams.

It was some days later that Will brought a letter to Eline. She stared down at it, a frown of bewilderment on her face. She quickly tore open the envelope and read the few words written upon a slip of paper inside.

'Listen to this, Will,' she said quickly. 'It says here that Arian is settled now with her husband, she is safe and well and thanks us for all we have done for her. It's signed by Gerald Simples.'

'Oh,' Eline sank down into her chair. 'But she was unhappy, she didn't want to live with him. Why should she suddenly go back to him? It doesn't make sense.'

Will shrugged. 'Her life here was not ideal, you'd be the first to admit that. Didn't you sense that she was becoming restless? I did.'

'I suppose so,' Eline said doubtfully, 'but how can we find out for sure?'

Will took her in his arms, lifting her from the chair so that she faced him.

'My darling,' he said patiently, 'you can't take on the cares of the whole human race.' He kissed her mouth. 'And don't you think we have enough to worry about trying to make a success of our business?'

'But if she's being held against her will we should do something to help.'

'What?' Will asked softly. 'She's married to this man. He has all the rights on his side. The law would see Arian as a recalcitrant bride, that's all, and how many of those are about?'

'I know, there are more marriages made in hell than in heaven,' Eline admitted reluctantly. Resting her head against his chest she listened to his heartbeat. 'I'm one of the lucky ones.'

'If it will help, I'll call in and see Arian when I next go to Swansea,' Will said gently. He tucked the letter away in his pocket. 'But I'm sure it's all right. The man wouldn't have given us his address if it wasn't, he wouldn't have bothered to write at all, would he?'

'I suppose not,' Eline replied, though she was still far from convinced. Will tipped up her face.

'I'd love to spend the afternoon in bed with you, my darling,' he said. 'I could hold you and kiss you all day long but we have work to do, both of us.'

Eline smiled. 'Thanks to you,' she said. 'It's wonderful that my shoes and slippers are beginning to sell again. Arian was right. The cape and matching boots I wore for our wedding have taken off. I have so many demands for them that I think we're going to need another cobbler around the place now that she's gone.'

Will looked at her thoughtfully. 'You know,' he said, 'this could all turn out for the best. Arian would make a fine contact down in Swansea. What if she was to act as an agent for us?'

'I don't know if she'd want to,' Eline said, 'or even if that husband of hers would allow it.'

225

'If I know Arian,' Will said smiling, 'the man will have very little say in the matter. She's got guts. That's why I think she's there with him of her own free will.'

Eline nodded thoughtfully. 'Well, you could be right and it wouldn't do any harm to talk to her about your idea. At least a meeting with her would prove of help should Arian need it.'

'That's settled then,' Will said. 'Now can we both get on with our work?'

Eline smiled at him mischievously and drew him close. 'Not yet,' she said. 'Our boy is asleep, we can work at any time.'

'In other words you have designs on me, is that it, you shameless wench?'

Eline didn't answer as she gently unbuttoned his shirt and slipped her arms around the warmth of his body, drawing him close. She kissed the hollow of his neck and then his shoulder and then his mouth.

'Have I told you that I love you?' she whispered against his lips. Will lowered her gently onto the huge sofa.

'Once or twice.' His mouth was hot on hers, his passion growing. Eline sighed softly and closed her eyes.

It was a week since Arian had taken up the clothes Gerald had left for her and acknowledged, in doing so, that she was also taking up occupation of his bed. In that week they had scarcely talked, he was out most of the day and Arian spent time alone, exploring the small but elegant house. She kept the fires well stoked, for the weather was chilly now, and for his return in the evenings, she cooked nourishing meals.

It was a time for coming to terms with her life and, strangely, she found she was enjoying the hiatus, the quietness of the surrounding hillside, the comparative peace of being cared for. She missed nothing of her old life. The walks up the hillside with the heavy basket over her arm, the cloistered feeling that living with Eline and Will had given her; they were all part of a past, a past that was over and done with.

Strangely, Gerald had made no move towards her, even though at night they lay side by side in the double bed. He had not turned to her, had not claimed what rights were his, the rights a husband had over his wife.

It had come to a point where Arian felt she must make a move herself, have the suspense of waiting for the inevitable over and done with.

Had he suddenly changed his mind, she wondered? Now that he had her in his power did he no longer want her? But that was too much to hope for. In any case, he was her husband and nothing could change that, so she might as well make the best of it.

Tonight she had cooked him a nourishing supper of rabbit and hot potatoes and she waited for him to come home, the dutiful wife, sitting in her chair in the kitchen as though this was a normal marriage. And why not? There was nothing else in life for her, no knight in shining armour to ride away with her. Gerald Simples was a crook but then Calvin had scarcely been honest.

Over the past days she had forced herself to look the truth full in the face. The man she loved was no good, a womanizer who slept with his rich exotic paramour while making a gullible married woman like Sarah Frogmore pregnant with his child. Oh yes, Calvin Temple was a man like the rest of them, out to gratify his own desires.

The door-latch lifted and Gerald Simples came into the kitchen carrying with him the coldness of the night air. He looked fresh and clean, his face weathered by the wind, his mouth strong beneath the dark moustache.

Arian looked at him objectively. He was a handsome man. Could she in time come to love him? She doubted it but perhaps she might at least make the best of things.

'I have news for you,' he said. 'I met with William Davies in town. He has a proposition for you which coincides with my own projects, as it happens.'

'Oh?' Arian didn't bother to conceal her surprise. 'How did he know where I was?'

'I wrote to him and told him, of course.' Gerald said calmly. 'I didn't want him alarming the constabulary or riding after you like an old-time vigilante.'

Arian digested this information in silence. What must Eline and Will think of her? But did it matter? Did anything matter now?

'Don't you wish to know what was proposed?' Gerald asked, taking off his topcoat and sitting in his chair.

'Yes,' Arian replied quietly, 'I would like to know, I suppose.'

Gerald appeared self-satisfied. 'Come, put out the meal and let us eat while we talk.'

Arian contained her impatience while she served him his food. She watched him taste the rabbit with a nod of approval and, absurdly, she was pleased.

'He wants you to be his contact in Swansea,' Gerald said. 'Initially, William Davies imagined you would simply spread the word about his boots and shoes by showing them off to folk. I had a much better idea.'

Arian looked at him, waiting for him to continue. It irked her that Gerald made no mention of Eline, as though Will Davies was in business on his own, but then Gerald rarely gave women credit for any intelligence.

He was infuriatingly slow with his meal but at last he put down his knife and fork. 'I had decided already that you should open your own emporium, that you should sell boots and shoes from a variety of sources which it would be your place to find. What I don't want is you thinking small; selling stock just supplied by William Davies isn't good enough, you must approach the big concerns as well. I told you I could present you with a new future if only you would give me the chance, didn't I?'

'It has nothing new about it,' Arian said slowly. 'It's an idea that has been used by Emily Miller and by Hari Grenfell, both of them talented ladies in their own right.'

'It will be a fresh departure for you, a fine opportunity. Are you afraid of the competition?' Gerald asked bluntly. 'Will you give up before you have begun?'

'No,' some of Arian's old spirit returned, 'I am not afraid of anything about the scheme but neither will I take on something that I feel is doomed to failure.'

'What do you suggest then?' Gerald leaned back in his chair. She knew that he was testing her, wanting to learn how committed she was to succeeding in business which meant, inevitably, remaining with him.

'On my rounds in Clydach, I thought about the future quite a lot, had plenty of ideas, and one of them I think is very good indeed. If you are willing to fund me then I wish to start up an agency.'

Arian paused and seeing she had Gerald's full attention continued speaking. 'I'll go to people's homes demonstrating the kind of boots and shoes I want to sell. I will make up a catalogue of designs, of various styles so that the customer can choose what he or she wants without leaving the house.'

She stopped talking, her breath had left her as she suddenly realized how good her idea sounded put into words.

'I would make some of the shoes myself,' she continued. 'I'm not brilliant but I am a good worker and I have learned a lot from my time with Eline. I *will* make a success of this, it's something I can really believe in.'

'Better idea than my own, I'll admit. You have imagination and flair, you also have enthusiasm. I like that.' He rose to his feet. 'Shall we go to our bed, Mrs Simples? It's high time.'

She tensed. She knew what his words meant, knew just what she had committed herself to. She looked at him for a long moment and then she rose to her feet.

In their room, he undressed unhurriedly and then, naked, slid beneath the sheets. He watched as she slowly removed her own clothing and then he held the sheets back for her to climb in beside him. He made no move in her direction and Arian realized he was not going to make matters easy for her – that was not his way, she had learned that lesson once.

She lay rigid for a moment then turned towards him and put her arm around his shoulder. 'I'm ready,' she whispered and Gerald stretched and sighed in the darkness.

'Well I am not,' he said. 'I am not a machine any more than you are.'

Reluctantly, she began to caress him. She closed her eyes as he began to touch her, his fingers familiar with her body. She suppressed a sigh, dreading his passion. But then, didn't most wives feel exactly the same thing? How many women loved their men? How many wives sighed over the chore of submitting to their menfolk between the sheets?

He seemed to rise above her and then he was pressing her back against the bed. He slipped his hands beneath her, pressing her close to him as though he might penetrate into her very soul.

She longed to push him away from her, to cry out in protest but she did none of those things. She had sold herself to him, sold herself for the price of a business. Catering to Gerald's needs was a part of that life; the bargain was made and she would not shrink from doing her duty.

CHAPTER SIXTEEN

Fon O'Conner set the table for her visitors with a strange premonition that nothing was as it seemed. She'd been pleased when she'd heard from Arian – pleased, if rather surprised, to know that she was married. Her husband, Fon assumed, was a man of means. He'd set up a business in Arian's name so he must be generous and very much in love with her.

Fon paused, her hand resting absently on the cutlery, straightening a fork without really seeing it. The feeling persisted that something was awry in Arian's life. She knew Arian well enough to read between the lines of the carefully phrased letter, which was brief, explanatory in a practical way but there was no mention in it of love or happiness.

It was quiet in the kitchen, the children were in bed and the silence that settled like a mantle around Fon was refreshing in its rarity. Well, Arian would be here soon, and then Fon would know a little more.

She put her best plates on the pristine cloth and stood back to admire the table that she had made bright and welcoming. She was proud of the sparkling china and polished cutlery. It was her way of supporting Arian, making a good impression on that new husband of hers.

She heard footsteps outside and looked up with a smile as Jamie entered the room. He kissed her upturned mouth and held her close for a moment before sniffing appreciatively.

'Something smells good.' He took in the neat kitchen and well-laid table at a glance. 'Sure and it's a lot of trouble you're going to, colleen, trying to impress Arian, is it?'

'*Duw*, there's soft you are.' Fon smiled up at her

husband, loving him more now than she did when she'd married him. 'I don't have to worry about Arian, she's like a sister to me, you know that.'

'Then it's the husband you'll be out to please, is that it?' He put his arm around her waist. 'I won't have you making eyes at any man but me, remember.'

'Shut up.' Fon pushed him away playfully. 'Fat chance I'd have of looking at anyone else with you around. A bossy, domineering man you are, mind.'

He drew her closer and kissed her mouth. 'Well, I can say the same about you. Boss me something terrible, make my life a misery with your nagging. Still an' all, you're not a bad wife, sure I'll grant you that.'

Fon put her hands on her hips. 'Kind of you to throw in a good word.'

'Don't get uppity, though.' Jamie touched her mouth with his fingertip. 'There's a little too much of the lip from you on times, but I'll forgive you, cos you're not slow when it comes to caring for your man.'

'Fine to have such watery compliments from a man who's supposed to love his wife to distraction.' Fon shook back a stray lock of hair. 'Can't you think of any sweet words to whisper to me, Jamie?'

'Well, I don't have to put anything into words, not with you, colleen. You know when you're well off. Won't get a better husband than me this side of the Irish sea, not if you looked from now till doomsday.'

'Well, I've got no intention of looking anywhere, so hush your nonsense and help me put the food on the table. Arian will be here at any minute now.'

'There you go, bossing me again. Sometimes I think it's a good hiding you need, my girl. Comes to something when a man can't so much as be master in his own house.'

Fon rested her hand on her stomach. 'Not master, eh? Then how come you filled me with child again so quickly after the last one?' Happiness flared through her, a son she'd given him this time, a brother to Cathie.

'Keep a woman well filled and poor shod and she'll never leave you, that's what they say.' Jamie moved to the pantry and brought out a crispy loaf of bread.

Fon dreamed for a moment, watching him deftly cut thin slices from the loaf. She was enjoying the moment of intimacy between them, the banter, the carefree affection they shared. These moments were becoming all too few.

The house was becoming full of children, fine and healthy they were too. Patrick was the big boy now. He was not her own son but she loved him as dearly as if she'd given birth to him. And April, well April was sometimes a thorn in the flesh, not an O'Conner at all but trusted to Fon's care, but was a dear child in spite of her tantrums. April, however difficult she could be, was part of the household.

'We'll have to build on to the farmhouse if this continues,' she said softly.

Jamie put down the bread knife and took her into his arms, holding her close, his chin against the softness of her hair. 'If you mean us having babies then building on is imperative. I have no intention of refraining from making love to you.' He tipped her face up to his. 'And if the result of that is you giving me fine sons and daughters, then I'm happy.'

Fon closed her eyes and pressed her head against Jamie's chest, listening to the strong throb of his heart. She was so lucky that sometimes she was afraid something might happen to take all her joy away from her.

The gate at the end of the path clicked open and, reluctantly, Fon moved out of Jamie's arms, patted down her apron and brushed back her hair.

'They're here,' she said. 'Now Jamie, be on your best behaviour, mind.'

Arian looked well, even to Fon's critical eye. She was neatly dressed, her skin shone and her hair was as if alight with silver and gold. What a contrast, Fon thought, to the girl who used to wander barefoot in rags around the countryside.

'Come here.' She hugged Arian and kissed her cheek and then stood back shyly to be introduced to Arian's husband.

Gerald Simples was handsome, there was no denying that. His manner was charming, open and friendly as he shook hands with first herself and then with Jamie, and yet Fon had her reservations – he was, perhaps a little too charming.

It seemed, however, that the two men had a great deal in common. Gerald Simples was knowledgeable about the land, asking all the right questions, interspersing intelligent comments whenever there was a silence.

In the flurry of serving the *cawl*, then the rich potato and beef roast Fon was not able to catch much of the conversation that flowed around the table but she was, covertly, able to study Arian closely. There was a droop about her mouth, a lack of light in her eyes that confirmed Fon's feeling that Arian was not happy. But later, when the men took a turn in the garden in order to smoke, she and Arian would be able to talk. Then she might learn the truth about the sudden marriage.

'So, tell me all about your business venture. I'm dying to hear what exactly you're doing.' Fon took her seat after serving a pudding of milk, rice and honey, glad that the meal had been a success, and happy that her obligations were over because now she could concentrate her attention on Arian. 'Something to do with leather, I expect.'

It was Gerald Simples who replied. 'My wife had this wonderful idea . . .' He sounded as enthusiastic as a man in love with his wife should be and Fon wondered if she was misjudging him. 'She has produced a catalogue – it's brilliantly written. Arian really has a gift for words.' He paused to smile at his wife. 'Our distribution covers the entire Swansea area and some of the outlying villages advertising Arian's own brand of boots and shoes.'

He smiled proudly. His gaze, meeting Fon's, was open and enthusiastic and she felt herself warm to him.

'So what you do is to take orders and then make bespoke shoes to any size, is that it?'

'That's right but it's not all,' Arian said quickly. 'The customers are given time to pay, six weeks in all.' Her excitement with the scheme shone in her eyes. 'This gives the poorer families time to get the money together. That people with a few children are taking up the offer is not surprising but, happily, we're also getting business from the rich.' She made a wry face, 'They like to hold on to their money as long as possible.'

'My wife is an astute business woman, you see, as well as being an industrious worker.' Gerald looked at his wife but Fon couldn't help noticing Arian was avoiding direct contact with him, even going so far as to ignore him.

'The idea seems to be working well but we need a bit more time yet to really get the scheme launched.' Arian's tone was brisk as though she'd talked enough about her business. She sat back in her chair, her hands resting on her lap like a prim child at a party.

'That was a lovely meal, Fon. No wonder your husband looks so well. My compliments to you, you can cook for me any time.'

Fon rose to her feet. 'You men can move to the garden if you want to smoke.' She began to clear the dishes from the table and stacked them in an enamel bowl.

The men wandered outside, their voices muted on the evening air. Arian made a move towards the dishes but Fon shook her head.

'I'll do those later when I've boiled up plenty of hot water.' She swept up the cloth and folded it away in the drawer and then, as there was nothing left to occupy her hands, she turned to face Arian.

'Right now,' she said, 'there's no-one here but me and you. Are you happy? That's what I want to know.'

'Happy enough,' Arian said and it was clear she was reluctant to be drawn.

'But you don't love your husband.' It was not a question, it was something that Fon knew instinctively.

'No, I don't love Gerald. I even left him once but he fetched me home again.' She shrugged. 'I can't say in the end that I was unwilling, in a way I was ready to come home I couldn't go on living the way I was. I was smothering, vegetating up in Clydach.'

'And do you share anything with him?' Fon was concerned. 'I don't mean to pry but you look so lost.'

Arian didn't dissemble. 'Oh, I sleep in his bed but there is no joy and no love in it.'

Fon reached out and took her hand. 'Come on, sit down by the fire with me. Look love, you were ill treated by one man and it'll take some time to get over it but it doesn't mean they are all beasts. Gerald seems good to you. He really cares about you, I can tell, and love might grow if you give it time.'

'Our marriage is only a bargain,' Arian said flatly. 'Gerald wants me, so he pays for me to live comfortably and is financing my business.' She smiled wryly. 'You see, I'm no better than the whore some folk have always believed me to be.'

'Rubbish! You're no whore. You have respectability, the chance to make something of yourself, don't decry it.' She paused. 'Many women do not like their husbands to . . . to possess them, it is no strange thing in a marriage but women endure it for many reasons.'

'You do not like Jamie to make love to you?' Arian looked her full in the face and Fon smiled.

'I'm in love with Jamie, he is my darling. I enjoy him in every way but then I am lucky, there are many who are not so lucky.'

'Well, in any case,' Arian said, 'the pact is made. I'm Gerald's wife, he takes me whenever he wishes. In return, he looks after me. I suppose I should count my blessings.' She sighed and looked down at her hands. 'One thing I've realized is that I don't want children.' She looked up beseechingly. 'Is there a way I can prevent it?'

Fon laughed out loud. 'Me who catches whenever Jamie comes near and you're asking me that. Look, my love, you know how afraid I was but it's the most wonderful thing in the world, to be a mother. You'll see when the time comes, trust me.'

'I don't want a baby.' Arian repeated. 'I don't want Gerald's child growing inside me, I can't bear the thought of it.'

'You will glory in it when it happens. A son or daughter would be a great comfort to you.'

'No.' Arian shook her head stubbornly. 'I don't want a child and I don't intend to have one, understand me?'

Fon put her hand over her mouth and stared at Arian's white face. Icy fingers of superstition crawled along her spine and suddenly Fon felt frightened, as though Arian's words could somehow bring harm to her own babies.

'Don't talk like that, please, Arian. It's not natural, it's not right.'

'Damn what's right!' Arian rose to her feet and moved to the window, her shoulders were heaving. She stood for a moment in silence and then suddenly she seemed calm. 'Perhaps we should have a nice hot cup of tea. We'll forget all I've said. I shouldn't talk like that, not to you.' She smiled and Fon, eager to do something for her, hurriedly rose and pushed the kettle onto the flames.

Arian wandered over to the dresser and picked up one of the books. It was only when Fon brought the steaming teapot to the table that she saw what Arian had been reading.

'Don't take any notice of that old herbal.' She felt a sense of panic. 'Old wives' tales, those are. They tell you how to prevent a baby and how to slip one, nonsense it is.'

'If you say so.' Arian took the cup of tea and silently began to drink it. She had become remote, untouchable and Fon felt she didn't know her any more.

The men returned to the kitchen and the talk became general. Arian joined in the conversation but her brightness was forced, her mind obviously elsewhere. It was a relief when Gerald Simples decided it was time to leave for home.

Obediently, Arian rose and kissed Fon's cheek in a perfunctory gesture before allowing her husband to help her with her coat.

'We'll see you again soon?' Fon asked but even though Arian nodded her agreement, Fon didn't believe she meant it. She frowned as the couple moved arm in arm down the pathway towards the road.

'They look happy enough,' Jamie said, his hand warm on Fon's shoulder.

'Aye,' Fon sighed, 'but then, not everything is what it seems, is it, Jamie lad?'

He turned her into his arms and kissed her mouth. 'Hush, colleen.' He kissed her again. 'You can't carry the cares of the world on your shoulders, haven't you learned that much yet?'

'I know.' She put her arm around his waist as, together, they returned to the brightness of their house and closed the door on the world.

'I have five more orders,' Arian said easily. 'Firm orders at that and some of them from previous customers.'

Gerald was seated at his desk, his shirt collar immaculate, his waistcoat pristine in its cut and style. He had found work with another rich client and Arian sometimes wondered quite how crooked Gerald's business was.

His investments seemed to bring in results, it was true, both for himself and for his employer and perhaps, she mused, he had simply been unlucky in the past, unlucky and perhaps a little careless.

Gerald looked over his shoulder. 'Very good,' he said but it was clear he was not really listening.

Arian left her own desk in the improvised office and moved to the kitchen at the back of the house. She wrinkled up her nose in disgust at the smell of the roots of fenwort boiling on the hob.

She looked down into the small pot resting on the fire. If the herbal was correct, the infusion of roots would make her miscarry. She rubbed at her eyes. Her courses were late, two weeks late and if she should be with child she would go mad. In any case, she intended to take no risks – she would drink the vile concoction if it killed her.

Resentment against Gerald Simples filled her. He had taken her life, altered it out of all recognition, shaping it to suit himself. Why, she asked herself, had she allowed him to do it?

'What on earth is that smell?' Gerald had entered the kitchen and was standing behind her. Arian glanced back at him almost with hostility.

'Herbs,' she said tersely. 'Medication for women's problems, don't worry about it.'

He put his hands on her shoulders and turned her to face him. 'Arian,' he sounded concerned, 'what's wrong?'

She shook her head. 'Nothing.' She sought desperately in her mind for an excuse, some words which would appease him. 'It's just my monthly pains, that's all. The herbs ease things of that sort.'

He tipped her face up and studied her carefully. He slid his hands down from her shoulders to her waist and then over her hips and stomach.

'Are you going to have my child? Tell me the truth, Arian. I have the right to know.'

She shook her head. Suddenly her heart was beating too fast, she felt she would choke. She tried to twist away from him but he held her.

'Speak to me, Arian. Answer me. Are you expecting my child or not?'

'I don't know, not for sure,' she said at last. 'I'm a little late in my courses, that's all. It could mean nothing.'

He released her and moved away from her, his eyes unreadable. 'You weren't going to tell me,' he said, 'because you don't want to carry my baby. You are planning to take this' – he gestured towards the pot on the fire – 'this herbal stuff in order to miscarry. I can read the truth in your face.'

Arian sank down into a chair, her legs trembling as if with the ague. 'It's the wrong time,' she said in a low voice.

'We are not in love, Gerald. We are married because you want to possess me; you can't want children under such circumstances.'

'Don't tell me what I want.' His voice was cold, hard. 'Do you know what you were about to do?' He continued speaking without waiting for her to reply. 'You were going to murder our child.'

She flinched as if he'd struck her. 'No . . .' she held up her hand as though to ward off a blow. 'I'm not going to have a baby, it's just a precaution, that's all. I never thought of it as anything else.'

'Well think of it now.' He moved to the door. 'Think clearly, Arian, with your head and brain, if not with your heart. You could do untold harm to yourself, has that occurred to you?'

She put her head in her hands. He was right; she was a cold unnatural monster.

Gerald stared at her for a moment. 'Oh, do what you will,' he said at last. 'I won't stop you.' The door slammed and he was gone. She was alone in the steamy kitchen with the herbs bubbling like poison in the black pot on the fire.

Arian cried until she was exhausted. Then she rose to her feet and taking up a cloth, removed the pot from the flames. She carried it outside and poured the greeny contents onto the ground. The mixture bubbled its way into the soil, sinking at last out of sight, leaving only a residue of scum to show where it had been. Then she went to the pump and ran the water over her hot cheeks and swollen eyes so that her salt tears were cleansed.

She was in bed when Gerald returned home. She stirred as he climbed in beside her. Her eyes were still red and swollen and she felt vulnerable and ill at ease.

'I threw the stuff away,' she said. 'I'm sorry, Gerald.' She lay dry eyed beside him and, after a moment, Gerald put his arms around her, not in passion, as he usually did, but as if he was suffering some of her pain.

Together, they lay in each other's arms and, though it might only be pity on his part and despair on her own, Arian was grateful to Gerald for his gentleness at a time when she most needed it.

As the weeks passed and the winter winds blew through the mountain sides, Arian woke one morning to the realization that she had been mistaken – she was not going to have a baby. She gloried in the knowledge, falling down on her knees beside the bed she shared with Gerald, silently thanking God for sparing her that ordeal and yet, at the same time, an edge of guilt crept into her mind and would not let her rest. She would have to speak with Gerald, tell him of her mistake, and she bit her lip wondering what his reaction would be. She was soon to find out.

'So you did your worst.' His voice was bitter. 'In spite of everything I said, you went ahead and got rid of my child.'

'No I did not.' Even as she spoke, Arian knew it was pointless. Gerald had drawn his own conclusions and nothing she said now would make him listen to the truth but she needed to try to convince him of her innocence.

'I did nothing, took nothing. It was a mistake, I was just late. I couldn't have caught for a child after all. Listen to me, Gerald.'

'I don't believe you,' he said flatly. 'In any case, it doesn't matter now, does it?' He walked out of the room and Arian stood staring at the closed door, her mind in a turmoil, her hands trembling. She was guilty, in a way. The intent was there to rid herself of the child and even if she hadn't actually done it, she had wanted to.

After that, Gerald was cold and withdrawn. He moved his things into the spare room and Arian breathed a sigh of relief; what did it matter what Gerald thought, so long as he left her alone. But strangely, she found it did matter.

She immersed herself in her business more than ever before. Most days, she worked mornings at the bench with the old cobbler she'd hired. Together, she and Vincent

241

repaired boots and shoes for their growing number of customers.

In the afternoons Arian wrote out orders to other firms like Clark's of Somerset and Lotus who made fine slippers, a favourite with the ladies of the town.

Later she would spend an hour or two walking around the streets of Swansea, collecting money due and giving out catalogues. She was always recruiting new customers, as though she felt the need to prove that she was making something of her life. The business, though the profits were small and the money sometimes slow coming in, brought her a small measure of independence, the feeling that she still had an aim in life.

One evening as she sat over her books, working out her profit margins, adding up her expenditure and balancing it with her intake, she sat back and took stock. She was not making a fortune – the repairs were a regular if small source of income and the catalogue business was just about breaking even. Still, all things considered, she was beginning to make some meaning out of her life. She was comfortable in the house Gerald had bought for them, even if she was often alone there. Her hours she could fill with things to do, new catalogues to design, new slogans to write, this was part of the work she really enjoyed.

Gerald came home early. She folded away her papers and sat back in her chair. She could hear him moving about in the other room and she wondered what had brought him home at such an early hour. There was nothing for him here, not now – he didn't even share her bed. Their marriage was no marriage at all.

Gerald came into the room and looked down at her. 'You know something? You look very desirable tonight.' He sounded a little worse for drink. She thought she could smell another woman's scent on him but she remained silent. What he did was no business of hers.

'Very desirable.' He rested his hand on her shoulder, his fingers moved down to her breast and she tensed, knowing by the light in his eyes that he wanted her and intended to have her.

'Gerald,' she spoke softly, urgently, 'please believe me, I'm sorry about everything, about the mistake . . . the . . .' Her words trailed off as he drew her to her feet.

'Let's not talk about that now.' He rested his hands on her shoulders, his tone was abrupt but he was roused and made no attempt to conceal it.

She had no illusions about him. Gerald wanted her, wanted her body. He did not care about her responses. He was a man after all. Love and gentleness did not enter into it.

He led her into the bedroom and undressed, dropping his clothes on the floor. He pushed her back on the bed and took her as he would take a whore, it was a quick coupling with no regard to her feelings.

When he had finished, he rose from her and disappeared into the other room. She could hear him pour water into a bowl and she lay there feeling used and angry. He returned after a few moments and stared down at her.

'Perhaps I should leave a few shillings on the bedside table.' The sarcasm in his voice brought the colour to her cheeks.

'You underprice me, Gerald.' Her reply was sharp. 'I demand much more than that for the sale of my body, you more than anyone should be aware of that.'

'Move over.' He climbed into bed beside her. 'I might as well have my money's worth.'

In the morning, Arian could not bear to stay indoors. Instead, she did her rounds of the nearby streets, taking so many orders that she wondered if she would have to employ a younger, full-time cobbler; the work was getting too much for Vincent and her to handle alone.

She was outside the house of one of her richer customers, busily writing in her notebook that, yet again, Mrs Willerby had failed to pay for the goods she'd received over a month ago when she became aware of a presence, a shadow falling over her.

Arian looked up into the eye of the cold sunlight and for a moment was blinded by it.

'Well, if it isn't Mrs Simples.' Calvin Temple's voice held a marked note of derision. He moved a shade and she saw him clearly; he was looking at her as though she was something distasteful to him. 'Happy are you with your well-to-do husband?'

'Calvin . . .' she began, but he made an impatient gesture which silenced her.

'You are looking well,' he said. 'Living off your husband's ill-gotten gains suits you.'

'Don't be so quick to judge. You are no angel, your sins are just different ones so why should you be anyone's judge?'

'Defending your husband are you? Don't say you've fallen in love with him now that he has lined his pockets.'

Arian lifted her head. 'Mind your own business.' She put her hands on her hips and her coat swung open. She saw Calvin's eyes move over her slender body.

'I suppose Simples finds you a worthwhile bargain.' His implication was plain and galled. Arian struck out at him, her words like stones. 'Don't act holier than thou. I happen to know that you made a Sarah Frogmore pregnant and she a married woman with a child. Is that the behaviour of a gentleman?'

She turned as though to walk away and then she was aware of his hand on her arm.

'You're right, of course,' he said. 'Who am I to judge anyone?' He dropped his hand. 'I could have loved you so much, Arian.' He said it so softly that she hardly heard the words. Then he was striding away, the line of his shoulders taut as though they carried a heavy burden.

Suddenly Arian was tired. She felt weak and rather ill. She moved slowly back along the streets wanting nothing more but to reach the peace and privacy of her own home. She hoped Gerald was out, that he would stay out. But he was there, seated at the dining table, his arms folded across his chest as though he was waiting for her. She took her place beside him and they ate in silence. He made no reference to the previous night and Arian hoped he'd been so drunk that he didn't remember what had happened.

The hope was short lived. That night Gerald again reached out for her, only now he was coldly sober. He took his time having his fill of her and his words, spoken in a drunken anger the night before, rang in her ears. It was clear he meant to have his money's worth of her. In the darkness, when he was asleep, Arian lay dry eyed at her husband's side feeling as though she was trapped in a web from which there was no escape.

CHAPTER SEVENTEEN

Sarah sat in Calvin Temple's sumptuous drawing room and knew that her visit had been a mistake. He was distant from her, even his expression was remote as though he'd much rather be somewhere else. She felt miserable, humiliated and she knew it was all her own fault.

She decided to be honest with him. 'I'm sorry, I shouldn't have come here,' she said. 'It was just that I felt so . . . so abandoned.' She paused, wondering if she was being silly and melodramatic.

'It's as though no-one in the world cares for me,' she added in a small voice. And why should Calvin be any different to the rest of the world? she thought, suddenly seeing their relationship for what it was – nothing more than a brief, casual encounter, at least to Calvin Temple.

'I'm sorry.' His voice held genuine sympathy. 'You are a lovely, charming lady, very persuasive too.' He smiled though his eyes did not meet hers. 'I was wrong to take advantage of your vulnerability. We were both very foolish. Still, you're a very attractive young woman. Don't underestimate yourself.'

She felt suddenly warmly grateful to him. She longed to go to him, rest her head on his shoulder, beg him to hold her, but she knew he wouldn't welcome such a move. Whatever had been between them was all her doing. He'd never wanted her, not really. He'd just been like her, needing someone to turn to in a weak moment.

She rose to her feet. 'I'd better be going. I'm sorry I troubled you but thank you for seeing me anyway.'

He rose quickly and opened the door for her, and his eagerness to see her go compounded the hurt she felt.

'There's nothing to thank me for.' He looked down at her, his brow creased. 'I was irresponsible, I shouldn't have made love to you.' He smiled then. 'But it was an experience I very much enjoyed.'

She knew it was a salve to her pride – he was a good, kind man – but the truth was, their encounter had been only a momentary dalliance on his part.

She left the house and began to walk slowly down the drive. She felt bowed down with humiliation but worse, she was so lonely, so alone.

Leaving the large gates behind her, Sarah headed for the town. She didn't know where she was going or what she intended to do next. She was at a loose end, wife and mother yet none of those things. There was no-one who cared for or needed her, no-one in all the world.

There was a hard lump in her throat and she wanted to cry, to tell everyone of her pain but who would want to know? She took a deep breath and held her head high, unwilling to make a show of herself in the streets of Swansea. She suppressed her tears – she was Sarah Frogmore, respected now by the community who had once looked down on her. She had at least achieved that much but it was a hollow victory.

In a desultory manner, she strolled past the shops, scarcely seeing what was inside the windows. She needed nothing. Her wardrobe was filled to capacity with clothes, so many clothes that she would never find time to wear them. Then her eye was caught by a sign in the window of one of the buildings advertising the catalogue of a Mrs Arian Simples, supplier of boots and shoes. Slippers, perhaps that was something she did need.

As Sarah stood there, idly looking at the bright picture on the front of the catalogue, the door of the building opened and a woman came out into the street. A lock of pale gold hair had escaped from under her hat and her eyes seemed large in her pale face. In her arm was a large bundle of catalogues. They were too heavy for the woman to hold and they slipped to the cobbled roadway into a fan of colours.

Sarah took a step forward. She knew the girl by sight, of course, knew her as Arian Smale, daughter of Bob Smale who had once owned the newspaper. There'd been all sorts of tales about Arian roaming wild over the hillside, living like a hermit in some hut or other but by her dress, Arian was far from the itinerant she had been branded.

Arian seemed to sway, putting her hand against the wall for support and Sarah found herself moving quickly to Arian's side. 'Are you sick? Here let me help you.'

Arian shook her head. 'I just need to sit down, rest a little. I feel so cold and tired.'

'It's all right,' Sarah said reassuringly, 'I'll call a cab to take you home.'

It was as if Arian hadn't heard her and Sarah, holding Arian upright, took a deep breath and lifted her hand, waving frantically towards the busy roadway. To her relief, a driver reigned his horse in to the kerb and she gestured to him to help Arian up into the cab.

'There, there,' she soothed, 'everything is going to be all right.'

'I can manage.' Arian's voice was faint and Sarah squeezed her arm reassuringly. As she sat in the cold leather seat of the swaying cab, Sarah realized Arian was looking at her strangely, almost as if she didn't want her help. But that was absurd.

'Are you in pain?' Sarah asked solicitously. She was, in a peculiar way, enjoying the experience. It was a change to be in control of the situation.

'I'm upset, that's all it is.' Arian spoke through gritted teeth. 'I've been let down. Rich people seem to be all the same, even Calvin Temple is a liar.'

Sarah was taken aback. This woman knew something about her and Calvin, she was sure of it. But how?

'You know Lord Temple?' her voice was strained.

'I doubt if anyone really knows him,' Arian said bitterly. 'You perhaps know him better than most.'

'Not really.' Sarah bit her lip. Did Arian know the truth about Sarah's sham marriage and her liaison with Calvin? And if she did, so what? What harm could she do? But no, Arian couldn't know anything. She was acting strangely because she was ill.

The sound of hooves clip-clopping along the streets seemed to have a soporific effect on Arian and she sank back in the seat, her eyes closed, her hand over her side.

Sarah regarded her thoughtfully. Here was Arian, sick and ill with no-one, it seemed, to care about her. The husband was probably an unfeeling brute who took his pleasure of her however bad she was feeling. Sarah bit her lip, would that were her problem.

There was no-one at home when Sarah knocked on the door of the plain sunwashed house in the hills. She pushed the door wide open and helped Arian inside.

'Come on,' she said, 'there's no need to worry. I'll get you into bed and call the doctor. He'll know what's up with you.'

'I don't want a doctor to tell me what's wrong,' Arian said flatly. 'I know what's wrong.'

'Why, what is it?' Sarah pushed the kettle onto the hob and looked round for the teapot. A cup of tea always seemed to help whatever the situation.

'I'm two months gone,' Arian said, her eyes hooded by her lids. 'I didn't want to tell my husband because last time I thought I'd fallen for a baby, I was mistaken. It caused nothing but bitterness between us.' She rubbed at her eyes. 'It's a punishment on me. I'm miscarrying the child, I just know it.' She shook her head. 'I don't know why I'm telling you this, I don't know what I think you can do to help.'

Sarah felt a sense of panic. No longer in control, she turned around as though searching for help. There seemed to be no house near by, no neighbourly old woman to call on.

'Come on,' she said with a firmness she didn't feel, 'I think you'd better get into bed.'

It was difficult negotiating the stairs. Arian kept crumpling under the pain but, at last, Sarah managed to get her into the bed. Breathing heavily, Sarah looked down at Arian; her eyes were squeezed together in pain, her knees drawn up to her stomach.

'There's a good girl,' Sarah said softly. 'It's going to be all right. Let's get your skirts off you, shall we?'

Arian looked at her with huge eyes. 'Help me, I don't want to be alone, not now.'

'I won't leave you, don't you worry.' Sarah swallowed hard. She'd been about to suggest running for help, she just wasn't equipped to handle such a situation. Her thoughts were confused, she was almost as frightened as Arian but at least she made a pretence of being calm.

She rolled up her sleeves, a gesture designed to infuse some confidence in both herself and Arian but inside, she was trembling. She remembered, with a feeling of pain, the time she'd miscarried her own child, hers and Calvin's, the baby she'd given up so much for. It had been an awful experience but at least she'd had an experienced midwife at hand, someone who knew exactly what to do.

She became aware that on the bed, Arian was straining against the cruel contractions. Sarah felt a momentary pang of fear, Arian cried out, and then it seemed Sarah was too busy to worry about making any mistakes. She looked for clean towels, ran up and down stairs with bowls of water. Someone had told her that cold compresses prevented heavy bleeding, it was worth a try.

At last it was over. Sarah found herself almost in tears as she sat back onto the bed. Arian, lying panting beside her, was exhausted, drained and pale but no longer in pain.

'It's finished.' Sarah began to clean up the bedroom. She knew that all she could do now was to make Arian as comfortable as possible. 'You'll be all right, you're a strong girl.'

Arian didn't reply. She seemed empty of feeling. Her face lacked any vestige of colour and tears slipped from under her closed lids.

250

Quickly, with a deftness she hadn't known she possessed, Sarah made up the bed with fresh, clean sheets and plumped up the pillows beneath Arian's tangled hair.

'Perhaps you should have the doctor now, just to make sure you're all right.' Sarah washed her hands briskly and rolled down her sleeves. 'I'll make you some tea, if you like.' She didn't know what else to suggest. Arian was so still, so silent, it was unnerving.

Arian didn't reply and it was with a sense of relief that Sarah heard the front door opening.

'Arian!' A strong masculine voice called out from below and Sarah hurried eagerly to the top of the stairs.

'Up here,' she said and found she was looking into the face of one of the most handsome men she'd ever seen. He took the stairs two at a time and when he entered the room Sarah saw he was very tall, with a tapering waist and hips, and fine strong legs beneath the good cloth of his suit. His hair was awry and his eyes, dark and magnetic, stared into hers. So this was Arian's husband.

He moved to the bed at once and knelt down, his hand reaching out to cover Arian's listless fingers.

'Are you all right?' he asked abruptly. 'I knew something was wrong. I was drinking in the Castle tap room when this driver came in with a story about a woman falling sick in his cab. I heard him mention our house and I came at once. What's wrong, Arian? Have you caught some plague, what?'

Arian's eyes flickered open. 'I'll be all right, Gerald,' she said with a touch of bitterness in her voice, 'I haven't caught any plague. Just give me time.'

Sarah moved forward and touched Gerald Simples's arm. 'Let her rest,' she spoke softly. 'She needs a bit of quietness after all she's gone through.'

'What exactly has happened?' Gerald's tone was almost threatening and yet Sarah knew she was strongly attracted to him. He was so masculine, so dominant – the complete opposite of Geoffrey.

'It happens quite often,' Sarah said placatingly, 'she's had a miscarriage but she'll be all right.'

Gerald moved away from her as though he had been bitten by a snake.

'Is she telling me the truth?' Gerald looked coldly at Arian who turned her head away from him.

'She's telling the truth. I couldn't help it, Gerald, believe me. I didn't want it to happen.'

Gerald slammed his fist against the wall and, alarmed, Sarah stepped back apace.

'These things can't be helped,' she spoke placatingly. 'It's nature's way. It will be all right next time, you'll see.'

Gerald didn't turn or speak, he just continued to stare down at his wife as though he hated her. Sarah moved downstairs, feeling it tactful to leave them together, but Gerald followed her.

'I understand you helped my wife home. I'm very grateful. Perhaps I could offer you some sort of compensation for your trouble.' He sounded businesslike, almost off-hand and Sarah was stung.

'No need for gratitude. I only did what any woman would do in the circumstances and as for money, I have more of that than I need.'

She was aware that Gerald Simples's expression changed but so slightly that she could not interpret what it meant.

'Please leave me your name and address.' He moved a little closer. 'I am grateful to you, I don't know what would have happened if you hadn't been around.'

Sarah warmed to him. It was good to be appreciated and Gerald Simples was an extremely handsome man. She held out her hand and he engulfed it in his.

'I'm Sarah Frogmore,' she said, 'a wife and mother myself.' She lowered her gaze. 'But my husband is away on business,' she lied blatantly, 'and he's taken our son with him.'

Gerald's hand tightened over hers. 'You're lonely,' he said, 'the man must be blind to leave a woman as beautiful as you. Please, let me at least pay for a cab to take you home.'

252

Sarah shook her head. 'No need. Geoffrey doesn't leave me short of funds, he's very generous in that way.'

'I couldn't persuade you to stay for a few days, could I?' Gerald was still holding her hand and Sarah felt that she would very much like to know him better. She looked round at the small neat house, so insignificant compared to her own home and a thought struck her.

'Why not come and stay with me?' she suggested with enthusiasm. 'Both of you. I have more rooms than I can fill and you would be most welcome. There we can be waited on by the servants, and Arian will be able to rest.'

'That's very kind, very kind indeed,' Gerald said, appearing to hesitate, 'but I wouldn't dream of imposing.'

'It wouldn't be an imposition,' Sarah said quickly. 'I would be glad of the company. Please say you'll come and stay, at least for a while.'

She would hire a nurse to care for Arian and that would leave her free to enjoy Gerald Simples's company undisturbed. She wouldn't be breaking anything up – by the look of it, the Simples didn't have much going for their marriage.

'I will explain the situation to my wife,' he said. The words stabbed Sarah with a sudden pain. He leaned towards her as though sensing her hurt, his dark eyes looking down into hers.

'Arian doesn't always understand that what I do is in her best interest. Has anyone ever told you how very beautiful you are?' He didn't seem aware of the abrupt change in his tone. He looked at Sarah with undisguised admiration and she felt the rich colour flow into her cheeks, felt alive for the first time in months, alive and attractive. While she was searching for something to say, Gerald was turning away from her, adopting a matter-of-fact tone as he spoke again.

'I would be very grateful for your help, Mrs Frogmore, and I won't deny it. I would be honoured to accept your kind invitation if you're sure it's no inconvenience. I have to work, you see, and I don't like to think of Arian left alone.'

'Sarah, call me Sarah. *Duw*, it's no inconvenience. It will be lovely to have a man in the house again. May I suggest something?' she added a little more decisively. '*Tell* Arian what we intend to do, don't ask her. She's in no frame of mind to make a sensible decision right now.'

He turned to look over his shoulder at her, his eyes warm. 'I think you are right, Mrs . . . Sarah. We shall make the arrangements between us, shall we?'

She felt suddenly happy. Her house would be filled again, filled with the healthy scents and the laughter of a real man. The fact that Arian would be there too scarcely rippled the surface of her mind.

'Let's do that, then,' she said smiling.

Arian sat in the warm, comfortable armchair near the window and stared out at the manicured gardens of the Frogmore house. Events had overtaken her, or so it seemed; one minute she was in bed in her own modest home and the next she was transported to what was virtually a mansion.

Her body still ached. She was weak and lethargic. She knew she was neglecting her business – there was money to be collected, boots to be mended, and none of it was getting done. Still, it was kind of Sarah to take them in and at least it spared Arian the awkwardness of being alone with Gerald.

As if on cue, the door opened and Sarah entered the room, a tray of tea in her hand. Arian smiled wanly. Sarah understood and was sympathetic – she had felt like this herself after the loss of her own child. She didn't try to persuade Arian to pull herself together. There was, as she said, a time to mourn what might have been. Arian knew her feelings were mixed; she hadn't ever wanted a child and yet she couldn't deny that the miscarriage was a trauma from which it would take some time to recover.

They sat and talked in a desultory fashion, about trivia, about nothing at all, really. Arian knew that Sarah would have little interest in business matters. When she did talk it was to praise Gerald to the skies for his patience and his endurance.

If the truth were to be told, Arian found Sarah empty headed, tedious even, and yet she had been so kind that Arian felt beholden to her.

'You're very quiet,' Sarah said, as though sensing a little of what Arian was feeling.

'I'm just tired.' Arian knew it was a lame excuse but she was too weary to think of anything else. In any case, Sarah got to her feet eagerly enough.

'I'll leave you, then. Is there anything you need?' She waited in vain for a reply and when Arian shook her head, Sarah left the room, closing the door quietly behind her.

Arian returned to her chair and resumed her contemplation of the garden. It was peaceful and sun-kissed and though the wind trembled through the leaves, it seemed warm and welcoming. Arian felt a desire to go outside but she hesitated. What if she came face to face with Gerald? She knew he blamed her for what had happened, which was unjust but she could hardly blame him. As yet, he'd respected her wishes and left her alone. Perhaps he hated her. There had certainly been more than anger in his eyes when he'd found out what had happened on that awful day, was it a month ago?

If only this tiredness would go. Sarah reassured her that she would get over it, would soon return to normality but Arian doubted she would ever feel normal again.

She closed her eyes and leaned back in her chair. Perhaps she didn't have the energy to go into the garden, after all. Perhaps the best thing would be to end it all, to walk into the embracing arms of the seas of Swansea Bay and never look back. It was a thought she had toyed with more than once, an intriguing, teasing thought. She went to the bed and lay down on the soft covers, closing her eyes as though to shut out the world.

Slowly, sleep, her only respite from the feelings of terror that plagued her, stole over her and Arian, temporarily, was at peace.

* * *

Sarah had tried all her wiles to entice Gerald Simples into her bed and so far she had failed. She knew he admired her – he made that abundantly clear. He flattered her with his words and with his eyes, he made her feel she was the most desirable woman in all the world and yet he still evaded her.

She was falling in love with him, she knew it. Even her feelings for Calvin Temple that had flared briefly into flames died into embers in the face of this new love.

She couldn't fathom Gerald Simples. She would have put her last penny on her success in having him succumb to her wiles and yet she had failed. His inaccessibility added a piquancy to the affair that excited her.

At dinner, she told him about Arian's continued tiredness, intimating she should see a doctor or perhaps have a nurse tend her for a time. He frowned, staring at her over the polished silver cutlery that gleamed in the candlelight.

'Do you think that's really necessary?' he asked and he appeared so concerned that Sarah hesitated, wondering if she'd overplayed her hand.

'I think it might be for the best,' she said softly. 'Arian's not well, it's her mind as much as anything. Perhaps a rest home would be the answer?'

She felt well pleased with her suggestion. It would leave her alone in the house with Gerald and with his wife out of the way, he would surely fall into Sarah's arms.

'You are very thoughtful,' Gerald said slowly. 'I could not expose you to the gossip that our being alone would invoke but thank you for caring, Sarah.' He was right, of course. There would be gossip if they were alone.

'I would like to talk to you on another matter, after supper will do,' Gerald said and a dart of hope filled Sarah's breast.

'Yes, of course. Can you give me a little hint of what it's about?'

'Later,' he said and his tone brooked no argument. That was part of what she loved about him. Gerald had an almost ruthless belief in himself and although he was a guest in her house, he never acted as though

Sarah was doing him any favours. It was almost the reverse.

She ate the devilled kidneys and the saddle of lamb which followed it with little appetite and some impatience but at last she rose and took her leave of him, moving into the drawing room while he sat back in his chair and smoked the cigars she had provided for him.

She tried to compose herself so that when he came into the drawing room some time later, she appeared engrossed in the needlepoint on her lap. It was all to create an effect. She was not adept at fine stitches and loathed sewing in any shape or form.

'Ah Gerald,' she smiled up at him, aware of his eyes going to the round firmness of her breasts beneath the silk of the gown. She smiled. 'Come and sit down. Tell me what it was you wanted to talk about.'

He drew his chair close to her and leaned forward, so that if she had reached out, she could have touched the dark hair that curled on his brow.

'I may not have told you quite how I feel,' he said, 'but I'm deeply grateful for all you have done, are doing, for me.' He paused, so close that she could see the sweep of his dark lashes as he glanced down at his hands. 'So grateful that I would like to be of service to you in any way that I can.'

Her heart leapt. There was one way he could repay her and that was to take her in his arms and make her feel wanted but she remained silent, waiting for him to continue.

'I've thought long and hard about this,' he said, 'and what I propose is that I advise you as to your investments.' He paused. 'You may know that I was adviser to Lord Temple in just that field.'

So now she had him. Money, or at least the manipulation of it, was what heated Gerald Simples's blood. Although he couched his words in fine phrases, Sarah knew naked greed when she saw it and she was quite prepared to give Gerald control over some of her money in return for his passion, and if possible his love.

She rose, resisting the desire to reach out to him and put forward a bold proposition; subtlety was the way forward with this man, she knew it in her bones.

'I will think about what you have said.' She smiled benignly. 'I do my best thinking in the comfort of my bed,' she added with a small lift to her eyebrows.

She left the room and made her way up the wide staircase, her heart pounding. Had she overplayed her hand? Had she totally misjudged him? Somehow, she doubted it.

Later she sat against the pillows, her satin gown clinging to her body, concealing and yet revealing. Sarah knew that she was a voluptuous woman, a healthy woman. Gerald must be growing more than a little tired of the pale, passionless wife he'd married.

She was not wrong. It was perhaps twenty minutes later, long minutes during which doubts assailed her, when she heard the door-handle turn. She smiled up at Gerald. His hair was damp and tousled, and he wore a silk dressing-gown and nothing else, if her eyes did not deceive her, and her heart rejoiced. She held out her hand.

'I've had an idea,' she said softly. 'What if I had an aged aunt come to stay here with me? That would silence any gossips.' Sarah had no aged aunts that she knew of but she could easily hire one. 'And what if you were to act as my house steward? In name only, of course. You could have one of the best rooms in the servants' quarters.' She laughed softly. 'Not that you would need to occupy it very often, it would be just for appearances' sake, you understand?'

He didn't seem convinced.

'Of course I would pay you far more than the usual steward's wages of a hundred pounds a year, much more.' Her eyelashes fluttered up at him in an open invitation.

Gerald didn't answer but she could see he was now considering her words carefully.

'All right.' His words were clipped but Sarah felt triumphant. It was the mention of wages that had done the trick and she knew it. Still, once he'd tasted of her charms he would be eager to come to her bed without extra inducement.

She smiled up at him. 'I've been waiting for you for so long.'

Waiting for far too long, she thought as he came towards the bed but now, she would have her fill of him. Tonight, he would make his first commitment to her and tonight was only the beginning.

CHAPTER EIGHTEEN

Arian worked over her accounts trying to push aside the mists of doubt and worry that nagged the edges of her mind but she couldn't escape the fact that her business prospects were not good. Sales had been static this past month and the position was made worse by the fact that she'd been unable to collect any money.

She put down her pen carefully, a frown creasing her brow. It looked likely that she would have to dismiss Vincent, difficult as that would be. She simply couldn't afford to pay him.

She sighed as she closed the books and sat back in her chair, looking round at the small office with a sense of despair. She'd rented the place with high hopes but that was before she'd been taken ill. At the time, she'd felt the need to have a place of her own, it was an assertion of her independence.

The office was sparsely furnished and the rent was accordingly low but still, she had no choice but to move out – it was a case of cutting back on everything that was not essential.

It was a great pity, though. The office had become her retreat from the world, an oasis of calm that was all her own, somewhere she could be free of Gerald.

Arian rose and moved to the window that looked out on nothing but a bare brick wall. She might as well face the truth. She was a failure. Even here in this office, with the smell of pencils and ink and old books, she'd not been able to arouse any enthusiasm for her job. It was as though with the loss of her child, her initiative had been lost too.

She put on her coat. It was time she returned home. Not that she was home – she was still living in that huge mausoleum of a place with Sarah Frogmore, who was no friend. Arian had overheard her suggestion that they send Arian to some sort of nursing home. Sarah, who had been unfaithful to her husband with Calvin Temple, was acting as if she was a saint. Well, Arian would stay no longer. Gerald could do as he pleased, the matter was one of complete indifference to her.

She took a cab. It was an extravagance she couldn't afford but she was impatient now to get her belongings, begin her return to some sort of control of her life. She sank back into the creaking seat. She realized she was still feeling weak and tired, and was glad she was spared the long walk through Swansea and the climb up the hill to the big house.

There was no sign of Gerald. Sarah though, was sitting in the drawing room, a tray of cordial on the table beside her. She looked at Arian as though she'd grown two heads.

'What are you doing home?' She had followed the silent Arian upstairs and was watching as she packed away her few possessions.

'I'm getting out of here,' Arian spoke softly. 'Thanks for all you've done, Sarah, but I can't stay any longer. I feel I'm suffocating.'

'You're not well,' Sarah's protest was feebly made and Arian smiled wryly. 'And you need someone to look after you. If you go back to your place you'll have to do your own cooking and washing. Are you up to it?' Sarah made the chores sound as bad as a term of imprisonment and Arian smiled.

'I'll manage. I managed before and anyway, it wouldn't hurt Gerald to get us some help, he can well afford it.' She hurried upstairs and hastily threw some clothes into a bag.

'I'm sure you should wait and consult Gerald. He's been very comfortable here,' Sarah said when Arian returned to the drawing room.

'I'm sure he has.' Arian's voice was dry. 'What he does is up to him, he can stay if he likes. I'm off home.' She waved her hand around the room.

'Anything I can't carry, he can bring me later.' She paused. 'I know you've been kind but I have to begin again, take charge of my own life. Please try to understand.'

Sarah looked down at her shoes like a small child sulking. 'I wish you'd wait a bit. There's no rush, is there?'

It was no good. Sarah was too self-centred to see anyone else's point of view. For a moment, Arian wondered just why Sarah had taken her into her home but did the reason really matter?

Arian made her way back to where the cab was waiting. The driver was feeding the horse an apple and smoking a pipe. He seemed well pleased with his expensive fare and was obviously of the opinion he could afford to take a break.

Arian sank back into the cab seat with a sigh of relief. She was out of there, away from the cloying kindness Sarah heaped upon her. She'd found that living with Sarah she'd begun to feel cloistered, weak, dependent, almost as though she was unfit to plan her own future. How dare Sarah suggest that Arian go to a rest home to recuperate. What precisely did she intend to achieve by it?

Anger swept through her afresh as Arian thought of the way she'd allowed Sarah to take over her life. It wasn't even that she liked Arian. Indeed, they had nothing in common. No, it was Gerald whom Sarah wanted to impress.

The whitewashed house seemed a haven of tranquillity; windows had been left open and the sun was warming the rooms. Arian paid off the cab driver and then went inside and stood for a moment drinking in the silence. She dropped her bag and sank down into a chair. It was good to be back.

It was much later when Gerald arrived. Arian could tell by his face that he was displeased with her.

'Couldn't you wait to discuss all this with me?' He swung his hands around indicating the cheerful fire in the grate and the kettle boiling on the hob. Arian resisted the temptation to be facetious and ask him did he mean the brewing of a cup of tea, and shook her head.

'I wanted to come home, there's nothing to discuss.'

'I see. So you're fit again, are you?'

Arian was slightly puzzled by his attitude. 'I'm feeling better, yes.'

'Good.' He went upstairs and she could hear him in the room they shared, putting away his things. She sighed. So that's what he intended, he would be sleeping in her bed once more. Well, that was the bargain they'd made and it was one she would honour.

Arian settled quickly into the routine of being home again. She had given up the office and had brought her books home and had begun, tentatively, to try to collect money from her customers. Slowly, her life was falling into some sort of pattern and she had at least made a start at hauling herself onto her feet again.

Arian considered one of the biggest disadvantages of leaving Sarah's house would be having Gerald in her bed again but after the initial move he'd made – the great show of storing away his belongings – he'd not come near her. Quite what his motive was in occupying the spare room Arian couldn't fathom, but she didn't intend to raise the issue with him. The great bonus of her return to her own house was being spared Sarah's endless, inane gossip, most of which seemed focused on Gerald.

It was all too good to last. One evening when Arian was sitting at the kitchen table with her account books spread out before her, Sarah arrived unannounced with a basket of fruit and cheese and a huge crusty batch of bread. She breezed into the kitchen and set the basket down regardless of Arian's protests.

'It's nothing, nothing at all. I felt like making you and Gerald a small gift, please don't thank me.'

Arian removed her books, carefully brushing away breadcrumbs from the freshly inked pages. 'How kind of you, Sarah. Please sit down, Gerald will be here soon.'

'Good, it's Gerald I want see. I need his help with my finances. I can't manage alone and he's so capable, you know.' Sarah paused and looked at her archly. 'You don't mind if I borrow him for a few evenings a week, do you?'

For Gerald to visit Sarah several evenings a week was an appealing thought. 'The arrangement would suit me admirably, Sarah. Feel free to borrow him any time you like.'

Gerald, when he returned home, was not quite so enthusiastic. 'I'll do my best, Sarah, but I'm very busy, you know.'

'Oh, please Gerald. There are some new investments I've been told about and I want you to look over the paperwork before I sign anything.'

Gerald, Arian could see, was hooked. He smiled warmly. 'In that case, I'll come back with you right now. No time like the present.'

It was quiet when they'd left and Arian picked up her pen. She still had work to do. There was the new autumn catalogue to plan – the production of it would take several weeks. She had already written most of the glowing advertisements, describing the latest fashion in boots and shoes, a task she always enjoyed.

Whether she could afford the outlay of having the catalogue printed was questionable but if she didn't advertise, she wouldn't get any fresh custom. It was a difficult decision but, in the long run, she felt she would benefit by taking the risk.

Some days later Arian packed up her notes and made her way to the village of Clydach. She had arranged to meet Eline and have a talk with her about the footwear business, ask her advice, if possible. At this stage anything was worth a try.

It was the first time she'd been back to the village since Gerald had virtually abducted her, and a feeling of depression fell over her as she saw the long street and the sloping hills surrounding the boot and shoe shop. She'd been unhappy here, lacking challenge, an aim in life, and even if things were difficult now, at least she was no longer vegetating.

Eline was looking well. She had put on a little weight and it suited her. She hugged Arian and pressed a cup of tea on her the moment she set foot in the kitchen.

'Tell me all that's been happening to you.' Eline leaned forward eagerly. 'Will and me, well we were worried until we got that letter from your husband. Fancy you going back to him, I thought that was over and done with.'

Arian could hardly tell her what had really happened, it all sounded so implausible. Nor could she explain that anything, even a life that included Gerald, had been preferable to tramping the cold streets, carrying heavy boots and shoes from house to house.

'We decided to try again, make a fresh start.' Arian smiled. 'Sorry it was all so abrupt but Gerald was impulsive, he was so anxious to have me home.'

'Well, anyway, is this a social visit or what?' Eline rose and lifted the teapot. 'Here, hold out your cup and, whatever your reason for coming, I'm very happy to see you.'

'Well, it's bit of both, business and pleasure.' Arian stirred some sugar into her tea. 'I'd like you to do some designs for my latest catalogue and I'd like to have some of your stock, as well.'

'Sounds interesting, but why now, Arian? I mean, I thought you dealt with Clark's and the like.'

'I'll be honest,' Arian felt it best to come clean. 'Yes, I've been buying from the big companies but they're expensive and I owe them money. The business is rocky and I need a breathing space.'

'I see,' Eline's voice was guarded. 'Well, if I can help then I'd be pleased to.'

'I've great hopes for the business,' Arian said quickly. 'I've let things slide for the last few weeks but I've great hopes for renewing my contacts, building up a reliable clientele again. It worked before I . . . before I was sick and I know it will work again.'

'I didn't know you'd been poorly. Of course I'll help, Arian. I'll do all I can for you. Come on, let's get down to business, see what we can work out.'

This was the old Eline, the good business woman and generous friend, and Arian bit her lip feeling her throat constrict with tears. 'Right, this is what I want – as much of your stock as you can spare and say, two or three designs to include in my catalogue and, Eline, I'm grateful to you.'

'Nonsense, let's see if together we can't put you back on the road to success.'

Later, as Arian made her way home, she brooded a little on the outcome of her visit. It had been unfair of her to talk about her sickness, it had put Eline under an obligation and yet she didn't see any way around it. How else could she explain the lack of progress over the last weeks? She certainly didn't want Eline to think she'd been slacking or that she'd made too many mistakes. Still, she had what she'd requested. Eline would send the stock down by van tomorrow and already, some of her designs were in Arian's bag.

When she arrived in Swansea, Arian breathed in the scents of the sea with relief. It was good to be back. She heard a bird singing, the piercing notes high and sweet on the evening air and felt a catch in her throat. Freedom; how beautiful was the word, how wonderful to feel unencumbered by ties.

Suddenly restless, Arian set out quickly towards home. She would forget about business. She'd worked hard enough this past week and her mind was becoming stale. She needed time to herself and, with a bit of luck, the house would be empty. She could pretend, for a while at least, that she was her own woman, obligated to no one.

The weather was warm and the air balmy, and as Arian left the streets of Swansea and started up the hill she saw a couple walking hand in hand. A sharp regret filled her, she'd missed out on so much in life. It would be wonderful to be with a man she loved, with Calvin Temple. She imagined him walking with her, holding her hand, looking down into her eyes. All that was just a dream. She had decided long ago that love was not for her. Now it was questionable if she would even succeed in business.

She'd once had such plans, such hopes, that one day she would make something of herself, that she would be fulfilled in one way at least. Surely she couldn't allow that dream to be snatched away from her too?

She sighed. She'd been happy once, hadn't she? She thought with a pang about her first love, Eddie, who had been so young and ardent, so eager to please. Arian had been so innocent about love then, she'd not really begun to experience the true depths of feelings. She had given herself sweetly and carelessly to Eddie, tossing away her favours as though they didn't mean anything. Eddie was a practising doctor now, she'd heard he had come back to Swansea with a comfortable wife and a brood of children. She hoped he was happy.

She felt a shrinking as she thought of her husband. She didn't love Gerald, would never love him. She knew she would resent his touch more than ever now. How could she go on living this lie and yet, how could she escape from the web of deceit she'd woven for herself.

She walked up the hill towards her home. Home, what an empty word it was. House, an empty house with no laughter in it, no light or joy, just a heavy sense of duty.

It was a long walk and Arian felt tired as she reached the brow of the hill and caught her first glimpse of the white building nestling among the folding hills. It was beautified by the sunlight and yet she felt no sense of homecoming, just relief that her journey was almost over.

She walked in through the open door, longing for a hot cup of tea and a chair to sit on. In the passageway, something, some intangible instinct made her pause and listen.

From upstairs came the low sound of laughter, excited laughter, throaty and somehow suggestive. Arian climbed the stairs silently and stood on the small landing. There was the laugh again, Sarah Frogmore's laugh but different.

Arian moved towards her bedroom and pushed the door open and, strangely, she was not surprised to see

267

Sarah in bed with Gerald, both of them naked, both of them looking at her in startled amazement.

'I know,' her tone was heavy with sarcasm, 'you're helping Sarah with her investments.' She retreated and made her way back downstairs. A great sense of relief filled her. It was over, her marriage, her obligation to Gerald. No longer need she feel bound to him; he had chosen to break their marriage vows and that released her from any promises she had made him.

Shortly, he appeared in the sitting room, his hair brushed, his demeanour showing no signs of embarrassment or discomfort. He looked down at her as she sat in a chair near the window and if she had expected a torrent of excuses, she was mistaken.

'Well?' she said softly. He glanced at her, eyebrows raised, as though she had spoken out of turn.

'Well what?' he asked coolly. He was not going to even try to excuse his behaviour, she realized with a sense of disbelief.

'Well, that's the end of our marriage,' she said coldly. 'I would like you to pack your belongings and get out of here and take Sarah with you.'

'I have no intention of moving out,' he said easily. 'This is my house and you are my wife or have you forgotten?'

'Have I forgotten?' she echoed. How dare he act as though nothing had happened.

Sarah entered the room and she was flushed, more with passion than with shame, Arian suspected.

'He's yours, Sarah,' Arian said. 'Gerald can come and live with you permanently, I don't want him.'

'You mean that?' Sarah said, her eyes shining. She caught Gerald's arm. 'Hear that, Gerry? You can come home with me. We can have a proper relationship. I'll look after you so well. Arian knows all about us now and I'm so glad.'

'This is my home,' Gerald said. 'I have no intention of leaving it.'

Sarah looked up at him anxiously. She had tensed and a frown creased her brow. After a moment, Gerald took her hands in his.

'Look, my dear, I am an independent sort of man, I don't want to live on your charity. I'd like to be with you all the time but I can't, it wouldn't be proper. Surely you can understand?'

'No, Gerald, I don't understand.' Sarah looked mutinous and Arian leaned back in her seat, watching the little scene, almost enjoying Gerald's unease.

'Come home with me. Arian doesn't want you here. What could be more simple?' She snuggled up to him. 'You do love me, Gerald, don't you? It isn't just the money, is it?'

Arian saw the warring of Gerald's feelings. He wanted control of Sarah's riches and yet he didn't want to relinquish his control of his wife.

'Gerald,' Sarah decided to assert herself, 'I'm not staying here a moment longer. Come with me. We'll be happy together. You know we will. She's no good – she's cold, unfeeling. She'll never amount to anything.'

'If you don't go, Gerald,' Arian spoke quietly in contrast to Sarah's excited tones, 'I will. It's over. Salvage what you can. You know what I mean?'

He knew what she meant; he wouldn't have her, so he might as well have Sarah and her money. He looked at her for a long moment and then, as though he knew he had lost, he turned abruptly away.

'All right, I'll go.' His voice was low with controlled anger. 'But I'll be back, I promise you that.'

Sarah cast a triumphant glance towards Arian and as Gerald hurried up the stairs, she spoke softly. 'You see, I've won. He'll forget you in time. I'll win him over to my way of thinking and then he won't want anything to do with you.'

Arian looked at her without expression. 'It's a relief,' she said. 'I never wanted him to touch me.'

'I don't believe that. Gerald is a handsome man, and any woman in her right mind would be happy to be in the same house as him.'

The two women stood in silence for a moment. Sarah glanced anxiously up the stairwell.

'Gerry, are you coming, I'm waiting.'

She turned to Arian. 'I'm not sorry to be taking him away from you. You never appreciated what a fine man you had, did you?'

'I never wanted Gerald,' Arian spoke flatly. 'You will make him happy, for a time, at least until your money runs out.'

'Right,' Gerald came quickly down the stairs, his eyes alight, he had found a way to hurt her. 'Money seems to be your obsession, not mine, but as we're on the subject I assume you won't need an allowance from me.' He paused for his words to sink in. 'You have your income from your business, and would probably prefer to be independent and manage on that.'

When she didn't reply he shrugged. 'It won't be easy living without my support. The day will come when you'll beg me to come back to you, mark my words.'

Sarah clung onto his arm. 'But you won't come back to her at any price, will you, Gerry? You've got me, you've always got me.'

Gerald caught her in his arms. 'Of course I have and I'll do right by you, Sarah, believe me. You're a warm natural woman and I'll give you fine sons, all the sons you could wish for.'

He glanced at Arian as though to taunt her. 'The only surprise to me,' he spoke slowly, deliberately so there would be no chance of misunderstanding him, 'is that you, Sarah, my darling are not full with my child already. We've made love enough times.'

If he thought to make her jealous, he was wasting his time. Arian, meeting Sarah's eyes caught the fleeting look of fear and remembered with stunning clarity the day at Calvin Temple's house when Sarah had flung into the room in tears. She'd miscarried of Calvin's child, she had cried pitifully that she could have no more children. Arian remained silent. That was Sarah's secret and if

Gerald wanted sons by Sarah, Arian could see problems ahead for her.

'You'd better go, both of you.' Arian's voice was cold. 'I don't think there's any point in delaying, do you? We've said all we have to say, we've both made our positions entirely clear.'

Gerald left the room without a word and Sarah followed him, glancing back with something like gratitude in her eyes. At the doorway she paused. 'I'll look after Gerry, and don't forget, if you need any help, *any* sort of help, I'm not short of money.' It was a sop to Sarah's belated conscience and Arian knew it.

After the outer door had closed the house fell into a dreaming silence. Arian sank into a chair, relief flooding over her. She was just glad that the unpleasantness was over.

It was true that now she had the responsibility for maintaining the house as well as the business but she would think about that later. For now, it was enough to be alone.

She felt suddenly sick and ill, perhaps she had a chill coming on. Still, whatever it was, she must shake it off. Somehow, she would have to make a living for herself. As for Gerald Simples, she only hoped she would never set eyes on him again.

Sarah lay in Gerald's arms. He was still now, his passion spent – if you could call what had happened an act of passion. Sarah caught her breath on a sigh as she looked at Gerald's dark head, turned away from her. He had taken her as a stallion takes a mare, with no sensitivity, no feeling except the need for his own release.

She had come to the conclusion over the last week or two that Gerald Simples loved his wife. He dallied with Sarah, had enjoyed her when theirs was an illicit arrangement but now that they were together permanently, their coupling had nothing of romance about it. He even complained about the old 'aunt' she'd hired to chaperone them.

And yet she was grateful to have him in her house, in her bed, for Gerald was the man she was in love with. She sighed softly. Why did she spurn worthy men like William Davies who once, when they were both young, had been her lover? Why did she fall for tough, hard-nosed villains like Gerald Simples? For he was a villain, she'd learned that much about him, and it made no difference to her feelings, she still loved and wanted him.

She reached out her fingertips. His strong neck and broad shoulders were exposed by the bedclothes and his dark hair curled on the nape of his neck in the most beguiling way. Oh yes, he was a crook, a crook of the first order. He had taken her money, quite a lot of it, and salted it away somewhere in so-called stocks and bonds.

But Sarah was no fool. In spite of her love for Gerald, she saw him clearly for what he was. Still, she reckoned it was a small price to pay and she would go on paying it for as long as necessary. It was ironic really. Her husband Geoffrey Frogmore was the one who was really paying and that seemed entirely fitting to Sarah, serve him right for leaving her alone. What he would do when he found out that she was living with Gerald she didn't know but neither did she care any longer.

She ran her hands over Gerald's back. His skin was like silk. His hair touched the back of her hand and a great tenderness filled her. He moved suddenly and rose from the bed, and stood looking down at her with an expression in his dark eyes she did not quite understand.

'I have to go out,' he said, standing naked and magnificent beside her. 'Send for the maid to bring water, would you?'

She stared up at him longing to snap at him that she wasn't his servant but she bit back the angry words, frightened that he would leave her if life proved difficult for him.

She rose, pulled on a robe and rang the bell for the maid to come.

'I'll see you sometime tomorrow,' Gerald said and she looked at him sharply.

'Tomorrow?' she asked anxiously. 'Won't you be back home tonight, Gerald?'

'No,' he said shortly. 'I have a business meeting that'll take quite a long time and I will probably stay at the club.'

'The club.' She echoed his words, dismay evident in her voice. 'But Gerald, there's the dinner party. It was for you I arranged it.' She was aware that her words sounded silly and trivial. He walked from the bedroom without answering.

'In any case, if you do have to go out, if your appointment is urgent, can you please try to come back? I don't mind how late it is. Please come home to me.'

'That's not what you said last time I was late.' There was the sound of water from the elegant bathroom and Gerald's voice rose above it. Sarah knew he was punishing her.

'I'm sorry if I was angry,' she said quickly. 'I was worried, frightened that you'd had an accident. I won't be like that ever again, I promise you.'

She hated herself for the abject pleading in her voice but she couldn't help herself. 'Please Gerald, come home. You can sleep in your own bedroom in the servants' quarters if you like.'

'All right,' he said quickly, too quickly. 'That way I won't disturb you however late I am.'

She had played into his hands, Sarah realized at once. This is what he'd wanted all along, an excuse to sleep alone. The club, of course, cost him money, his own room did not. A taste of bitterness filled her mouth, the feeling that she wasn't wanted, that she was nothing more than a whore but instead of being paid for her services she was the one doing the paying.

She turned away from him when he returned to the room, too hurt to speak, and she heard him close the door behind him with a feeling of dread. She should tell him to go, she should salvage what little was left of her pride but she knew she would go on taking the crumbs Gerald offered for as long as he was willing to provide them.

She watched from the window as he strode away down the drive, nodding curtly to old Peters who opened the tall gates for him. Then he was gone from sight. Sarah sank into her chair with tears streaming along her cheeks. She was hurt, so hurt she thought she would die of it.

What was wrong with her? Why couldn't she find a man to love and cherish her? It was not much to ask, was it? She closed her eyes and thought for a moment of all the men who had, briefly, been part of her life. None of them, not even Sam Payton, the first man she had really loved, not one of them came up to Gerald Simples's shoulder. She wanted him and so she would put up with whatever treatment he meted out. Unless the scales fell from her eyes and she saw him for what he really was. But that day, she felt, would be a long time coming.

Gerald strode from the town towards his house in the hills. He had been kept informed of Arian's comings and goings. He paid his informers well. The young village girl whom Arian had employed to help her in the house would do anything for a few pennies. Women, they were all whores, all to be bought – all, that is, except Arian.

He smiled. Soon she would ask him to come back to her. The business was falling deeper into debt, she'd given up her office, and even let old Vincent go. And now it seemed she was unwell, suffering from some sort of chill. She was vulnerable; this perhaps was the time to forgive her and go back to her.

Gerald had made it his business to buy out her debts, so it was to him she owed the money now though she didn't realize it. He would catch her at a weak moment and he would get what he wanted, just what he wanted.

He entered the house without knocking; it was his house still and Arian was lucky to be living in it.

She looked up startled as he entered the kitchen. She was flustered. Her hair was tangled around her face and she was still dressed in her night clothes. He felt his pulses quicken, God how he wanted her. But he must bide his time, he would get her back on his own terms.

As for Sarah, he'd taken almost all he could from her. He had supplemented his income very nicely from her funds and enjoyed the luxuries of her home but, by way of repayment, he'd had to act the stud and had found Sarah a very demanding woman. Now he'd had enough of her cloying, clinging, nature to last him a lifetime.

Arian was always dignified and, strangely, her lack of passion for him enhanced his enjoyment of her. He loved lying with her, caressing her, forcing her into an unwilling response. It gave him a sense of power that was heady and satisfying. And he loved her too, in his own way.

'What do you want?' She spoke baldly, with no welcome in her voice.

'I want to help you.' He smiled, 'I heard you weren't feeling too well. Are you worried about business?'

'You heard? You mean you've been spying on me. Well you won't hear any more. I sacked the girl a few days ago. She didn't do much work anyway, as you can see.' She didn't look at him and he moved closer, determined to get her full attention. She was very thin, worryingly so.

'Are you getting enough to eat?' He resisted the urge to take her into his arms.

'Eat?' she appeared vague. 'I don't know, I suppose so.' She rubbed at her eyes wearily. 'I've just finished doing the books, it'll all come right given time. Don't you worry about me, I don't need your help.'

Gerald took her arm. 'Sit down,' he said. 'I shall cook you breakfast and then I shall put you to bed.'

'No!' She sounded almost panic stricken. 'I don't want anything from you,' she said, 'but I would like to sleep, just for a while. I was up most of the night finishing a pair of boots. The money comes in straight away for repairs, you see.'

Arian moved towards the door. She seemed half asleep already. She stumbled and Gerald caught her arm, holding her around her slim waist with a feeling of such protectiveness that he knew he must have her back, whatever it cost him.

'Go to bed,' he spoke softly, knowing he had to play his cards carefully. To frighten her now would be the worst thing he could do.

'Thank you, Gerald. Please go, I'll be all right.' Arian mounted the stairs without a backward glance and crossed the landing into her room. There, she fell upon the bed and drew the tangled clothes over her.

Gerald returned to the kitchen and closed the door behind him. Arian would sleep for a while and in the meantime, he would just take a look at her books; there were bound to be one or two little items there to interest him.

After a time, he put the books away and, well satisfied, looked around him. Perhaps it would be a good idea to straighten the place up a bit. It was like a pig sty; as she'd said, the village girl hadn't put herself out to clean the place properly. Arian clearly couldn't cope, that's what happened when she was without him. The thought gave him an immense feeling of satisfaction.

A little while later, a cheerful fire roared in the grate and the table was scrubbed and covered neatly with a cloth. The brasses shone and Gerald settled back into his chair with a glow of pride. He seemed to be getting what he wanted out of life – money, position and a beautiful wife. If he played his cards right, he would even have a son, that would be the one thing to make his happiness complete.

Oh, there had been difficulties on the way. He'd needed to leave Arian for a time in order to consolidate his financial position but then most men went away on business. His mouth curved into a smile. That his business included sleeping with Sarah Frogmore was his burden but some things just had to be done, some sacrifices made. Arian would understand that, in time. There was no need for her to be jealous, no need at all. Sleeping with Sarah was a chore, nothing more.

It was a few hours later when he heard footsteps on the stairs and Arian appeared, her eyes still heavy with sleep. She looked around her and took in the neatness of the room with surprise.

'What's happened to the place?' She sank into a chair and Gerald rose at once and made her a hot cup of tea. She took it with gratitude, her eyes soft as they looked up at him. It was the first sign of warmth he'd ever had from her.

'I'm not entirely useless in the kitchen, you see.'

'Thank you for your kindness, it's very much appreciated.' Arian's face clouded. 'That doesn't mean I want you back, Gerald. You do understand it's over, don't you?'

'You're not well, I *do* understand that. All these business worries are too much for you, but then you brought it all on yourself Arian, too much expenditure and not enough income – that way leads to disaster. I could always help you out.'

It pained him to rub salt into her wounds but then it was necessary for she must be made to realize that she needed him.

She shook her head. 'I'll manage, Gerald.'

He doubted it. She looked as though she was about to faint. Gerald hardened his heart.

'I'll be off then, I'll call again in a few days' time, see how you are. Take care, Arian.'

He walked away without glancing back over his shoulder but he knew he had left Arian feeling weak and indecisive and with too much on her hands. She was a woman of spirit but she was not as self-sufficient as she believed. She was too worn down by worries about the business and her health hadn't been too good since she'd suffered the miscarriage.

It was much later when he returned to Sarah's house and he found that her dinner party was in full swing. In his anxiety to advance his plans for Arian's future, he had quite forgotten about it.

The actual meal was over and the guests were assembled in the music room. Calvin Temple was seated in the big chair near the pianoforte and he seemed quite at ease. His eyes, though, were guarded as he saw Gerald but he didn't move.

The other guests were people Gerald knew only by sight; Sarah's father, John Miller and his wife Emily, the old 'Aunt' Sarah had employed and one or two other guests who seemed to Gerald to have come simply to make up the numbers, none of them prominent citizens in any way.

'I'm sorry I'm late, Mrs Frogmore,' he said, formally bending over Sarah's hand. 'But I have been working hard on your behalf.' It didn't do to allow too much of his private life to show in public – that was one dictum he always followed.

'I'm pleased you're here, Simples.' Sarah was in high spirits. 'I wanted to introduce you to my guests as both my wonderful house steward and the financial genius you are.' A strained silence followed her words and Sarah rushed on, 'Lord Temple has been entertaining us with such beautiful music,' Sarah said. 'He really is the most talented man. He does so many things well.'

Gerald caught something in the tone of Sarah's voice that warned him he would have to tread carefully, at least for a while longer. Sarah and Calvin Temple had, obviously, been lovers at some time and she was issuing a warning that it was a relationship easily renewed.

Even while Gerald joined in the small, polite conversations and laughed in all the right places, he was showing by touches of his hand and by meaningful glances that Sarah was, for the moment at least, his property.

In response, she sparkled even more than usual, her eyes bright, her skin flushed. She even seemed desirable. Gerald made up his mind that for tonight, the comfort of his own room would be forgone in favour of Sarah's bed. He must make sure that he pleased her, at least for as long as it took to make Arian beg for his help. The thought filled him with such pleasure that he felt quite generous towards Sarah and actually squeezed her hand in full view of Temple who appeared not to notice.

'Naughty boy,' Sarah whispered in Gerald's ear, 'I'll make you pay for that later, mind.'

'I can't wait,' Gerald said and if there was irony in his voice, Sarah was too happy to notice.

At last the guests had gone and they were alone. Gerald took Sarah in his arms and drew her close. 'I've been all sorts of a bastard lately,' he said, looking down at her, 'but I can't help being moody when I'm worried about money.' That was inspired, for Sarah immediately loosened his hold, went to her desk and took out a bag of chinking sovereigns.

'Never worry about money, my darling,' she hugged him. 'I have enough for both of us. Come on, let's go on up to bed.'

He concealed his irritation. If only, once in a while, she would be a little subtle about her desires, it would be so refreshing.

Still, he was out to charm her, he reminded himself and so he threw some cushions down on the floor and pressed her down against them.

'I want to make love to you here, in the firelight,' he said softly, his lips pressing against the warmth of her neck. She sighed happily.

'That's one thing I like about you, Gerald,' she whispered pressing his hand to her breast. 'You are so daring, so greedy for my love that you can't wait.'

He surpassed himself that night. True, he pretended it was Arian beneath him, although Sarah's loud moans detracted from that fantasy for Arian never made a sound while he took her, but he had achieved what he wanted by convincing Sarah his moods had passed for, afterwards, she turned to him and looked him full in the face, her eyes soft and dreamy.

'I think I must make you an allowance, all legal-like,' she said in a whisper. 'I don't want you to worry about money, not ever again. It must not be allowed to come between us.'

He was so pleased that he felt himself becoming aroused once more and Sarah's look of joy was the seal of approval on their pact.

CHAPTER NINETEEN

Eline sat opposite Arian studying her carefully, concern for her mounting. Gone was the light from her eyes and even Arian's silver-gold hair seemed to lack lustre.

The chatter of the tea-rooms ebbed and flowed around them and Arian sat listlessly in her chair, hands folded in her lap, subservient, as though awaiting instructions. She presented a picture of a supplicant rather than the eager-for-success business woman she was.

'More tea?' Eline asked over the noise of tinkling tea cups and the conversational tone of the ladies on the next table.

'Yes, please,' Arian said, but it was as though she couldn't really care less either way.

Eline put down the pot and leaned forward. 'Arian, what is wrong with you?' The question was blunt and Arian's eyes flickered on Eline's face for a moment before looking away.

'Nothing's wrong. What should be wrong?' She didn't even sound defensive, Eline thought worriedly, just hopeless.

'Something is *very* wrong,' Eline persisted. 'Your husband, is he all right? He's not sick or something, is he?'

Arian's eyes slid away from her. 'No, it's not Gerald's health. He's all right, he always is.'

Eline reached out and touched her hand. 'Come on, we'll go into the foyer. There are some comfortable chairs there and it's not so crowded, we can talk then.'

Arian followed her from the room and obediently took a seat beside Eline, her hands clasped tightly in her lap, the knuckles gleaming white, revealing how tense she was.

'Tell me,' demanded Eline and Arian shook her head in silence for a moment. Then she seemed to gather her courage and, slowly, she began to talk.

'There is something wrong,' she spoke with great difficulty, 'something very wrong.' She took a ragged breath. 'Gerald has bought up my debts. I discovered it only this morning when I got a letter from him demanding payment.'

'Your husband is demanding payment from you?' Eline couldn't conceal her sense of shock. 'But he's responsible for your debts, isn't he?'

Arian shrugged. She was under a tremendous strain, that much was clear.

'He's walked out on you, hasn't he?' Eline probed gently.

Arian nodded. 'In a way, I suppose you could say that but, in any case, I don't love him and I don't want him near me.'

'I knew it.' Eline sighed. The man was taking his revenge for something Arian had done, some injustice, real or imagined. 'Gerald Simples is trying to do to you just what Calvin did to me. Your husband wants to ruin you financially.'

Arian didn't reply and Eline tried to reassure her. 'Don't worry about the business. I'll help out all I can, me and Will are doing quite nicely now.'

'I don't care any more about the business. What's the point in even trying? I'm a failure, Eline. Whatever I do goes wrong.'

'Don't be so downcast, it's not like you,' Eline spoke softly. 'I think you must have gone back to work too soon after you . . . you lost your baby. You've haven't been yourself for some time. Come on, cheer up. Nothing will seem as bad once you feel well again.'

Eline sought for the right words. She didn't know what to say to take the look of hopelessness from Arian's face. It was obvious that whatever she said to the contrary, the break-up of her marriage had left her bereft. All Eline could do now was to offer practical suggestions.

'Would it help if I took over your business commitments for the time being?' She knew that Arian had let matters slide almost beyond redemption. Orders had not been filled, people waited in vain for deliveries and the complaints had been flowing in.

'I suppose so,' Arian said quietly. 'But I don't want to get you involved. Why should you take on my troubles?'

'It will give you time to take stock.' Eline smiled encouragingly. 'Make it up with your husband – you're obviously unhappy as things are.'

Arian shook her head. 'I don't want anything to do with Gerald, not now, not ever.'

'Sometimes,' Eline began cautiously, 'it's hard to get things like this into perspective. Give yourself a chance to think about it all calmly. Forget business, leave all that to me. Rest is what you need, a good rest.'

Arian shook her head. Her lips trembled and she looked so vulnerable that Eline wanted to take her in her arms and hug her. Instead, she spoke firmly.

'You'll be all right, Arian. You have more courage than most women I know. Look, why not see a doctor? Perhaps it would help if you had some sort of medicine, a pick-me-up. You're far too pale.'

Arian looked up. 'Can a doctor put me out of Gerald's reach?'

Eline tried again. 'Come home with me for a bit, then. Stay for as long as you like, William wouldn't mind.'

Arian shook her head. 'No, there's no point.' She swallowed hard. 'But I will accept your offer to take over the business. Perhaps Gerald will be more reasonable about the debts if he's dealing with you and Will instead of me.'

'Right, we'll take a cab to your house and I'll collect all your books and things. I'll get down to sorting things out right away.' Eline was relieved to be able to do something positive. She led the way outside and saw Arian blink a little in the sudden light.

Eline glanced covertly at Arian. She was so pale, her skin was almost translucent. She might not admit it but her husband had hurt her more than she realized.

When they arrived at the small whitewashed house, Arian went through the kitchen and into the room at the back of the house. Eline followed her, biting her lip worriedly.

'Here's all the information you'll need about the business. It bears out all that I've told you. Take it, it's no good to me.'

'Arian,' Eline said doubtfully, 'you won't do anything silly, will you?'

'I don't know what you mean.' Arian didn't meet her eyes. 'I'm just so tired, that's all, and with you taking all this off my hands I'll be able to rest.'

'Well don't worry about anything, not even your husband. He'll come round, you'll make up with him, you'll see.'

'I'll manage all right without him.' Arian spoke with a touch of her old spirit and Eline smiled.

'That's better, that's the Arian I know. You see, you'll be all right, just give it time.'

'Time, yes.' Arian sank into a chair and closed her eyes. 'Time, there's so much of it.'

'Where is your husband now?' Eline asked. 'I mean, where exactly is he staying?'

'With Sarah Frogmore in her fine mansion, of course,' Arian said quietly. 'She's welcome to him.'

That was as may be, Eline thought, it was probably bravado talking, but in any case Gerald Simples should be with his wife. She needed him right at this moment and Eline was inclined to be the one to tell him so.

A sudden sense of resolution swept over her. There *was* one thing more she could do, she could speak to Gerald, tell him how ill Arian was.

'I'm going now but you know where to find me if you need me. I'm sure everything is going to be just fine. Indeed, I mean to see that it is.' She left Arian seated in a chair in the kitchen, her head back, her eyes closed. She hated leaving her alone but it wouldn't be for long, not if Eline had her way.

Gerald concealed his triumph as he faced Eline Davies over the vast expanse of carpet in the sitting room of the Frogmore residence. He was fully aware of Sarah, her face dark with anger, watching the interview in silence.

'I think she might do something foolish if you don't go back.' Eline was intent on pressing home her point, just in case he didn't get the message. 'I've never seen her like this before, so lacking in spirit. You really must go to her.'

Gerald stroked his chin as though he was considering what she'd said and Eline rushed on, nervous but determined.

'I shouldn't interfere in other people's marriages I know, but I'm so worried.'

'You did right to come,' Gerald said at last. He smiled, determined to impress this woman with his sincerity. She was, after all, telling him to do just what he wanted to do. Sarah would just have to take it or leave it. She had served her purpose, had provided him with funds, unlimited funds, by her trust in his business acumen not to mention the generous allowance she made him, and now he found her possessiveness getting too much to bear. He wanted to be with Arian and Eline was giving him every excuse.

'I will go home, I'll talk to her at least.' He was aware of Sarah's sharp intake of breath and he glanced at her apologetically. 'There's nothing else I can do, is there? She is my responsibility, after all.'

Later he would lie to Sarah, tell her this was only a temporary measure, that soon, when Arian's health was improved, he could once again be her lover. He'd better not burn any boats.

'Perhaps you will share my cab?' Eline was nothing if not persistent and that was all to the good. Gerald rose at once and bowed to her, excusing himself from the room.

Sarah followed him upstairs as he knew she would and he took her in his arms at once. 'It won't be for long,' he said. 'I promise you that, but how would it look if I ignored Mrs Davies's entreaties?'

'I don't care how it would look,' Sarah said petulantly. 'I just want you here with me, that's all.'

'And if Arian *were* to do something foolish, how would we both feel then, my darling?' Gerald spoke persuasively, his lips against her hair. 'I'll be back before you know it, my sweet. I can't live without you, you know that.'

'Can't live without my money, you mean,' Sarah said acidly. Gerald drew away from her at once, his expression stern.

'I will not touch another penny of your money, Sarah.' He had put just the right amount of injured innocence into his voice and Sarah was regretful, her arms going around him, her eyes pleading.

'I'm sorry, Gerald, I didn't mean it. I love you, you know I do and you love me, don't you?'

'Of course,' Gerald said, 'but there's such a thing as duty, you know. Arian is sick. How can any decent person ignore such a responsibility, inconvenient though it might be?'

'I know.' Sarah, he saw, was ashamed. Inwardly he smiled. She was so easy to manipulate but then, so were most women. Not Arian however, at least not until now. Triumph filled him. Right now his wife needed him and the thought was a heady one.

Quickly he packed a bag and then, taking Sarah in his arms once more, he kissed her soundly. He could afford to be generous with his flattery – he was getting away from her. It had suited him to live with her for a time, to make sure of his power over her, but enough was enough and now he was going home.

Arian looked dully out of the window. The rain was sliding into the garden, dripping monotonously from the trees, echoing her own feelings of despair and futility. Gerald had been home for more than a month now and they had fallen into a pattern of behaviour that was more reminiscent of an old, devoted couple than a pair who were together out of a sense of convenience and duty.

She went to his bed and did his bidding as a good wife should. She had been grateful for his presence, his strength, his love that had seemed like a balm in her days of black moods and fearful depressions. He had brought her out of the dark horrors with patience and understanding and even though she still couldn't feel happy with him, at least she no longer felt threatened by some unspeakable sense of disaster.

The business under the expert hands of Eline Davies was beginning to prosper once more. Some repayments had been made to Gerald, as well as arrangements for further monthly instalments.

Arian suspected that a great deal of effort was being injected into the sale of catalogue goods by both Eline and her husband. She was grateful and yet she had no urgent need to be involved herself; it was more their business now than hers.

She was content to stand back from life and allow everything to pass her by. It was good to have nothing to worry about, no debts, no challenges, nothing.

Her mind, these days, felt calmer. Acceptance of the inevitable, Gerald's power over her, seemed to help but her body, strangely, was weak and vulnerable. She had no energy, no will to live.

She awoke one morning and knew that she was very sick. It wasn't her mind, or her spirits – she was really physically sick. She struggled to sit up but it was too much of an effort and she sank back against the pillows. Her throat hurt and when she tried to focus her eyes, she felt them blur as though she was going to faint.

Gerald came into the bedroom, his hair damp, his cheeks glowing from washing. He was so robust, so healthy that somehow she couldn't bear to face him and she turned her head away.

'Arian, what is it?' He came to the bedside and looked down at her and then he turned on his heel and hurried out.

Arian tried to lift her head, to tell him she didn't want him to call anyone, she just wanted to be left alone. It was no use. She couldn't speak and she fell back against the pillows, her eyes closed. What did it matter if she died alone? Wasn't that the way she'd always lived?

She must have drifted off into unconsciousness because when she opened her eyes again she was aware of a tall figure standing in front of her, blotting out the sun from the window.

She shaded her eyes with her trembling hand and looked up in sudden recognition. 'Eddie.' Her voice was a croak. 'Oh, Eddie.'

He hesitated for a moment and then took her wrist in his hand, his touch light.

'Arian, I've just come back to Swansea and I find my old love sick in bed. That's not a very good welcome, is it?' He turned to look over his shoulder.

'This means complete isolation of course – it's scarlet fever. Didn't you realize how ill she was? How long has she been like this?'

'Eddie,' she whispered, 'I've not been well for a very long time.' He leaned close to hear her whispered words.

'It's the scarlet fever,' Eddie smiled down at her. 'You've obviously allowed yourself to get run down. You've not taken care of yourself properly, have you? I'm afraid I can't be of very much help either. I can give you something for the pain and discomfort but this is something that has to take its course.'

She tried to smile up at Eddie but his image was fading. She closed her eyes and sighed softly, giving herself up to the darkness that washed, comfortingly around her.

When she woke, it was dark. There was a lamp burning somewhere in the room and Gerald was beside the bed, bathing her face with tepid water. Eddie was there too, looking down at her anxiously.

She studied him. He'd changed over the intervening years but only a little. Once, when he had been her lover, his features had been softened by love and passion. Now, he was older and his face had hardened. He was no longer a boy but a man.

287

He moved forward and put the back of his hand against Arian's forehead. 'Don't try to talk. I want you to rest as much as you can. The fever will break tonight and after that, well, we'll see.'

In the bed that she shared with her husband, Arian lay wide eyed, staring up at the cracked, whitewashed ceiling. She was thinking of Eddie, imagining them together, rolling in the fields, full of joy and laughter. But then her father was there, his horsewhip raised in anger, and he was bringing it down again and again on Eddie's shoulders. Arian cried out.

She heard Gerald open the door. He came into the room quietly. The bed creaked as he sat down beside her and she felt the warmth of his hand against her cheek.

'It's all right, my darling, it's all right. Look, I've got cool water for you to drink and I'll bathe you to keep the heat down. I'm not going to let anything happen to you. I love you, Arian, you must believe that.'

He was tenderness itself. Perhaps, after all, he did really care. Why else was he bothering? She had nothing to offer him – she was a dismal failure, destroying everything around her, bungling anything she tried to do. He should wash his hands of her and go back to Sarah Frogmore.

For only a few moments her mind was lucid, then the dreams came, the nightmare images, devils conjured up from hell, and demons with blazing eyes and torches set a fire that burned her body. There was grit in her eyes, hot and burning into her skull. She was in hell.

'Is she going to die?' Gerald had never felt so lost in all his life. Sickness was a stranger to him. He never felt ill and he had never before witnessed anything as terrifying as the sight of Arian tossing and turning on the bed, her eyes wide open and staring.

'I don't know, that's the honest answer.' Eddie Carpenter was a stocky man, quite heavily built with premature grey streaking his hair. 'She's very weak, hasn't been eating enough by the look of her.' He paused and ran

288

his hand around his collar as though it was too tight for him.

'Can't you try leeches or something?' Gerald felt desperately inadequate and his anger turned itself towards the doctor.

'Leeches are very useful in some cases. In many cases,' Eddie corrected himself, 'but not in this one. Look, even if she gets over this, Arian's going to need careful nursing. She should have plenty of liver to enrich her blood, she certainly doesn't need blood taken from her.'

'Well, you're the doctor, I suppose.' Gerald's acceptance was grudging.

'Yes, I'm a very tired one, and I've a wife and children who'll be worried about me, too. I'd best slip home for a while but I'll be back. In the meantime, just keep her as cool as you can.'

'Will that work?' Gerald picked up the bowl and moved to the door.

'As good as anything else. You could try praying if you're that sort of a man.'

When the doctor had left, Gerald returned to the bedroom with fresh water and sat down beside Arian. 'I'm going to take care of you, I won't let you die. Do you hear me, Arian? I'm not going to let you die.'

It was morning. The pale sun was streaking the sky. Arian's eyes were clear. She felt weak but she knew that she was over the worst of the illness that had plunged her into the gates of hell.

She became aware of Gerald beside her, leaning over her. His face was grey with fatigue, a rough stubble graced his normally clean-shaven chin. He'd been crying.

She reached out a hand and he took it gently as though he feared his touch would hurt her.

'Arian . . .' his voice shook. 'Thank God, the fever's broken.' He fell down on his knees beside her and touched her cheek with the tips of his fingers. 'Tell me you're going to be all right, just tell me.'

'I am, Gerald, I'm going to get better, I promise.' She tried to smile but she was far too tired. 'I'm going to have a little sleep,' she whispered, 'but stay with me, Gerald, don't leave me.'

'It's nothing short of a miracle.' Eddie Carpenter stared down at Arian as she slept peacefully, her breathing even. His mouth stretched into a triumphant smile. 'The crisis is over. She's pulled through.'

'Between us, we did it, doctor.' Gerald felt so tired he could hardly think straight but it had all been worth it. Arian was not going to die.

'I didn't do anything, old boy. It was all your work. You must love your wife very much.'

The words penetrated the mists of Arian's mind. She sighed softly as if carrying a great burden and then, once more, peacefully, she slept.

The scourge of the fever spread a dark cloud over Swansea. There was scarcely any family who was not affected by the epidemic. In the peaceful hillside house on Honey's Farm, Fon and Jamie O'Conner sat at Patrick's bedside listening to the awful rasping sound of the child's breathing.

Fon held the small hand. It was brown from the open air and calloused, for, young as the boy was, he helped his father on the farm – a little man if ever there was one.

'We're losing him.' Jamie bent over the boy, his eyes moist with tears. 'God, Fon, we're losing him.'

'No!' Fon protested but her words fell into a sudden, ominous silence. The laboured breathing had stopped. Patrick O'Conner, Jamie's first-born son, was dead.

CHAPTER TWENTY

Sarah Frogmore stared at her reflection in the mirror that hung over the fireplace in the large sitting room and sighed. Her expression was petulant and there was a frown between her finely drawn brows. She was, she thought bitterly, growing old. Well, not old exactly but too old to be alone, too old to go looking for a fine young man to fill her dreams. In any case, there was one man she wanted so much that it hurt to think about him.

Gerald Simples had been only a dalliance at first, a sop to her passionate nature, a fulfilment of her desires. He was tall, handsome and with a quality of ruthlessness that had always fascinated her, even way back in her youth.

Her face softened as she thought of Sam Payton – he had been ruthless all right. Sam had drawn her into all sorts of escapades, even going so far as kidnapping a child and holding him for ransom. Sarah had gone along with it all, like the blind fool she was when it came to men.

In those days she could have her pick, and often did. She smiled now at the recollection of the men who had coloured her life, not many of them rich and respectable but all of them a boost to her self-confidence.

Good lovers she'd had aplenty, able and eager between the sheets. Any that were failures, she had shrugged off very quickly.

She touched her hair. She had a sensuous nature, she couldn't help it. It was the way God had made her, if there was a God at all.

One failure she was stuck with. She was married to him. Abruptly, she moved away from the mirror, unable to face herself. She was deceiving Geoffrey, lying to him, telling him that Gerald Simples was nothing more than a steward. He accepted this. He'd met Sarah's 'aunt' and, predictably, liked the old lady, believing she was a steadying influence on his wife.

Perhaps, Sarah thought miserably, she was losing her charms. Gerald had walked away from her so easily, run home to his wife on the flimsiest of pretexts. And yet she found him irresistible, would give anything to have him back in her bed.

Being married to Geoffrey had given her money, a certain standing in the community, but even all that hadn't been enough for her. She wanted more, always wanted more.

She had offered to share everything with Gerald. She would give up everything to be in his arms but it seemed that whatever she offered wasn't enough to hold him, and Gerald, she knew, was the one man she could spend her life with.

Quite suddenly she was angry. What was wrong with her? Was she going to give him up without a fight? She'd taken what she wanted up till now, what did she have to lose by going out to win Gerald back? That mealy-mouthed wife of his was nothing but a pale, passionless shadow constantly moping about the place.

Sarah moved quickly, her mind made up. She would go to visit his house, and would let Gerald see how much he was missing. By now he must be tiring of Arian's spiritless attitude which surely must be reflected in the bedroom. Gerald was a man of urgent needs, he liked a bit of spice and she was just the one to provide it.

The cab that carried her into town and up the hill to the east where the copper smoke hung like a pall was so slow that Sarah could have screamed. She was impatient now to see Gerald, to be able to touch him, to watch his mouth lift, his eyes light as they rested on her. He loved her, she was sure of it. As for the fever, it held no fears for her. She'd recovered from it as a child; hadn't the doctor insisted that she was the lucky one, she would never get the sickness again?

The cab was slowing down and, impatiently, Sarah hung out of the window. She saw that a funeral procession was up ahead, and sighed in exasperation. The coffin was small, that of a child no doubt, and Sarah felt a momentary pang of fear for her own son. But no, Geoffrey was taking good care of Jack. He had the finest attention any boy could wish for. Geoffrey was a good father, she would give him credit for that, at least.

She stiffened. Among the small band of mourners she caught sight of Gerald's tall frame. His dark head was bowed. Sarah's hand went to her cheek. She hesitated and then called sharply to the driver to stop. She paid him the cab fare and alighted outside the windblown churchyard.

She stood for a moment, wondering what to do and then she followed the small cortège through the gates of the cemetery. Then she saw Arian and disappointment swept over her. She had to be there, didn't she? Why couldn't this have been *her* funeral?

At once, she made the sign of the cross. Of course she hadn't wished Arian dead – it was unlucky to wish ill on anyone.

Sarah remained in the background, watching as the vicar intoned platitudes designed to comfort the bereaved parents. The couple were standing a little to the side. Sarah recognized them, they were the O'Conners from the farm up on the hill. The woman was weeping and her husband stood at her side, straight and strong, like an oak tree.

The small coffin was lowered into the ground and Fon O'Conner's hand reached out towards her husband for support. A man in the crowd was bending over Arian, talking to her solicitously. He was a stranger to Sarah but she guessed he was an old friend by the way he was looking at Arian with some concern.

He waved to the driver of the coach Sarah had just left and the man, eager for another fare, quickly dismounted. Arian was helped into the coach and the stranger climbed in after her.

Sarah's eyes moved to Gerald. He was speaking quietly, looking in through the coach window, then he nodded and stood back. It was clear he was to remain at the cemetery while the rest of the service was being conducted.

As the coach drew away, Sarah, uncaring that Arian's face was framed in the window, moved forward to stand at Gerald's side. He didn't seem to see her until she touched his arm briefly.

Gerald looked down at her and then he smiled and it was like the sun coming out. 'Come home with me, later,' she whispered. 'I've got a little present for you.' He bent his head towards her, his lips brushed her cheek and then he turned to listen to the vicar but Sarah was satisfied, fate had put Gerald in her path and she would not let him go again.

'I feel so guilty.' Arian looked up at Eddie. She still felt ill, as though she wasn't quite in touch with reality. 'I never meant to disrupt little Patrick's funeral. I should have been a comfort to Fon but I was so useless.' She bit her lip, 'Poor Fon, she looked so lost, so bereft.'

'No-one noticed you and you didn't disrupt anything, so don't give it another thought. Anyway, it's about time you gave yourself some consideration.' Eddie spoke quietly, soothingly. 'You seem to forget you've not been up from bed for very long. I strongly disapproved of you going out in the cold, I told you that. At the very least it was ill advised.'

She looked out of the window, at the countryside quickly moving past the coach windows and didn't reply. Eddie took her hands in his.

'What's worrying you, Arian? There's something more on your mind than you're telling me. Perhaps I can help.'

'Didn't you see her – Sarah Frogmore? She came just as you helped me into the coach. She went right up to Gerald, bold as anything, took his arm and, in front of all those people, he kissed her.' She shook her head. 'I thought their affair was over. I believed him when he told

294

me he wasn't seeing her any more. I was a fool to think he'd changed. Men like him never change.'

'Gerald having an affair?' Eddie quickly suppressed his surprise. These things happened to the best of men and he should know.

'Whatever you think, he loves you, Arian. No man could have cared for you better when you were ill. Look, men do things. They are ruled not by sense but by their senses. It doesn't mean he loves you any less.'

'He only loves money.' Arian spoke with bitterness. 'I can't live with him any more,' she said flatly. 'My days with Gerald Simples are over. I must get out, get away from him before I lose all my spirit.'

'Perhaps you do need a break from him. Come home with me for a few days, I have plenty of room in my house.'

Arian shook her head. 'No, Gerald would make trouble for you. I've got to stand on my own two feet, again. Find the courage I once had. Can't you see that, Eddie?'

'It's very soon after you've had a serious illness to be making a big decision. It's all very well giving voice to brave words but you are lucky to be alive. You will need help, at least give yourself time to recuperate.'

Arian was silent for a long moment. 'All I know is I'm not willing to have Gerald flaunting Sarah Frogmore under my nose. I won't be humiliated by him any more. If you want to help perhaps you'll take me to my friends?' She didn't wait for him to reply.

'Eline and Will Davies will take me in just until I decide what I'm going to do.'

'I'll take you anywhere you want to go but don't you need to fetch some things from home first?'

Arian leaned back against the cold leather. 'No,' she said flatly, 'that's never been my home, not really. I don't want to go back there.'

Eddie gave in and leaning out of the window, gave directions to the driver. The man grumbled under his breath at the vagaries of passengers who didn't know their own minds but he turned the horse's head, guided the animal away from Swansea and headed east towards the small village of Clydach.

Arian sat in Jono's warm kitchen and drank her tea appreciatively. 'Thank you for being so kind these last few days. It's about time I told you why I came to Clydach.' She paused and looked into her cup. 'I've left my husband for good. I don't know what finally did it. Perhaps it was being at the funeral of little Patrick, realizing how uncertain life is for all of us, or perhaps it was seeing him with that woman again, but I suddenly had had as much of Gerald Simples as I could take.'

Jono was gripping the huge brown teapot so tightly that his knuckles shone white.

'That man better not show his face round here. Husband or no, I won't have him bothering you whatever the law's got to say about it. No, you just depend on me. I'll keep you safe, *cariad*, and no-one will make you do anything you don't want to, not when Jono's around.'

Arian smiled at him. 'But I can't stay here indefinitely, Jono,' she said. 'It was kind of you to take me in but if I'd known Eline and Will were away on business I wouldn't have come. Now they're back I must go to see them, sort something out.'

Jono shook his head. 'Stay by here with me as long as you like, you know you're welcome.' He paused. 'Bridie's here now, her old nanny, too, so there's enough women about the place to make it all respectable like.'

'I'd only be in the way. Your relatives want to have you to themselves, Jono, it's only natural.'

'It's a bit of peace our Bridie wants. Grieving over her dad, she is, see. Be glad of your company she would, me too, mind.'

Arian had been surprised when she'd met Bridie James, a wealthy young woman by all appearances, well educated too, and not at all the sort of cousin she'd have expected Jono to have.

Bridie was likeable enough, though a little childish yet, clinging to her childhood nanny for support at a time when most women were out earning their own living. Still, she was sympathetic to Arian's plight but quite distant, wanting to spend time alone, which was entirely reasonable in the circumstances. One thing was sure, she wouldn't mind a bit when Arian moved out whatever Jono chose to think.

'What did her father do for a living?' Arian asked, turning her mind determinedly from thoughts of her own troubles. 'Did he work on the planning of the new works with you?'

'*Duw*, no, love. Her dad owned a fleet of ships, a real sea-going family are the Jameses. No son to take over the business, mind. Tragic really.' Jono grinned. 'As her only male cousin, I'm supposed to share it all with Bridie but I told her to keep it, I'm not going to sea for anyone.'

'But shouldn't you think it over?' Arian was concerned. 'It could mean a lot of money, a change of life-style for you. Wouldn't you like that?'

'What do I want money for, girl?' Jono asked cheerfully. He shook his big head. 'Don't want none of it. In any case, so long as Bridie marries within the year, her husband can take charge of it all, so the lawyer chap said.'

Arian smiled, rarely had she met anyone so lacking in avarice, so patently honest. 'You are a nice man, Jono. Do you know that?'

'Don't be daft, girl,' he said blushing. 'I'm nothing of the sort, I'm a rough-necked working man and that's all I'll ever be.' He took her hand shyly. 'But I'll watch out for you, mind. That man is not going to make you go back to him, not again. Jono will see to that.'

Arian leaned back and closed her eyes. She felt safe here. Jono, with his simple honesty, had made her feel protected and cared for, valued for herself alone. He seemed to want nothing in return or if he did, he concealed it well.

As for Gerald Simples, she had written him a letter, telling him the marriage was finally over, finished. She wanted no more to do with him, wanted nothing from him. She had received no reply but she expected none – she had given no address. Still, Simples was a clever man and it wouldn't take him long to work out where she'd gone.

Well, if he turned up, she would deal with that problem when it arose. For now, she was glad of a small oasis of peace, a quiet time, a chance to come to terms with her own failures. She had even failed as a mother, lost her child before it came to full term. It seemed that whatever she touched, she destroyed.

'Come on, *cariad*,' Jono's gentle voice brought her out of her reverie. 'Time for bed. Bridie's gone up hours ago.'

'Aye, you're right,' she said. 'Bridie's a sensible girl, about time I learned some sense too.' She rose and lightly dropped a kiss on Jono's cheek. 'Thank you for your help.'

He caught her hand. 'Not used to that, are you *cariad?*' He smiled. 'People helping you and wanting nothing back. But I don't want you to feel obliged. I'll always be here for you, I can hope but I don't expect anything, just remember that.'

As she climbed into bed, Arian pondered on Jono's words. What he was trying to tell her was that he would be ready and willing to step into Gerald's shoes if ever she should want him to. She smiled ruefully. Poor Jono, he was a fine man, a good man but she'd had her fill of men. From now on, Arian Smale, for she refused to think of herself as Mrs Simples, Arian Smale would go it alone.

'Why don't you have the marriage annulled?' Sarah was sitting with Gerald in the elegant drawing room of her house. She was looking her best in a new dinner-gown of cream satin and with a string of fine, creamy pearls around her throat. 'Come to that, the marriage might not even be legal, not in this country.' Hope rose within her. 'Those foreign laws are not the same as ours, mind.'

'Then what?' Gerald asked, and Sarah could see he was hiding his impatience. She would have to tread carefully, she knew it. Gerald wasn't the kind of man who appreciated interference.

'Well, then you would be free, that's all,' she said quietly. He looked at her for a long moment and she thought she saw a touch of a smile on his mouth.

'But you, Sarah, you wouldn't be free, so what's the use?' He shrugged and she bit her lip hard. He was right, of course. Even if Gerald was to shake himself loose of Arian, Sarah would still be tied to Geoffrey. But then, it would be enough for her that Gerald was out of the clutches of that clinging vine who called herself his wife.

An idea struck Sarah. If Gerald didn't want to go through the bother of freeing himself from an empty marriage, perhaps Arian did. It was something worth pursuing.

'Where is she, Arian, I mean,' Sarah asked with feigned indifference.

'Oh, I know where she is and when she's been punished enough, I'll go and fetch her home. Clydach is not where she belongs. Arian belongs with me, she'll learn that in time.'

Sarah tucked this bit of information away carefully and then changed the subject. 'Would you like more tea, Gerald or perhaps some porter? It's very good, I believe.'

She had been very careful of late. She'd realized that Gerald was a man not to be pushed, that he liked a little reluctance in a woman and her mistake had been to be too available.

Since she'd met him at the funeral of the little O'Conner boy, she'd restrained herself, been very careful not to be effusive, presented herself as nothing more than a friend and she felt she was beginning to arouse Gerald's interest by her attitude of indifference to his charms.

This evening would be the testing point. She was having another dinner party. Sarah liked to feel she was in the swing of the best of Swansea's society. So far, she had succeeded in covering up her failed marriage and if Geoffrey's absence was noted, none of her guests were impolite enough to question the matter, especially as she was the daughter-in-law of the influential Emily Miller.

There would be other ladies present, of course, but Sarah had made sure that none of them were overly blessed with maidenly charms.

She alone would shine, the respectable Mrs Frogmore who was rich enough to run a fine establishment.

Gerald's position in the household had now been elevated from steward to adviser and though she knew he wasn't considered socially acceptable, no-one would be unmannerly enough to complain.

She would flirt, of course she would, though she wanted nothing from the young men she was inviting. Her aim was to draw Gerald's attention to herself once more, to inspire him with jealousy and make him feel he would be lucky to have her in his arms. It had worked once before, the night when Calvin Temple came to dinner, for Gerald had sensed that Calvin and she had something between them and it made him hot for her.

'I'm glad you came early, tonight,' Sarah said. 'I feel so close to you, Gerald. You have become such a good friend.' She looked away from the fleeting expression of displeasure on his face with a feeling of triumph. He might be a very clever man but it took a woman to run rings around him.

Her plan was working. By pretending she was no longer interested in him, she was fanning his desire. His need to possess was strong and he had the usual man's reluctance to give up that which he deemed was his.

That it was this self-same emotion that held him to Arian was a truth Sarah couldn't deny, but by the same token, he couldn't rid himself of his proprietary feelings towards Sarah.

The doorbell chimed and a flurry of guests arrived together as often happened. Eddie, the handsome young doctor recently come down from London, was among the first. He kissed Sarah's cheek and held out his hand to Gerald though his expression was guarded.

'Evening, Mr Simples. Bearing up, I hope.' He didn't enquire after Gerald's wife for which Sarah was profoundly grateful.

She was busy then, involved in the business of greeting her guests. She smiled up at Paul Marchant, a handsome man by anyone's standards. He owned a shipping fleet, a small one perhaps but thriving, by all accounts. He was still very young but a man to be reckoned with all the same.

'Good of you to come,' Sarah smiled up at him. 'You must be so busy with all those ships to see to.'

Paul shrugged and bent to kiss her hand, and Sarah's nerve ends tingled. He was extraordinarily handsome with deep, almost violet, eyes and hair bleached blonde by the sun. His fair skin was tanned and beneath his well-cut jacket his shoulders were broad and straight. She could admire him as she would admire a fine painting but Sarah's interest was never far from Gerald. He was talking to one of the simpering young ladies who blushed furiously, dimpling up at him.

Sarah felt a flash of jealousy wondering what he was saying to the girl but she forced herself to ignore him. She mustn't let him see that it irritated her to see him hold court over such an admiring audience.

She deliberately slipped her arm through Paul's as the gong sounded. 'Will you take me in to dinner?' She flashed him her most enchanting smile.

'I'd be delighted.' He moved beside her, so tall and well made, and Sarah knew that before Gerald had come along she would have been eager to get Paul between the sheets. She glanced up at him and he was looking down at her, his eyes knowing, as though he had read her thoughts. She smiled up at him like a conspirator; they were two of a kind, she and Paul Marchant.

As they moved towards the dining room, she hoped fleetingly that the staff had risen to the occasion and that nothing would go wrong, she so wanted this evening to be a success.

She deliberately sat next to Paul, chatting animatedly to him, drawing him out about his business. 'What sort of goods do you carry on your ships?' She put

301

down her knife and fork and leaned towards him, fully aware that Gerald was watching her. Paul leaned closer.

'You are not really interested in me, are you, Mrs Frogmore?' he said in a conspiratorial whisper. 'I think I know just who it is you *are* interested in, however, and I'm quite happy to play your little game with you.'

She smiled. 'You are too clever by half, Mr Marchant. I just knew we would see eye to eye from the first moment I saw you.'

He took her hand and lifted it to his lips. 'I don't mind taking the part of the adoring admirer, I'm only sorry there won't be the sort of conclusion that I could wish for.' He winked. 'Catching a man is the usual reason for such magnificent acting. He must be a very special lover because I'd say you're a lady who would know the difference.'

'How right you are,' Sarah said playfully. 'I think you will go far in all sorts of ways.'

'Not so far as your bedchamber alas,' Paul said and though he sounded regretful Sarah was well aware that a man like him would never lack for female company.

Dinner passed very pleasantly. The food was good, the choice of courses provided something every guest could enjoy. Later, as she led the way into the drawing room, Sarah chose a seat where she had a good view of everyone present and took stock of the situation.

Gerald, she noticed, was sitting with young Miss Cummings and her disapproving mother. Mrs Cummings wanted some eligible young man to be paying court to her rather plain daughter and, to her irritation, the best the girl could do was to employ the half-hearted interest of a married man.

Sarah smiled to herself. By the end of the evening, Gerald would be putty in her hands. Miss Cummings with her simpering ways would bore him within half an hour.

She felt light-headed although she had drunk very little wine. Her evening was a success. Mentally, she thanked her stepmother, for it had been Emily who had indicated the sort of food she should serve to the people she was entertaining in her home.

Emily had been taken aback by Sarah's insistence that the unmarried girls she invited should be among the plainest in the area, but then Emily knew Sarah of old and was more than a little grateful that she and John were to be spared from participating in the evening. As a staid married couple, at least in Sarah's eyes, they were dispensable.

Sarah's gaze rested on Paul Marchant who had moved away to talk to the uninteresting, though obviously wealthy, Miss Bridie James.

Bridie might have been Emily's one mistake. She was very young, newly come to the neighbourhood and staying in the most unsuitable premises with some relative or other on the outskirts of Swansea, and though not striking in appearance, her figure was well formed and comely and her hair was a glorious shade of red.

Sarah concealed a smile. At one time she might have been piqued to lose the attention of a handsome young man like Paul but now, all she wanted was to have Gerald at her side.

Sarah moved among her guests with an ease born of an inner sense of satisfaction; when Gerald was in the room, close to her, she was happy. She caught his eye and he smiled and she allowed herself to return it for a brief moment before turning away. She congratulated herself that she was playing just the right sort of game. Gerald was beginning to be puzzled by her behaviour, not quite sure of her any more. That he was intrigued was obvious because she could feel him watching her.

Deliberately, she moved towards Paul and the young Miss James and sat alongside them. Bridie smiled an ingenuous smile, not at all upset that her cosy chat with a handsome young man had been interrupted.

She was the sort of young woman who was so naïve as to believe that infidelity was something that would never shadow her own life. Sarah could see it in the innocent upturn of her eyes. For a moment she felt almost sorry for Bridie James. She had a great deal to learn about men.

'I hope you're enjoying my little get-together,' Sarah said pleasantly and Bridie smiled. Her face was immediately transformed from plainness to beauty. Dimples appeared in her cheeks and her eyes seemed lit from within.

'It's kind of you to invite me,' Bridie said in a soft voice tinged with an Irish accent. 'I don't know many people in the area as yet.'

'Oh?' Sarah examined her carefully. Bridie's clothes were of good quality and a fine diamond pendant hung around her throat. She was from a well-heeled family, no doubt about that.

'I thought your parents owned a shipping line operating from Swansea,' Sarah concluded.

'That's right,' Bridie said, 'but I've been away from home for some time now. My father wished for me to be convent educated, he thought it for the best.' Her voice faltered and Sarah remembered that Bridie had recently lost her father.

'I'm sorry.' She reached out instinctively to touch the other girl's hand. 'I know how precious my father is to me. You have all my sympathy, my dear.'

Paul Marchant leaned towards Bridie and Sarah saw his look of concern, expressed with just the right amount of respect, and a sceptical smile touched her lips. Bridie would be a good catch for Paul; they were involved in the same sort of business. It was probably one of the reasons Emily had cleverly included them both on the guest list.

'Do excuse me,' Sarah said in her best voice, she didn't want Bridie to have any reason to feel superior to her though in all fairness, she didn't seem to be that sort anyway. 'I must try to share myself with all my guests.'

After that, the evening seemed to drag. All Sarah wanted was to have Gerald on her own. She felt sure that the first thing he would do would be to take her in his arms. She warmed at the thought and her blood seemed to tingle in her veins. She loved him with a passion that in all her passionate life, she had never known before.

It was Bridie who made the first move to leave and Paul Marchant was on his feet in an instant. 'Perhaps we could share a carriage?' He suggested and Bridie smiled up at him.

'Don't you think that would leave us open to gossip and speculation?' A small smile curved the young woman's lips and Paul Marchant hesitated for a moment, uncertain about the situation.

Bridie relented. 'It will be very kind of you to share a cab with me,' she said. 'Maria my nanny is waiting for me in the kitchen. She will be more than adequate as a chaperon, I'm sure.'

It seemed an eternity before the last of the guests departed and when she heard the front door close, Sarah looked across the room at Gerald. She longed for him to come and take her in his arms, to kiss her mouth, to carry her upstairs and to lay her on the bed. Instead, he stared at her morosely, his hands in his pockets.

'I suppose it's about time I was going too.' He seemed disconsolate and Sarah felt she was melting with love for him.

'You needn't go, Gerald,' she said softly. 'I know how lonely you must be these days.' She didn't dare mention Arian's name. She moved towards him and put her hand on his arm.

'No strings attached, mind,' she lapsed back into her Welsh accent. 'There's plenty of room here and you needn't even see me, if you don't want to.'

'Thank you, Sarah,' he said but he seemed abstracted, far away from her and Sarah resisted the impulse to put her arms around him. If she wanted to win him, she must be careful not to rush him, not to make him feel obligated or trapped.

'Well, I'm tired, I'm going to bed.' She moved to the door. 'Why bother to take a carriage home? Stay the night at least, choose your room. Take the east side of the

305

house if you like, it's quiet there, private too. You won't be disturbed.'

He met her eyes, recognizing the meaning beneath her words and for once there seemed to be genuine gratitude in his dark eyes.

She blew him a kiss. 'That's settled then. Good night, Gerald.' She floated upstairs knowing that she had won a battle, however small. She opened the door of her room and then closed it firmly with a click of finality. For tonight, she would sleep alone, but soon, very soon now, all that would be changed.

CHAPTER TWENTY-ONE

Arian sat outside in the garden of Jono's house and stared across the valley at the hills beyond. She felt at peace for the first time in many months, cosseted and warmed by Jono's regard for her. He asked nothing in return but she knew he gloried in the fact that she was looking well, her thin frame filling out, her face losing its high-cheeked gauntness.

Arian sighed softly. Today she had the house to herself. Jono was working and Bridie had gone on a shopping spree, taking her old Maria with her. She leaned back in the seat and closed her eyes, feeling relieved there was nothing she need do, just sit and rest and recover from the sickness that had upset her mind as well as her body.

She heard the sound of light footsteps coming around the side of the small house and smiled, expecting Fon to come into view, her hair ruffled by the breeze, her skirts whipping around her ankles.

She and Fon had needed each other these past weeks, Arian to talk about the failure of her business, not to mention her marriage, while Fon spoke mostly of Patrick, how she missed the boy, how lonely the farm seemed without him and how grateful she was that the other children had not fallen prey to the fever.

Arian's sense of anticipation faded as she saw not Fon rounding the corner of the house but Sarah Frogmore. As usual, Sarah was well dressed, her hair beautifully coiffured.

'Arian,' Sarah's voice was surprisingly warm, 'I felt I just had to come and see how you are. Over your sickness now, I trust?'

Arian rose to her feet. 'How did you know where I was?' The question was clipped, her voice full of apprehension but Sarah didn't seem to notice.

'Oh, Gerald knew you would be here, in Clydach, I mean.' Sarah smoothed down her skirts. 'It took a bit of hard work on my part to find exactly where but I'm not one to give up easily.'

She sat on the wooden bench, arranging her skirts carefully and Arian stared down at her. 'What do you want?' She told herself to be calm. There was nothing Sarah could do, nothing she could say to hurt her. That part of her life was over for good.

Shakily, Arian sat opposite Sarah wondering what she could possibly want with her. She was soon to find out.

'Look, I want to help you, Arian. I mean you no harm, please don't look so worried. I wondered if I might help you to prove your marriage was not really legal.'

'Why do you want to do that? You wouldn't benefit either way, would you?'

'Oh, no, certainly not,' Sarah said breezily. She was at her most ladylike today. Sarah enjoyed pretending she was from the upper-crust society of Swansea, choosing to forget that her father had been a humble cobbler before his marriage to Emily Grenfell. 'I wondered why you didn't go to France to try to find out the truth about this so-called marriage.

Arian looked at her suspiciously. 'Why do you care?' She knew the question was direct, blunt even, but she was past being polite. 'What's in it for you? Even if Gerald turned out to be a single man he couldn't marry you.' As she spoke, Arian felt a pang of hope. What if the marriage wasn't legal? She would be free, free of Gerald Simples and free of the past.

'There's really nothing I could gain from all this,' Sarah said softly. 'I am, as you know, a married woman myself. It's just that you are obviously unhappy in this marriage and so is Gerald. It would surely suit you both to be released from vows you made under duress.' She produced a piece of paper.

'Look, I copied this name down from some certificate Gerald had in his possessions. It's the name of a priest and of a church, it might just be of help.'

'But we weren't married in a church.' Arian looked at the name Sarah had written. It was one she didn't recognize. The so-called priest who had married them was Father Alain, a name imprinted on Arian's mind, part of the nightmare she'd experienced in France.

She tried to think clearly. She didn't trust Sarah. She must have some ulterior motive for wanting Gerald's marriage to be illegal. Probably, she just wanted Gerald Simples all to herself, without any encumbrance. Well, Sarah was welcome to Gerald.

Arian rose to her feet and took the paper. 'Thank you for calling.' Arian moved away. 'Now if you'll excuse me I really am . . .' Her words were interrupted by Bridie who came into the garden carrying a tray.

'I'm home. I've stripped the shops bare and now I thought we'd have some tea.' She glanced politely at Sarah and nodded. 'You don't mind if I intrude into your conversation?'

'Of course not.' Sarah moved to help Bridie with the tray. 'You are the reason I called, actually.' She chose to ignore the fact that she had been handing out advice to Arian. 'I'm having a small afternoon sometime next week. The invitations will come out formally, of course, but as we hit it off so well the other evening, I took the liberty of calling on you unannounced.'

'Very kind of you, I'm sure,' Bridie said. 'We don't stand on ceremony here. Visitors are more than welcome, with or without leaving a calling card.' It was a mild rebuke but Sarah was thick skinned enough to ignore it.

'You got on so well with that young captain, I thought you two might like to meet again.'

Arian stood for a moment listening to the inconsequential chatter of the two women. She wanted no more discussions with Sarah Frogmore and yet she liked Bridie and it would

309

be rude to refuse to take tea with her. Reluctantly, she returned to her seat.

'You two know each other well?' Bridie placed the tray on the garden table. 'I suppose it's inevitable that your paths should cross, both of you coming from Swansea.'

'Of course we know each other,' Sarah gushed. 'We have been through some trying times together, haven't we Arian?'

Arian was tempted to blurt out the truth, that she had caught Sarah in bed with her husband, but she thought better of it. She didn't wish to embarrass Bridie.

'You could say that.' She took the elegant bone china cup that Bridie had bought to replace Jono's crude pottery and drank some of the tea gratefully. What had promised to be a peaceful afternoon had turned out most unexpectedly. Still, Sarah had raised a doubt in Arian's mind. Perhaps a trip to France would be worth it. There was a faint hope that her marriage to Gerald was invalid.

She would discuss it later with Bridie who knew quite a lot about the shipping that went in and out of the port. Perhaps she could arrange for them both to take a short trip across the channel.

Arian sat back and listened as the two other women chattered together, making polite small talk. It was quite obvious to Arian that Bridie was not impressed by Sarah's affected manners but Bridie was nothing if not a lady and so she offered more tea and smiled encouragingly, listening to the inane things Sarah said as though they were pearls of wisdom.

At last Sarah rose to her feet and brushed down her skirts. 'Well, I'd better be going. I shall walk into town along the canal bank,' she dimpled, in what she hoped was a charming manner. 'Once I return to civilization I can get a cab back home.' She turned to Arian. 'Think about what we discussed, my dear.' Her tone was patronizing and Arian saw Bridie's mouth quirk a little at the corners. 'I'm sure the advice I gave was good.'

Arian didn't choose to reply. She watched as Bridie walked with Sarah round the corner of the house, listened to the muted chatter as the two women went towards the gate and sighed with relief when she heard it creak shut behind Sarah.

Bridie returned fanning her face. 'That lady is really quite hard to take,' she said smiling. 'I suppose as a good Catholic girl with convent manners I should be more tolerant but an hour of Sarah Frogmore is as much as I can stand.'

She sat down and rested her hand on Arian's shoulder. 'What was this advice she was so keen to give you?'

Arian bit her lip before answering. 'It wasn't bad advice, really,' she said at last. 'She thought I should go to France, find out if my marriage to Gerald Simples was legal or not.'

'Do you want to know?' Bridie asked slowly and Arian looked up, meeting her eye.

'If I found I was free of him, it would be the happiest moment of my life.'

'Then I'll arrange it, if I may,' Bridie said. 'I would love to go to France again. My father used to take me with him when I was little.' Her voice trembled and Arian looked at her quickly.

'I'm sorry,' she said, 'I know you miss him badly.'

Bridie clutched her hand. 'I'll get over it, it's about time I grew up. I can't be a daddy's girl for the rest of my life, can I?'

Arian suppressed a smile. 'I like you, Bridie James. You're like a breath of fresh air, mind.'

'You'll embarrass me if you go on like that.' Bridie rose to her feet. 'I'm going inside now, put all my shopping away, but I'll see to our trip to France, you can count on it. I'd regard it as an adventure.' A sudden smile lit her face. 'I might even get that handsome Paul Marchant to take us, that's what I'd *call* an adventure.'

When she was alone, Arian looked around the garden as though with new eyes. Perhaps she was a free woman – the thought was heady indeed. She had no idea of Sarah's motives in coming here today. They were probably inspired by self-interest but she didn't care. She had been handed a sliver of hope and now she felt invigorated as though, suddenly, she had a reason for living.

It was two weeks later when Arian and Bridie and a reluctant Jono prepared to set sail from Swansea docks. The ship, predictably, belonged to Paul Marchant. It had been the first of his vessels sailing for the French coast and when he and Arian were introduced, they recognized each other at once.

'Ah, Mrs Simples, going to France on another visit then?' his smile was tinged with speculation. 'I hope this trip will be happier than the last.'

Arian looked at him, wondering how much he knew about her arrest and marriage. Not very much, she supposed.

'Mr Marchant is coming with us on this trip, by way of a small holiday.' Bridie couldn't conceal her delight and Paul Marchant couldn't have failed to be aware that Bridie was more than a little interested in him.

'I'm honoured to have you both aboard.' Paul's tone was warm, his eyes sparkling as they rested on Bridie. 'I can only hope you'll find everything in order.'

'I'm sure I will,' Bridie said. 'But don't you think that deckhand should get out of the way of the anchor line?'

Paul shrugged. 'See? Finding fault already.' His tone was dry but he moved quickly to the side of the ship and shouted instructions to the men on the deck below.

'Perhaps you ladies would like to go to your cabin?' Paul returned to Bridie's side. 'Mr Morgan too?'

'Want to get rid of me, do you?' Her smile widened. 'I admit I've been a thorn in the side of more than one sailor when travelling with my father's fleet. As to poor old Jono, leave him be, he'll cling to the rail until we leave the docks, he hates the sea.'

Arian followed Bridie below, she seemed as much at home on the ship as she was on land.

'Who is running your father's fleet now?' Arian asked curiously and a shadow fell over Bridie's open face.

'I should be doing it,' she said, 'but just at the moment, I can't cope. Perhaps later on . . .' Her voice trailed away and she swallowed hard. 'I keep expecting to see my father everywhere, at the wheel, reading his charts . . . Oh, I don't know, I suppose I'm being silly. Come on, let's both rest. It won't do to arrive in France in tatters, will it?'

She climbed into her bunk, unlaced her boots and flung them onto the floorboards. 'I'm going to close my eyes for half an hour till we're at sea,' Bridie said, 'and I'd advise you to do the same.' She smiled. 'Poor old Jono will be sick the minute we set sail. It's only his concern for you that made him come along in the first place.'

Arian climbed up into the bunk, lifting her full skirts and lay wide eyed, wondering if she was wasting her time going to France at all. She felt the rocking motion of the ship, lulling her into a sense of unreality. Soon her eyes closed and she slept.

It was in the captain's cabin later when Arian saw Paul Marchant again. She realized that he was an exceptionally tall, very handsome man and for a moment, in a trick of the light, he reminded Arian of Calvin Temple. Calvin – how she'd missed him all these long months. What was he doing now? she wondered. Was he still womanizing, deceiving? Probably so. Men didn't change their ways that easily.

Arian sat on Paul's right hand and Bridie on his left; of Jono there was no sign. As Bridie had rightly pointed out, Jono was no sailor.

'I hope you find what you want in France, Mrs Simples.' Paul Marchant leaned towards her. He was smiling but the look in his eye was full of challenge.

'Do you know something I don't know?' Her tone was blunt and she saw Bridie glance at her in surprise. 'I'm sorry to appear rude but this trip is important. I have to find out if my marriage to Gerald Simples was legal or not.'

'I won't say I'm surprised to hear that,' Paul said in a low voice, 'and perhaps I can help. I do have my contacts.'

Paul, young as he was, was used to flirting outrageously with women passengers, very used to exerting his charms.

313

Arian looked at him speculatively. He was probably about the same age as she was, in his early twenties, perhaps.

'You're very young to be the owner of a shipping line.' She was embarrassed that she'd spoken her thoughts out loud but Paul didn't seem the least bit offended.

'I've been in the shipping game a while now, Mrs Simples.'

'Please, call me Arian.' her tone was brisk. 'Sorry, I hate being called Mrs Simples.'

Bridie broke into the conversation. 'I was wondering about you, too, Paul. Inherited the fleet, did you?'

'No. Indeed, I built up the business myself. I've been at sea since I was a boy. No-one gave Paul Marchant a gift of anything and all I have I've worked hard for, believe me.'

He paused, his eyes looking mockingly into Arian's. 'As for my age, let's just say I'm old enough.' His meaning was unmistakable and Arian felt her colour rise. Once, she would have equalled his teasing, would have joined him in clever repartee but now, she was unused to laughter and suddenly she realized how dry her life had become. She stared down at her hands feeling dull and foolish. Bridie came to her rescue.

'Arian hasn't been too well. She's had a difficult time of it, lately. A bit of sea air will do her good.'

Arian smiled at her gratefully. 'I'm fit enough now, you and that cousin of yours have seen to that. And, if I'm a free woman, that's all the inspiration I need to begin a new life.'

'And what does Mr Simples say about all this?' Paul seemed genuinely interested.

'I don't know,' Arian said honestly. 'I've left him, now he's found consolation with someone else, at least I hope he has.'

'So it wasn't exactly a love match?' Paul asked. 'Forgive me for being so inquisitive but I wondered why you were married so suddenly last time you came to France.'

'It's a long and complicated story.' Arian had no intention of launching into an explanation of the events leading up to her marriage.

'Arian is full of mysteries,' Bridie said and if she hoped to divert Paul, she was disappointed. He smiled at her briefly and then returned his attention to Arian.

'Some mysteries are worth unravelling,' he said. He pushed his plate away and rose to his feet.

'Would you ladies like to accompany me for a stroll around the deck before you turn in?' he asked. 'It's our last chance to talk. We dock with the tide in the early morning.'

Arian rose to her feet. 'I intend to get some rest.'

'Well I'm not tired,' Bridie said 'I'd love a walk, Paul.' She looked at Arian apologetically. 'I feel I need some air.' Arian left the couple alone together, that's what Bridie wanted and, as for her, she would be glad to get some rest. In the cabin, Arian lay on her bunk but sleep wouldn't come. She felt restless, unsettled by the day's events. One minute she was full of hope and the next her spirits were plummeting.

'Damn you, Gerald Simples!' she said but her voice was drowned by the creaking of the timbers and the roar of the engines.

Bridie looked up at Paul. 'I think Arian's offended because I didn't want to go to bed yet.'

'Surely not,' Paul said. 'I think Arian has more sense than that. Come along, let's enjoy a last look at the sea before we turn in.'

It was cool on deck with a soft breeze blowing across the channel. Bridie shivered and was tinglingly aware that Paul had put his arm around her in a protective gesture.

'I find you very attractive, Bridie James,' he said, 'but then I don't have to tell you that, you are not so stupid that you haven't guessed already.'

She stood in the circle of his arm wondering what it would feel like to enjoy a man's kiss. She knew that if she so chose, she could find out, here and now in Paul Marchant's arms. But she was frightened, she was so inexperienced, she wouldn't know how to respond if he did make an advance.

'Bridie, don't look so worried, I'm not going to harm you.' He leaned forward and then his lips touched hers, softly at first, experimentally, then his mouth hardened in passion, his arms tightened around her. She stood quiescent in his arms. The scent of him moved her. She felt transported with joy into a world of excitement.

'Paul, don't . . . I've never . . .'

He put his finger over her lips. 'Hush, I will take care of you, trust me. I won't do anything you don't want me to.'

She tipped back her head. The skies were above her, the stars dazzling, the moon a glorious orb ringed with light. Bridie felt as though she had drunk a great deal of wine.

Paul edged her backwards and, in the shadow of the wheelhouse, drew her down onto the boards that creaked and groaned beneath her as though with life of their own. Paul was stretched out beside her, his hand on her breast, and she drew a ragged breath, her hand on his, drawing it away from her in sudden fear.

'I could take you back to my cabin,' he said softly, 'but it seems so romantic here, under the night sky and with the sea lapping against the ship. Can you feel it, Bridie, the life force around us? Don't be frightened by it. I'll teach you, I'll take care of you.'

Slowly, she put her arms around Paul's strong neck and drew his head down towards her. His breath was sweet, tinged with the taste of wine, as he kissed her. His hands were on her naked breasts though she didn't remember him opening her buttons.

'Paul,' her voice was a whisper, 'I'm frightened.' He drew away from her a little.

'I'll not hurt you, Bridie James. I'll teach you about passion, teach you about love. You don't want to be a maiden for the rest of your life, do you?'

She was torn between her desire for him and her conscience. All her convent teachings had not prepared her for a moment like this when the sea was in her pulse, the air was heady and love was a glittering prize to be grasped.

She turned towards him and he tipped her face back, kissing her eyelids, her throat, her breasts.

His kisses lifted her into a world of magic, a world of heightened senses. She pressed against him, feeling the breeze lift her hair, drift across her face, and as the tide of passion rose within her, she clung to his young strong shoulders.

He brushed her thigh with his fingers and suddenly, she pushed him away, rising to her feet and straightening her clothes. She was trembling.

'It's not right, Paul. I'm sorry, I just can't do this. Not now, not like this.'

'All right, all right, my little darling. I promised I wouldn't do anything you didn't want me to and I meant it. Come, sit by me, we'll just talk.'

They didn't talk, they simply sat together in the darkness, hand in hand. The waves lapped the sides of the ship and the moon dipped behind clouds. Paul leaned on an elbow and looked down at her. 'Are you cold, lovely, sweet Bridie?' he spoke softly, like a man in love.

'I'm so cold I want you to hold me close again,' she said, reaching up and touching his face. 'Look, the dawn will break soon. Let's not waste a minute of this lovely night.'

Paul laughed low in his throat. 'A woman after my own heart. I want you Bridie, not just for tonight but for as long as I can have you. Sail the seas with me.'

Bridie felt her throat constrict. She felt she'd never been so happy in the whole of her life, never been as alive as she was this moment. 'I love you Paul.' Her words fell softly into the darkness and he took her hand and kissed her fingertips.

Arian was awake when Bridie at last returned to the cabin. She edged restlessly about on her bunk but didn't look up. She was being tactful, Bridie realized.

She undressed and washed quickly, though it was hardly worth going to bed but once she was beneath the blankets she closed her eyes, drowsy with sleep. She felt dazzled, in love. Whatever happened in the future, wherever fate led her, she would always remember this night as the best one of her life.

Later that morning, Arian woke heavy eyed. She sat up to look into the flushed face of Bridie James.

'You slept so long, I wanted to wake you up, talk to you. I'm so happy. I'm in love Arian, really in love.'

'You took all the water for washing,' Arian said, rolling out of the bunk, 'but then a woman in love doesn't always think rationally.'

'You know what I've done? I've allowed Paul to take what my mamma would have called liberties. Do you think Paul will consider I'm loose because I was so forward? I just couldn't help it, I wanted to . . . I wanted him to make love to me. I just stopped myself in time, I don't know how.'

'Hussy.' Arian's voice was stern but she was smiling. 'I had my first lover when I was about sixteen. It seems worlds away now, though I remember it as if it was yesterday, that feeling of wonder it gives you to be loved.' She glanced at Bridie. 'I suppose I did play fast and loose but then I wasn't a nice convent-trained girl like you.'

'Well, I know I let him be . . . intimate in a way that would have shocked the nuns but I mean to have Paul for a husband one day.'

'You deserve to get what you want and I hope you do.' Arian studied Bridie. She was a natural wife while Arian was not meant for marriage. From the day she had taken Eddie into her arms, she'd felt her role was to be a lover not a respectable married woman, and being tied to Simples had been enough to put her off marriage for life.

Love, now that was a different thing entirely. She allowed herself to think about Calvin. She had felt real love for him but it had all come to nothing. Men were usually false, self-seeking, and no, she would never want a serious relationship with a man again. She would use them as she'd done when she was so young. In those days, she'd known what was good for her.

318

'God, I hope my marriage isn't legal. It would be wonderful to be free, to be my own woman again, to do what I want to do instead of what I'm supposed to do.'

Bridie touched her arm. 'Poor Arian. I'm sad that you haven't found love but it will come. One day it will happen and then you'll feel as I do now, so happy.'

At daylight, they stepped ashore at Calais, Arian flanked by Bridie and Jono. At least she felt safe this time, sure that she was not going to be flung into a French jail:

Her first stop, however, must be the church of St Catherine; it was from there the priest had come to perform the marriage ceremony, at least according to the information Sarah Frogmore had given her.

Jono asked the way of some young men, pointing to the written word with his thick finger. One of the men made a gesture and pointed ahead. 'Gauche, the left, one half mile, perhaps.' He smiled and doffed his hat and Bridie's colour rose.

'Come along, Arian you can't trust these foreign gentlemen,' Bridie dimpled. Since last night, she'd become aware of herself as a woman, and about time Arian thought dryly.

They followed as Jono turned left and then walked briskly for about twenty minutes. They turned a corner into a rectangle of houses, and there at the end of the block, Arian saw the spire of a church reaching above the rooftops.

She paused for a moment, her heart beating swiftly. Now, perhaps, she would know the truth about her marriage and for an instant, she was afraid. Bridie jogged her arm.

'Come on,' she said softly, 'there's no turning back, not now.'

There was no turning back. The words rang in her ears as Arian went slowly forward towards the arched doorway of the church.

CHAPTER TWENTY-TWO

Calvin lay beside Daphne in the large bed and knew with a feeling of sadness that what had once been between them was no longer there.

Daphne sat up and stretched her slender white arms, and her breasts, beautiful breasts, jutted forward in a way that once would have filled him with desire. Now there was nothing, just a feeling of disquiet as he wondered how he could sever the ties between them. But Daphne was nothing if not perceptive.

'It's over, isn't it?' she said, slipping out of bed and standing naked before the long window. She sounded sad.

He wondered for a moment if he should protest, tell her how much he had enjoyed her company and her body. But it would all seem like faint praise. He'd merely be going through the motions and Daphne was too intelligent to be taken in by pretence. In the end he said nothing.

'I know it's over, my dear, and I don't want you to worry about it. The best things must come to an end.' There was a hint of laughter in her voice and he knew she wanted to end it as much as he did.

'Daphne,' he began but she held up her hand. He subsided against the pillows rubbing his hair from his eyes.

'It's that girl. You are in love with her. I don't know why you don't just admit it to yourself and go and find her.'

'It's not as simple as you seem to think,' he replied. 'In any case, how can you know my feelings so well when I don't know them myself?'

'You are like most men in that respect,' Daphne said softly, 'you won't face up to the truth, you'd rather hide your head in the sand and pretend that everything is all right.'

'I see.' Calvin attempted an indulgent smile but he knew she was speaking the truth. If he were honest, he would give anything to have Arian beside him now, sharing his bed.

'She's married,' he said at last. 'Now, I can't get more realistic than that, can I?'

'It's an obstacle, yes,' Daphne conceded, 'but not an insurmountable one as you've proved in your own life.'

'Divorce, you mean?' Calvin said. 'I've had a belly full of that, I can tell you.'

'Then take the girl away somewhere and live in sin,' Daphne said impatiently. 'It's not like you to admit defeat, Calvin my dear.'

Daphne was right. He wasn't one to accept defeat easily and yet there was something about Arian that baffled him. Calvin wasn't at all sure that she would welcome his attentions. She was a woman with her own views, an independent strong woman. She might not even want him. Daphne might have read his mind.

'Every woman wants love and protection,' she said. 'She wants the man to be the hero, to take charge, to make decisions. Wake up before it's too late.'

Daphne disappeared into the dressing room and Calvin heard the sound of running water. He closed his eyes for a moment trying to imagine Arian's face, her silver hair, her slender figure. She had such a fragile beauty, her eyes seemed to look right into him, to read his thoughts almost. But then, many women had that gift, had other gifts too, so what was so special about Arian?

He climbed abruptly from the bed. He was becoming introspective and it was about time he pulled himself together, time he cleared his mind of all the nonsense evoked by Daphne's words.

It was easier said than done. His thoughts returned to the subject of Arian and, in spite of himself, his emotions seemed to take charge. He must find out where Arian was. She had moved out of Swansea, that much he knew.

She had left her husband; this bit of information had been the subject of gossip at quite a few dinner tables recently.

Gerald Simples, it seemed, had become 'adviser' to Sarah Frogmore. He was doubtless more use in her bed than he was handling her finances.

Sarah – Calvin was well out of that tangle. How ill advised he'd been to be taken in by her charms. She was nothing but trouble, tainting whatever she touched. His mouth curved into a smile. She had done him one favour at least; she had split Simples from Arian apparently for good and all.

Arian might have returned to Clydach to work with Eline and her new husband. Hope rose within him. There was every likelihood he would find her there . . . if he decided to pursue the matter.

Daphne entered the room on a cloud of perfume. She was fully dressed and her eyes sparkled as though she had found a lover and was not losing one. He admired her greatly. What a pity they were not in love with each other.

'Well darling, it's bye.' She blew him a kiss with the tips of elegant fingers, 'I shall see you at some supper party or other I dare say.'

'Daphne,' he began, and she waved aside his words. She was smiling but there was a tear trembling on her dark lashes.

'Now don't spoil things, Calvin. Let me remember you as you are now, naked and magnificent, the strong silent sort of man that I most admire.'

She sailed out of the room, the scent of her perfume lingering in the air. Calvin sighed. Why couldn't a man fall in love at will? Daphne was a beautiful, sensuous woman, she was open and honest about her lust for life, she had breeding and money of her own. In short, she would be an ideal partner for him.

He closed his eyes and he could see Arian's fragile beauty and he knew he wanted her more than he had ever wanted anything in all his life.

Arian walked along the French street, breathing in the strange evening scents, looking at the glazed pastries as she passed the open door of a shop. She tried to force her mind

322

to concentrate on anything, anything but the unshakeable fact of her marriage. She felt in a daze, close to tears, unable to speak. It was Bridie who was the first one to break the silence.

'It isn't the end of the world, Arian, dear. So your marriage is legal. That doesn't mean you have to live with the man.'

Legal husband; the words echoed inside her head. Now, she would never be free of Gerald Simples. Father Alain was a properly ordained priest, he'd been kind and sympathetic but somehow it didn't help to make the truth any more palatable.

She sighed heavily and Jono tentatively put his arm around her.

'I'll protect you from him, don't you worry. That man had better not come near you or I'll break his bluddy neck.' His face reddened. ''Scuse language, mind.'

Arian forced a smile. 'Well, that's that then. At least I know, now. No more uncertainty. I'm a married woman, tied to Gerald until death do us part.'

'Don't upset yourself,' Bridie said. 'There's worse things than that in life, at least you have your health and strength. The trip seems to have done you some good. You're looking better and there's colour in your cheeks now.'

Bridie's voice held a note of happiness. She was clearly anticipating the return journey when she could spend more time with her new love, Paul Marchant.

As though Bridie had picked up on Arian's train of thought she spoke softly, the features of her face transformed so that she looked beautiful.

'Paul will be taking us on the voyage home,' she leaned close to Arian so that Jono wouldn't hear her. 'I can talk to him again, let him hold me in his arms, feel his mouth on mine. I can hardly wait.'

Arian felt a pang of envy. She wished she could feel such a burning desire to be with a man instead of the grudging acceptance she'd come to know with Gerald.

They were to stay in a small pension that night because the ship wasn't leaving until the morning. It was irksome to Arian, who wanted to shake the dust of France from her feet for ever.

'We'll have supper together,' Bridie said, 'and then perhaps take a walk along the dockside.'

Arian glanced at Bridie. It was clear she was hoping to catch a glimpse of Paul. Bridie seemed to have fallen in love with him far too quickly and Arian hoped she wouldn't end up being hurt.

She was tired now and longed to lie down and close her eyes but there was a last-minute hitch; the pension was full and their rooms no longer available. The concierge was most apologetic but her elegant shrug told Arian plainly that there was nothing she could do.

'We'll sleep on board,' Arian said decisively. 'That's the only alternative. We can hardly go looking for accommodation at this time of night.'

She set out purposefully towards the docks with Jono and Bridie coming along behind her, arguing about what had gone wrong with the arrangements for the night's accommodation, questioning each other's competence.

'I thought I made it clear that we meant to come back. I *know* I booked the rooms for two nights,' Bridie said positively. 'I don't understand what can have gone wrong.'

'I do.' Arian turned to look over her shoulder. 'Madame had the choice of a big party or the three of us and she thought of her cash book first.'

'You are so mercenary, Arian.' Bridie caught up with her, her heels tapping the cobbles loudly, 'I'm sure it was just a genuine misunderstanding.'

Was she mercenary, Arian wondered? She thought not. Money was not a prime consideration in her life. But she did want to be a success, she was sure of that and yet success continued to elude her.

She sighed, what would she do now? She had tried to go into business several times and for one reason or another had failed. Perhaps she would be better off working for someone else, just doing her job and taking her monthly salary with gratitude like most people did.

But that wasn't her way. She would never be satisfied with second best. She would prefer to make a little money working for herself than a lot of money working for someone else.

Paul Marchant was not on board but Bridie called a command in her halting French to one of the deckhands to lower the gangplank. The ship creaked and groaned against the harbour wall and Bridie fumed impatiently. Once the gangplank was in place, Bridie mounted it as though ready to do battle with someone and sheepishly Jono indicated that Arian should precede him.

'Don't take any notice of our Bridie's moods.' He followed Arian up the shaky gangplank. 'She's got a lot of growing up to do yet. Spoiled she's been, all her life.'

Arian found herself on the moving deck and smelt the salt of the air with a sudden sense of excitement. She was going home. She would accept what she couldn't change. She was married but she wouldn't allow the fact to ruin her life.

She was surprised, later, when Paul Marchant asked her to go to see him in his cabin. Bridie looked at her in astonishment, her pique showing in her expressive face.

'What does he want you for?' Her voice was sharp.

'Well, there's only one way of finding out.' Arian left the cabin almost able to feel Bridie's anger. She smiled. Bridie needn't worry. Paul was an opportunist and he would find Bridie James and her shipping line much more attractive than anything Arian could offer.

When she knocked, he called to her to come in. He was seated behind a desk, a pen in his hand, a book open before him.

'Mrs Simples,' he spoke in a businesslike tone, 'I've a proposition for you.

Later Arian returned to the cabin she shared with Bridie. She appeared to be asleep. Arian shrugged. She was pleased not to have to talk, she had a lot on her mind.

Her mind was on the edges of sleep when she made her decision – she would do what Paul Marchant asked. It would be an adventure. Another thing, from now on, she would enjoy men when and as she could. She would never be a wife to anyone again, she would be forever a mistress. Her last waking thought was of Calvin Temple and when she woke in the morning, her eyes were still damp with tears.

Calvin was riding over the hills above Honey's Farm, glad to be out in the open air with the tang of autumn in his nostrils. He'd had enough of women, he told himself, of would-be wives – good ladies all, but so earnest and boring. In any case, he'd had one marriage and that had ended in disaster. It was a mistake he was in no hurry to repeat. Of course, had Arian been free, the whole issue would have taken on a different complexion, but she was not. She was married to Simples, a man who was a thief and a villain. So much for the judgement of women, he told himself bitterly.

He rode high up the hill and reigned in the mare, pausing to look down into the valley below. The blue of the sea contrasted with the russet-leaved trees that lined it and far out on the horizon was a ship in full sail making for the arms of the harbour.

It was a fine day for a man who was lonely. He smiled at his own self-pity and lifted his head to look above him at the light racing clouds.

The thunder of hooves vibrated beneath him before the big white stallion came into view over the hill. Calvin's heart thumped unexpectedly as he saw the bare legs and long flying hair of the woman riding the animal bare-back.

'Arian,' her name was carried away on the wind and then she was coming towards him, slowing the mad gallop, drawing the sweating horse to a halt.

Like adversaries, they eyed each other in silence and then Arian smiled. It was like the sun washing the landscape in light and Calvin dismounted.

Arian jumped lightly to the ground and he saw with almost a sense of pain that her feet, tiny, exquisite feet, were bare.

'Little gypsy.' The words sounded like an endearment. She stood before him, looking upwards, her lashes thick and golden, her eyes flecked with sunlight. He wasn't sure who moved first but then she was in his arms.

He kissed her deeply, passionately and she clung to him. He could feel her slender body trembling and with a thrill of joy he knew she wanted him as badly as he wanted her.

'Let me take you home,' he said, holding her close, smelling the sunlight in her hair and the freshness of her skin. 'I don't know what brought you up here but by God I'm glad to see you.'

'Make love to me here, under the sun.' She took his hand and drew him down into the coarse grass and quickly, with complete abandon, she loosened her skirt and bodice. She lay like a nymph, naked against the grass, a creature from another, ethereal world. In any other woman, the act would have jarred but somehow, with her, it was so right.

He stretched beside her and touched her wonderingly, her flesh was firm and so white, dappled by late, mellow sunlight. He buried his face in her hair and closed his eyes, knowing that he had never wanted anything in the world as much as he wanted Arian.

She lifted his head and deliberately kissed his mouth. He felt a fire begin to burn within him. He knew he must possess her. He drew her close. She shuddered, closing her eyes and he was still for a moment, wanting the joy of anticipation never to end.

It was Arian who began to move beneath him and the fire encompassed him. He could no longer resist the temptations of her sweetness. It was so right, so natural. He cradled her and even as he took her a great tenderness mingled with his passion.

When it was over, they lay together still, Arian clinging to him, unwilling to let him go. He knew then he could never have enough of her. Until now, he'd only tasted of love, this was the reality.

He twined his fingers in her hair and she looked up at him, questioningly. 'Will you come to live with me, Arian?' His voice was humble and he held his breath until, slowly, she shook her head.

'No, Calvin, my love, I won't come to live with you.' She was rising, drawing her skirt over her nakedness. 'I'm still a married woman and there's been enough scandal in your life.'

'Do you think I'd care about gossip? I want you Arian, I—' She stopped his words by putting her hand over his mouth.

'No, Calvin, don't spoil things, don't say any more.' With a suddenness that took him by surprise, she was astride the waiting horse. She looked down at him for a long moment, her face softened by passion and then, she turned the animal and was racing away across the hills, hair streaming behind her like a silver cloud.

He sighed. She was like a wild creature; there was no taming her. He didn't want to tame her, he just wanted to be with her for ever, to love her, to cherish her, to make her smile at him so that the sun would perpetually shine on them both. It was nothing more than a dream, perhaps the entire thing had been a dream and Arian a figment of his imagination.

He lifted his head to look up at the sky, shadowed now as if in tune with his feelings. 'Arian, I love you.' His voice was carried away by the breeze and it didn't matter. He was the only one to hear it.

'Did you enjoy your ride?' Fon was busy over the black-doored oven. 'Hope you brought our poor horse back safely.' Her face flushed with the heat, she glanced at Arian and then looked away again.

'If I didn't know different, I'd say you've just been with a lover.' Her words were soft, with no hint of censure and Arian smiled.

'Good thing you know different then.' She moved out to the yard, divested herself of her clothes and stood close to the pump, sluicing cold water over her body. She returned into the kitchen naked and stood for a moment looking at Fon.

'Can I borrow some of your clothes?' She smiled at Fon's raised eyebrows.

'I think you better had and quick about it,' Fon said. 'I don't want my husband seeing you like that. It would be too much of a temptation, even for Jamie.'

'I don't believe that.' Arian hurried upstairs and took a faded blue skirt and a white calico bodice out of the drawer. She felt clean and fresh and her hair hung damp and curling to her waist as she looked at herself in the mirror.

What sort of woman was she? She put her head on one side. A young, healthy woman with healthy desires, she told herself. So what, if she didn't live by the rules that others held so dear? What if she had decided to give herself to Calvin one last time before she went out of his life for ever? It wasn't much to ask, was it?

She ran lightly down the stairs and returned to the kitchen. 'Where are the children?' she asked and Fon grimaced.

'I persuaded Jamie to take the little ones with him up to the top field. April is seeing to the cows, a real help she is these days.' For a moment, Fon's eyes were clouded. 'I'll never forget Patrick and neither will Jamie but God's been kind to us, there's another baby on the way.'

Arian moved towards Fon and embraced her. 'I'm so happy for you, Fon, I know you've had your troubles but you have such a lot to be thankful for. Sorry for the sermon. I'm going now,' she said. 'Wish me luck on my adventure on the high seas, won't you?'

'Are you sure you know what you're doing?' Fon asked, hands on hips like a mother. 'Because if you ask me, you're having your doubts about all this.'

'Sure enough that I want to get away from Swansea, for a while at least. Perhaps when I come back I'll have sorted myself out. Perhaps then I might even know exactly what I want to do with my life.'

Fon shook her head. 'I don't understand you, Arian. You're like a wild spirit, as changeable as the breezes that blow in from the sea.'

'I agree with you. It's doing me the world of good too, better than being stuck in a rut, vegetating as the wife of a man I could never love.'

'But there are other ways out of all this. You could still settle down, live here on the farm or go back to shoe-making.'

Arian shook her head. 'No, I'm a failure at that sort of business and I might as well accept it. I must shake the dust of Swansea from my feet for a little while at least.' She kissed Fon's cheek warmly. 'See you when I get back, it's a promise. And Fon, thanks for everything.'

'There's daft you talk!' Fon said pushing her away in mock anger. 'I haven't done anything at all. Now take care of yourself, right?'

'You take care, too, old mother hen.'

She left Honey's Farm without looking back and moved quickly over the familiar, beloved hills to where the farmlands sloped downwards to meet the outskirts of the town. The streets were quiet now, the traffic a mere trickle of vans homeward bound, horses eager now for food and rest and one or two cabs touting for late business.

Arian looked around her at the shop fronts and the doorways, innocent now of the merchandise that usually adorned them and for a moment she wondered if she was indeed being foolhardy and impetuous, throwing aside all she knew for a life of uncertainty.

But then life was full of risks, and anything was better than a life filled with Gerald Simples's shadow. She had been grateful to Jono and, in a way, to Bridie for their kindness, but she had begun to feel stultified in the small village of Clydach, smothered by Jono's obvious adoration and tired of Bridie's insistence that she find an occupation worthy of her talents.

When Bridie had learned of Arian's plans, she had turned a little pale, her blue eyes had been full of hostility. Arian tried to tell her that the trip was nothing but business but Bridie's mouth had pursed into a sulk. Arian knew that Bridie was piqued but she couldn't help that, she had her own life to live.

She made her way now through the darkening streets towards the docks and the smell of tar and salt and ships hung heavy in the air bringing Arian a sudden sense of adventure.

The ship was a huge shadow in the harbour, the lights already swinging on the port and starboard as the crew made ready to sail.

She saw Paul Marchant waiting for her at the rail and raised her hand in greeting. He didn't move but she heard him issuing orders to his men.

As she boarded the ship, he took her hand and led her towards the cabin. 'I have work to do,' he said. 'So have you. I want you to go over my books with a fine toothcomb; I am losing money somewhere but I'm damned if I can find out why.' He smiled. 'It won't all be work. Once we are well out at sea, I'll be back. Have a bottle of wine ready.'

'I thought sailors only drank rum.'

'I can see I'm going to have to change many of the misconceptions you have about sailors,' he said. 'Remember one thing, Arian. At sea, my word is law.' He laughed lightly and touched her cheek. 'But I think you'll find me a good master.'

'Don't delude yourself,' Arian said quickly. 'It's not you who will be boss, but me.'

When she was alone, she stared around her, listening to the crack of the wind in the unfurling sails and feeling the swaying of the boards beneath her. She was a good sailor and that was just as well because she had committed herself to sharing a trip with Paul Marchant that would take her away from the shores of Wales for a very long time.

His excuse had been that he had no office on shore, couldn't afford such a luxury. Until now he'd worked on his own books, not with much success. Because she had wanted to get away from Swansea, Arian had accepted his offer without really thinking it through. Had she been foolish? Paul had been very convincing in his arguments and yet for the first time, Arian wondered if his intentions might not be strictly honourable.

CHAPTER TWENTY-THREE

'Where is she?' Gerald Simples spoke in a low voice but he was feeling angry and apprehensive, all at the same time. 'Where is my wife?'

Bridie James looked at him with a level gaze, her blue eyes appeared slate grey in the early morning sunlight. She beckoned to him to come inside the whitewashed cottage and, reluctantly, Gerald followed her through the long passage and into a quiet, restful sitting room.

'I've been hearing rumours,' Gerald began, 'rumours that Arian is behaving no better than a common slut.'

Bridie indicated a chair and seated herself firmly, her back against the straight wood of the old armchair. She was not a woman to be flustered, that much was obvious to him even though Gerald was finding it difficult to control his temper.

'I can't answer for rumours.' Bridie James was composed, her hands folded together in her lap over the neat cloth of her skirt. She was a plain woman but there was a dignity about her, even though she was young, which Gerald recognized with a reluctant feeling of respect.

'I realize you can't answer for rumours,' he said more calmly. 'But I know she was living here and I was satisfied that she was safe with you and your brother.'

'My cousin, Jono is my cousin. Arian was going to work for Will Davies but she changed her mind.'

He could have struck her for her pedantry. She was determined to be of as little help as possible.

'I don't know what my wife has told you about me,' he said, 'but I am not an ogre. I didn't beat her or ill use her in any way and it wasn't my choice that we separated. I'm simply concerned about her, about the talk I've heard. I want to know where she is.'

He saw that Bridie was considering his words and after what seemed an eternity, she replied.

'I don't know where she is, not exactly. She's at sea, that I do know, somewhere between here and the West Indies.'

Gerald was silenced. He stared at Bridie in amazement. He'd been expecting to be balked, he'd expected aggression even, but this blunt stating of the facts completely threw him off balance.

'She's with a man.'

It was a statement and Bridie squared her shoulders and stared straight at him.

'I expect she is with a number of men. There usually are many sailors aboard ship.'

'That is insulting my intelligence, Miss James.' Gerald felt anger grow again in the pit of his stomach. Bridie James was not the meek and mild woman he'd first thought her to be, plain she might be but she had character. He tried again.

'She has taken a lover from among the crew of this ship, is that it?'

'How should I know the details of Arian's private life?' Bridie lifted her chin defiantly. 'What Arian does is no business of mine. I'm not her keeper. We were strangers until a few months ago.' She rose to her feet, effectively dismissing him. 'I don't think I can be of any more assistance to you, Mr Simples,' she said. 'If you'll forgive me, I'm busy.'

Gerald fought to control his temper. He had never struck a woman but right now he felt like doing just that. He even made a move forward but Bridie stood her ground.

'At least you could tell me the name of the ship and who is the owner.' He felt he was grinding the words through his teeth.

'I have nothing more to add to what I've already told you,' Bridie said, and he could see he'd rubbed her up the wrong way with his hostile attitude. He might have done better to employ a little charm.

'Bitch!' he said, and just then the large figure of Jono Morgan moved into the room. He calmly caught Gerald by his collar and shook him as though he was a dog with a bone.

'Apologize to the lady,' Jono said roughly, 'or I'll break your bluddy neck.'

'I do apologize,' Gerald said quickly. He was no coward. Under other circumstances he would have tackled this man, big as he was, but it was clear Gerald would learn nothing by abuse and aggression. 'It's not usual for me to lose my temper this way and I apologize most humbly, Miss James.'

Jono released him and Gerald straightened his tie.

'It's just that I'm very worried about my wife. She's behaving most strangely and I've been going out of my mind thinking about her.'

That was true. Gerald wanted Arian back, much as he'd tried he couldn't put her out of his mind. She was an itch in his blood, an itch that Sarah Frogmore, for all her trying, had failed to dispel.

'Why now?' Jono's harsh voice penetrated into Gerald's thoughts. 'Why should you be worried about her now, when you haven't cared a toss about her for months.'

It was a question Gerald found difficult to answer. He decided to be honest. 'I tried to put her out of my mind. I felt she wanted to be free, but I can't forget her. I gave her every chance to straighten herself out but she's my wife, for God's sake, and I don't want her running round the world with some sailor!'

'She's your wife all right,' Jono said heavily. 'We went to France with her to find out the truth. Didn't like it, mind. She wanted rid of you.'

This was news to Gerald. 'I could have saved her the trip – I knew the marriage was legal. I'm her husband and as such I have rights.' Gerald changed tack. 'I love her, I've given her every chance. Come on, man, be reasonable. You know I speak the truth.'

'Aye,' Jono agreed, 'you have rights but if you try any force I'll bluddy kill you, understand?'

'I'm wasting my time here,' Gerald said, 'I might just as well give up and go home.' He heard the sadness in his own voice and then Bridie peered round her cousin's big shoulder.

'Arian's fit and well, I do know that,' she said, 'so you needn't worry about her. She's working, employed to sort out the master of the shipping fleet's finances. I understand she's very clever at that sort of thing.'

Gerald turned away. 'If you believe that load of rubbish, you'll believe anything!' He saw the look of doubt on Bridie James's face and savoured the moment, it seemed she had a personal interest in this man whoever he was and Gerald's barb had struck home.

He stored the information away. It was clear he would learn nothing more from Bridie or her cousin.

He strode from the house without a backward look and made towards Swansea and the docklands. There perhaps he would learn what ships had headed for the West Indies in the last week or two. What he would do once he knew, he wasn't sure, but one thing he *was* certain of, was that when she returned home to Swansea, Arian would find him waiting.

'*Duw*, there's a bully boy for you.' Jono shut the door of the cottage and made his way into the kitchen. 'No wonder she ran away from him, mind.'

'He's a strange man, true enough,' Bridie agreed, staring at her cousin thoughtfully, 'but he does have rights.'

'Well, she don't want nothing to do with the man so there must be something wrong with him.'

'Not necessarily.' Bridie knew she was being argumentative but something in Gerald's appearance had made her wonder why Arian didn't want to stay with him. He seemed quite personable, indeed, he was very good looking. True, he'd been aggressive but she'd seen very real anxiety in his eyes.

'He loves Arian. Whatever else he's done wrong,' Bridie said, 'at least he loves her.'

'Humph.' Jono pushed the kettle on to the fire. 'Well, I don't blame the girl. If she don't want him, there must be some reason for it that we don't know about.'

Bridie sighed. Jono was biased in Arian's favour, of course. What was it about the girl that inspired men to fall at her feet? Bridie smiled, she was suffering from the green eyed monster, she might as well admit it. She would have liked to be sailing the high seas with Paul herself. She wondered uneasily if there was something between him and Arian, but no, Paul had said he loved Bridie, that she was the only woman in the world for him. He wanted to marry her when he returned from his voyage, that was the only reason he was getting his accounts in order, wasn't it?

'Well there's no chance of him finding her for some time.' She looked up at Jono. 'Perhaps by the time she returns to Swansea her husband will have forgotten all about her.'

'I doubt that,' Jono said in a low voice and on an impulse, Bridie kissed his cheek. 'You are a darling man,' she said softly. 'Why don't you come into the shipping business with me? It's about time I picked up the reins I suppose.' About time she consulted her father's lawyers, found out just where she stood. She didn't want to come to Paul empty handed.

'No bluddy fear!' Jono said. ''Scuse my language, Bridie, but you won't get me to sea again. That trip to France was enough to put me off boats for good and all.'

Bridie laughed. 'But I need a man to be in it with me,' she said. 'No-one takes any notice of what a woman says or does.'

'Why don't you get that Paul Marchant to go into business with you then?' Jono said dryly. 'I'm sure you'd be good partners, even if he is smitten with Arian.'

Bridie bit her lip. Jono was wrong, of course he was. Damn Arian, Paul was hers. Still, she'd been a fool not to protest at the suggestion of Arian sailing with the *Marie Clare*. There were plenty of men around who could have worked on the accounts much more efficiently.

But Jono's words had struck home, Paul was a man after all, an easy target for a pretty woman. She'd seen enough with her father, whom she had adored, to know that men were led by their needs not by common sense. She'd been indulgent where Daddy was concerned. She wouldn't be so easygoing with Paul, not when they were married.

Perhaps it would be more provident to go into partnership with Jono rather than handing Paul her father's fleet as a gift. She smiled wryly. There was an element of insuring against his ever wanting to stray in her reasoning, but a bit of cold common sense never came amiss, especially when applied to affairs of the heart. She well remembered how generous her father had been with his money, handing out expensive gifts to his women if they pleased him enough. It was only her own steadying influence that kept him from being downright foolish.

She had inherited a large fleet, a much bigger fleet than Paul owned, but if they were to be partners, the margin of profits could be adjusted accordingly, and would be, she would see to it. In that way she would have some power, just in case she ever needed to wield it.

'You know, Cousin,' she said, smiling, 'you have straightened out my thinking. I was in danger there of being improvident but I do believe you've cured me of that.'

She smiled at the bewildered look on Jono's face. 'Pour me a nice cup of tea, Cousin. I think I'm going to need it.'

Sarah was not happy. Gerald had been moody of late, snapping at her with uncalled-for irritation in his voice. She was forbearing, loving him as she did, but now, her patience was wearing thin. She glanced in irritation at the old woman sitting in the fireside chair, eyeing her with a knowing look. 'Watch your manners, you're dispensable and don't forget it.' The old lady lowered her eyes without replying.

Gerald came into the sitting room and, ignoring the old 'aunt', slumped into the chair opposite her. Sarah rose and lit the lamps. The shadows were lengthening, the sky outside the windows growing dark. Without a word, she poured him a glass of porter and without a word, he took it from her.

'Gerry, darling,' she began and he frowned, his dark eyes not really seeing her.

'You know I hate the diminutive of my name. For God's sake call me Gerald if you must use my Christian name at all.'

She sighed, toying with the idea of telling him to get out of her life for good, to end this charade and yet she knew she couldn't do without him.

'Try to relax, my love. Here, let me refill your glass.' She looked at him, loving him so much, wanting his arms around her, his mouth to touch hers. She tried, with her eyes, to tell the old woman to leave them alone but her look was ignored.

They sat in silence for a time and then Gerald rose. 'I'm going to my room,' he said. 'Good night, Sarah.'

She watched him go with a feeling of relief. At least he was staying with her tonight. Sometimes he went out, quite where, she was not told. Perhaps he stayed in the house he'd shared with Arian but it was full of bad memories and Sarah thought it unlikely. The more feasible answer was that he had found another woman but she didn't want to believe that.

Had she known the truth she would have been surprised and relieved because the nights Gerald was away, he was waiting on the dockside for the night tide to bring in the ships from the bay, hoping that this was the night the *Marie Clare* would dock and with his wife on board. The sailors in the harbour were most co-operative once he'd bought them a drink of ale. He felt he knew a great deal about Paul Marchant and his small fleet. He was the self-same man who had sailed with them to France, the time he'd married Arian. The swine must have had his eye on her even then. Well he would find that it didn't pay to cross Gerald Simples.

But Sarah was kept in the dark about his nightly excursions and she was distressed by Gerald's strange behaviour. She loved him more now than when she'd first slept with him. She knew he didn't love her but then he only loved himself; other people, he used.

In her bedroom she studied herself in the long elegant mirror. She was dressed in her finest satin nightwear and her hair hung loose to her waist. Were her breasts a little too full? Was her waist broadening? Oh, God, was she losing her charms? But no, the lamplight was kind. She looked as young and beautiful as ever, the fault was not in her but in Gerald.

With an air of determination, she crossed the gracious landing and went into Gerald's room. It was in darkness and she could hear his regular breathing from the direction of the bed.

As her eyes grew accustomed to the gloom, she made her way towards him and climbed beneath the covers, clinging to his shoulder.

'Gerald, wake up. I've had such a bad nightmare, I'm so frightened.' It wasn't very plausible but drastic action was called for. One thing she had learned about Gerald was that he was more inclined to be amorous after he'd been drinking.

She pressed herself against him and he groaned a little shifting his position to accommodate her. She snuggled against him and spoke in a small voice.

'Will you hold me, Gerald? Please, just until the nightmare fades a little. I'm so frightened alone in the darkness.'

The scent of her perfume seemed to bring him fully awake and his arms tightened around her. 'You know what you are, Sarah,' he said and there was a touch of indulgence in his voice. 'You are a scheming hussy.'

He kissed her throat and she drew a ragged breath as his mouth moved to her breasts. She arched against him hungrily.

'You are such a fine, vigorous man, Gerald. Is it any wonder I can't resist you?' Like any man on earth, he liked to be flattered. Just at this moment, Sarah would have said anything to have him hold her and tease her to a pinnacle of passion.

She ran her hands over his nakedness and knew, with a sense of satisfaction, that he was roused. He wanted her, the knowledge was as heady as wine singing in her blood.

He slid the straps of her gown from her shoulders, his touch expert, practised. She kicked the satin material away from her, glad to be free of it. Now she was as naked as he was and sighing, she pressed closer to him.

'Please, Gerald, don't keep me waiting.' She moaned softly and then he was obeying her wishes, he was possessing her and she felt like swooning with the joy of it.

Afterwards, they lay side by side and Sarah caressed his cheek gently. 'You are a fine man, Gerald,' she whispered. 'If only you were free of that woman, we could be so happy.'

He sat up abruptly. 'I don't want to be free of her,' he said harshly. 'Can't you understand that, Sarah?'

She felt pain bite deep into her soul. 'Gerald . . .' she began uncertainly, 'I didn't mean any harm.'

He sensed her hurt and leaned over her. 'Sarah, I want you, I always want you, but Arian is my wife. Try to understand that.'

Sarah told herself that she did understand. He was not a man to let go of a possession lightly. That's all Arian was, a possession, and it hurt Gerald's pride to have her snatched away.

She comforted herself with the crumbs of his words. Hadn't he just said that he always wanted her? Well that must be enough and on the subject of his wife, she must keep her own counsel.

'I do understand, Gerald,' she said softly. 'I am married too, don't forget. I think a lot of Geoffrey, in my way. Whatever he has done, he *is* my husband.'

Gerald seemed to relax. He lay back against the pillows, and it was clear he wanted to talk. 'I won't have her going off at will, gallivanting out of the country. Do you know she even checked up on the legality of our marriage?'

Sarah held her breath. She didn't want Gerald ever to know that she'd had a part in that. He would be furious if he realized it was Sarah who had put the idea of going to France into his wife's head.

'There's a strange thing to do then.' As always, Sarah's Welshness asserted itself when she was troubled. 'I think she's the luckiest woman alive having a fine man like you.' She risked touching Gerald's hair but he turned away from her hand impatiently. That was the trouble with him; he was passionate enough and yet afterwards, once he had possessed her, he was a cold stranger.

'Now she's gone off somewhere else. God knows what she's up to,' Gerald continued as though he'd not heard Sarah speak. 'A law unto herself, is Arian Simples.' There was a touch of pride in his voice and Sarah felt she knew the secret of his devotion to Arian. She kept him guessing. He didn't know where he was from one day to the next.

Yes, Sarah saw it now. The one time she was able to take him away from Arian was when his wife was sickly, docile even. Then Gerald had found her tedious. Perhaps she, Sarah, should play the game of indifference with Gerald, just as she'd been doing for the past weeks. The ploy had worked, she'd got Gerald back into her bed again.

She sighed, she must be careful with Gerald, not let him know how eager she was to please him. She turned her back on him and sighed as though she was sleepy and she felt him stir at her side. He seemed restless. Well then, let him be restless. She would not bow to his every wish.

He put his arms around her from behind and drew her into the crook of his body. She felt his warmth, knew his desire for her was reawakened and forgetting all her resolutions, she turned once more into his arms.

The next morning when Sarah woke, Gerald was gone. She sat up in bed staring at the rumpled sheets and wished that he was there with her, his eyes warm with love, his arms reaching for her. She gave a short laugh. She must be content with what she had, with his occasional passion.

Gerald Simples was not a man to give very much of himself to anyone.

Arian was glad that the voyage was over. She saw the arms of the pier come into sight and sighed with relief. Paul came to her side and smiled down at her. 'I thought I'd enjoy this moment with you. I'm leaving the captain to do his job and bring us safely into harbour.'

'Was the trip worth it?' he continued. 'Did you enjoy your voyage?' Arian saw how handsome he was in the early light. No wonder Bridie was madly in love with him.

'It had it's dangers.' Her voice was dry. 'But once we understood each other, I think it was a success. At least the trip got me away from Swansea, gave me time to think.'

It had been difficult convincing Paul she'd come aboard thinking there really was a job for her. He'd been incredulous at first.

'But you've left your husband, and a beautiful woman like you was made for love. I find you very exciting Arian, very desirable. I thought we would have a good time together.'

'A fling before you finally settle down, that sort of thing?' Her reply had been a little sarcastic. 'Under any other circumstances I might have been tempted to have an affair with you, you're a very good-looking man.'

'But?' He raised his eyebrows, smilingly aware of her irony.

'But, Bridie is in love with you. She trusts you. Don't you realize how lucky you are to have her, Paul?'

He'd taken her hand, capitulating gracefully. 'I expect you're right. In any case, I can take no for an answer. Perhaps, as you're here on board, it really would be useful for you to go over my accounts. We can tell Bridie how clever you were when we get home.' If his words held a double meaning, Arian had chosen to ignore it.

After that, they understood each other and Arian had been free to enjoy the sights of the exotic islands of the

Caribbean Sea – the white sandy beaches, the rugged hills surrounding azure lagoons, the quaint sugar mills.

At St Kitts, they went ashore and spent the day wandering around the tiny town with its shanties laced together by fronds from the coconut trees. Lying there on the sunkissed beach, Arian closed her eyes and imagined Calvin here at her side; the island then would truly have been a paradise.

The cold spray struck her face. Swansea docks was not far away now; she could almost smell the tar and the aroma of the fishmarket. Once she stepped ashore, the holiday would be over, she would step back into the unhappy realities of her life.

But it was time now she returned to her roots. While at sea she'd taken stock, faced her failures head on. The one thing she had succeeded at was writing for the newspapers. Writing she was good at, she enjoyed it, but alone it wasn't enough to make her a living.

Slowly, her thoughts had crystallized. A newspaper. She could surely do that sort of job? She had worked enough times with her father, watched him write his leader articles. Ink was in her blood, wasn't it about time she realized that was where her future lay?

'That's a pensive look if ever I saw one,' Paul teased. 'Well, I'll leave you to your thoughts. I'd better check on the captain, he's not all that familiar with these waters.'

She leaned against the rail and stared overboard at the sea washing against the ship. The question of her future came into her mind once more. Up until now she'd been an abject failure. She had tried to make her name in the leather business but she might have known, early on, it wasn't for her. Oh, she could tap a boot and shoe, carve a heel from leather, do a fairly competent job but there were many who were more skilled than she was in that trade.

She was the daughter of a newspaper man, for heaven's sake. Surely she could find work in one of the local newspaper offices? She had helped to set the type as a young girl. She remembered finishing off her father's news items often enough when he was drunk. Words, she was good at words. If only she could find backing, she might even be able to start up her own newspaper, in a small way of course.

The *Cambrian* newspaper had been taken over by someone else when her father had died but the offices had been abandoned. Somewhere in the bowels of the building the old machinery would still be there, rusting probably. A thought filled her head, an extravagant thought, that perhaps she could do something more ambitious than simply work on a newspaper. She could start her own.

A sense of adventure filled her. She knew just enough about the newspaper to get by. She would need help, certainly. There was the problem of distribution; she would need boys to stand on the street corners. She would need a good typesetter, she would need lots of things, but at least now she had an idea that might just work.

The pilot boat drew alongside and the voices of the sailors calling to each other echoed over the waters. What about a ladies' journal? Arian bit her lip. She could write most, if not all, of the items herself. She would need advertisers, perhaps people like Emily Miller and even Hari Grenfell. There were other businesses – drapers shops, book stores, many business people in Swansea she could approach.

She remembered then, with mixed feelings, how she had stood in Calvin Temple's library, how he had shown her a directory of business people. Dare she approach him and ask him for help?

The ship was nosing into the docks now, the pier amazingly close and Arian held her breath, wondering if the inexperienced captain had made an error of judgement. But no, the pier arm was successfully negotiated and the anchor was being lowered.

Arian waited, watching the sailors begin to unload the cargo. She must see Paul, say goodbye to him. She had enjoyed being with him and was grateful for the respite, the chance to evaluate her goals. He was a man of ambition and meant to go far in his sea-faring enterprises, and if she wasn't mistaken, he was about to make Bridie James his wife.

'Time to go ashore.' Paul was at her side, his hand resting on her arm. 'Thank you, Arian, for your company and if you need anything, another voyage perhaps, just say the word.'

'Thank *you*, Paul.' She bent to pick up her bag but he took it from her and led her down the gangway.

'Take care of yourself, Arian.' Paul smiled and handed her the bag. 'When you go back to Bridie James's house will you give her my love?'

Arian smiled at his impudence. 'I'll do that. I'm hoping Jono is here to meet me. He said he'd look out for the return of the *Marie Clare* and he's a man who keeps his word.'

Even as she finished speaking, she caught sight of Jono shouldering his way through the crowd with Bridie clutching his arm.

'Arian!' he waved and then he was standing before her, smiling down at her, his open face a picture of welcome.

Arian hugged him and then kissed Bridie's cheek. 'It's good to see you, I'm so glad you came to meet me.' But Bridie's eyes were looking past her, hoping no doubt to see Paul.

Jono took her bag. 'You're looking bonny,' he said. 'The sea air did you good. There's pleased I am you're home again though. I've missed you something awful.'

Bridie disappeared and, looking over her shoulder, Arian saw she was with Paul. They were talking quietly together and after a moment, Bridie smiled brightly, her plain face transformed.

'Paul is coming to have a bit of supper with us tonight.' There was an excitement in her voice that brought a catch to Arian's throat. Bridie was a lucky girl, she was going to marry the man she loved.

'I've got us a cab waiting,' Bridie said, reluctantly withdrawing her hand from Paul's fingers. 'I thought Arian would like a ride home for a treat.'

Paul laughed. 'Good idea. It'll take a bit of time for her to get her land legs back again, I expect.'

He winked wickedly at Arian.

'Goodbye.' She shook his hand formally. 'And Paul, many thanks for all your kindness.'

Sandwiched between Jono and Bridie, Arian made her way through the throng of people on the dockside and her spirits were lighter than they'd been for some time. She had hope for the future now, some sort of plan. She felt strong again, her own woman. She had shaken herself free of Gerald's oppressive influence and had begun to think for herself again.

As though conjured up like a bad dream, Gerald stood before her. 'Arian,' he said forcefully, 'I've been waiting for you. I've come to take you home.'

CHAPTER TWENTY-FOUR

Calvin Temple stared out of the window into the night-shaded garden, not seeing the rain dripping from the glossy-leaved laurels or the way the intermittent moonlight washed the ground with light. He was taking stock of his life, trying to make sense of his feelings, wondering at the despair he felt whenever he thought of the future.

It was the latest gossip about Arian that had unsettled him, of course. Arian had managed to get right away from that charlatan Simples. She had married the man for all the wrong reasons and now, it seemed, she had walked out on him. It appeared she'd run away to sea with Paul Marchant, the young shipowner, the darling of the matrons who hoped for a respectable marriage for maiden daughters.

Talk was that Arian had sailed with him for the West Indies, had spent long weeks aboard his ship. He could just picture her on some sunwashed island, her and the handsome Marchant together. He clenched his hands into fists. Why didn't he forget her? Why didn't he just forget her, start a home and family with someone who would be suitable to his sort of life-style? He'd tried marriage with a woman out of his class once before and look how that had ended.

The latest news was that Arian had just returned home to Swansea but where she was now, no-one seemed to know. He sank down into a chair and closed his eyes, his mouth curving into an unwilling smile. Arian led the most amazing life, he had to admit that much. She had guts enough to do what she wanted to do, not what people expected of her. She certainly wasn't one to conform as other women did, settling for domesticity and the quiet life. This, Calvin recognized, was part of her charm.

He rose from his chair abruptly. It was about time he made some decisions, stopped idling about like a young untutored lad. If he wanted a home, a family, he'd better start thinking seriously about finding himself a wife.

He thought briefly of Daphne but dismissed the idea at once. He knew without a shadow of doubt that motherhood did not feature as any part of her plans. Daphne was a mistress, a damn fine mistress but she did not want the responsibilities of marriage and children and frankly he didn't blame her.

Arian wasn't cut out to be a wife either, sweet fragile Arian, perhaps too frail for childbearing. What Calvin needed was strong heirs and a good woman to rear them. Families needed stability, a sense of continuity. And yet, without doubt he would take Arian on any terms, he would pay any price, he would even settle for her being his mistress, any children they might have being illegitimate. No problem was insurmountable if there was the will to overcome.

Why didn't he find her then, tell her of his feelings? What did he have to lose? She might laugh in his face, might turn him down flat, but on the other hand, she might just want to be with him. He could set her up in a nice house somewhere. They could live together, fall in love together, because she would love him, given time, he knew it in his bones.

The clock in the hall chimed the hour, ten o'clock. He turned towards the window, staring out at the darkness. It was too late now to go making social calls but tomorrow he would look for her, find out where Arian had gone. It would be easy enough to track her down, surely?

With an impatient movement, he rose and drew the heavy curtains against the night, his thoughts racing like a rat in a trap. He was losing his mind, becoming obsessed. He covered his face with his hands. 'Arian.' The name fell softly into the darkness of the room that was lit only by the dying embers of the fire.

* * *

'It's a lovely house.' Arian looked up from the long dining table and stared round at the pictures hanging on the walls. Bridie had good taste, that much was obvious and the money with which to indulge her wishes.

'I thought you'd have a nice surprise.' Bridie smiled amiably, putting down her napkin. 'It was high time I gave Jono back his privacy. I couldn't live there in his cottage for ever, could I?'

'I don't see why not,' Jono grumbled amiably, lifting the glass which looked ludicrously tiny in his big hand.

Arian could see that Paul Marchant was impressed. He hadn't realized quite how well-set up Bridie was or how extensive her shipping fleet. Early in the evening, Bridie had mentioned casually that she and Paul must get together some time with a view to joining forces; as she'd said, a woman needed a man as a figure-head, especially in something as hazardous as transporting goods overseas.

Arian knew Paul's love of the sea, of ships, and she had seen the blaze of interest in his eyes. If Bridie had set out to bribe him into marriage, she couldn't have chosen a better inducement.

Marriage and a partnership with Bridie would be a step up for him; Paul would be extending his enterprises and the merger would be more to his advantage than Bridie's. And yet, what could be more sensible? It was what Bridie really wanted. Arian secretly revised her impressions of Bridie. She was growing up, losing her petulant, almost childish behaviour. She intended to keep a reign on her business and by doing so, keep Paul in check.

Arian genuinely liked Paul. The voyage and his company had helped her find her sense of adventure that she thought had died. Somehow she had been cleansed of her past mistakes and failures by her absence from Swansea. She supposed that going away to other lands had given her a sense of perspective.

'Glad to be home, *cariad*?' Jono's voice was gentle, and Arian felt a momentary pang of guilt. Jono was a kindly man who thought the best of everyone. It was Jono who'd

350

blocked Gerald's path when he'd threatened to take her to his home by force, Jono who'd warned Gerald that if he ever saw him near Arian again he'd give him such a thrashing that he'd never bother anyone again.

Arian had expected Gerald to put up a fight – he was a powerful man and no coward – but he'd stepped aside and allowed them to pass, more for appearances' sake than anything else; he was a man who liked to be respected, it wouldn't become him to be seen brawling on the docks like a common drunk.

'I am glad to be back,' she smiled. 'I've got plans now, Jono. I'm going back to Swansea to set myself up in the newspaper business. I'm going to stop wasting my life.'

The look of dismay on Jono's open face would have been comical had it not been so sad. 'Oh, no, girl, not going to leave us, are you?'

She smiled and put her hand on his arm. 'I can hardly stay with you now, can I? Not with Bridie set up in her own home?'

'I wouldn't care what folks thought,' Jono protested. 'Let 'em gossip. Sticks and stones won't hurt me and I won't let anything hurt you.'

Arian shook her head. 'We needn't lose touch altogether, Jono. Perhaps you can help me, when you're not working on the Mond building, that is.'

She smiled, touched by the relief in his eyes. 'My father's presses will have gone rusty, they will all need maintenance. The typeface should still be all right; it was always kept well greased to prevent rusting.'

'You'll need money,' Jono said slowly. 'I have some. I can give it to you, if you like. I have no use for it.'

Arian was silent for a moment. 'I wasn't thinking of money but practical help. I don't want to take anything from you, you've been kind enough already.'

'You'll need backers.' It was Bridie who spoke, her voice firm. 'Let Jono and me put some money into the enterprise – it sounds like a good one from what you've told me.'

351

'I am going to need backers,' Arian agreed. 'If you really want to risk some of your money then I'm only too glad of the help, from you too Jono, if you really meant it.'

'I meant it all right.' He was eager to keep a foothold in her life. 'I don't want much to live on, you know that, and Bridie insists on giving me a share of the profits from the ships.' He smiled. 'So that's fixed then.'

'Aye, that's fixed.' On an impulse, Arian kissed Jono's cheek. He flushed scarlet with happiness.

'Perhaps I may be permitted to get in on this new business, too?' Paul was leaning back in his chair. 'Like Jono here, my input will not be very large but it all helps when you're starting out.'

'Thank you, all of you.' Arian felt overwhelmed. 'You've given me more than just the promise of money, you've given me a chance to start up my newspaper business sooner than I'd thought possible.'

Jono beamed. 'I always knew you and me was meant to be together.'

Arian bit her lip. 'Don't read too much into all this, mind,' she said. 'I need backing. You'll be a wonderful asset to me in many ways but, Jono, don't forget that I'm married, will you?'

'I won't forget, girl.' His voice was heavy. 'But if that man tries to interfere in your life again, I'll send him packing, don't you worry.'

Bridie and Paul had moved away from the table and were seated close together, heads bent, engrossed in conversation. She half smiled. Paul was nothing if not an opportunist and could she blame him? Bridie was alive and glowing, her very skin seemed to radiate happiness and suddenly Arian felt lonely. Was she forever to be locked in a loveless marriage?

Stop feeling sorry for yourself. She almost spoke the thought out loud and glanced quickly at Jono. He was staring at her with a love-sick expression in his eyes. The sooner she was away from Clydach the better, she thought ruefully.

* * *

Arian, Jono and the small army of people he'd somehow roped in to help, took little over two weeks to renovate the top rooms of the old *Cambridge* offices. The building was very run down but the rent was cheap. Fresh curtains provided by Bridie hung at the windows and an old desk, covered by a cloth, served as a table. The kitchen had always been there. The sink, old and cracked, needed to be replaced but the stove on which the workers at the newspaper used to boil water was, after a thorough cleaning, still functional.

The privy was the main problem. It was all the way down three flights of stairs and out at the back of the building. Not something to look forward to on a cold winter's morning, Arian thought sombrely. Still, she would live quite comfortably and, at last, she would be independent.

While she worked scrubbing the floors of the offices free of years of dust, Jono was downstairs in the bowels of the building attending the old presses. His presence during the day was something of a comfort but Arian worried that he was neglecting his own work and that he might be dismissed from the newly opened nickel works if he took too much time off.

'Don't you worry about that, girl,' Jono reassured her, while they stopped for a brew of tea and some thick slices of bread. 'They need me too much. Good with the engineering, I am, see and no-one knows how to make things work like Jono Morgan. 'Well, it's coming into shape, now,' Jono looked at her over the edge of his cup. 'Bit o' paint on the outside next, is it?'

Arian nodded absently. 'Once the worst of the clearing work is over, I'll face the most difficult task of all, Jono. I want suppliers willing to provide paper and ink and prepared to wait for their money.'

'What about the money you've got in the bank then, love?' Jono asked, biting a huge chunk out of his bread.

'Most of that will be needed to pay the wages of a typesetter and reporters.' Arian knew she could do much of the actual writing herself, but she would need a young eager man who could go into areas where she would stand out like a sore thumb. She would also want an editor, and a sub, two if possible.

'We must find advertisers, Jono.' She put down her cup. 'They pay part of the costs of publishing the paper. I'll need to approach the owners of furniture stores and general emporiums, that sort of thing. There's an awful lot to do before we get this thing off the ground.'

'It'll come, girl,' Jono spoke with an easy confidence that she envied. 'It will come, don't you worry.'

The first night she slept in her own home right on the top of the tall building, Arian felt such a sense of release it was almost like a rebirth. She was her own woman at last, about to make her own mark on the world. It was a heady feeling.

She slept well and in the morning, dressed in her neatest clothes, made her way around town in a hired cab.

It might seem an extravagance but the expense was worth it for the time she would save, and to arrive in style would make a good impression on prospective advertisers.

It was easier than she'd expected. Her rates were competitive and her first approaches were made to people with whom she'd had dealings before.

Craig Grenfell's foreman at the leather company took notes and assured her that she would have some business from them and the fact that his eyes were taking in every detail of her appearance didn't deter her at all. Indeed, if men found her attractive, so much the better for her business.

John Miller spoke to her personally. 'I will be very happy to place an advertisement with your new newspaper, Miss Smale. Anything I can do to help, just let me know. It's people like you, with a bit of go in them who deserve a hand up.' Arian warmed to him; tactfully, he had accepted her maiden name without question. She had no intention of being known as Mrs Simples; she and Gerald were married but that didn't mean he owned her.

It was the owner of one of the smaller boot and shoe establishments who struck the one and only sour note.

'Aren't you the young lady who lost a whole load of French calf in the most odd circumstances? No, I don't think I shall be advertising in your newspaper. No, indeed not.'

In spite of that one incident, the entire day passed swiftly and fruitfully and, feeling weary and a little overwhelmed by the ambitious nature of the task she'd taken on, Arian decided to sit for a while on a bench in Victoria Park.

It was a fresh day. The trees around her were swaying in the salty breeze coming in from the sea. She glanced along the path and with a shock of recognition saw a familiar figure making his way towards her.

'Eddie Carpenter, what are you doing here? Taking time off from doctoring?' She studied him. Eddie was more mature, obviously more polished in his behaviour and manners but he was still the same old Eddie who'd lain with her in the grass.

'Arian, you look better. You're well over your fever now, and to answer your question, yes, I'm having a day off. I'm entitled you know.'

'Eddie, come and sit down by me, let me tell you all that's been happening lately. I feel like getting an objective view on my chances of making a success.'

'A success of what? When I know what you're talking about I might be able to offer an opinion.' Eddie listened quietly as she described the way she'd set about starting up the paper and when she'd run out of breath, he leaned over her.

'We could do with another rag in Swansea.' He smiled and she knew he was teasing. 'I might even be persuaded to give some small financial backing to this wonderful newspaper *and* I have a good lead story for you to kick off with.'

'What? Tell me.'

'Patience, Arian, but then that was never one of your virtues, was it? Come to think of it, you had no virtues at

355

all.' He dodged her fist. 'All right, keep calm. It's just that I've arranged a meeting next month of doctors from the surrounding areas. I want them to come to a conference in Swansea. I'll invite other responsible delegates such as our MPs and the members of the Chamber of Commerce so that we can all discuss the appalling conditions that still exist in parts of Swansea. Shall I go on?' Arian nodded.

'We have too many slums. Even in these so-called enlightened days some people are still living in uninhabitable hovels, drinking water from stagnant ponds, even from the canals. We want better water supplies and more efficient sewage works if we're to stamp out fever and pestilence.'

'Quite a speech.' Arian regarded him steadily. 'Can I use all this as a personal interview?'

'I don't see why not.' Eddie frowned. 'I don't suppose it will make me over-popular in certain circles but then I never did care what anyone thought, did I?'

'Eddie, I could kiss you,' Arian said sincerely, and he raised his eyebrows in mock alarm.

'You'd better not. My wife and four children might not understand.'

'Eddie, I'm so pleased for you. A family man, a fine doctor, but still with fire in your belly. I couldn't be more delighted.'

'Ah, but you helped make it all happen,' Eddie said. 'You it was who got Calvin Temple to put up the money for my training. I owe you a great deal for that.'

'You don't owe me anything,' Arian said, 'but if I can't kiss you, can I at least give you all my thanks?' She embraced him and realized that her feelings of weariness had been replaced by a burning enthusiasm to write up all that Eddie had told her. It would make a fine lead for her first issue – controversial and yet caring for the people.

A month later, the first edition of the newly named *Swansea Times* appeared on the streets. Ragged boys stood on corners shouting the news, posters papered to walls gave out the headlines, LOCAL DOCTOR SPEAKS OUT.

Arian was deeply in debt. She had paid her workers for the next two weeks and after that, unless the paper made a profit, she was lost.

She leaned out of the window of the *Swansea Times* and felt excitement build up within her. All she needed now was for the townspeople to buy, then she would be on her way.

It was a tense day. Her young reporters sat around sharpening pencils, trying to think of the next week's news. In the bowels of the building typesetters worked to meet the deadline but Arian felt too overwrought to write or even think.

But, by the end of the day, she knew it was going to be all right. It was Eddie who broke the news. He came into the office and held up a bottle of champagne.

'Congratulations, Arian. The first printing is sold out on the streets. There's not one copy of the *Swansea Times* to be had anywhere and I should know, I've scoured the town.'

She hugged him and he lifted her from her feet and swung her round. 'Tomorrow,' Arian said breathlessly, 'the letters should start coming in. You must give me more quotes Eddie, keep me up to date with your progress. We'll make a local hero of you yet.'

'God forbid,' Eddie was smiling. 'I've had my hand shaken so many times today, I don't think I'll ever use it again.'

Arian worked late that evening. It was as though she was inspired. It was only when Bridie and Jono came hammering on the door and burst into her rooms carrying bottles of ale and plates of sandwiches that she raised her head from her writing.

'We've come to help you celebrate,' Jono said hugging her. 'I bet you've had nothing to eat all day.'

Bridie was more restrained but just as pleased. 'You're on your way, Arian,' she said. 'I can see the *Swansea Times* becoming part of everybody's life.'

Arian made a wry face. 'Aye, all I need now is to keep up the good work, find the stories, keep the adverts coming. Not much if you say it quick.' But as she took a glass of ale and lifted it to clink glasses with Bridie and Jono she felt a sense of warm achievement sweep over her. She had done it, at least made a good start, a very good start. It was ironic, really, that by following in her father's footsteps, she was finding a sense of fulfilment. Even if she was never going to know happiness with a man, then she would work her fingers to the bone for the *Times*, make news, and people who made the news her living. It was a heady prospect.

'I've never seen you looking so well and happy,' Bridie observed. 'You have obviously done the right thing, setting up this paper.'

'I couldn't have done it without your help, I'm grateful to both of you.' Arian, looking at Bridie, wondered how much she guessed about her past. Bridie had never asked questions, had taken Arian on face value but she must have heard stories, been told the scandal of the lost load of French calf, not to mention the way Arian had lived her life, flaunting all the conventions, running wild about the countryside. But she was not a woman to judge.

Bridie met her eyes and smiled wanly. She didn't speak but Arian had the distinct impression that not much missed Bridie's shrewd eyes.

As the days passed, the *Swansea Times* became part of the fabric of the town. Circulation continued to rise and Arian knew that she must take on a more senior reporter. There was no way she could administer the business side of things and seek out the stories too.

She wrote out an advertisement which would appear in several editions of the paper and specified that the reporter must be a woman. She wanted no more complications in her life, no more men cluttering up her offices.

She would be breaking new ground, possibly antagonizing many with her views, but it was high time women were given a chance to break into what hitherto had been a man's world.

She was putting on her coat, intending to walk to the shops when the bell on the office door clanged. Arian expected to find someone wanting to advertise in her paper and hurried downstairs, her coat flapping around her legs. She stopped in the doorway, drawing a breath sharply as she recognized the man standing near the counter.

'Arian,' he spoke her name softly, 'Arian, it's taken me so long to pluck up the courage to come to you. I never thought it would be easy but I didn't know how difficult it would be to face you.' He paused and looked down at her as though he would leap the counter and take her in his arms.

'Calvin.' She said his name on a sharply drawn breath. She longed to take him in her arms, to hold him and kiss him and tell him that without him, her world, her achievements, were empty. She'd filled her life with work and yet, now that she saw him again, she knew she wanted more, much more. And then her strong feeling of common sense asserted itself. 'What are you doing here?' she asked more calmly.

'I want you to come and live with me. I'll give you the finest house, I'll give you anything you want, you can come to me on your own terms.'

How she had longed to hear him say those very words but not now, not just when she was beginning to make something positive out of the ruins of her life.

'You forget something, Calvin. I'm still a married woman. What sort of reception would I get, would we both get, from the people of Swansea if we lived openly in sin?'

The door swung open and a young boy placed a note on the desk and hurried out. 'It's from an advertiser, I expect,' Arian opened the paper and saw that she was right. She dropped it into her file and looked up at Calvin.

'Come upstairs. We can't talk here.' She walked briskly around the counter and slid the bolt on the door into place. She felt his nearness, sensed his longing to reach out to her and she moved quickly towards the stairs.

He followed her and soon, they were standing together in her apartment. He made a move towards her but she held up her hand and he stopped, looking at her, waiting for her to speak.

'Calvin, I'm married. Nothing can change that,' she said shortly. 'I don't want to be a mistress, not any more.' She

359

looked up at him knowing that she loved him but the price she would have to pay for his love was too high.

'Arian, I'm offering you my love, my protection. I won't treat you as a mistress, I'll treat you with the respect I would give my wife. You'll *be* my wife in everything but the law. I'll make a will and you will be cared for. I love you, Arian.'

It would be so easy to give in to him, to fall into his arms, to let him take charge of everything, but then she would be nothing more than a kept woman. She shook her head.

'It wouldn't work, Calvin.' She knew now she must hurt him. He was silent, waiting for her to continue and she swallowed hard.

'You've had mistresses. You know full well it's not the same as having a wife. And I've been a mistress, and a wife. Now I want more out of life. Having you that way wouldn't be enough. Can't you see that, Calvin?'

He stepped back a pace, hurt as she knew he would be by her bald refusal of him. She spoke quickly in a brisk, businesslike voice.

'What I am looking for is backers for my newspaper. If you should be interested in risking your money with me again, please don't hesitate to get in touch.' She turned her back on him and there were tears in her eyes as she heard him leave the room.

His footsteps on the stairs were heavy. She heard his measured tread, listened to the outer door being opened and knew she'd turned away the only man she'd ever love.

'Goodbye, Calvin.' Arian took off her coat. She was in no mood for shopping, not now. She sat in a chair, curled her legs beneath her and tried not to remember the look of pain in Calvin's eyes. Was it worth it, the newspaper, the whole damn shooting match? Was anything worthwhile if she was never to know a man's love?

CHAPTER TWENTY-FIVE

It was a fine day. The sun was breaking through the clouds and the birds were singing when Bridie walked out of St Peter's church on the arm of her new husband.

'Happy?' Paul looked down at her and Bridie longed to reach up and kiss him. He was so handsome, his eyes so bright as they looked into hers, his tanned, lean face turned towards her as though she was the only thing in the world he wanted to see.

She nodded, unable to speak. Of course she was happy. She had just what she wanted, Paul at her side, his ring safely on her finger. Admittedly she'd schemed a little, seduced him with promises of their business merger and yet, she was vain enough to think that in the intervening weeks since they'd met, he had fallen in love with her, if only a little.

Bridie was nothing if not realistic. Had she been Jono's poor relation, Paul wouldn't have found her in the least interesting but then she was not a beautiful woman. She was the first one to admit it. She would be a good wife to him and a good mother to their children when they came along and she would always love him, whatever he did.

She wasn't a stupid woman. She knew that there had been relationships before; he wasn't a man to live as a monk. That he was experienced in affairs of the heart was as plain as the nose on her face. She smiled a little at her own self-deprecating joke. Paul touched her ringed finger gently.

'I can see you are happy by the look in your eyes and I promise to try always to keep you feeling that way.'

She looked up at him wistfully. 'Just love me a little, Paul,' she said. 'Just a little, that's all I ask.'

'You have that already,' Paul said. 'I do love you Bridie. You are gentle and honest and good. I know I will always be the only man in your life, you are that sort of woman.'

'You read me well,' Bridie said. 'There'll never be anyone else only you.'

He smiled down at her. 'Something worth more than gold or diamonds,' he said, 'a faithful wife.'

Why did the words make her sound so dull? Bridie wondered. She was so different to the women Paul must be accustomed to, so different and yet wasn't that what attracted him? Well, he was her husband now and his ring was on her finger. They were bound together by the ties of the church and the law, and by her devotion for Paul.

She held onto his arm and felt a wave of joy flood through her. She was a bride, something she thought never to be and beside her was the most handsome man in all the world.

As the days and nights of her marriage slipped by, Bridie discovered that she was a passionate woman. Her love for Paul was more than matched by her desire for him, something which seemed to give him great happiness. He delighted in giving her pleasure and though she was still a little shy of being naked before him, he was not offended. Indeed, he seemed to relish her modesty.

He was to return to sea within the week and Bridie arranged a dinner for two in their home. She wanted the atmosphere to be just right; it would be her farewell to him, after all, this would be their first parting since they were married. They sat close together at the long dining table, the candlelight shimmered over the silver and glass and Bridie felt a deep contentment fill her. The only cloud on the horizon was that soon Paul would have to leave her.

They talked quietly as they ate and Bridie scarcely tasted anything of the fine dishes the cook had prepared. She watched Paul's expressive face, admiring him so much. He was still very young and yet so wise in the ways of the world.

'Why do you keep looking at me?' Paul asked at last. He rose from the table and held out his arm to take her into the drawing room.

'I want to savour this moment.' She was near to tears. 'I want to imprint you on my mind as well as on my heart.'

He drew her close and looked down at her earnestly. 'I love you, Bridie. Remember that always.'

That night, as she lay in his arms, Bridie listened to the strong beat of Paul's heart and wished he never had to go away from her. But the sea was part of him. She'd known that when she met him and there was nothing to be done about it. She wanted to stay awake, to savour the last night they had together but slowly sleep claimed her and when she awoke, she was alone.

It didn't surprise Bridie to find, as the weeks went by that she was with child by her new husband. Paul was a virile, vigorous man and she was a healthy young woman. Any day now, he would return to her arms and then she would tell him the wonderful news. But before that happened, there was a long weary time to wait, endless days and even longer nights to live through.

She spent her days shopping and sewing, preparing for the new baby. She didn't want to share the news with anyone, not even Jono, not until she'd told Paul.

She followed the *Swansea Times* faithfully, buying every edition, turning to the tide tables and the shipping news. Always she feared storms. Ships were lost at sea but she tried not to dwell on it.

Arian had begun a new column. It was trivia, really, gossip about the prominent people of Swansea but Bridie could see how it would appeal. Most folks were nosy and wanted to pry into the lives of others.

Paul wrote, but often his letters took weeks to arrive. Bridie ordered a crib and lace covering for it in pure white decorated with rose buds. Would it be a boy or a girl and did it matter?

The days passed pleasantly but Bridie was only marking time. Her entire being yearned for Paul and she longed to be in his arms, to tell him all that had happened since he'd been away.

363

At last, the news came. His ship was to dock at first tide. Her husband was coming home.

She dressed with care, concealing her thickening waist-line with a full jacket of fine worsted that hung past her hips. She'd had it made especially, knowing it would be useful for the coming months. Her hair was glossy and her eyes bright; impending motherhood seemed to have given her a bloom that even she couldn't fail to notice.

She stood on the dockside and waited impatiently while the pilot ship nosed into port like a fussy hen leading a stately matron.

Then he was coming towards her, his hair lifting in the breeze and she was in his arms, breathing in the very scent of him.

'I can't believe it.' She clung to him. 'I can't believe you are here at last.'

The salt breeze lifted her hair. He glanced down at her, his eyes shrewd. 'You look different, what's happened?' He brushed her cheek with his lips and lightly kissed her mouth.

All her fine resolve to tell Paul the news once they were home in their own house faded away. 'Guess what, my darling? You're going to be a father.' Paul stopped quite still, his eyes searching hers. She nodded.

'It's true, Paul, we're going to have a baby.' She felt her heart beat swiftly. What would his reaction be? Would he be upset that she had conceived before they'd had a chance to enjoy their marriage?

He swept her into his arms and held her close. 'My dear girl, that's the most wonderful welcome home I could have had. We'll have a son, you'll see, a fine boy to follow in my footsteps.'

Bridie laughed but her eyes were moist. 'It could easily be a girl, mind,' she said softly, 'but we'll love the baby whatever it is because it's ours.'

'Of course we will. Come on, let's go home so that I can show you how happy I really am.'

* * *

The *Swansea Times* was continuing to grow in popularity. As a weekly, it was eagerly awaited and was snapped up the moment it was in print. The advertising was paying its way and the only problem Arian experienced was finding enough news to fill the pages. She'd not yet found a reporter; the women in the town were either not adventurous enough to come forward or were not qualified for the post. She placed a fresh advert in the paper, wording it differently. The inducement offered a senior reporter a partnership some time in the future.

The advert bore fruit. The man who entered the offices was older than Arian had expected him to be, almost fifty she supposed. He was also somewhat eccentric in his dress.

He entered the front offices with a flourish of his hat and put down a sheaf of notes on the desk as though presenting her with the Holy Grail.

Arian indicated that he should take a chair and began to read. She forgot the sounds of the office around her, the chatter of the young reporters, the scrape of pen on paper, the to and fro of people coming into the office with advertising, blocked out everything but the work before her.

Her spine tingled. She saw at once that this man had a flair for writing that was outstanding. His syntax was original and pithy, his style brisk and newsy.

'You are very good, Mr . . .?' she smiled up enquiringly.

'Machynlleth Brown,' he said. 'Some quirk of my mother's mind, apparently. Most people shorten the name to "Mac" – more digestible.'

'You can certainly write . . . Mac, but I need someone to go out and look for the news. Would that be within your . . .' she had been about to say capabilities, but somehow the word seemed insulting, – 'scope?' she ended lamely.

He gave a broad smiled revealing unevenly spaced teeth. 'I am not as sear and ancient as I appear, madam,' he said with humour. 'I make it a rule to walk ten miles at least every day. I think I would be able to get around Swansea and its environs without too much trouble.'

'In that case, you've got the job.' Arian rose and held out her hand, establishing their relationship as a business one at once.

He took her hand and shook it warmly and then leaned from his great height over the desk. 'I inferred from the wording used in your advertisement that you are looking for more than a reporter,' he said. 'Was that simply a hook, a sprat to catch a mackerel, to use a much maligned cliché?'

'It was a genuine offer,' Arian replied. 'I want a partner, in due course, but first we must see how things work out.' She looked at his shabby clothes doubtfully. 'Do you have money to invest in the paper?'

'No', he said bluntly, 'I have nothing but my talent which is considerable, as you can see.'

Arian smiled. 'I like the modesty . . . Mac.' She paused. 'Right then, can you start at once?'

'I can start at once,' he affirmed, 'and might I say you have made a wise decision, madam.'

'Yes,' Arian said slowly, 'I think I have.'

Mac proved to be a tireless worker. He found the news with an unerring instinct, ferreting out serious items along with scandals about people in high places and writing the stories with verve and spice. Soon the *Swansea Times* was now even more successful, bought by even the poor who relished the reports of court cases along with the stories of the vagaries of the social set who lived in the big homes of Swansea.

It was Mac's idea that the paper become a daily and Arian considered the matter carefully. 'Do you think we could manage it, though?' she asked. 'There's so much more work to a daily. I'd have to employ more people, more junior reporters – you and I couldn't cope with the admin alone. As well as that, poor old Billie Bishop would need more than a little help on the typesetting and printing side.'

'Granted,' Mac said, 'but we would increase our sales enormously if we brought out six editions as opposed to one. It's worth the risk don't you agree?'

'Hmn, let me think about it.' Arian chewed her lip as she tried to control the excitement that was like wine in her blood.

'It's worth considering then?' Mac prompted and Arian smiled at him in a sudden surge of determination.

'Oh, yes, it's certainly worth considering.' She held out her hand to Mac and he took it with a slow smile that revealed his uneven teeth.

'Then that's good enough for me.' He gripped her hand tightly. 'You and I, madam, are going to own the biggest newspaper in the whole of Wales, do you realize that?'

'I think you could be right, Mac.' Arian smiled warmly. 'And you know what else I think? I think it was my lucky day when I met you.'

Gerald was in the comfortable sitting room in Sarah's house looking down at the *Swansea Times*, the page of print washed with sunlight. A feeling of anger gripped him. So Arian was making a go of it, and alone without him, her husband. If it wasn't for that oaf Jono Morgan, he would be with Arian now, close to her taking her to his bed, as was his right. Oh, she had been glad to marry him to get out of that French jail, hadn't she? She'd given herself to him so sweetly, so submissively and now she had turned into someone cold and hard, someone he didn't know.

Sarah came into the room and looked at him carefully, and Gerald became aware that he'd been twisting the cord of the curtains in his hands almost as though it was a noose.

'Gerald, are you all right?' Sarah asked softly. 'You haven't been drinking, have you?'

'No, I haven't been drinking,' he said sharply, 'but if I want to drink, I don't need to ask your permission do I?'

'Of course not.' Sarah's tone was conciliatory. 'But Gerald, something is wrong. You've been behaving so oddly of late.'

'I don't know what you mean,' he said in a flat voice but he did know, exactly. It worried him too that his moods seemed to take a tremendous swing. Sometimes he was buoyant, full of optimism and then the next moment he would be plunged into despair, as though the world was about to cave in on him.

'Do you think you should see a doctor?' Sarah asked in a tone meant to placate him but which instead angered him.

'For God's sake woman, I'm all right. How many times do I have to tell you?'

'I'm sorry.' Sarah turned away and Gerald realized that she was afraid of him. He was suddenly contrite. He moved towards her and held out his hand to touch her shoulder and she actually flinched.

'Sarah, what is it? Have I suddenly become repulsive to you?' he asked, feeling bewildered and uncertain, feelings that were new to him and unwanted.

'You mean you don't remember?' she asked tremulously. 'You don't know that last night we had a terrible row? You looked at me as though you would kill me, even raised your hand to me, and all because I mentioned Arian and that blasted newspaper of hers. Does she have to pick on people like me, writing about me, spreading trivial gossip about my love life?'

Gerald shook his head. 'You're exaggerating. I don't recall being angry.' That's what worried him, he didn't seem to be in complete control of his mind sometimes. It was probably nothing to worry about, nothing at all. And yet he was afraid and Gerald Simples knew why he was afraid. In his family, and more markedly in his cousin Price Davies, there had been a streak of strangeness that some might call madness and some might describe simply as evil. Gerald didn't know if it was a trait he might have inherited and for a brief moment, he was tempted to confide in Sarah but he hesitated, some stones were best left unturned.

'I'm sure you are concerning yourself about nothing,' he said, 'and I'm sorry if I was moody. I'll try to control my impulsive nature.' He smiled and put his arm around her waist, his mouth against the warmth of her neck. 'But not in all respects.' His voice was muffled as he felt Sarah's immediate response to his caress. He smiled to himself.

368

Women were so easily pleased, show them you wanted them and they would forgive you anything.

Later, Gerald decided to take a walk into town, his mood one of dissatisfied restlessness. He would talk to Arian, tell her to keep her nose out of his business. If she didn't want him as a husband then why write these insinuations about him and Sarah. Oh, it was cleverly couched, of course. No-one was mentioned by name but everyone in Swansea knew who the woman in the piece was. How many wives lived apart from their husband and only son? It was vindictive and cruel, pointing the finger, disturbing his comfortable life-style. If it went on too long, all this publicity, Geoffrey Frogmore might make difficulties for his wife and her lover.

He walked briskly along the Stryd Fawr and made for the tall buildings of Wind Street. The offices of the *Swansea Times* were situated in Green Dragon Lane, the small strip of cobbled roadway that led to the Strand. Gerald doubted if he would find Jono James there but even if he did, the man couldn't prevent him from making a perfectly justified complaint.

The windows of the offices were freshly painted with the name of the newspaper and Gerald peered through the glass, seeing the wooden floors and the long counter within, with people walking about busily, or sitting at desks writing.

'Good God!' He realized suddenly that this was no twopenny-halfpenny concern but a real, thriving business. Perhaps it was time he took an interest in it, he had his rights after all.

Of his wife, there was no sign but at a desk near the front an older man was working, bent over a sheaf of papers, a frown of concentration on his high forehead. Another man, a much younger one, sat at the counter and Gerald felt a dart of jealousy. How dare his wife work in the company of other men like a common hussy? Where was she skulking, anyway? Could she be shut away somewhere with a lover? He wouldn't put anything past her.

He remembered then with startling clarity what the row with Sarah had been all about. She had told him that Arian had taken a lover, Paul Marchant, owner of a shipping line.

'They were lovers while she was at sea with him, everyone was talking about it.' Sarah had a gleam of triumph in her eyes. It was then Gerald had remembered his own doubts about the voyage Arian had taken with the man.

'You are talking rubbish,' he had protested weakly. 'Bridie James is married to the man, it was in all the papers, wasn't it?'

'Well, he married Bridie after he dropped Arian,' Sarah had continued remorselessly, 'Arian was a married woman. No future in that, was there? Oh, no, Paul Marchant knows which side his bread is buttered. Bridie has her own shipping line, much bigger than his. She's money, is Bridie and he wanted a share of it so Arian was dropped like a hot cake.'

It was then that Gerald had shouted abuse at Sarah, had, as she'd claimed, raised his hand as if to hit her. It had only been the stricken look on her face that had brought him to his senses but in that moment, he had been close to murder.

He pushed open the door of the *Swansea Times* offices and strode inside. 'Mrs Simples, I must see her at once. 'The young lad at the counter looked at him uncomprehendingly.

'I don't know any Mrs Simples,' he said laconically. 'You must have the wrong address.'

Gerald leaned across the counter and caught the young man by his lapel. 'Don't be high handed with me. I know she's here and she's my wife, I demand to see her.'

Quietly, the man at the desk had risen and come to the counter. He eased Gerald's hands away from the collar of the frightened young clerk.

'Take it easy, sir,' he said. 'I'm a partner here, Mac Brown. Can I help you?'

'Arian,' Gerald said, 'Arian Simples is my wife. I want to see her, now.'

'Well, sir, perhaps if you could call back another day we might be able to sort this little matter for you. Could you do that, sir?'

'Don't patronize me.' Gerald was trying to keep his temper under control. 'Is Arian here, or is she not?'

'It's all right, Mac. I'll see him.' Arian was standing in the doorway and Gerald was struck at once by the paleness of her skin. She was visibly upset and the thought gave him a certain sense of satisfaction.

She led the way upstairs to her own quarters and closed the door firmly behind them. Calmly she turned towards him, her face still pale but her features composed.

'What makes you think you have the right to come here and make a nuisance of yourself?' she asked coldly. 'You are openly living with Sarah Frogmore, everyone in town knows about it. It's only because I'm still married to you that your name hasn't appeared in the gossip column of the newspaper.'

'You've made enough insinuations though haven't you, Arian? Everyone knows who you write about in your nasty little column.'

She was so lovely, so desirable, he didn't want her looking at him as though he was an unwelcome stranger. He wanted to own her, to possess her, to make her submit to his will as he'd done so many times before.

'I am your husband and deserve some respect,' he reminded her.

'Do you think you're worthy of respect, then?' There was a heavy irony in her voice and anger poured like wine through Gerald's blood.

'You can cast no stones. Haven't you taken a lover? And don't think you can lie to me, I know the truth.'

'I have no intention of lying to you,' she said. 'What I choose to do with my life is my own business. You have made your own way and I have made mine, let's leave it like that.'

He was at her side in a few quick strides. He caught her in his arms and lifting her easily he carried her through the open door of her bedroom. He dropped her on the bed and then locked and bolted the door.

'How dare you?' Her voice was still low but filled with anger. 'How dare you treat me like this?'

He didn't answer. He pushed her back onto the bed and undid her bodice, his fingers finding the buttonholes with ease born of long practice.

'You are my wife,' he said, 'and I have rights. I mean to exercise them, so shut your mouth before I shut it for you.'

He saw the look of alarm and horror on her face but he was pulling at her skirts, listening to the tearing of the material with indifference. She must be taught a lesson. She was his, his alone and she would obey him in all things.

He climbed astride her and she looked up at him, her eyes suddenly hard with anger. 'You said you would never force me against my will,' she reminded him. 'I believed you were a man of honour, Gerald, a man of your word.'

He hesitated. He wanted her. Nothing else in the world seemed so important as having her, if only for one more time. He heard her muted cry as his hands gripped her, felt her twist and turn in an effort to get away from him. His head was filled with pounding blood. He could not let her go. He gripped her more tightly.

She was still then, accepting, her arms were no longer pounding at him. She knew she was helpless against his strength. He wanted to hurt her, to give her pain as she had given him pain. His hand tightened around her neck. He was the victor, triumphant in his power over her. She was here, lying naked before him; all he had to do was to take her.

A tear rolled from beneath her lids. Her eyes were squeezed tightly shut. He wanted to hurt her but he could not. Slowly, the haze cleared from his head and he slumped to the floor.

When he turned his head to look at her, she had turned on her side, her shoulders heaving. Her neck was turning blue with bruises and one of her eyes was swollen from where he had slapped her. There were bruises on the whiteness of her thighs and on the softness of her belly and when he met her eyes he saw only loathing there.

In an agony of remorse, he put his head down on her body. He could not believe his own brutality, he could not believe that he had almost raped and killed his own wife.

'I'm sorry,' his voice was a croak, 'Arian, I'm so sorry.' He heard his voice as though it was that of a stranger. 'I don't know what's happening to me. I'm losing my mind, Arian.'

She didn't move but lay quietly crying. He had lost her, lost her for good. He rose and in a dream fetched a bowl of water and tenderly sponged her shrinking body. He held a cold cloth to her bruised eye and then, tenderly, he tucked her into the sheets.

'I don't know what happened then but it won't happen again. I'll stay away from you, I promise you.' He tried to plead with her to forgive him but she remained still, her eyes turned away from him, as though she couldn't bear the sight of him.

'I know I'm not fit to live, Arian. Please say that you forgive me.' He knelt on the bed and took her face in his hands and made her look at him. He saw, by the look in her eyes, there would be no forgiveness.

He rose and left the room and walked slowly down the stairs and into the office. The older man was busy once more at his desk and the young man was opening the drawer of a cabinet. Obviously none of them had been aware of what had been taking place upstairs.

'You'd better call a doctor, Mr Brown,' he said slowly, his tongue feeling thick in his mouth. 'I don't think . . .' his voice trembled, 'I don't think my wife is very well.'

The older man took one look at him and turned and made for the stairs. Slowly, Gerald walked out of the building and he knew he was walking out of his wife's life, for good.

CHAPTER TWENTY-SIX

Eline sat looking down at the books on the table before her. She rubbed her eyes wearily and then looked up to see Will watching her.

'Put those away, love,' he said softly. 'You've done enough for tonight. You'll ruin your eyesight if you go on like that.'

She smiled. 'My eyes are fine, so don't fuss.' She shut the books with a snap. 'The business is doing well,' she said, 'and I keep forgetting that it's not our business, it's Arian's. She thought of the idea and she put it into practice. It was she who found the customers, invited them to order goods from her catalogues, and we have no right to take all the profit.'

'Not all, I agree,' Will said, 'but we've earned a good percentage of the takings for the work and effort we've put into it. Without you, the catalogue business would have failed.'

'I know you're right, Will, but I must see Arian and talk it over with her, sort out exactly what is hers and what is ours. Even if we split the proceeds in half, we will all have done well out of it.'

'Half and half is more than generous to Arian. It's your ideas have kept the catalogue going, Eline, your styles, your designs and both of us have put materials and workmanship into making the shoes.'

'I'll go and see Arian soon. Mind, she's doing very well with that newspaper of hers, I shouldn't think she'd have too much time for this catalogue business anyway.' She paused thoughtfully. 'Perhaps she'd like to be a sleeping partner.'

'Talking about sleep, isn't it time we went to bed, Mrs Davies?'

Eline looked up at him mischievously. 'Are you making improper suggestions, Mr Davies?'

'Well, no, I don't think so. Once my suggestions would have been most improper but then we weren't married.' He smiled with mock regret. 'These days, of course, all my suggestions are treated with mirth, that's what happens when you make an honest woman out of a mistress.'

Eline threw a pencil at him and Will made a wry face and addressed the walls as though they could hear him. 'See what I have to put up with from this shrew I married?'

She launched herself at him and he caught her in his arms and kissed her. The kiss deepened. They clung together and Eline felt the old sweet feeling of love and desire that Will always roused in her.

'Come on, love,' she whispered in his ear, 'we're wasting time.'

Will lifted her easily in his arms and carried her into the bedroom, gently kicking the door closed behind him.

The offices of the *Swansea Times* were clean and neat. Eline was impressed. She breathed in the unfamiliar scent of beeswax mingled with ink and, as she moved forward, she saw Arian talking to an older man seated at a desk. Arian glanced up at Eline and smiled in recognition.

'Eline! Come upstairs and have a cup of tea with me. It's lovely to see you looking well. How's Emlyn and how is that handsome husband of yours?'

In spite of her cheerful chatter, Arian looked pale and there was a suspicion of a bruise around one of her eyes. Eline was introduced to the older man who stood very tall to shake her hand, and she liked Mac instantly in spite of his rather eccentric appearance.

Several young men were seated at desks further back in the office, most of them busy writing. The whole feeling of the place was of efficiency and industry and Eline felt a new respect for Arian.

Upstairs, the rooms were tasteful and quiet, the furniture good but old, the curtains on the windows adding a touch of freshness.

'So this is where you live now,' Eline said, resisting the temptation to ask Arian about her private life.

'Aye, this is where I live,' Arian agreed. 'Sit down, Eline. I'll make us a cup of tea and I think I've got some biscuits here somewhere.'

'You know why I've come,' Eline said smiling. 'It's about the catalogue business. It's doing very well, Arian, it was a wonderful idea of yours.'

Arian looked at her in surprise. 'I'd forgotten all about it, to be honest.' She poured the tea and then sat down opposite Eline. 'It's more your business than mine, let's face it. You've done all the work.'

'We have worked hard at it, Will and me,' Eline agreed, 'but part of it is still yours, Arian. We don't want to cheat you out of anything that's owed to you.'

Arian smiled slowly. 'I don't think for a minute that you'd do that.' She sighed. 'But it's yours, I gave it to you. I didn't put very much of myself into it, did I?'

'You must have your fair share of the profits,' Eline argued. 'You started the business, after all.'

'I let it run down, too,' Arian said. 'It would have died the death if you hadn't stepped in and saved it.'

'I suppose so.' Eline was unconvinced. 'Still, you must look over the books and decide what we are to do about it all.'

'I'm doing very nicely here,' Arian said. 'I don't want any part of the catalogue business. You've built it up, you and Will, you deserve the rewards.'

Eline bit her lip. 'I can't accept that, Arian. I'd feel guilty for the rest of my life thinking I'd cheated you.'

Arian's face brightened. 'All right, what if you advertise in my paper then? That way we'll both benefit.'

Eline was silent. It was a good idea. The catalogue would be brought to the attention of everyone who took the *Swansea Times* and Arian would be paid for the advertising.

'Don't you like the idea?' Arian asked, leaning forward eagerly. 'I think it's the perfect solution.'

'Well, if you think that'll be enough,' Eline said doubtfully. 'I don't think it is, myself. I'd rather you take some of the money from the business.'

'Look, we had a gentlemen's agreement,' Arian said. 'There was never anything on paper, either way. I had the idea, it's true, but you and Will have done all the work. The business is rightly yours.'

'If you're sure, then . . .' Eline said slowly. 'I . . .' Her voice faded away as Arian touched her arm.

'Let's talk about something else. How are you? Happy, obviously and quite prosperous, too. Tell me all about it.'

Eline smiled and relaxed a little. There was nothing more she could say at this point but she would talk it over with Will again, find out what he thought.

'Our son is doing well,' Eline said. 'Growing up fast, mind and under my feet all the time.' She drank some of her tea. 'We're on our feet, now. We've had difficulties but there's every chance that we're over most of them now. I needn't ask you how you're doing, Arian. The paper is a success, and you seem happier than you've been for a long time.'

'Happy is a funny word,' Arian said thoughtfully. 'I'm content, fulfilled in my work. It's enough.'

Eline saw then by the stubborn set of Arian's chin that she would say no more. In any case, her private life was her own business.

Arian's husband had been working for Sarah Frogmore last time Eline had heard of him. It was quite obvious that Arian didn't want anything to do with him, didn't even want to speak of him. What a pity Arian seemed destined to be alone. Eline had William, she was so fortunate, life would have been empty without him.

'So now you are respectably married to William,' Arian said as if she had read Eline's mind. 'It must be a wonderful feeling to be with the man you love. That's something I'll never experience.'

'I know a bit of what it's like to be tied to a man you don't love,' Eline said quickly. 'When I was married to Calvin, I was so unhappy, so guilty that I didn't love him.'

'At least Calvin Temple was no crook, no maniac either.' Arian said briskly and then, as if she regretted her hasty words, she rose to her feet.

'I'm glad we've sorted out the business,' she said smiling warmly, 'but I really have to get on and do a bit of work otherwise I'll have my reporters revolting.'

Eline put down her cup. 'Arian, if ever you need a friend, you know where I am. I accept that you're an independent woman, that you like to sort out your own problems but sometimes it does help to talk, mind.'

'I'll bear it in mind.' Arian led the way back downstairs and towards the front door, but as Eline left the building she turned back briefly and caught sight of Arian's pale face looking out of the window, and it was as if she was trapped there, within the glass like a fly in amber.

Arian opened the envelope that had been delivered to her offices by hand and there, inside, she found a roll of banknotes and a letter. She smiled. It was a gift from Eline and Will, their payment to her for her share of the profits from the catalogue business.

She shook her head. 'Obstinate devils, the pair of them.' But she put the money away in the heavy safe with a warm feeling of gratitude. In return for their generosity she'd put a series of advertisements in the newspaper; she would make Eline's catalogue service famous throughout the town.

'Going out?' Mac looked up at her enquiringly as she moved through the front office. She nodded briefly.

'I'm going to see Gerald,' she said, her voice matter-of-fact. 'I want to divorce him.'

Mac frowned. 'I'd like the bastard to rot in hell,' he said in a low voice and Arian smiled.

'Language, Mr Brown, one of our customers might hear you.' He didn't apologize and she hadn't expected him to; Mac was a law unto himself. In any case, she was inclined to agree with him. Pity Gerald Simples couldn't just vanish off the face of the earth.

The new young trees at the gates of the Frogmore estate were fresh and green and the ornate front entrance smelled strongly of pine needles. Gerald was certainly being kept in style.

She asked the maid who opened the door for Mr Simples and was invited into the hallway.

Sarah Frogmore bustled out of the drawing room, her face flushed, her shoulders tense. She looked at Arian with open hostility.

'I blame you for this,' she said gesturing towards the staircase. 'He was all right when he left me. What did you say to make him so sick?'

'He's sick? I didn't know that.' Arian stared at Sarah's angry face. 'I came here to ask him to divorce me.'

'Well you've chosen a fine time to make up your mind to that,' Sarah said, 'but perhaps he'll talk to you. Come upstairs, we'll see what he says.'

It was obvious that Arian's words had surprised her, the set look on Sarah's face had vanished, to be replaced by a pleased smile.

On the landing Sarah paused. 'Why now, why didn't you ask him for a divorce when he came to see you the other day?' she asked and for a moment Arian was tempted to tell Sarah the truth – that Gerald had tried to force himself on her, had struck out at her like a madman.

'He was angry,' she said, 'very angry. It didn't seem the right time to talk about divorce.' She shook her head. 'What else do you expect me to say?'

Sarah stared at her furiously. 'You never loved him, never wanted him. I bet you wish he was dead.'

Did she? Arian asked herself. Did she wish Gerald dead? But no, she wanted to be free of him, of course, but she couldn't wish anyone dead.

Sarah led the way into the opulent bedroom. The rich drapes were half closed across the windows, shutting out most of the light. As if hearing their voices, Gerald stirred.

He looked firstly at Sarah and then turned beseechingly towards Arian.

'Help me,' his voice was desperate. 'I'm not well, Arian. I need a doctor, a good doctor. I'll go mad if I don't get help.'

Arian felt a chill run through her. He seemed pathetic somehow, his arrogance vanished. She leaned forward and touched his hand.

'I won't allow that to happen.' She tried to smile encouragingly. 'You'll be all right, Sarah will look after you.'

Looking at her, Arian knew that Sarah was like a leaf in the wind – when there was any sign of trouble, of Gerald being sick with a serious illness, she would simply drift away.

'Here Gerald, drink this. You know the doctor told you to take it regularly.' Sarah held a glass of coloured fluid in her hand. 'Come on, Gerald, be a good boy now and take it quietly, won't you?'

Gerald's eyes were angry but he took the medicine and swallowed it and the look he gave Sarah was one almost of dislike.

'I think she's trying to poison me,' Gerald glowered. 'Can't you take me away from here, take me back home to our house?'

Arian looked at him helplessly and then glanced at Sarah who was frowning in irritation.

'He doesn't know what he's saying half the time.' Sarah slammed the glass onto the table. 'I wish to God he'd buck up. Go on, tell him what you came for, while he's still awake.'

Arian bit her lip. How could she speak sensibly to Gerald when he was in this state? Even while she stood there, he seemed to be drifting off to sleep and with an exclamation of annoyance, Sarah marched from the room.

Arian followed Sarah outside. 'It's up to you,' Sarah said before Arian could speak. 'Why don't you go ahead and divorce him? He's not in a fit state to do anything about it, is he?'

Arian shook her head. 'I'll think about it. In the meantime, don't you think you'd better have the doctor take another look at him. He doesn't seem right, to me.'

Sarah sniffed. 'He's malingering. He's a baby, like most men are when it comes to sickness. If he'd only pull himself together, he'd be all right.'

Arian moved to the door. 'Well, it's up to you but I don't think he's malingering. I think there's something badly wrong with him.'

She heard the door slam behind her and, with a sigh, Arian began the long walk down the hill back towards the town.

It was a week later when Sarah walked into the offices of the *Swansea Times* and asked to see Arian.

'He's worse,' she began without preamble. 'I can't cope with him any more. It's about time you took a hand – he's still your husband isn't he?'

Arian stared across the counter at her in silence. The cheek of the woman left her speechless.

'I suppose you think I'm abandoning him?' Sarah lifted her chin. 'But he's not my responsibility, not really, is he?'

'I should tell you to go to hell your own way,' Arian controlled her voice with difficulty, 'but I'll see if Eddie Carpenter can call up to your house. He's a wonderful doctor.'

'You should come and take him out of my house altogether.' Sarah's voice was hard. 'He's mad. I've had enough of his nonsense, I can tell you.'

'Forget it.' Arian's voice was just as hard. 'I'll get you the doctor and that's all I'll do. You took Gerald on, you deal with him.'

Sarah seemed defeated. 'I'd better go, then.'

Arian stared her out, feeling slightly sorry for Sarah. She was an overblown siren and yet she was still a woman who wanted only to be loved, and Arian suddenly felt a kinship with her.

'Look, I'll see what Eddie says and then we'll talk some more, right?'

'I suppose so, but make it soon. I can't stand him and his tantrums for much longer. Thinks I'm out to harm him and me doing all I can for him, it's just not fair.'

Arian watched her leave with a sense of disquiet. Everything had seemed so clear cut. A divorce would be a scandal, a sin in most people's eyes. Look what had happened to Eline; she'd been driven out of Swansea. But it would have been preferable to remaining tied to a man she hated. Now there were complications. Gerald was sick, perhaps very sick, and Sarah all set to cast him aside.

'Come in here.' Eddie Carpenter appeared troubled as he welcomed Arian into his office. 'Sit down, we've got to talk.' He indicated a chair near his desk. 'It's not good news, I'm afraid. You look pale, Arian. I'm sure you're not taking good care of yourself.' Eddie sat on the edge of the old desk and stared down at her, his eyes full of sympathy. 'Gerald is a sick man but you know that, of course.'

Arian nodded. 'I want the truth, Eddie. What is it and will he get better?'

Eddie pursed his lips. 'Better, yes. Full recovery, it's doubtful. In any case, he needs to go into hospital. For a time at least, he will have to be placed somewhere specially suited to such cases.'

'Specially suited? What do you mean?'

'I mean his sickness isn't of the body but of the mind. It's complicated, Arian.'

'You want to put him in an asylum?' Arian's voice was unsteady. She saw Eddie pick up some notes and study them in silence for a moment and she knew he was giving himself time to think.

'We don't know very much about the mind,' he said at last, 'but we have learned a little bit.' He paused. 'Gerald is suffering from an illness which I believe to be inherited, never mind the name, it's long and complicated and it doesn't really matter what you call it, the man is sick.'

'Are you telling me he's dying?'

382

Eddie shook his head. 'No, on the contrary. Gerald could live a normal span of life.' He paused. 'But, he will be unstable, always.'

'You can give him medicine?'

'Yes, I can do that and so long as he takes it, his moods will be contained, I say *contained*, not cured.' He leaned forward and touched her arm.

'Let go, Arian. You can't cope with this, it's too much to ask of anyone.'

'He *is* my responsibility, he's my husband. You know I can't just let him rot in an institution.' She shuddered.

'He will be dangerous,' Eddie said. 'If he fails to take the medication, he could harm himself or someone else, think of that, Arian.'

She felt her breath dragged inward. 'Is he dangerous now, right now?'

Eddie hesitated. 'I don't think so, the illness hasn't progressed too far but it could be accelerated by anything.' He shrugged. 'We know so little. I can't give you firm assurances of anything.'

Arian rose. 'Thank you for taking so much trouble, Eddie.'

'Give yourself a few days to think this thing through.' Eddie rose too and stood beside her, resting his hand on her shoulders. 'He left you for this Sarah woman, it's her problem now. In any case, you must consider every angle before you make a decision.'

Arian left Eddie's office and set out towards Sarah Frogmore's house. She had to talk to her, warn her about Gerald's illness. She had no doubt what Sarah's reaction would be; she would wash her hands of the matter without compunction.

Sarah was sitting in the drawing room with Gerald seated opposite her. He appeared his normal self, his eyes were bright and alert and there was no sign of him being anything but normal.

'I wanted to talk to you, Sarah,' Arian felt uncomfortable. Sarah was smiling as though nothing was wrong.

'I don't see any point, now that Gerald is better. We have nothing to talk about.'

'But Sarah,' Arian lifted her hands in exasperation, 'we have a great deal to talk about.'·

'No. Please leave. We don't want you here, do we Gerald?' Sarah rose and pulled at the silk bell-rope. Gerald stared at Arian with a strange expression in his eyes.

'Sarah told me what you wanted,' he spoke suddenly, his voice harsh. 'If you'd had your way, you would have put me away in a mental institution, don't deny it.'

Arian looked at Sarah, who shrugged. 'Well you didn't want him, did you? Went to the doctor about him. Thank God he's got me, that's all I can say.'

Arian tried again. 'Sarah, it would be better if we could talk in private.'

It was Gerald who answered. 'Get out of here and don't come back, do you hear me?'

Arian left the house and without a backward glance made her way down the hill and into Swansea. Sarah was a fool to herself. Did she know what she was taking on? Arian doubted it. Well, for the moment, there was nothing else she could do; Sarah would just have to find out her mistake in her own way.

Mac was furious when she told him what had happened. 'Too good you are, Arian, too good by far. Leave them to it, the pair of them. Both mad as hatters if you ask me and don't deserve your help, either of them.'

'Never mind,' Arian squared her shoulders. 'Let's talk about something else. What have we got for tonight's leader, Mac? Anything interesting?'

Soon she was caught up in the business of the newspaper and Arian felt the blood flow through her veins with renewed vigour. She had this, her work; the words had become her life-line. Getting the story on the page and the page to the press, was an excitement. It took the place of love in her life and Arian realized that, for the moment at least, she was content to leave things the way they were.

'Throw that old medicine away,' Sarah stood looking down at Gerald as he lay in her huge bed. 'Makes you dull, that does. Stops you being the randy devil that I know and love.'

Gerald smiled and put down his glass. 'Come on then, it's about time I remembered I'm alive.'

He pulled her down beside him and carefully took off her bodice, his hands going to her breasts, his mouth hot on hers. Sarah sighed. This is what she wanted; her man, strong and wonderful, making her feel so desirable, so good. She put her hands on his cheeks and lifted his face from hers.

'They don't know what they're talking about those doctors. There's nothing wrong with you, Gerry. They're a lot of fools, just out to get money from suckers like that Arian. Well let her be taken in, she deserved it. Me and you will have our fun and to hell with the lot of them.'

Gerald's love-making was all that Sarah wanted. She felt him move within her, strong, as vigorous as he'd ever been. She cried out as he gripped her hips, thrusting himself deep, possessing her in the way she loved.

'Gerry, Gerry, my darling, I love you so much!' He fell away from her and she lay gasping in delight. Her hand reached out to catch his and together, they fell asleep.

Arian moved from the doorway and crossed the street, staring back at the two buildings, both of which she was utilizing for her growing business.

The windows and doors were freshly painted and above the façade, the name of the newspaper stood out in black: *The Swansea Times*. Within the grey stone walls were housed the tools of her trade; the printing presses, the brand-new guillotines for cutting the paper, the indian ink in bottles. The very smell of the place excited her.

Housed in the original building were the offices, the front desk where the public came to place advertisements; the reporters' rooms equipped now with the new typewriting machines and above, Arian's private rooms, enlarged and extended with new drapes and a brand-new bathroom.

She was so engrossed in her thoughts that she was not aware of the man coming to stand beside her until he spoke.

'Arian.' The name fell into the quietness, the voice was so familiar, so masculine, so loved and the sound of him saying her name had the power to thrill her.

'Calvin.' She wanted to go into his arms, to tell him how much she loved him but she stood quite still, looking at him as if he were a stranger. 'You startled me.'

'I understand you've had problems with Gerald Simples. He's sick, Eddie Carpenter told me. I hope you don't mind, he was concerned about you.'

'Let's walk.' She was filled with a complexity of feelings; she wanted to be with Calvin, was pleased that he cared enough to come to find her and yet what sense was there in talking? There was nothing to say that hadn't already been said.

He led her towards a waiting carriage and helped her inside. She sat next to him on the cold leather seat, savouring the moment, breathing in the scent of him, the rich aroma of his tobacco and she felt herself melt. It was a long time since she'd felt like a woman, she realized suddenly.

He took her to his house and when he opened the door and she saw the familiar, gracious hallway, she remembered with a pang of longing how happy she had been working for Calvin, being under the same roof with him. What a long time ago it all seemed now.

In the drawing room, she sat down in the large up-holstered chair near the glowing fire. She took the glass of porter he handed her and closed her eyes for a moment, sighing with a sense of release.

'Talk to me Arian.' His voice was mellow. She opened her eyes and looked at him.

'I don't know what to say, I don't even know what I'm doing here. I can't say anything except that I went to ask Gerald for a divorce. I wanted to make a new start but he's sick, very sick.'

She looked into the glowing liquid in her glass. 'He could be violent, dangerous even. I tried to warn Sarah Frogmore but she doesn't believe me.'

'Gerald Simples is not your problem,' Calvin said reasonably. 'Why should you be responsible now after the way he has treated you?'

'He's my husband.' She looked directly at Calvin. 'I wish to God things were different but they're not.' She wanted to hold out her hand to him, beg Calvin to hold her close. She needed love so badly. But what was the use? She was no good to him. She must keep her distance, allow Calvin to find a wife, to have the son he always wanted.

He came towards her quickly and took her in his arms. His mouth was on hers, searching, thrilling. His hands caressed her. He bent and kissed her throat, her breasts and she took a ragged breath, her eyes closed, wanting him so much.

He drew away and spoke to her softly. 'Why did you want a divorce, Arian? Was it so that we could be together?'

She shook her head. 'I don't know. I really don't know, Calvin. Perhaps I just wanted to be free.'

He moved away from her and stood staring at her, his eyes warm. 'Tell me you don't love me and I'll never bother you again. Go on, Arian, tell me.'

She looked away from him. 'I can't, Calvin, I just can't tell you a lie.' She stared up at him in anguish. 'That's what you wanted and that's what you've got – you've forced me to admit to my feelings, but it doesn't change anything, can't you see that?'

She turned and moved away from him but he caught her up in a few strides and drew her back against him, his hands gentle.

'We love each other, Arian. For now, that's all that matters, everything else can be sorted out, just leave it to me.'

She put her head backwards onto his shoulder. Her eyes were closed and hope washed over her. Perhaps, just perhaps, Calvin could make everything right, just as he said he would. But, no, she was only fooling herself. Slowly, she drew away from him.

'I'll speak to you some other time, Calvin. For now, I must be alone to think things out.' She didn't look back, otherwise she might have been tempted to go with him and damn the consequences. And in the back of her mind, the thought of Gerald rose like a big dark cloud.

CHAPTER TWENTY-SEVEN

Sarah wandered around the room, picking up first one expensive piece of china and then another, replacing the objects without really seeing them. She thought of Gerald, how he'd held her in his arms, made love to her as he used to. Doctors, they didn't know everything. She loved him, she knew what was best.

She smiled to herself. By throwing away his medication she'd done him a favour. He was out now, in town, buying himself a new suit and a few shirts. She'd insisted that he go to the best shops and put the goods on her account. He'd lost a little weight and his old clothes no longer fitted him but he was looking well, his eyes were clear again and he seemed to be more and more in love with her each day.

She paused and looked at herself in the mirror that hung over the ornate fireplace. She was getting older, not really old, not yet, but there were creases around her mouth and lines around her eyes. Gerald didn't seem to notice. He was grateful for her love and support. She was the only one who cared, that's what he was constantly telling her.

One thing she needed to make her life complete was to have her son home again. She missed Jack terribly. She should be settled down now with a husband and family like any other woman but there was no way her husband, Geoffrey, would ever release her. She knew that even if he did, she would have no means of support. Gerald was not earning anything these days and sometime, even his seemingly endless source of funds would dry up.

Gerald was one of the finest men to come her way, and there had been many men in her life, too many if the truth were told. None of those men who had been her lovers –

and somehow the word lovers comforted her – none of them had brought her more than a passing happiness, none except Gerald.

Abruptly she moved away from the mirror. It told the truth too starkly, it told her things about herself she would rather not know.

She glanced at the clock. Gerald would be a while yet and she was bored on her own. Perhaps it would be an idea to go round to see her son. Geoffrey would not be best pleased about a surprise visit but she had rights and it wasn't often she exercised them.

The morning air was chill when she stepped out onto the small drive of her house. Sarah glanced up at the lowering skies and shuddered. It would rain soon. Over the bay of Swansea hung a string of clouds like washing on a line; dirty smudged washing, ragged and grey.

The sea ran ceaselessly reaching for the shore and then receding, pewter in the dying daylight. Even the sand on the beach appeared colourless, as though the world had been robbed of light.

Sarah almost laughed. She was being fanciful in her old age. Stop it! she admonished herself. She was not old and mustn't even begin to think that way.

After she left the train, the walk to Geoffrey's modest retreat was not a long one. It would have been pleasant if the weather had been a little more kind. She passed a small wooded field, heard the tinkle of the stream running over smoothed stones, saw the contours of the land as though for the first time.

Sarah felt, quite suddenly, that her eyes had been opened to the world around her and for a moment she was frightened. She didn't want to see too clearly, for then she might learn that no-one really loved her at all, that she was just being used.

As she reached the house, she saw a lamp glimmer in the window. There was a silence about the place and as she raised her hand to the knocker, Sarah felt a sense of being outside an empty building.

The maid who opened the door to her was red eyed with weeping and Sarah felt a dart of alarm.

'What's the matter?' She pushed her way into the hall and looked around her fearfully. 'Is it the boy? Is my son hurt?'

The maid shook her head. 'Mr Chas.' Her voice broke with emotion. 'I still can't believe he's gone. Living in those awful draughty rooms by the docks has done for him. He's dead. The master's down at Oystermouth church. He's been there every day this past week.'

A sense of relief washed over her, and Sarah bit her lip. She'd imagined that Jack had fallen sick with some dreadful malady and the fear had made her almost fall into a swoon. She clung to the banister in the hallway and tried to get a grip on herself, trying to sort out her mixture of feelings. She should have heard about Chas, would have heard had she not been so engrossed in Gerald.

She should feel pity for her husband and yet there was a sort of triumph in knowing that he was free, free of the love that had bound him so tightly. She realized he must be sad. He'd lost so much, the man who in all the world had been his dearest friend. And lover, said a sharp voice within her.

'When are you expecting Geoffrey back?' she asked, standing up straight, feeling she needed to be strong. Somehow, all along, she had felt this to be a day of moment, a day when the world had grown a dark place, with sorrow round the corner waiting to pounce. And yet it wasn't her sorrow, it was Geoffrey's.

'He'll be in the cemetery a while yet, Mrs Frogmore.' The maid tried to dry the tears that persisted in running into her mouth. 'Can't bring hisself to leave Mr Chas alone in the ground, if you ask me.'

'My son, where's Jack?' Sarah heard her voice take on a note of panic and the maid visibly stiffened.

'He's safe in my care. Gone to bed, he has, Mrs Frogmore. Worn out the poor child is, sick from all that crying.'

Sarah glanced upstairs. She must see him, make sure her son was safe. Then she would go to her husband and comfort him. He would need her now more than he ever did before. Somehow the thought gave her a strong sense of power; no-one had ever really needed her. Perhaps in the last few weeks Gerry had clung to her but now he was recovered, he seemed to want to stand on his own two feet again.

She felt happy, reassured; if she so wished, she could resume her rightful place in her husband's life. They could never give each other physical love but there would be a strong warm bond of friendship between them. And if the day ever came when Gerry no longer wanted her, Geoffrey would be there, to care for her as he always had, in his own strange way.

Arian was outside the buildings that housed her newspaper, her very own newspaper. It seemed she never grew tired of admiring it, this, the solid proof of her growing success. The newly painted façade was old but gracious, the windows arched by stone, that appeared now like eyebrows raised in question. The windows shone, the paint on the woodwork new and fresh. And yesterday in the vaults, she had found the deeds that had proved the building was hers, something her father had left her, a building he'd thought worthless, not even valuable enough to gamble away at cards or dice. Now, it was worth everything to Arian. It offered her security, a future.

She stepped back a pace, watching the passers-by glance with interest at the sign above the door. It gave her a sense of pride to know that her name was there, hers alone: Arian Smale, proprietor. It was an achievement, of course it was. Why then, did she still have a sense of being unfulfilled?

She heard the clock on the Guildhall chime and knew it was time she got some work done. There was an obituary to write, a difficult one about Geoffrey Frogmore's friend, his lover if what Mac said was correct and it usually was, but what to say about a man who seemed to have no identity, no job, no aim in life?

Mac had refused outright to write the obituary. 'Don't like that sort of man, spot 'em a mile off. Should be tolerant, I suppose, but I can't understand it myself.'

Arian had taken the task upon herself, not knowing quite how tactful the younger reporters would be in such a situation and she wasn't about to risk either bringing her paper into disrepute or harming Geoffrey Frogmore's reputation, perhaps even condemning him to a prison sentence into the bargain.

When she knocked on the door of the modest house where Geoffrey Frogmore lived, the maid who opened it looked at her suspiciously. 'Yes?'

'I would like to talk to Mr Frogmore. I'm from the *Swansea Times*.'

'I'm not sure. . . . Mr Frogmore isn't in at the moment, you see.' The maid hesitated and Sarah appeared in the doorway behind her.

'Arian, do come in.' Sarah's eyes were alight with triumph. 'I should like to talk to you, anyway.'

Arian stepped inside the neat house. The place smelled fresh, the furniture glowed and in the polished grate, a warm fire was burning.

Sarah led the way into a tiny sitting room. She stood, arms folded, looking at Arian as though she'd scored a victory over her.

'Gerald is better, much better.' Sarah's cheeks dimpled coyly. 'The doctors were wrong, quite wrong. His recovery is the result of living with me. I care about him, you see, really care. Oh, I know he can be difficult at times but he really is a wonderful man. You've never understood him.'

'He's taking his medication, is he?' Arian asked and Sarah laughed out loud.

'That rubbish! It made him dull and boring. He's fine without it.'

Arian felt a pang of alarm. 'He can be dangerous, Sarah. For God's sake, take the advice of the doctors. Make sure Gerald takes the medicine regularly.'

'There's no need. I don't know what trick you're trying to pull but Gerald is fit and well. I look after him properly, which is more than you ever did.'

'Look, Sarah, I haven't come here to quarrel with you about Gerald. All I wanted was to talk to Mr Frogmore about his . . . his friend.'

'Why?' Sarah looked at her challengingly. 'What are you going to say about Chas?'

'I don't know.' Arian shrugged. 'Perhaps you can tell me a bit about him, something flattering that I can print in my paper, an obituary.'

The door behind her opened and Geoffrey came into the room. Arian felt herself melt with pity for him. Geoffrey Frogmore had been crying, his eyes were red and swollen and his hair was tangled about his forehead.

'What's going on here?' He looked from Sarah to Arian. 'What are you both doing in my house?'

'I came to see Jack.' Sarah moved to her husband's side and slipped her arm through his. 'This, this woman has come to write about Chas. Tell her how we both cared about him as friends should, go on Geoffrey.'

He disentangled himself from his wife's arm. 'I loved him, as a friend.'

The simple words brought a constriction to Arian's throat. She smiled sympathetically. 'I know you did but I need facts about him; his age, occupation, the names of his parents, where he was educated, that sort of thing.'

'You'll be sympathetic?' Geoffrey looked at her appealingly. 'You won't write anything speculative?' He shook his head. 'I'm not ashamed of caring for Chas but there's so much to consider, my son for a start.'

'I know,' Arian took out her pencil. 'That's why I came myself, so that I can be sure of writing a suitable obituary.'

'Don't listen to her, Geoffrey. She'll make a scandal of it all, expose you to ridicule. Be very careful what you say. In any case, I'll be a witness for you, Geoffrey, should she tell any lies.'

'Please, Sarah, be quiet.' He spoke with authority. 'I want Chas's name to be honoured in Swansea. He was born here and he died here and I don't think Miss Smale is going to do anything underhand or scandalous, so leave it to me, will you?'

Geoffrey's dignity impressed Arian and as he talked she wrote rapidly. Chas, it seemed was the son of a rich copper baron, his father was a man of means and of stiff-necked pride.

Arian folded her notebook and looked up at Geoffrey. 'I'll be very careful how I write this obituary,' she reassured Geoffrey, 'don't worry.'

She left the house and turned once to see Sarah framed in the window. Perhaps, Arian thought, she should have made another attempt to convince Sarah that Gerald could be dangerous. But then Sarah had made up her mind that he was fit and well, it was pointless talking to her. And yet, even as she walked back into Swansea, Arian's sense of unease was growing. Gerald was at large a dangerous man who might strike anywhere, anytime and Arian knew that she was afraid.

The house smelled of paint and brand-new drapes, the carpets were deep and rich, and the good heavy furniture was waxed and fragrant. The Hollies was Arian's new home, rented for now but once she had enough money, she intended to buy it and live there for ever.

The elegant house looked over the sea at Swansea. The large windows facing the curving bay allowed the sunlight into every room. There were no dark corners at the Hollies and better still, no dark memories.

'You've done well for yourself, girl.' Fon hugged her baby daughter to her breast and stared across the room admiringly. '*Duw*, I'd never have thought to see you so prosperously set up, mind.'

Arian looked towards Fon who had settled in the depths of the chair. Everything about her seemed to gleam with happiness, from her bright hair to her even brighter eyes.

It was good to see Fon again, Fon with her ever growing brood of children.

'I'm successful, after a lifetime of failure,' she agreed. 'I haven't got what you've got, though, the love of a fine man and lovely family. I can see the happiness shine from you right across the room.'

Fon blushed. She would always be the simple girl from the village of Oystermouth who had married her farmer, never be sophisticated, never be a career girl like Arian and yet it didn't seem to matter.

'Me and you, we shared some good times and some bad times, mind.' Fon lifted her baby to the other breast and a pearl of milk beaded the child's mouth. 'But we've come through it all and none the worse for it.'

Arian wasn't too sure of that. Her past had marked her and there were memories that would always haunt her, memories that sometimes even now reared up in the night.

She realized with surprise that she hadn't thought of her husband in weeks, since she'd visited Geoffrey Frogmore and spoken with Sarah.

Arian had not heard a word from him or about him and she didn't want to. Still, the feeling persisted that he would always be there, at the back of her mind, at the back of her life, waiting to pounce.

'The paper's doing well, got to be the best one this side of Cardiff.' Fon's soft voice interrupted Arian's unhappy train of thought. 'Everyone reads the *Swansea Times*, see it everywhere I go.'

Arian concealed a smile. The places Fon went were few indeed, a visit to her relatives in Mumbles and perhaps a supper with friends now and again was about the limit of her social life. Fon needed no-one. She had her family growing up around her. Above all, she had Jamie, in love with her still in spite of the new plumpness in her hips and the roundness in her cheeks.

'Jamie coming to fetch you, is he?' Arian asked pouring a fresh cup of tea.

'No, I'm meeting him in town. He doesn't believe in me being away from him and the little ones for too long.' She smiled mischievously. 'Not trying to get rid of me are you? Haven't got an assignation with a lover by any chance?'

'Not by the slightest chance,' Arian said firmly. 'There's no man in my life now, which is a relief after Gerald, I can tell you.'

'Everybody needs someone,' Fon said softly. 'You can be too independent, mind, turn the men away, make them frightened of you. Ease up a bit, Arian they're not all wasters, believe me.'

'I do,' Arian forced a smile. 'I've seen you and Jamie together but as for me, I'm all right as I am, I don't need anyone. I've got my job.'

'The paper can't tuck you up into bed at nights,' Fon shook her head disapprovingly. 'Can't tell you it loves you or give you a bit of a cuddle when you're feeling down, and you are feeling sad, I can see it in your eyes.'

'I'm all right, just envious of you.' Arian coughed to cover the sudden rush of tears. 'And I'm never lonely, it's difficult to get any time alone, in fact. This evening now, I've got Mac coming round, Mac's my senior reporter.' She paused. 'I'm going to ask him to start up a new features section to the paper, see what he thinks.'

'All right, you're good at changing the subject so I'll be good and ask what sort of thing do you have in mind for this new part of the paper?' Fon held the baby upright on her knee and rubbed the small body.

'Well, it will principally deal with women's interests, sewing, cooking hints, budgeting, that sort of thing.'

'Will that go down well in Swansea?' Fon sounded doubtful. She buttoned her bodice and cuddled the baby, making small rocking movements even though the child was asleep.

Arian couldn't help staring. She would have no child of her own, not now. It wasn't that she was old, not really, but she couldn't envisage being a mother even if her life had turned out differently. As it was, she was tied to Gerald.

She couldn't marry anyone else and she was not interested in casual alliances. Not now.

'I don't know if a women's page will be well received or not,' Arian answered Fon's question truthfully. 'I never will know unless I try it. Anyway, I trust Mac's judgement. I'll see what he says about it.'

'But you'll go ahead with the idea whatever?' Fon said smiling and Arian smiled too.

'I expect so.' She watched as Fon rose to her feet and picked up the closely woven shawl which she wrapped around her own body, tucking the baby inside like a neat parcel.

'Better be on my way,' Fon said. 'Jamie will be waiting for me in the market.' She smiled. 'I don't like to leave the children for too long, April isn't the most patient of girls.'

She stood for a moment on the front step with Arian and it was clear she wanted to say something more. Arian smiled indulgently. 'Come on, spit it out.' She watched the frown on Fon's brow and knew that something she didn't want to hear was about to be said.

'I saw that Sarah Frogmore,' she said. 'In the market she was, with him, your husband. He had the cheek to ask about you, where you were living. I didn't tell him anything, mind, but he was that persistent.'

Arian felt she was facing a great chasm. 'Damn and blast,' Arian said softly. 'I hoped I'd never hear from either Sarah or him again. Did he look well?'

'You owe him nothing,' Fon spoke sharply. 'They might make a show of being respectable but he left you to live with that Sarah Frogmore. You can't feel responsible for him any more.'

'I wish I didn't.' Arian bit her lip. 'But tell me, Fon, was he all right?'

'Seemed a bit agitated, if you must know. Eyes staring at me in a strange way, frightening really.'

Arian sighed and stared up at the sky without seeing the slowly moving clouds.

'I wish I hadn't told you now,' Fon's voice was low. 'I should have kept my mouth shut but I thought you should be warned about him. I think he's going to come and see you from the way he was talking.'

Arian forced a smile. 'Don't let it worry you, I can cope with Gerald.' She watched as Fon walked away from the house, her baby wrapped close, her tawny hair shining in the sunlight. Slowly Arian turned and moved back into the house and suddenly, her hands were trembling.

CHAPTER TWENTY-EIGHT

Calvin Temple sat in the garden staring out over the curving sweep of the bay far below him. The scent of roses was all around him and the sun was warm on his face. He should feel on top of the world, he told himself. He had everything; a fine home, an easy life-style and most of all, he had a new mistress.

Ellie was sweetness itself; golden of hair, soft of nature and passionate in the bedchamber. She was a pale imitation of Arian Smale and Calvin knew it.

Arian. A success now, her newspaper flourishing. Everyone, including Ellie, was avidly reading the new feature pages within the *Swansea Times*, an innovation by anyone's standards and guaranteed to make the paper more popular than ever.

Calvin recognized Arian's hand in the leader articles in the women's pages; these were always well constructed and full of controversy. He saw none of her in the gimmicky pieces on cooking and budgeting the household expenses, those were things that would not interest Arian in the least.

Ellie now, she read them with delight, sitting in the apartment he'd bought for her. She even ventured to try some of the recipes, much to her cook's chagrin. Ellie was cut out to be a wife, a homely girl who wanted a husband and a brood of children around her skirts. He'd toyed with the idea of marrying her, of course he had. He needed heirs but he always balked at the asking. More than anything he needed the spice that Arian alone brought into his life and he might as well face the fact that it was Arian he loved and longed to spend the rest of his days with.

He knew of her husband's sickness, something wrong with the man's mind apparently. He'd heard about it with a sense of dismay; he knew Arian, she had too much conscience to abdicate responsibility for her husband and he wouldn't put it past her to take the man back in spite of everything.

If Calvin hated anyone, it was Gerald Simples. Simples had tricked Arian into marriage, he had stolen Calvin's money and had got away with it scot-free. Revenge when it came, would be sweet indeed.

Bella came into the garden and bobbed a curtsy. 'A lady here to see you, sir.' He caught a glimpse of the curiosity in the maid's face before she stepped aside and allowed Ellie to enter the garden. She stood before him with a hangdog expression on her face.

'I've got to talk to you, Calvin, love.' She spoke softly, her Welsh accent lilting and delicate, her voice was one of the things about Ellie that most pleased him.

He met her eyes and warning bells rang in his mind. Ellie looked pale, strained even. She had never come to his house unasked and he wondered if she had found another lover, a man who wanted to marry her.

He was surprised by the feeling of relief that swept through him at the thought. He knew, quite suddenly, that after an initial sense of pique, he would not be too worried if Ellie were to leave him.

'That will be all, Bella.' He waited for the maid to leave.

'Go on, then Ellie,' he encouraged, 'spit it out, I won't bite.' He patted the wrought iron seat but she remained standing like a small girl about to be rebuked.

'I'm with child.' The words fell into the silence, softly spoken words, almost an apology in themselves. Calvin became aware of the singing of the birds, the rustling of the leaves in the tree, as his mind, for an instant, refused to accept what Ellie was saying.

She had begun to weep softly, her head down, her hands hanging to her sides. He rose and took her in his arms and patted her awkwardly. Guilt seared him. He hadn't expected this. But why hadn't he? It was the thing women

401

did best, getting with child, usually in order to trap a man into marriage.

Immediately, he dismissed the thought as unworthy. No, not Ellie, she wouldn't even think of trapping him. She was innocent, a lovely girl with not one ounce of guile in her make-up.

He drew her towards the garden seat and took her on his knee and smoothed the hair from her face. 'It isn't your fault, Ellie,' he said softly, soothingly. 'It isn't anyone's fault. These things happen.'

He was suddenly calm. After the initial shock, his first thought had been to offer marriage but he had been down that road before with Eline and would not take that path again.

'What am I to do?' Ellie asked in a whisper. 'You won't want me. I'll grow fat and ugly and you'll hate me for what has happened.'

'Of course I won't hate you,' Calvin reassured her. 'I'll take care of you, always. I promise you that.'

'But you don't want to marry me.' Ellie had said the words that were in his mind and Calvin felt his defences rising.

'No,' he said as gently as he could, 'I have been married. I don't want to marry again, Ellie, you always knew that.'

'I know.' She turned away as though afraid for him to see her face. 'But you'll still let me live with you?' She was pleading.

'Of course I'll let you live with me,' he said. 'We have our own little love nest, our apartment in town, don't we?' He was avoiding the issue. She wanted to live with him, not in the apartment but here, in his own house.

'I'll get a nurse for you, you won't ever be alone, I promise you.' He was promising a great deal and yet nothing at all and they both knew it.

Ellie turned and clung to him, he could feel her hot tears against his neck. He felt his being melt but it was with pity not love. He held her close and kissed her hair but his mind was working on practical matters. He would set up a trust

402

for the child when it came. If it should be a son, he would adopt him as his legitimate heir.

Excitement filled him; he was to be a father at last. Ellie had been nothing if not faithful to him. She was the truthful kind who would have broken off the relationship at once if someone else had come along. Not like Eline. He pushed away the bitter thoughts of the son she'd borne, the son he'd believed for a short time had been his.

'Don't worry,' he soothed, 'let me give you some money and you can choose some baby things. That will make you happy, won't it?'

She put her hand on his face then and kissed his lips. 'If it makes you happy, there's nothing more to be said.'

He watched as she rose to her feet and moved slowly, gracefully away from him. In that moment, he realized how he'd always treated Ellie as a child. In reality, she was a woman with an insight he'd never given her credit for.

'You're going home?' He hated himself for the feeling of relief that filled him. 'My carriage will take you, I'll call the groom.'

After she'd gone, he moved restlessly from his seat. He would walk into town, take a stroll past the offices of the *Swansea Times*. It was possible, just possible that he might catch a glimpse of Arian. Why he should think of her now, he couldn't understand. Unless he wanted to say goodbye to her, finally.

Gerald was growing cunning. He knew now when the bout of temper was going to come upon him. He felt the stirrings as though a rage at all the world was about to take him over and suffocate him. It was then he would take a dose of the laudanum that he had secreted away in the drawer beside the bed he shared with Sarah.

The laudanum always helped. He knew it would bring on a calmness akin to sleep, he would dream away the hours for God knows how long and then, he would wake and the rage would have passed.

Dr Carpenter had been pushy enough to track him down, to call on him at the Frogmore residence. He'd been puzzled by Gerald's apparent cure. He'd thought Gerald ready for the mad house and here he was, apparently confounding all the doctors' learned theories.

The trouble was, Gerald thought wryly, that he was beginning to crave the laudanum even when the bouts weren't threatening but he could control that, just as he had controlled everything in his life, including the women.

Especially the women. Even now, he lay in an hotel room waiting for a beautiful girl, the seventeen-year-old daughter of Eddie Carpenter, the doctor. That was rich and Gerald stretched and smiled to himself.

Candida Carpenter was the one who supplied him with laudanum in return for vows of true love and marriage one day in the future.

She was sweet and gullible and very passionate beneath the sheets. Having another woman was a situation which suited Gerald admirably, for Candida had a splendid young body, an eager young libido. In addition, she believed herself to be very modern and felt, with a growing number of other women, that equality was the name of the game between a man and a woman.

Candida was training to be a nurse because of a whim. She was from the privileged classes and her duties were inordinately light; her father, after all was a well-to-do doctor who adored his first-born child. So, well placed to open the right doors, Candida would doubtless make it to the top of her profession, if she stuck it that long.

He heard the knock on his door and sat up, a knowing smile on his face. It was growing dark outside and this was the time of day that Candida visited him after she'd come off shift in the hospital. They had a regular arrangement, one paid for by the generosity of Sarah Frogmore, if she but knew it.

She slipped into the room, her starched apron rustling and Gerald imagined Candida, so pristine in her uniform and yet with the black stockings hidden seductively beneath the fresh linen.

He pretended sleep and heard her come to the bed. She leant over him and brushed his mouth with hers. He felt her breasts against his arm and resisted the temptation to reach up with his mouth.

'Time for your blanket bath, sir.' Candida was nothing if not predictable. 'Let's see how your muscles are working tonight.' She drew back the bed-clothes. 'Oh, *very* good.'

He opened his eyes to see her divest herself slowly of her uniform, hanging the clothes over a chair, careful not to crease them. When she was naked, she came to him and climbed astride him.

'You look tired tonight, darling.' She smiled, her small white teeth pearly in the dim light. 'I think I will have to administer to your needs. We must look after you, mustn't we?'

Gerald suppressed a sigh, he wished she'd shut up, she was not a conversationalist. Then he gasped. She had stopped talking and was doing what she was best at and he gave himself up to what he knew was going to be an hour of sheer delight.

Later, when he was alone, Gerald relaxed into a comfortable sense of well being. In his possession was a fresh supply of laudanum. Perhaps, he thought, he should take some before he faced the ordeal of going home to Sarah.

She imagined he'd been out shopping, stopping at some public bar on the way home. She would question him about which shops he'd been to and what he'd bought, who he had drunk with, but then he'd always been adept at lying.

There was just one worry that tugged at the corners of his mind. What if Sarah should find out about Candida? He didn't want to lose the money she heaped upon him. On the other hand, he meant to hold onto Candida, too. She was his means of obtaining the laudanum he needed so badly.

He would have to be very careful with both his ladies. Candida accepted that he had a wife, but a mistress she would never tolerate. If she even so much as guessed at the situation, he would never see her again, for Candida had a very great sense of self-preservation.

He took some of the precious laudanum and lay back, his senses sated. He felt exultant. In time, everything would fall into his lap. A little patience, that's all he needed. His blood quickened. He was making his plans soon, very soon now, and then he would seek out Arian, his wife.

'When are we going to have this great civic "do", business, then?' Mac as always was surly and Arian suppressed a smile.

'I don't know the exact date but you should be happy that the city fathers are honouring our newspaper with a supper at the Guildhall. It's some achievement to be the highest selling daily in South Wales.'

'Dunno about that,' Mac picked up his pen. 'There's other papers just as good. Better, in fact.'

'Maybe so,' Arian felt it polite to agree with Mac, as he hated any show of pride, 'but none have such a fine writer as you on the staff.'

'Stuff and nonsense.' The words were harsh but none the less, Mac was pleased, that much was evident by the colour that flooded up his neck to his ears.

'*Duw*, I don't believe it,' Arian teased, 'the hard-bitten reporter is actually blushing.'

'I am not.' Mac didn't look at her but bent his head lower over the page on which he was writing. 'Go away, I have work to do even if you haven't.'

Arian had no work, at any rate nothing she wanted to get on with right now. Right now she needed a walk in the fresh air, needed to get out of the aura of ink and pencil sharpenings and raise her head from work once in a while, if only to stay sane.

Sane. The word brought to mind unwelcome thoughts of Gerald. She had caught sight of him leaving an hotel yesterday evening. He appeared slightly dazed and she'd hidden in a doorway, feeling foolish but praying he wouldn't see her.

He was well dressed and prosperous looking, no doubt courtesy of the gullible Sarah. He could charm any woman he chose, any woman except his wife. Perhaps it was this that had made him want her so much, the fact that Arian alone saw him as he was.

'I'm going out.' She put on her coat.

'I'm relieved to hear it.' Mac glared up at her. 'I'll be able to get some real work done in peace.'

'And I will have a rest from your moaning.' Arian moved to the door. It was all banter. She would never manage without Mac, and in any case, she really was very fond of him.

It was good to be outdoors. The sun was warm and the breeze coming in from the sea was scented with salt. It was a day when Arian felt, almost, that she was a young girl again. But she wasn't so young now, she would never see twenty-five again.

Her life had been eventful. She had known men, not all of them kind. She was married to a man whom she had never loved, tied to him for the rest of her life. It was a sombre thought.

But, at least in one thing she had made her mark, she was a newspaper proprietor and one on whom the city fathers were about to bestow a singular honour. She should feel proud. Why then, did she feel empty and unsatisfied?

'You look as downhearted as I feel.' The voice was one she recognized at once and Arian felt her senses quicken. She glanced up to see Calvin Temple, his eyes holding hers were without laughter. She made to move away.

'Don't go, Arian,' he spoke softly. 'Talk to me, just talk. That's all I ask.'

'All right.' Arian followed him as he led the way along the street in the direction of the bay. They walked for some minutes in silence, finally facing the sea as the long arm of the pier came into sight.

'I'm not happy, Arian.' He began without preliminary as they stood beneath the struts of the pier, the sand soft beneath their feet. 'I don't think I'll every be really happy, not without you.'

He held up his hand. 'I know it's impossible. You're married, you've told me that a hundred times, but it doesn't stop me wanting you.'

'Doesn't stop you having a new mistress, either, does it?' There was not much about the doings of the privileged classes that Arian didn't know thanks to the diligence of her reporters.

Calvin looked at her quickly. 'Add this to what the gossips tell you, Ellie's having my child.' He sounded proud and Arian felt a bite of jealousy.

'You'll marry her?' It was a question that she had no right to ask and yet she wasn't surprised when he answered. 'No.'

'You don't love her.' This was a statement. It was clear that he didn't love the girl, not enough anyway, otherwise he wouldn't be talking to Arian this way.

'I'll take care of her, of course,' he avoided the question. 'I'll make sure that she never wants for anything.' He looked levelly at Arian. 'Ellie is a nice girl, looks a bit like you. A substitute, I recognize that.'

Arian was absurdly pleased though she had no right to be. 'If I was good, and generous, I'd wish you every happiness with this Ellie, I would wish for you to fall in love with her.'

'But that's not what you want, is it, Arian?'

'I can't say it is.'

'And you still won't come to live with me, even though you'd be everything in the world to me, my wife in every way possible.'

Arian smiled ruefully. 'Except in law. I couldn't do it, Calvin. I think my wild ways are gone now I'm getting older. You see, I'm settling into a routine, I'm compromising with life, isn't that what it's all about? It's what we all seem to do in the end, even you with your Ellie.'

'I suppose so.' Calvin fell silent, he stared at the sea receding now, moving insidiously away from the shore. Arian watched him covertly. She loved him, she wanted him physically, wanted to be in his arms, to know him intimately as a woman should know the man she loved. She'd had so little of him and yet he was scarcely far from her thoughts.

He felt her gaze and turned to look at her. Slowly, he leaned forward and carefully pressed his mouth against hers. She felt that this was a goodbye, perhaps a last goodbye and she wanted to cry.

'I must go.' His voice was brisk. 'Come along, let me walk you back to the highway.'

It was far too short a walk. Soon, they reached the bottom of the Strand and after a moment, Calvin turned on his heel and walked briskly away from her. Arian watched until he was out of sight and then she made her way slowly towards the press, it was better than going home to an empty house.

Mac was obviously in a bad mood. He looked red in the face and there was a streak of ink across his cheek. Arian wanted to hug him; he was so dear, so ordinary, so reliable in spite of his eccentric ways.

'There's trouble.' There was no preliminary, just like Mac to get right to the heart of the matter. 'Seems that some rich bitch is suing us.'

Arian was not alarmed. 'How can that be?' She shrugged off her coat, aware that there was sand in her shoes. She kicked them off impatiently. 'We haven't written anything defamatory, have we?'

'Of course we have. It sells papers and usually no-one complains.'

'How bad is it? Who is the lady in question and does she have a case?' Arian sat down at her desk and leaned her chin on her elbows, she could still feel Calvin's mouth on hers.

'It's Mrs Sarah Frogmore,' Mac glanced away in embarrassment and suddenly he had all Arian's attention.

'And?'

'And I sort of hinted, only hinted, mind you, that her husband is of, shall we say, a deviant disposition.'

'Oh, my God, Mac, you didn't?' Arian didn't know whether to laugh or cry. 'How could you do such a thing?'

'It was too good a story to miss. It's not an acceptable way of life, never will be. Not here in Swansea, anyway.'

'Mac, that was taking unfair advantage of the man's weakness.' Arian bit her lip. 'I was so careful writing the obit.' She sighed. 'In any case, it is not our policy to preach or lay down the law about anyone else's private behaviour, we are not here to judge.'

'Balderdash!' Mac stared up belligerently. 'It's what we do best, my dear. We stand in judgement on someone every time we write a story. You don't object to me writing about a man taking a mistress, do you?'

'I do as a matter of fact,' Arian was surprised at her own reaction. 'I think a man's love-life, or a woman's come to that, is their own business.'

'That's a new one on me.' Mac had risen to his feet. 'Since when have you been so God-awful pompous about a bit of gossip? You haven't taken a lover yourself, have you?'

'No, but if I had, I'd make sure I didn't tell you or I'd find it splashed all over the pages of the *Times*.' She was aware her voice had risen. 'Anyway, you should have been more careful over a story like this. You should know that Geoffrey Frogmore could end up in prison over it; it just isn't on to ruin a man's life in that way.'

'Oh, so now I must cover up for perverts, must I?' Mac was coldly angry. He began picking up his pens and stuffing them into his pockets. Arian watched him for a moment, pride prevented her from asking him what he was doing.

'It seems to me that I no longer have a place on this paper,' he said. 'I suppose now that the *Times* is a success you don't need an old hack like me.'

'Well, I think you are just leaving a sinking ship, myself.' Arian was too stubborn to beg Mac to forget his anger and stay. 'Running out on me when I most need you, letting me deal with the mess *you've* made of things.'

'I'll stay then, just until I sort this out for you. Then, my dear lady, I shall be off, away. I see I've outworn my welcome.'

Mac left her sitting there at her desk. He didn't, as she'd expected, slam the door behind him. Instead he closed it with a quiet finality that frightened her more than his anger.

'Mac, don't do this to me.' She covered her eyes with her hands. 'I need you, you are the one stable thing in my life.'

Now why hadn't she said that to his face instead of getting holier than thou and lecturing him? The office was silent except for the popping of the gas lights. Suddenly Arian felt lonely, so lonely. She ached to be with someone who cared about her. There was no point in fooling herself, she ached to be with Calvin. How wonderful it would be to tell him her problems, have him take her in his arms and reassure her.

She found herself almost running from the offices and out into the street. She paused and stared round hoping for the sound of carriage wheels. She walked to the end of the street and there at the kerbside, the driver of a cab was just helping a well-dressed lady onto the pavement.

'Wait,' Arian moved towards him, 'are you free to take me on just a short journey?'

'No trouble, Miss.'

'So it's you, Arian Smale.' The voice was harsh with anger and Arian looked back over her shoulder, her foot on the step of the cab.

'Sarah, I can't stop.' She climbed into the coach. The last thing she wanted now was another confrontation. Sarah wasn't letting her go so easily and hung on to the door of the cab.

'You'll pay for your slandering remarks.' Sarah's face was white in the moonlight. 'I'll see you in the law courts.'

'Drive on,' Arian commanded and slapping Sarah's hand away, closed the door of the cab firmly. The coach jerked into motion and Arian's last glimpse of Sarah was of her furious expression as she stood in the street, her fist raised.

Half way up Mount Pleasant Hill, Arian regretted her hasty actions. She was suddenly frightened, realizing what her appearance at his door would mean to him. He would naturally assume that she was ready to be his mistress, and was she?

The thought of being taken care of, being loved was a comforting one and yet would she ever be really happy in such a role?

When the coachman dropped her at the entrance of the drive she looked across the lawns and saw the lighted windows of the big house with a feeling of nostalgia. She had been happy here until Gerald Simples had interfered in her life.

She felt the cool night air on her cheeks as she walked along the tree-lined drive. It was spotting with rain, soft rain like tears. Arian's step quickened, she moved towards the door and then paused, seeing a light warm the windows of the sitting room to her right.

Arian stepped across the crazy paving and stood outside the long window looking in. Calvin was in his chair with a glass of porter in his hand. Across from him sat the woman he had described as similar in appearance to Arian herself. Arian could see no likeness. All she saw was a fair-haired girl, little more than a child. The girl, Ellie, was laughing, her eyes alight as they rested on Calvin. In her hands she held a small garment, a baby gown hung with ribbons.

Slowly Arian turned away, she couldn't break into his life, not now. She began to walk back along the drive, her footsteps quickening until she was running. It was as though her dreams of being loved had finally been torn in tatters before her eyes and Arian, like a wounded animal, was running for cover.

CHAPTER TWENTY-NINE

Sarah was fuming, her hands clenched into fists. She stood in the roadway watching the receding cab and all the foul epithets she had learned in her varied life came flooding out. A woman passed and stared at her, her ragged skirts lifted as if in disdain. 'Whore!' she said loudly.

Sarah drew herself up. She was Mrs Geoffrey Frogmore, she must remember that and no-one, no-one was going to shake her life to shreds, not again.

She and Geoffrey had come to an understanding since Chas's death. They could even learn to live together again, given the chance. The main obstacle between them though was Sarah's relationship with Gerry and she was fast coming to the conclusion that to finish it might just be the right thing.

Gerry was different these days, he seemed preoccupied. She could almost believe there was someone else in his life. She'd made up her mind to follow him on one of his jaunts to town but at the moment more pressing matters were taking her attention.

That bitch Arian had written awful things about Geoffrey in that rag of a newspaper of hers. She'd insinuated that Geoffrey was some sort of pervert. Well she would pay for that. How dare she try to ruin the reputation of folks who were her betters?

There was Jack to consider. The little boy was happy to be reunited with his mother and Sarah would kill anyone who tried to ruin her son's life. Jack would not grow up with the stigma of a jailbird father hanging over him, she would not allow it.

Apart from anything else, it was unthinkable that Geoffrey should be accused openly of being a . . . being a . . . Her lips refused to frame the crude word that leapt to the forefront of her mind. It was too painful to have her husband branded publicly in that way, even if what was said about him *was* true.

She moved along the street and stood for a moment outside the offices of Church, Evans and Grove, solicitors, and then, with a decisive movement, pushed open the door.

Later as she made her way towards her home, she smiled to herself; she had set the wheels in motion. Arian would soon learn not to tangle with Sarah Frogmore's family. Now she could concentrate on finding out what Gerry was up to. In a way, she was looking for an excuse to end the relationship. It had become sour, the passion spent, and Gerry's moodiness was getting on her nerves. He seemed lethargic sometimes, as though unaware she was even in bed beside him. His love-making had become less than a pleasure and whatever they had had between them, they had lost.

It was a week later when Gerry, freshly bathed, wearing his best clothes, announced he was going out and might not be back until late. Once she would have accepted it without question, eager to have whatever he gave her of himself. Now with the possibility of Geoffrey returning to the fold, she felt more confident, more in charge of her life.

When Gerry had set out towards town, she drew on her coat and followed him, keeping at a safe distance behind the trees that flanked the curving drive. He walked slowly with a slightly unsteady gait and Sarah wondered if he'd been drinking.

Once on the perimeter of the town, she hailed a cab and moved towards the door gratefully.

'Follow that man,' she said dimpling at the surly driver. 'I think he's up to no good, and I want to catch him at it.' Oblivious to her attempt at a beguiling smile, the driver shrugged and climbed up into his seat, flicking the reigns so that the horses jerked into motion. He saw a great many strange things in his job and found it wise to keep his nose out of other people's business.

Gerald stopped at the door of the Castle Hotel and without even a cursory glance around, went inside. Sarah paid the driver and went inside the foyer. She was just in time to see Gerry disappear up the curving, red-carpeted stairway. He acted as though he was familiar with the place and a flash of anger brought the colour into Sarah's cheeks. He must have another woman, no wonder his love-making lacked lustre.

A few minutes later, a pretty young nurse in uniform entered the hotel and Sarah scarcely noticed her. It was only when the girl hurried up the stairs without pausing at the desk that she became suspicious.

She approached the young clerk at the desk and smiled at him. 'Excuse me, I'm supposed to meet Mr Gerry Simples here today. Can you tell me which room he's in?'

The clerk looked at her steadily for a moment and then, apparently reassured by her good clothes and respectable manner glanced at the open book before him.

'Number forty-five, first floor, madam. That's the room he always has. Shall I send a page to fetch him?'

'No, it's all right, I'm his sister. He's expecting me.' Sarah mounted the stairs with slow, deliberate tread. She was angry, very angry. Gerry was a regular here, so he'd been carrying on for some time. Her hands clenched into fists. He was so sure of himself, of *her* that he hadn't even given a false name to the clerk.

The door to number forty-five wasn't locked. Sarah opened it and at once saw the figure of a young woman lying beside Gerry. Her magnificent body was naked and she was smiling, her eyes closed, her head thrown back as Gerry cupped her breasts.

'So you *are* carrying on.' Sarah's voice was low. 'I hate you, Gerry Simples. I've finished with you, for good.'

He looked up at her, his eyes almost drowsy, he didn't seem to care that she was there, watching him betraying her. 'Why don't you go home, Sarah. You're too old for all this excitement.'

The girl was watching her, triumph written all over her young face. Gerry leaned up on one elbow and without releasing his hold on the girl, nodded towards the door. 'Close it on your way out, I'll be glad to see the back of you.'

'You bastard!' Sarah said, her breath seeming to leave her body. 'Don't you dare come near my house again or I'll set the constables on you. You are finished, do you understand?'

She left the door open and hurried downstairs and at the desk she stopped, her fury at being made a fool, getting the better of her.

'Do you know you are keeping a bawdy house, here, my good man?' she said in a loud voice. The clerk looked up at her startled.

'Upstairs, there's a man in bed with a girl young enough to be his daughter. Disgusting behaviour, that's what it is and I'm going straight to the offices of the *Swansea Times* to tell them what sort of establishment you have here.'

She left the hotel, her head high and once outside began to hurry towards home. Suddenly she was frightened at what she'd done; the last thing she wanted was to cause a scandal and involve herself in it. She would no more think of going to the newspapers than fly to the moon. Apart from anything else, Gerald was not a man to cross.

She would go to see Geoffrey at once, beg her husband to come home, then she would be safe. She would pack up Gerald's belongings, get rid of them and him for good. Her mind was made up, she would go to Geoffrey's house now, talk to him, convince him he must come home.

She took the train, fuming with impatience all the while and then let herself into his modest house without knocking on the door. She wouldn't give him a chance to rebuff her before he'd heard her out. The warm scents of the kitchen rose, tantalizingly mingling with the clean smell of beeswax polish. Geoffrey's house was well kept.

But he would come home once she asked him and she would be Mrs Geoffrey Frogmore, a lady with a husband's protection.

To her surprise and delight, Sarah found Geoffrey seated in the drawing room, his son playing at his feet. He looked up as she entered the room and for a moment, a light of welcome flickered in his eyes.

Sarah went to him and kissed his brow. He smiled up at her like a lost dog and she knew he was missing Chas badly. 'I want you to come home,' she said almost pleadingly.

'There's nothing I'd like better. I'm so lonely,' he replied. 'But what about . . .'

'There's nothing stopping you, *nothing*,' she said firmly. Gerald wouldn't dare show his face now and as for the newspaper article about Geoffrey, well it would all be disproved if they lived together again as man and wife.

'If you're sure . . .' Geoffrey said pitifully and Sarah smiled warmly, feeling an overwhelming urge to protect him.

The first thing Sarah did was to fire the old 'aunt'. The next thing was to move Geoffrey and Jack back home where they belonged.

As she'd expected, there had been no sign of Gerald. She'd relented over his clothes and had them delivered to the hotel. From his ensuing silence, it was clear that Gerald was accepting her decision as final.

It was about a week later that she woke in the early hours of the morning to hear pitiful sobs coming from Geoffrey's room. She left her bed and moved towards the door, pausing for a moment, her hand on the knob, her heart beating swiftly. Dare she intrude on his grief? Would she be doing more harm than good?

She went silently into his room and climbed into bed beside him, and winding her arms around him began to rock him as though he was a child. He clung to her, his face buried in the warmth of her neck, his tears hot against her skin.

'There, there, my love, it's all right. Everything is going to be all right, believe me. I'll look after you.'

Her hand slid along his belly and he seemed, at first, to cringe from her touch. She persisted, whispering softly to him, coaxing, encouraging him, her experienced fingers arousing him in spite of himself.

He moaned softly and she could feel his heart beating against hers. 'There's nothing to be afraid of, lovely,' she whispered. 'I'm here. I'll see that no one harms you. I'll always care for you, don't you worry now. I'll give you ease, you'll see.'

In his ecstasy of release, he was blind and deaf, his long abstinence from physical love clouding his judgement. He didn't seem to realize that he was giving himself to her, so deft was Sarah in manipulating him.

At last he fell away from her, turning from her over onto his back, his breathing ragged. She smoothed his brow, her triumph overwhelming. That was the first time, and if she could make it happen again, it wouldn't be the last. True it was not a satisfactory coupling, not where she was concerned, for she'd needed to make him mad with the need for release before she'd taken him to her. It had been over in seconds but at least, this way, she would have what she wanted, power over her husband.

That night she slept in his bed and this, she determined, was how it would be from now on. He didn't have anyone but her. He needed her strength now and like a good wife, Sarah would be there to care for him.

Arian opened the thick envelope and took out the document from inside. The paper crackled as she unfolded it and it was some moments before Arian realized that the document was summoning her to appear in court to answer the charge of libel. Wordlessly, she handed it to Mac who stared down at it with his mouth pursed.

'I suppose I'd better print a retraction.' He spoke without meeting Arian's eyes, he was still angry with her. 'It's my problem, leave it with me.'

'No, it's my problem. I'm the proprietor of the newspaper. I'll go and see Sarah Frogmore myself.'

'I don't see why—' Mac began but Arian cut into his speech abruptly.

'I'll deal with it. Sarah needs another woman to handle her. You'd be outclassed my dear Mac, devious though you may be you don't understand what sort of person Sarah Frogmore is.'

'What if Gerald Simples is there, what will you do then?' Mac frowned.

'For once your gossips seem to have let you down. Gerald has left Sarah and is staying in an hotel with a young, very young, lady.'

'I see, very well.' He wasn't pleased but he sank back in his chair accepting her right to take charge.

'I'll be clearing out my desk at the end of the week.' He leaned back and dropped his pencil on the pad in front of him. 'I can see you don't need me, not even to clear up this business of the Frogmores.'

'No,' Arian said carefully, 'I don't need you for that, I don't even need you to make decisions for me. I can stand or fall by my own mistakes. But what I do need you for is to write my leader articles for the main paper. I need your talent for gossip – no-one can ferret out scandal like you.' She smiled ruefully. 'Just consult me occasionally when there's a story that's doubtful, like this one.' She tapped the summons.

He didn't reply and Arian went up to Mac and hugged him. 'I want you and I need you, Mac,' she said earnestly. 'You take care of me, you make me feel safe.' She kissed his cheek and felt the bristles hard against her mouth.

'I'm sorry if I was angry, Mac. Please stay, please?'

For a moment it seemed he would refuse then his craggy face broke into a smile and he nodded slowly.

'Right, I'll stay. I don't see why I should miss the "do" the city fathers are putting on for us, do you?'

'Mac,' Arian hugged him and tutting, he unwound her arms from around his neck. 'Mac, I love you.'

'Stuff and nonsense!' he said gruffly. 'Now get on and

419

sort out that Frogmore person. There's real work waiting for you instead of placating silly women – waste of time, I call that.'

With lightened spirits, Arian let herself out of the offices of the *Times* and hailed a cab. The sooner she spoke to Sarah Frogmore, the better. Arian had no doubt she'd convince Sarah to drop her foolish notion of taking the matter to court. Once the disadvantages were pointed out to her, she'd see reason.

From the outside, Frogmore Hall was imposing and within the huge arched doorway, the real splendour of the old house was evident. Domed ceilings were deeply corniced and the frieze above the picture rail was decorated with Greek urns and swags of olive leaves.

Arian became aware that the door of the sitting room had opened and Sarah appeared in the hallway. It was clear from the mutinous look on her face that Arian's presence was not welcome.

'You've got the cheek of the devil himself coming here to my house,' she said, her face flushed. 'Go away, I don't want to talk to you. If you're going to beg for mercy, forget it.'

'No, I was going to ask you to reconsider, though.' Arian moved closer. 'I think it better if we talk privately, don't you?'

Sarah led the way into the sumptuous drawing room where Geoffrey Frogmore was seated in a chair. He was a sad-looking man, Arian thought afresh, his sallow complexion not flattered by the dun-coloured smoking jacket, and the knotted cravat around his neck of a green and gold pattern gave him a definitely foppish appearance. Still, his personal tastes were no business of hers.

'What's this about, Sarah?' The question could have been aggressive but the mildness of his voice belied the words. Sarah shrugged and took a deep breath.

'There was a silly story about you and . . . and Chas, in this woman's rag of a newspaper.'

'I thought you said it would be all right.' His pale skin took on a pink flush and Arian bit her lip.

420

'Mr Frogmore,' she began but Sarah interrupted her.

'It was slanderous, Geoffrey. That woman shouldn't have written about you like that.'

'Libellous, I think you mean, Mrs Frogmore,' Arian corrected absently. She turned to Geoffrey. 'The article, I'm afraid, hinted at your preference for your gentleman friend. I'm sorry.'

'It's absurd and untrue.' Sarah put her arm around her husband's shoulder as he seemed to diminish in his chair. 'Indeed, it might interest your readers to know that I am with child by my husband for the second time. Does that sound like the sort of man you make him out to be?'

Geoffrey Frogmore's look of surprise was not lost on Arian, she realized Sarah's story was an attempt to cover up but it didn't really matter one way or another.

'I've come to ask you not to take any action of this sort.' She took the summons out of her bag. 'I think it would cause more problems than it would solve.'

'For you, yes, and for your newspaper,' Sarah said venomously. 'You might find you have to pay us some money for the hurt you've caused.'

'If our story was proved to be the truth then Mr Frogmore could face a prison sentence, have you thought of that?'

Sarah was silent and, after a moment, Geoffrey rose to his feet. His dignity was impressive.

'We will leave well alone.' He looked at Sarah. 'It was foolishness to take this course of action and if I'd been consulted about the matter, I'd have forbidden you to do it.'

'But Geoffrey . . .'

'No buts, Sarah. Leave it.' He moved to the door. 'I think that brings our discussion to a close, Miss Smale.'

Arian inclined her head.

'I can only apologise, Mr Frogmore,' she hesitated for a moment, 'I take full responsibility for what appears in my press and I assure you, nothing like this will ever be used again.'

Geoffrey Frogmore didn't reply. He appeared white and strained and Arian realized how much grief he was suffering over the loss of his friend.

It was a relief to be out in the air once more. Her cheeks were hot and yet a sense of having averted disaster washed over her as she set out along the drive. She had learned a lesson today, that vulnerable people were to be protected. Mac might be a hard-headed reporter, a brilliant reporter but from now on, he would be careful not to aim his barbs at people who could not strike back.

He was bent over his desk when she entered the office and he looked up, his eyebrows raised in question.

'It's all right,' Arian took off her hat and hung it on the stand, running her hands through her hair wearily. 'Geoffrey Frogmore doesn't want to proceed.' She sank down into a chair and leaned on the ink-stained desk. 'He's a pitiful sight, Mac. He's so cut up about the loss of his friend.'

'Shouldn't go about doing unnatural things then, should he?' Mac spoke in a surly voice, clearly he was on the defensive.

'If we all were saints there wouldn't be much to write about, would there?'

Mac smiled and his craggy face was transformed. 'Point taken, boss.' He rose to his feet and thrust his hands into his pockets.

'Glad you solved one problem because we have another one. The typesetter's had an accident.'

'Oh, God, not on the premises?'

'No. Silly fool fell over after a session down at the Mexico Fountain and broke his arm. Can't operate the damn machine.'

He paused and Arian knew there was worse to come. She wasn't wrong.

'He tried, mind, when he came into work this morning. Daniel pied two lines and all hell's been let loose down in the print room.'

Arian groaned, one line pied – the printers' term for

dropped type – caused a great deal of confusion but two lines to reassemble with the separate letters, not to mention spaces and punctuation marks meant hours of work.

'Why didn't I stay in the leather business?' She put her hand to her forehead. 'It was not such hard work as a newspaper, believe me.'

'But you were no good at it,' Mac pointed out reasonably. He was nothing if not blunt but then Mac saw no merit in dissembling.

'Right, let's go and see if we can help sort the mess out, then.' Arian rose to her feet and stood looking at Mac who remained at his desk.

'Not me, boss. I got a leader article to write, remember?'

'I remember.' Arian moved towards the door of the office. 'But thank you, Mac, for reminding me.'

It was later that Arian left the office and made her way towards the hospital. She'd had a note from Eddie Carpenter asking her to call to see him and she wondered what was wrong. She had a nasty suspicion it was something to do with Gerald Simples.

It was a long walk from the centre of town up the hill towards the yellow-stoned institute. The hospital was set well out of the way of other buildings, along a seemingly endless drive and then, the imposing structure came into sight, sprawling and somehow intimidating.

Within the walls, there were many doors, all of them locked. It needed the company of an orderly to lead the way to the hospital wing where Eddie was working. Eddie himself met her at the door to his office. He looked sombre as he invited her inside and offered her a chair.

'What's wrong?'

'That bastard! Do you know what he's done?' Eddie sat on the edge of the desk, his arms folded, his shoulders tense.

'He's seduced my daughter!' He gestured helplessly. 'She's visiting him at some hotel, she won't tell me which one. Whatever I say, I'm wrong, I'm trying to thwart the course of true love. True love – the man doesn't know the meaning of the word.' He didn't wait for Arian to comment.

'It's against my express wishes. I've told Candida the man's dangerous but she won't listen. Simples has somehow managed to fool everyone about his condition. His acquaintances have even spoken up for him and my daughter is the one protesting his sanity most loudly.

'He's been examined by our top man here. He came in voluntarily and to all intents and purposes he's as sane as I am.' He stood up and ran his hand through his hair. 'But he's cunning. It's an act. I'm not quite sure how he's getting away with it but that's what the man's doing.'

Arian clasped her hands in her lap and tried to think rationally. 'Is your daughter in danger, then?'

'Everyone he comes in contact with is in danger; one wrong word and the whole thing could blow up into a disaster.'

'Is that a possibility or is it a likelihood?'

Eddie shook his head. 'I just don't know, Arian. I don't know anything any more. Perhaps I'm wrong, God I hope I am for all our sakes.'

'Perhaps he's cured.'

'Perhaps hell will freeze over.'

'I'll go to see him,' Arian said decisively. 'Tell him to give your daughter up. He might just listen to me.'

'I hoped you'd say that. Normally I wouldn't advise it,' Eddie shook his head, 'but Candida is so young, so headstrong. I'm frightened for her, Arian.'

Arian patted Eddie's cheek. 'Don't worry, I'll speak to him, try to make him see reason and I'll take Mac with me, he's a tower of strength.'

It wasn't difficult for Arian to find out where Gerald was staying. In the event, she didn't involve Mac but decided to see Gerald alone.

He was sitting in a chair close to the window. He was clean-shaven and fully dressed and he appeared well, if a little tired. His eyes were heavy, almost as though he'd been sedated.

'Gerald?' she hesitated at the door of the room and he smiled slowly when he saw her.

'Arian. I presume you've come to ask me to come back to you.' Gerald moved from the bed and leaned a little heavily on the cabinet at his side.

She sifted her words carefully, aware he might still be dangerous. She trusted Eddie's judgement above that of the other doctors.

'I'm not sure about that. I didn't think you'd want to give up the full life you seem to be leading without me.'

'I've always wanted to be with you, Mrs Simples, you know that.' He spoke quietly, as if his throat was a little sore.

It was a long time since she'd been called Mrs Simples and Arian shuddered. 'Does that mean you're growing tired of your young lady?' she said, taking a deep breath.

'If I say yes, you will arrange for me to come home, after all. You are doing very well now, aren't you, and don't you think you owe it to me to share some of that success with me?' He was not letting her off the hook, she could see he was determined to make her commit herself.

'Gerald, there's a lot has happened to the both of us in the last months. We can't pick up the threads, not just like that.'

'You don't want me, that's it, isn't it?' He was making an effort to control himself, she could see by the set of his jaw. 'Don't try to side-step the issue.'

'There's a lot to think about,' she said desperately. 'I think you should break off the relationship with this young lady before we talk again. It's up to you. I can't solve anything for you, Gerald. It's not as easy as that. You were the one to go off. You've had other women since we married. You must put all that behind you, prove you can be faithful to me before we can think of starting again.' She had no intention of starting again but at least if he thought she would he might break off his affair with Eddie's daughter.

'You never loved me, did you?' He was growing angry, she could see beads of sweat on his brow, he was frowning, his eyes were boring into hers and she was afraid. She rose to her feet and glanced at the door. Gerald made a move towards her and she held up her hand.

'We'll talk again, Gerald. Don't excite yourself, it isn't good for you.'

He sank back into his chair. 'All right, I'll think about what you've said.'

With a sigh of relief, she left the room and hurried down the stairs, almost colliding with a young nurse. She recognized the girl at once, she was Eddie's daughter.

'You're Candida.' Arian saw how very young the girl was with a pang of pity, she was just the right age to be taken in by a man like Gerald.

'So, and who are you?' The girl was on the defensive and Arian shook back her hair. 'I'm Gerald's wife.' She watched the antagonism fade from Candida's face. 'He's not cured, he's holding himself in check; somehow he's managing to control his anger but it's there, it's still there, all right, I've just seen a touch of it.'

'You're just saying that because you're jealous of me.' Candida lifted her chin defiantly.

'I'm not jealous. I don't want to ever see Gerald again. He can be brutal, I know that and if what your father says is right, he could be downright dangerous.'

It was a mistake to mention Eddie. The girl's eyes sparkled. 'I see, so Daddy's been talking to you, has he? Well I won't listen to either of you, why should I? I know Gerald better than all of you. I'm the one who cares about him, really cares. I'm the one who gives him the laudanum. That's all it takes, a small dose to keep him feeling great. The doctors, they look for trouble. What do they know?'

She hurried away, her shoulders stiff with anger and Arian knew she had lost.

Later she spoke to Eddie and told him what had happened. 'Your daughter, she's giving Gerald laudanum.' She paused as he looked up at her sharply. 'Is that bad?'

'Good Lord, we haven't used the stuff in years. Candida must be stealing it from the hospital's old stock.' Eddie rubbed his brow. 'God, so that's the answer, that's what's keeping the man's condition more or less stable.'

'Will it help him?'

'For a time, until he becomes so used to it that he can't live without it.' Eddie took Arian by the shoulders.

'Keep this to yourself. I will talk to my daughter again. She must stop supplying him with the medication, she'll get caught sooner or later and then she'll be in trouble.'

'What will happen if he stops getting the laudanum?' Arian watched Eddie's face carefully. He looked levelly into her eyes.

'God help us all.' His voice was filled with despair.

Arian left Eddie and made her way back home. Everything seemed to be falling to pieces around her. Would she never be free of Gerald Simples? She lifted her head to look up at the skies but all she saw were the scudding clouds that heralded a storm.

CHAPTER THIRTY

Ellie stared down at her hands. She was flushed and unbelieving. The midwife was rinsing her hands in the ornate china bowl, singing softly to herself.

'You're sure?' Ellie lifted her head, a feeling of excitement replacing the disbelief. 'You're sure it's twins?'

'Sure as I can be, lovie,' Nurse Parnel smiled. 'Been at this job nigh on thirty years, mind. Should know when I can feel two babbas instead of one.'

She lifted her strong hands. 'See these? Brought hundreds of little ones into the world, they have. Fine healthy infants so don't you fret, now. I'll look after you when the time comes.'

'I wonder what Calvin will say.' Ellie spoke her thoughts out loud. 'I hope he'll be pleased.'

'Well it's two for the price of one, isn't it, lovie?' The midwife dried her hands and then rubbed them over her clean apron as though to straighten out any creases. 'Usually tickled pink are the husbands, think they're something special to beget twins.'

Ellie felt a sinking of her heart. She wasn't a wife, only a mistress, and now she was going to be a mother of twins, illegitimate twins. Calvin would marry her now, he must do, mustn't he?

'I'll say good day, then,' Mrs Parnel smiled cheerfully. 'I'll come back again when you need me, right?'

'Thank you, nurse,' Ellie said. 'I'm sure Calvin will want you to keep an eye on me.'

'There's a sensible man for you,' Mrs Parnel approved. 'He knows a woman with child needs a lot of care. There's not many as thinks that way, mind.'

When the midwife had left, Ellie made her way from

the room and sought out Calvin, itching to tell him the news and yet frightened too. Still, the sooner she got it over the better.

He was reading the paper, looking quite at home in her apartment and he smiled when he saw her in the doorway.

'Am I disturbing you, Calvin?' She hesitated on the threshold and he gestured for her to come in, closing the *Times* and setting it down.

'This is *your* home remember? Now what did the good nurse have to say? Are you fit and well?'

Ellie nodded. 'Everything is as it should be, except . . .' she hesitated and Calvin frowned.

'Except what? There's nothing wrong, is there?'

'It's twins,' she blurted the words out. 'Calvin, we're going to have twins.'

He smiled. 'That's splendid.' His voice was strained. He didn't seem to be overjoyed by her news. Ellie felt silly tears come into her eyes, she longed for Calvin to say that they must be married straight away but she knew he wouldn't do anything of the sort.

Plucking up her courage, she broached the subject herself.

'Calvin, couldn't we get married? It needn't be a fussy service, just something simple, quiet. Nobody would know.'

He rose from his chair, thrusting his hands into his pockets, his shoulders were hunched as though he wanted to get away from her. She knew she was pressing him unwisely but she couldn't stop herself.

'The babies, they are going to be . . . to be . . .' She couldn't bring herself to say the words and he turned round and looked at her levelly.

'Illegitimate. You knew all along I didn't want to marry again,' he said quietly. 'I don't want to be tied to any woman, Ellie, not even you.' He took her in his arms.

'I'll always care for the children and for you, I promised you that much and I meant it but I'm afraid that is going to have to do.'

Ellie swallowed hard. She didn't want to cry. It was weak and Calvin would only be impatient with her and yet it was so difficult to keep the tears at bay.

'I'm going to leave you then, Calvin.' Her mind was suddenly crystal clear. She didn't want Calvin's charity, she wanted his love and if she didn't have that, she had nothing.

Instead of protesting, he looked at her in silence for a long moment and she knew he was waiting for her to retract the words but she couldn't.

'If that is your final word then leaving me is your prerogative,' he said. 'I'll care for you financially but I cannot change my mind about marriage.'

'So be it, Calvin,' she said regretfully.

'I don't want you to go away from me, Ellie,' his voice softened. 'If you reconsider, I'll understand. You'll always be welcome to live here at my expense but that's all I can offer. I'm sorry. Now, I'm going out. I'll be going home for supper so don't wait up for me.'

She wanted to go into his arms, beg him to forget her hasty words but something held her back, perhaps it was the knowledge that she had meant all she'd said, perhaps it was the distant look that had come into his eyes, but she remained silent.

She watched from the window as he strode along the street. He was walking into town instead of taking a cab, obviously he wanted to clear his thoughts, forget about Ellie and the problems she caused. When he was out of sight, she sank back into a chair and looked around her at the elegant room, a cheerful fire burning in the ornate grate. Calvin could offer her luxury, he had everything he wanted in life except perhaps one thing, the woman he loved and she, Ellie, couldn't fill that gap.

Ellie knew more about Calvin than he realized; she knew that in the night, when he was asleep, he sometimes murmured a name, so softly and so lovingly that she felt her heart sink with the pain of it.

She must accept things as they were, she told herself briskly and not brood on what was not hers. But she couldn't help remembering his voice when he was asleep, so full of tenderness and regret. He spoke in a way he never spoke to her and the name he uttered so lovingly was Arian.

Calvin was unsettled by Ellie's news. He wanted children, he wanted sons, just as most men did but not like this. It was Arian who should be the mother of his offspring, Arian he wanted at his side at all times, in his bed and in his arms at night.

He walked briskly into town and made his way deliberately towards the imposing offices of the *Swansea Times* and stood across the street, looking up at the windows as if expecting Arian herself to appear there. But of course she didn't.

After a while he turned to walk away, striding along the roadway with his head bent. He almost collided with a woman hurrying towards him and there she was.

'Arian!' They stood for a moment staring at each other and then she smiled at him, her eyes sparkling with light.

'Arian, I love you.' He didn't know for a moment if the words were in his head or if he'd spoken them out loud but Arian was blushing, the contours of her face softening.

'I love you, too, Calvin. It's just a pity we didn't both do something about it a long time ago.'

He held her in his arms, there in the street, and she rested her head for a moment against his shoulder. They were close, so close. Calvin closed his eyes, breathing in the clean scent of her. She moved away from him then but he held onto her hand.

'Please, stay with me for just a little while. Let's walk in the park, go to the tea-rooms, the Castle's just down the road. Don't leave me, not yet.'

Side by side they walked along the street unaware of the people around them, happy just to be together. It was magical. With her hand in his, the day was brighter, the air sweeter, the sea coming in to the shore soft and friendly. Calvin led her into the hotel and they sat surrounded by potted palms, listened to the sweet sounds of the string quartet and quietly, inconsequentially, they talked.

'I had you there in my house and I let you go, allowed you to be taken in by a charlatan like Simples. What a fool I was.'

'It all seems so long ago now.' Arian's voice was soft with the remembering. 'I was too gullible for my own good. But then, I thought I could make the best of things, be a success in business and, yet for all my strivings, I turned out to be a failure, most of all in my marriage.'

'It wasn't your fault, none of it. I was the fool, I should have kept you when I had you.'

'It's all in the past now, behind us. We can't change anything. I'm married to Gerald whether I like it or not.'

'Marriage to a dangerous madman is an awful fate for anyone. Let me take you away from here, we could make a fresh start.'

'Could we?' Arian's voice was so low he hardly heard her words. 'What about Ellie? She needs you. She's a sweet trusting girl. And remember, Swansea is my home, I don't want to run away from it. In any case, I love the newspaper business and I am, at last, making a success of something. I feel a sense of fulfilment every time an issue comes out, that's some compensation for all the other disappointments I've suffered.'

'So philosophical,' Calvin smiled ruefully, 'and so young into the bargain.'

'Am I young?' Arian looked up into his face and he longed to hold her close to kiss her sweet mouth. 'I feel older than the hills.'

'You're beautiful, all I could ever want in a woman.' Calvin took her hand. 'Arian, I want to be with you so much, in any way I can.'

'But you have your Ellie,' Arian withdrew from him. 'You are going to be a father.'

Calvin sighed. 'I know.' He sensed Arian's hurt and looked at her levelly. 'I make no apologies. I'm a man, I have needs but I've never been false. I've never told Ellie that I'd marry her. I'll take care of her always, look after her always, she'll want for nothing.'

'Except a husband and a father for her children,' Arian said softly.

He watched her expression. 'Are you telling me I should marry, then?' He felt a pang of anger, anger which had nothing to do with Arian and a great deal to do with his own guilt.

'I'm not in a position to tell you to do anything, Calvin,' her voice trembled. 'We've both made so many mistakes, just be careful you don't make another one.'

'If I married Ellie for the wrong reasons,' Calvin said calmly, 'I would be making a mistake.'

Arian hung her head and Calvin, watching her, felt a rush of pain that he would never hold her, never make love to her, never make her his wife. It had been a wonderful dream but it was only a dream.

Arian touched his hand and her fingers rested light and cool against his own.

'Oh, Calvin, why couldn't we have done things differently?' She sighed and he knew she was feeling the same sense of hopelessness as he was.

He wanted to persuade her to come with him now, to abandon everything and flee abroad, the Canary Islands perhaps, where the sun shone most of the time or further afield in America, far from the grey streets of Swansea. The words died on his lips as Arian spoke.

'I must get back to the newspaper, Calvin. I've been away too long as it is.'

'Is it that important to you then?' He sounded a little bitter and she shrugged.

'It's all I've got and I must make the most of it.' She stood up and he rose to his feet at her side. She looked up at him.

'Calvin, there's going to be a reception at the city hall in my honour, please say you'll come.'

'I'll be there.' He felt dismissed, a feeling he didn't much like but Arian was wiser than he was. There was

433

no running away, not for them, not now. It was far too late for that.

He turned, hearing a sound, and saw Gerald Simples walking across the foyer, he must have been eavesdropping on their conversation. He made to speak to Arian, to warn her but she'd gone and all he could see was the door swinging shut behind her.

When he returned home, it was to find a note lay on his desk and he opened it, straightening out the paper, reading the words slowly so that he would understand them clearly. Ellie had gone home to her parents. They, she told him, would take care of her and the children. She wanted no further contact with him.

He sighed as he crumpled the paper in his hand. It was a time of change, might it not be also a time of new beginnings?

The reception was held in the Guildhall. The steps beneath the splendid facade with its Grecian pillars were awash with people. Ladies in splendid gowns stepped from carriages and swept under the portico. Gems glittered at throat and arms and in glossy hair. It was a spectacular occasion when the owner of the newly formed *Swansea Times* was being fêted by the city fathers.

And yet Arian felt alone, even though she had Mac at her side and her staff, from reporters to machine operators around her, she felt isolated from the crowd.

The mayor came forward and shook her hand and spoke some words of congratulation. Arian nodded and made the right responses and accepted his offer to help her greet the guests.

Arian knew most of them, they were the élite of Swansea. In the crowd she could see Emily Miller and her husband John, with them was John's daughter Sarah and her husband Geoffrey Frogmore. Looking at them, no-one would suspect the secrets of their strange marriage.

'Arian, how lovely to be invited to your reception.' Hari Grenfell took her hand and squeezed it, she had always been a warm, generous person and her delight was genuine. At her side, Craig Grenfell was tall, elegant and imposing, a handsome, positive man, who clearly loved his wife dearly.

It seemed that most of the guests had arrived and the mayor excused himself and moved to join a group of other dignitaries. Arian felt free now to look out for Calvin. If he didn't come, the evening would be empty.

She felt Mac take her arm. 'Would you like a drink, Arian? It's champagne, the best.'

Arian sipped the drink. 'I've never tasted better champagne but you, Mac, I expect you are an expert at that sort of thing.'

He winked at her mischievously. 'I'm an expert at a great many things, my dear boss.'

Just when the mayor was preparing to make his formal speech of congratulation, she caught sight of Calvin from the corner of her eye. She smiled at him and for a moment it was as though there was no-one but the two of them in the spacious elegant room. Arian made her way to Calvin's side and her eyes met his.

'Don't look at me like that, Arian,' he said huskily. 'I might forget myself and take you in my arms right here in front of everyone.'

'As I feel now, I wouldn't care one little bit. All I wanted was for you to be here. I'm so glad you could be with me tonight.' He took her hand and looked down at her his eyebrows raised. She put her finger over his lips.

'Don't ask questions. Let's just enjoy what we have now, at this moment.' She was so happy, so keyed up with the excitement of it all. Tonight, anything seemed possible, even that she and Calvin might one day be together.

Gerald Simples stood in the elegantly furnished room in the Castle Hotel and stared at himself in the mirror. He looked well, he thought with satisfaction. He chuckled and yet the sound was menacing. Earlier, Gerald had gone to the bank and taken out quite a large amount of cash. With some of the money he'd bought himself a new outfit. It wouldn't do to turn up at Arian's party looking anything but a gentleman.

All he needed now was for Candida to bring him his fresh supply of laudanum. He'd taken none, not in the last few hours and by now, he was itching for it – it would make him feel good, confident at the Guildhall reception.

He would have to go soon, the reception would be in full swing by now. He smiled. His dear wife would have the surprise of her life to see him. His appearance would undoubtedly prove to her that they were meant to be together, she was half convinced about it already, he could tell by the way she had jealously begged him to rid himself of Candida.

It would be a relief to leave the avid Candida behind him, to put her out of his life. He was tired of her advances. Indeed once or twice lately, he had been unable to fulfil his duties towards her beneath the sheets. She had tried to make him go easy on the laudanum, blaming that for his reluctance rather than take the blame herself.

He rubbed at his head. He wished the clouds would leave him alone. They came like a grey mist, unbidden and covered his mind. He shook his head for a moment he couldn't see his own reflection in the mirror and then his vision cleared.

The door opened and Candida came in and to his surprise, she didn't even notice he was dressed to go out. He'd expected her to make a fuss, to beg him to stay in with her, she was nothing if not possessive.

'Gerald, darling,' she seemed agitated, 'I've got some bad news for you.' She closed the door and came towards him, her hands held out almost in supplication.

'They found me out, took away my key to the medicine cupboard. I'm sorry, my darling, I can't get you any more laudanum.'

She was babbling. He caught her shoulders and held her fast. 'What are you talking about?' His throat hurt his mouth was dry, she must have something for him, some small bottle perhaps.

'You've got me some, just for tonight, until I can arrange to buy some for myself? You wouldn't let me down like that, would you?'

She shook her head. 'I couldn't get it, Gerald, you don't understand.' Her eyes were moist, her face seemed to dissolve. 'I might be dismissed from my job and I did it all for you.'

'You've got nothing for me, nothing at all?' He stared into her face and watched with horror as she shook her head. He put his hand around her throat. 'You must have something, just a little laudanum. You're just teasing because you want to have me beg. All right, I'll beg. Please, please, Candida, give me the medicine, I need it, you know I need it.'

She was shaking her head, trying to get away from him but he couldn't allow her to go. He must keep pressing, pressing. She struggled helplessly and he pressed harder, he wouldn't release her, didn't she understand, he couldn't let her go, not until she closed those terrible eyes.

She struggled, kicked at him, hurt him, she should never do that, he'd always been good to her. She tried to speak but her tongue seemed to be in the way. She was ugly, grotesque, why had he ever thought her beautiful?

He shook her and heard something snap and then she was quiet and that pleased him. She was slack in his arms and he set her down on the bed and straightened his clothes. He didn't have time to talk to her any more, he had something important to do, what was it? Ah, the celebration, his dear sweet wife's night of triumph. She would be anxious, wanting him there at her side. He must go.

He left the room and closed the door, locking it carefully. He didn't want anyone prying into his private possessions. Someone might steal his money, might come in and see Candida in his bed, that would upset Arian.

His knife he had put in his boot, the cold steel was against his leg. It gave him a sense of power and he needed his power tonight for this was going to be his great moment. Tonight Arian would be his again.

Arian was standing close to Calvin. He secretly touched her hand, twining his fingers in hers. Happiness filled her, so much happiness, she knew it couldn't last, it was a dream and yet didn't she deserve to dream, just this once?

There was a sudden feeling of someone standing uncomfortably close to her. She glanced over her shoulder. Gerald Simples was so near he could have touched her. She shuddered. He was watching her, his eyes strange and he licked his lips as though he had difficulty in finding words to speak to her.

He appeared a little nervous but otherwise quite in control. He was well dressed, his clothes elegant and obviously new.

'Arian, I'm here.' His voice was a croak and Arian flashed an anguished look at Calvin who was suddenly tense, his jaw clenched together, his eyes hard.

Gerald took her in his arms and Arian, aware of the curious, staring eyes, accepted his embrace.

In the silence, Arian heard Mac deliberately begin a conversation. In minutes, the room was back to apparent normality, the guests chattering as though nothing had happened.

'What are you doing here?' Calvin said in a low, hard voice. 'You must know you're not welcome.'

'You don't understand,' Gerald's voice was a threat. 'She wants me back.'

'Please, Calvin, don't make a scene.'

Arian turned to Gerald. 'Let's go into another room, we must talk.'

He looked at her and the look made her shiver. 'You're not, not . . .' He put his hand to his head. 'What was I going to say?'

438

'Look Simples, this is neither the time nor the place,' Calvin spoke quietly. 'Why don't you go away and allow Arian to enjoy her evening?'

Gerald didn't turn round. 'Keep out of this!' He was facing Arian but it was as though he didn't see her. His eyes gleamed, his voice was rising. 'You've always wanted to bed my wife, think I don't know a ram when I see one?'

People were turning, staring. Quite a few of the guests who had been the subject of Mac's gossip column were enjoying Arian's embarrassment.

'Gerald, be quiet,' Arian spoke angrily. 'I will not have a scene here, do you understand me?'

As soon as the words sunk into his mind, Gerald became enraged. He caught Arian by the throat and held her against the wall, a knife suddenly appearing in his hands.

Arian felt the cold steel against her skin, saw the madness in Gerald's eyes and she was afraid.

'You are coming home with me,' he ground the words out between clenched teeth. 'I'm going to show you that I am master of my own wife, do you hear me?' He shook her and the blade of the knife drew a line of blood across the whiteness of her skin.

She knew then what she must do. 'Yes, I'm coming home with you, Gerald, let's get out of here, shall we?' It was obvious that he was not answerable for his actions, if she didn't get him away others might be hurt.

'No,' Calvin made a move towards her but Gerald lashed out and a patch of red appeared on the pristine white of Calvin's shirt. Some women screamed and Gerald stared around him, his expression fierce.

Arian addressed the crowds. 'Please be calm, we're leaving now, we're going home. To my house.' She flashed Calvin a warning look as she took Gerald's hand. He still had the knife raised, he was looking round him, his head moving from side to side like a caged beast but he allowed Arian to lead him across the room towards the door.

She was frightened, very frightened but she forced herself onwards towards the carriage that was waiting for one of the guests.

'Driver, take me to the Hollies, Mount Pleasant Avenue please.' She tried to warn him with her eyes but it was dark and the driver couldn't see what was going on.

'Sorry, madam, I'm waiting for Mr and Mrs Grenfell. I'm their driver, not for hire.'

Gerald growled and held the knife high. The man started back in his seat and Arian spoke quietly, trying to calm him.

'Please, just take us home and no-one will be hurt.'

In the carriage, Arian tried to talk to Gerald, offered to take the knife away from him but he shook his head. He slumped against her, his energy seemed spent and she sat still at his side, praying that he would fall asleep.

Just as she was about to take the knife from his hand, the carriage jerked to a halt. 'We're here, madam.'

The driver remained in his seat, unwilling to help, watching in silent fear as Arian led Gerald from the coach. The streets appeared silent, the carriage was fast disappearing, she was alone with a madman.

She led him inside the house wondering just what she would do next. He slumped into a chair, his eyes were ablaze with a strange light but it was as though he didn't recognize her.

'You're my wife.' His voice was thick and she saw him lift the knife and look at it and then look at her as though he was debating what to do.

'Come here,' he ordered and she moved towards him, clenching her hands together to stop them from trembling. 'Shall I kill you or shall I take you to bed?'

He reached out and drew her down onto his knee and held the knife against her breast. She felt the steel hard against her flesh, cutting through the thin cloth of her gown. She was going to die, she thought, die and not know what it was to enjoy life.

Gerald pushed her down onto the floor and slumped down onto his knees beside her. 'I don't think you've ever

oved me. You hate me, don't you, Candida? You didn't
bring me the laudanum, you let me down, betrayed me to
my enemies. You think I don't know what your little game
is but I know all right.'

Arian felt real fear then. He didn't even recognize her,
he was lost in some nightmare world of his own. She saw
the knife poised above her, she reached up and caught hold
of the blade to prevent Gerald from plunging it into her. She
didn't feel the knife cut into her hands but she saw the blood
run down her arms, staining the silk material of her sleeves.

The sight seemed to madden Gerald. 'You bitch, get
me laudanum, get it now or I'll kill you.'

'Yes, I'll get it, Gerald, just let me get up then.' She
struggled to her feet but he caught her round the waist
and hauled himself up beside her, leaning on her heavily.
He was breathing unevenly, his chest heaving.

'You haven't got any laudanum. You think I'm a fool,
but you won't escape me. I thought I'd finished it in the
hotel room but you were pretending to be dead. Very
good, my dear, but now I'll do it properly.'

'Gerald, what have you done?' her voice trembled with
horror. The blade was near her neck. Arian looked into
Gerald's eyes. He was unseeing, crazed. He twisted so that
her back was to him, he lifted the blade deliberately until
it was beneath her ear. 'I'm going to cut your throat, you'll
really be finished then, you bitch.'

She closed her eyes, she couldn't move, he was gripping
her so tightly. It was over, he would do it, nothing on
earth could prevent him now from killing her.

The door burst open, the rush of cold air bringing her
eyes wide open. Suddenly she was released. She fell back
against the wall and she saw Calvin grasping Gerald by
the throat, dragging him away from her.

Calvin held Gerald's arm in a lock behind his back, the
knife fell to the floor with a clatter and Gerald winced in
pain.

'Calm down now, Gerald,' Calvin spoke soothingly as
Gerald heaved and strained to be free. 'Everything is under

441

control, don't you fret now, you're going to be all right. We've got some medicine here for you, just be still now.'

The calm monotone of Calvin's voice seemed to have the desired effect and Gerald stopped struggling. 'Laudanum, I need laudanum.'

'Of course you do, it will take away the sickness.' Calvin paused and glanced warningly at Arian. 'Tell the doctor he can come in, slowly now.'

Eddie Carpenter came into the room. His face was grey; he looked like an old man. He gave Gerald a liberal drink from the bottle in his hand and slowly, Gerald slumped downwards, his eyes closing.

Other men entered the house and Gerald was lifted onto a stretcher. Eddie took Arian's hand, his eyes were anguished. 'She's dead, my lovely daughter's dead. They wouldn't listen to me, no-one would believe the man was dangerous.'

Arian held Eddie close, knowing the hell he must be suffering. He moved away from her. 'I must see that he's never allowed to be free, not ever again. I'm sorry Arian, so sorry.'

He left the house and Arian heard the sound of the carriage wheels move away down the road and she closed her eyes, feeling a sense of unreality. She must get out of the house, breathe in some air.

Outside in the cool of the night air, Arian felt tears on her cheeks. She had been inches from death and she'd realized suddenly that she wasn't immortal.

Calvin took her in his arms. 'I knew you'd bring him here.' His arms were supporting her and Arian leaned against him gratefully. She began to cry, the tears were hot and bitter.

'I'm taking you home to my place,' Calvin said decisively. 'You can't stay here, not now. Don't protest, we can think it all out in the morning.'

Arian slept that night in Calvin's arms. When nightmares woke her, he was there to hold her close and reassure her that nothing would ever harm her again.

The next day, she woke late and Mac was there, sitting on the edge of the bed, a newspaper in his hand.

'Mac, what are you doing here?' Her voice was heavy with sleep.

'I wanted to be the one to tell you. The paper's a smash hit. We broke the story of a lifetime, or at least I did.' He looked a little shame faced. 'If we hadn't done it the other papers would have.'

He held the paper towards her and she saw the headlines covering half the page: MURDERER LOOSE ON THE STREETS OF SWANSEA.

'Mac, you didn't . . .'

'Read on, boss then throw the book at me.'

But she didn't need to, she knew what Mac would have written and any reporter worth his salt would have done the same thing. She returned the newspaper to him.

'It's all right,' she said. 'It's news, you had to print the story. Go away now, you've got a paper to run.'

'What do you mean, to run? You are the owner, you run it.' Mac rose from the bed and moved towards the door. 'Sure I'll fill in for you until you've had a break, I grant you deserve that much. Right, don't say any more, I'm on my way.'

Arian fell back against the pillow. It smelled of Calvin's pipe tobacco and she turned her face breathing in the very essence of him. He came into the room, his eyes alight.

'I love you, Arian. I'm not going to leave your side, not ever, so don't ask.'

'But there's Ellie,' Arian said weakly, 'and there's Gerald. I'll never be free of him, you know that don't you?'

'Shut up, let me talk.' He took her face in his hands. 'Have faith in me, Arian, and in our future together. You very nearly didn't have a future so let's be wise and decide what is important, shall we?'

He kissed her mouth with infinite tenderness. 'It's easy. Just say one little word. Just say, yes.'

Arian put her arms around him and pressed her head into his shoulder. It was so good to feel alive, so good to know that Calvin would always be there to take care of her. Suddenly, the world was filled with hope, with life. Achievement, success they were empty things if there was no-one who cared enough to share them with you. Nothing had changed, and yet everything had changed, now that she'd faced death she knew how precious life was.

There would be problems, always there would be problems for her and for Calvin but there was nothing they couldn't overcome so long as they were together. She burrowed closer into his arms as though she could never get close enough. She breathed in the scent of him and joy flowed through her.

The sun was warming the earth. Outside the birds were singing in the trees. The world was beginning anew.

'Yes.' The word fell softly into the sunlit room and it was the most beautiful sound in all the world.